RAVEN SON: VOLUME ONE

Raven Son: Volume One

Nicholas Kotar

WAYSTONE
PRESS

RAVEN SON: VOLUME ONE

(*The Song of the Sirin* and *The Rusted Blade*)

Cover Design by Stuart Bache

Published by Waystone Press 2025

 Formatted with Vellum

Contents

The Song of the Sirin

THE RUSTED BLADE

THE CURSE OF THE RAVEN

The Song of the Sirin

Raven Son: Book One

To my princess

The song of the Sirin can overthrow kingdoms. I know. I have seen it. I have seen the song make gods of men. The song carved the eternal city of Vasyllia out of the mountains. The song transformed queens into healers, so that thousands were made well with a single word. But ever it comes as a harbinger of affliction. Only in the fire of adversity does the pure water of healing flow.

-from "The Journals of Cassían, Dar of Vasyllia"
(The Sayings, Book II, 3:35-43)

CHAPTER 1

THE SONG

The song teased Voran at the first hint of sunrise. His sister Lebía still slept, and he rose quietly, trying not to wake her. Outside his window, the trees were encased in overnight ice. Branches, like freshly-minted blades, clanged against each other in an almost military salute. As Voran leaned against the sill, the sun breached the summit-lines, and the ice-encased branches glowed from within. The song rose in a vast crescendo, then faded again. It stopped his breath short like a punch to the chest.

"Ammil," said Lebía from across the room, her hair rumpled from sleep.

"Ammil, little bird?" he whispered, hoping she would turn over and fall asleep again. It cut him deeply that she still could not sleep on her own, despite her sixteen years.

"The sun's morning sparkle through hoarfrost," she said, laboring through a yawn. One of her eyes remained stubbornly closed. "That's how the Old Tales call it. Ammil. The blessing of Adonais, you know."

Voran smiled, though there was little to smile about in the purple shadows under her eyes. She needed to sleep if she were ever to find her joy again.

"What is that?" She indicated the parchment lying on the sill, garish in its profusion of purple and red.

"One of the Dar's huntsmen claims to have seen the white stag." Personally, Voran doubted it.

Her second eye opened. "The white stag? Dar Antomír wishes to hunt the deer of legend?"

"He's anxious to begin as soon as possible," said Voran. Too anxious, he thought, but kept it to himself. "His advisers are less sure. The Dar's called together a small council this morning."

Privately, Voran wondered at the Dar's eagerness. Yes, catching the white stag was supposed to bring prosperity to the hunter's city for seven generations. But although legends grew in Vasyllia with the same profusion as lilac trees, they mostly stayed bound to the page.

"Why does he want the approval of his advisors? Couldn't he just announce the hunt, and be done with it?" she asked, rubbing her right eye with the heel of her palm.

"It's complicated..." Only last week, the Dar's head drooped in sleep during a small council. "Dar Antomír is of a different time. Most of his advisers are young, and they would prefer to leave old tales and superstitions behind. In fact, I think there are some who wouldn't mind so much if Dar Antomír retired from public life and allowed Mirnían to take a more active role in Vasyllia."

"I see. Meddling nags."

Voran laughed. "I agree with that sentiment wholeheartedly." He would much rather wander the wilds than sit in council with the representatives of the three reaches of Vasyllia.

"Do you have to be there? Why not stay at home for once?"

She looked away as soon as she said it. His conscience pricked him. Lebía was practically begging him, and he knew how much she hated to beg. It had been far too long since he stayed with Lebía at home, helped in the kitchens, took a long walk through the family vineyards, or actually read something with her. But Dar

Antomír depended on him. Even more than he depended on his son, Mirnían.

"I wish I could…"

"Oh well." She put on a feeble smile like a mask. "Never mind. Only please don't stay at court the whole day. You can't imagine how oppressive this house can be."

Yes, I can, he thought. Why do you think I avoid it so much? Nothing like an empty house to remind you of your parents' absence.

"I expect I'll be back before evening," he said, and his conscience pricked him again. He doubted he'd return before night. "Sleep now, my swanling. You need to rest."

She looked at him without blinking for what seemed an inhumanly long time.

"Voran, do you think…maybe if I had done something differently—"

"Lebía, don't." He hurried to her and sat by her on the bed. "You were the least problematic child in Vasyllia. Mama's disappearance wasn't your fault."

"I remember there were times when Papa looked at me with those heavy eyes, you know? Like he was trying to remember what it was like to love me. To love Mama. Could he have really—?"

"Lebía, don't believe the gossip. The bruises on Mama's arms were part of the disease."

She nodded, thoughtfully.

"I don't know why she left when she did, swanling. But the fact that he went to find her proves that he loved her, don't you think?"

Her look only mirrored his own thoughts. *He didn't love us enough to stay.*

"Please, Lebía, you need your sleep."

She hugged him and turned over. Within a minute, her breathing had deepened into sleep.

May all the Powers damn him for leaving you, Lebía.

The curse did not give him the pleasure he hoped. It gave him no sudden illumination about the nature of Aglaia's disease. It suggested nothing new about Otchigen's madness and subsequent disappearance after implication in the mass murder of other Vasylli. Nothing but questions, as always.

At this early hour, he went out the back door of the wine cellar, chary of waking the servants. He managed to close the door with no noise, but the gate at the end of the overgrown back garden moaned like a thing diseased. It always did, but Voran always forgot. Cursing inwardly, Voran looked back at the house. No one seemed to stir within.

The house's two stories lurched over him, the shadows thrown back by the morning sun, threatening him. As though the house itself were angry that Voran was master instead of his lost father Otchigen. As though it were Voran's fault that his mother had fallen prey to a strange illness, then disappeared inexplicably.

The song appeared again, hardly more substantial than the red alpenglow on the underside of the clouds. Voran's heart swelled as he turned away.

Otchigen's house was nestled among the other estates of the third reach of Vasyllia. Voran loved to walk the flagstoned road through the reach as it crisscrossed the cherry groves of the noble families. Amid the trees, the mansions—each a fancy in carved gables, lintels, and columns—stared at each other as though they, like their masters, were jealous of each other's status. Some of the most extravagant even sported gilded cockerels on the roof. Voran was grateful that it was generally considered in bad taste.

Every house was built on a small mound, to better overlook the other two reaches that extended downward and outward along the slope of the mountain, like the skirts of a great dress. Voran knew that, if looked at from below, the houses sparkled like jewels every morning: a reminder to the lower reaches that such opulence was as far out of their reach as the Heights themselves.

Voran stopped at a crossroads where stairs carved into the mountain led down to the second reach. Just to his left was the Dar's palace, its seven onion-domed towers carved out of marble blocks, each larger than a single man. He hesitated, unwilling to brave the nagging of the small council yet. The second reach spread out beneath him in clean lines of austere homes set apart by stone hedges, staircases, and canals, all in keeping with the military calling of most of the inhabitants.

"Make way," said a voice behind him. Before Voran could turn around, a mail-shod shoulder pushed him off the path. Voran landed knee-first in mud.

"Well, well, it's the son of Otchigen," sniggered Rogdai, the chief warden of the gates of Vasyllia. "You seem to have lost your warriors' edge. No graduate of the seminary should ever allow himself to be surprised by an enemy in the open. I'll have to speak to the elders about it. Maybe they can find you a post in the Dar's library."

The two sub-wardens flanking him laughed, but their knuckles were white on their pommels.

"Ever the paragon of civility, Vohin Rogdai," said Voran, forcing his tone to remain calm. He would have preferred to knock the idiot's teeth into the back of his head. "Thank you for pointing out the weakness in my defense. I will gladly accept your further instruction in the sword-ring." *Where I'll poke more holes into you than a sieve.*

"A pleasure. It's been years since my sword has tasted traitor's blood. Shall we say... this evening? I've always thought sword-fights are best done in torchlight."

Where fewer people can see how bad you are, Voran thought, *or how you cheat.*

"I'm afraid today I'll be too busy hunting and catching the white stag."

"You?" Rogdai spit. "You'll catch that beast as soon as the sun sets in the middle of the day."

"I smell a wager," said Voran. "My father's entire wine collection if I don't bring it back by midnight."

Rogdai's face twisted in indecision. The superstitious idiot was afraid of drinking the wine of a suspected traitor. On the other hand, it was the best wine in Vasyllia...

"Done," growled Rogdai. "I wager a public feast hosted in the central square by my family in your honor."

"No, in my father's honor." Voran smiled at the way Rogdai twitched. Voran was sure he would just walk away. The coward.

"Done." Rogdai's teeth sounded ready to break from the strain of his jaw. "Not one minute past midnight, mind."

Voran inclined his head.

Rogdai and his flunkeys walked by, their shoulders not quite as straight as before.

The wind picked up and whipped Voran's hair into his face. Annoyed, he pulled it back. As he did, the song rose as though it were carried by the wind. He gasped for a moment, it was so intense. And it seemed to whisper a thought to him.

Go now. Forget the small council. Go find the stag now. Leave the blind to lead the blind.

Voran was running even before he realized it, but not toward the palace. He angled away away from it, toward the headwall of Vasyllia Mountain.

Voran avoided the streets, sprinting along dirt paths behind the gardens of the third reach. Here, the trees were wilder—native fir and spruce for the most part. Sometimes avoiding the paths outright, Voran veered toward the largest of many canals that watered the three reaches, all of them fed by Vasyllia's twin waterfalls. As he reached the canal, all signs of domestication faded, replaced by mossy rocks and tree roots. Even the air smelled differently here. The spicy smells of the nobles' kitchens gave way to the cool scent of pine. Though he knew the way well enough, it took him a moment to find the ivy-encrusted archway that led to a staircase going up, away from the city.

Dar Antomír would forgive him, Voran was sure. Especially if he found the stag. An honor for his family, a boon to his disgraced name. Seven generations of prosperity to his city. If the legends were to be believed, of course. Did he believe them? Voran wasn't sure any more.

The wind gusted, dousing him with the spume of Vasyllia's twin waterfalls, thundering on either side of the ancient stairway. With it came the music, louder than ever. He closed his eyes, savoring. Only when he clung to the face of the mountain was the melody this vivid. It sounded as if the mountain, the trees, the clouds all sang. And only for him.

He reached a ledge and pulled himself up. He was soaked from the exertion and the mist. Falling on one knee, he raised both arms toward the rising sun.

"Adonais, accept the prayer of this scion of the dishonored house of Voyevoda Otchigen. May my hunt not prove futile."

The song hung on the air like a memory, then faded. He leaned back against one of the stone chalices that collected the water from the falls, each taller than Vasyllia's famed birches. The chalice hummed with the steady rhythm of the waterfall pounding it. At Voran's feet, a stone mouth faintly reminiscent of a dragon's head spit the gathered water toward the city's canals.

How mad and beautiful, he thought, considering the dragon. In the old times things were made with beauty in mind, not merely usefulness. How unlike these times. With the passing of the song, Voran felt emptied, hungry for a recurrence of the song. It did not return.

Voran stretched his shoulders, relief flooding into the popping joints. He sat at the ledge's lip, resting his feet on the dragon's ears. Miles upon miles of the woods beyond the city lay carpeted at his feet. It was the perfect vantage point.

As he stared into the spaces between the trees, Lebía's shadowed eyes kept intruding on his thoughts. He really should spend more time with her, not conjure up excuses to remain at the warrior seminary after hours, training the boys. Her plea pained him. He had not realized that she was so lonely at home. But of course she was. She had few friends, tainted as she was with their father's assumed guilt, their mother's inexplicable disappearance. He promised himself he would take her to the forests more often. Maybe even let her spend the night under the stars with him, as he so loved to do.

He was so wrapped up with the image of her smiling at the innumerable falling stars on a late summer night that he nearly missed it. Something gold flashed in the woods far beneath him. Voran's heart stopped, then raced forward. A white streak passed through the trees. Fearful of moving even a muscle lest the vision fade, Voran continued to stare. It moved again, now clearly visible. A white stag.

It took Voran a maddening hour to get through the city's reaches and out the gates. Another half hour away from the paths as he tried to get his bearings in the forests beyond the city. He was intent on his path like a pointer on the scent. But when the howling started, his blood turned to ice in his veins.

He had heard wolves before. This was no mere wolf. The sound was deeper and darker, like the buzz of a hornet compared to a fly. He tried to recall the details of the many stories of the white stag. Was there a legendary predator to accompany the legendary quarry? Not that he could remember.

A blur of white raced before his eyes, so close he could spit at it. In an instant, it was gone.

The sun showered the foliage with dappled light. Something that was not the sun—a strange golden mist-light—flickered through the trunks, as though the stag had left a trail of light behind it. The mist beckoned him deeper into the forest.

Voran plunged headlong into the deepwood. The strange light continued before him for a mile or so, then blinked out. Voran looked around and realized he had never been in this place before. He stood on the edge of a clearing awash in morning sun, so bright compared to the gloom of the woods that he could see nothing in it but white light. He stepped forward.

The light overwhelmed him, forcing him to crouch over and shield his eyes. Fuzzy at first, then resolving as Voran's eyes grew accustomed to the light, the white stag towered in the middle of the clearing, almost man-high at the shoulder. Its antlers gleamed gold, so bright that they competed with the sun.

Voran froze in place and adopted the deep, silent breathing pattern that an old woodsman taught him in childhood. Inch by inch, he reached for his bow. His quiver hung at his side in the Karilan manner, so taking the arrow would be the work of half a second, but extricating the bow strapped to his back was another matter. A single bead of sweat dropped from his forehead and slid down the side of his nose, tickling him.

The deer turned its head to Voran, showing no inclination to flee. As though Voran were nothing more than a fly, it flicked both ears and continued to graze.

The howl repeated, just to Voran's right. Out of the trees crept a black wolf the size of a bear, its fur glistening in the light of the antlers. It paid no heed to Voran, leading with bristling head toward the grazing deer. It lunged, blurring in Voran's vision like a war-spear, but the stag leaped over it and merely moved farther off to continue grazing. The wolf howled again and lunged again. Back and forth they danced, but the stag knew the steps of this death-dance better than the wolf. His nonchalance seemed to infuriate the hunter.

The wolf charged so fast that Voran missed its attack. The deer flew higher than Voran thought possible, and its golden antlers slammed the wolf's flank like a barbed mace. The wolf screamed. The sound ripped through Voran, an almost physical pain.

The stag trotted to the other end of the clearing. Looking back once more, it waited. Gooseflesh tickled Voran's neck. The stag called to him, teasing him to continue the hunt. Voran ran, and the deer launched off its back legs and flew into the waiting embrace of the trees.

Voran stopped. His body strained forward, intent on the

hunt, but his heart pulled back. The wolf. He could not leave a suffering creature to die, even if it was the size of a bear, even if it would probably try to kill him if he approached. With a groan for his lost quarry, Voran turned back.

The wolf dragged itself forward with its forepaws. Each black claw was the size of a dagger. As Voran approached, its ears went flat against its head, and it growled deep in its throat. Voran's hands shook. Gritting his teeth, he balled his hands into fists and willed himself to look the wolf in the eye. Its ears went up like an inquisitive dog's. It whined.

In the eyes of the wolf, Voran saw recognition. This was a reasoning creature, not a wild animal.

"I can help you," he found himself saying to the wolf as to a human being. "If you let me."

The wolf stared at him, then nodded twice.

Voran pulled a homemade salve—one of Lebía's own making—from a pouch on his quiver. Tearing a strip from his linen shirt, he soaked it with the oils and cleaned the wound of tiny fragments of bone. The wolf tensed in pain, then exhaled and relaxed. Its eyes drooped as the pungent odor suffused the air, mingling with pine-scent. Soon the wolf was snoring.

As Voran watched the sleeping wolf, something stirred in his chest—a sense of familiarity and comfort he had only felt on rainy evenings by the hearth. For a brief moment, the wolf was a brother, closer even than any human. Perhaps it was better that he had given up the chance to hunt the stag. This stillness was enough.

A rustle of leaves distracted Voran. He turned around to see the white stag returning into the clearing with head bowed. Voran could not believe his good fortune. He *would* be the successful hunter. His family's dishonored name would be raised up again on Vasyllia's lips. Trembling, he reached for his bow.

The stag stopped for a moment, as if considering. More boldly, he walked to Voran. Voran's heart raced at how easy this kill would be, but the excitement died when the stag didn't stop.

He stared right at Voran as he strode. Voran pulled out an arrow and nocked it. The stag walked closer.

No. He couldn't do it. This beast was too noble, his eyes too knowing. Killing him would be like killing a man in cold blood.

The stag stopped close enough that Voran could touch him. To Voran's shock, he bowed his two forelegs and dipped his antlered crown to the earth, a king of beasts making obeisance to a youth of a mere twenty-four summers. Gathering courage, Voran approached the stag. His hands shook as he reached out to touch the antlers.

Something shook the branches in the trees ahead. Voran looked up, shoulders tensed. Something, some sort of huge bird, much bigger than a mountain eagle, perched in the crown of an orange-leaved aspen. No, not a bird, something else. Then Voran understood, and terror and excitement fought inside him, leaving him open-mouthed and rooted to the ground. The creature had a woman's face and torso, seamlessly blending with the wings and eagle body. Her head was adorned in golden-brown curls, and each feather shone like a living gem. A Sirin.

She opened her mouth and sang. It was *his* song, but he had never heard it like this.

Voran no longer felt his body. It soared above the clouds; it plumbed the depths of the sea; it hovered on the wings of a kestrel. The song pinioned him like a spear to the earth, but raised him on a spring breeze above the world's confusion. He was once again in the arms of his mother as she nursed him, her breath a soft tickle. He was inside the sun, and its music weaved him into existence. The earth shuddered, and he knew that he could turn it inside out.

The song of the Sirin stopped, and life lost all meaning. It was all grey, ugly, useless without her song.

When he came back to himself, the stag, the wolf, the Sirin were all gone, though her song lingered on the air. It seemed he would never rest, never sleep until he found her again.

The prince, beguiled by the aspen grove, sat down to sleep. A sleep that lasted three hundred twenty-seven years...

From "The Sleeping-Wood"
(Old Tales: Book I)

Chapter 2

The Pilgrim

It was a few hours after midday on the same day, as far as Voran could tell in the enormous dark of leaves. He walked in a direction he hoped would lead him back to known paths, but he still recognized few of the trees or hills. The undergrowth was so thick that Voran suspected he had stumbled on a true wildwood. He didn't know there were any left in Vasyllia, for though there were few outlying villages outside the city proper, many Vasylli had been woodsmen in their time, and hardly an inch of copse, plain, or grove was undiscovered.

One thought niggled the back of his mind, where he tried in vain to keep it contained. It whispered that he was no longer in Vasyllia at all, that he had entered a different realm from the human. Though he had just encountered not one, but *three* legendary creatures, Voran was not yet ready to believe all the Old Tales to be true.

He stumbled out of the murk of oaks into the breathing space of an alder-grove. He was exhausted. Laying down his bow, quiver, and sword, he sat at the base of a young tree and leaned back.

He should be more worried about losing his way. His provisions were few, he had drunk all his water before midday, and poor Lebía would be frantic with worry. But he found he cared little for any of that. He was not even anxious to find Vasyllia. Nothing mattered so much as finding the Sirin, as hearing her song again.

A kind of echo of the music thrummed through him stronger than his own heartbeat. Whenever he stopped moving, everything around him moved with the rhythm of the Sirin's song. The wind tossed the branches in her cadence; the birds chirped in unison. His own heart and breath began to move with it, until he thought he would go mad with its insistence.

It was not the music itself, he realized. It was the incompleteness of it. The Sirin had sung, but not to him. To the trees and the beasts, perhaps, to the summits and rivers, but not to his heart. The thought held a creeping dread. If her incomplete song had caused him to go half-mad, what would happen if she directed her song at him? Nevertheless, to contemplate the possibility of not hearing the song again terrified him, like a childhood dream of a parent's death.

As for finding her, none of the Old Tales were particularly helpful. The Sirin were capricious, appearing in their own good time, in their own chosen place. You did not seek out the Sirin, they sought you out. But he had no intention of waiting patiently for the song to return. He needed to do something.

The stag. Somehow, the white stag and the Sirin were connected. He couldn't exactly understand how, but it made sense on a level of intuition. The stag was of a different world, the world of the tales, the world that never encroached on everyday life. At least until today. If he found the stag again, perhaps it would lead him to the Sirin.

His heart accelerated. Why had he not considered it before? The Dar would have already gathered the hunting party to search for the stag. All of Vasyllia—rich third-reacher and poor first-reacher alike—would be lounging in pavilions and on wool blankets before the city, feasting and awaiting the return of the hunters. Perhaps they had caught the trail already? He must stop them at all costs.

He tried to jump up, but found that his limbs were not responding to the commands of his mind. His eyelids were heavy, his head drooped, hungry for sleep. What had come over him? He had hardly been out for half a day!

Then the realization speared him. He was stuck in a sleeping-wood. By the Heights, surely *that* old story wasn't true as well?

Out of the corner of his vision, a hairy creature waddled toward him. He couldn't move his head to see it clearly. He heard a porcine snuffle, though it was far too large to be a tree-pig. It stood up on two hind legs, growing in the process, all matted hair and dirt and encrusted leaves. It growled.

Something changed in the music of the grove. At first, Voran couldn't place it, then he realized it was the birds. They no longer sang in rhythm to the Sirin's song, but to another music, more somber and ancient. Every branch in his vision hopped with purple, red, golden, brown songbirds. There was even a firebird trilling on one of the larger branches. The hairy creature snuffled back into the oaks.

"You shouldn't amble through these woods, young man. The Lows of Aer are not to be lightly entered. All manner of strange things are possible here."

Voran strained to move his jaw, and realized that nothing held him in place any more. He jumped up so suddenly that the speaker took two alarmed steps back and raised a walking stick in warning.

"I'm sorry, master," said Voran, eager to make amends. "I didn't mean to startle you."

"No harm done, young man." The voice was as harsh as rock grating on rock, though it had an uncanny melody. It oddly harmonized with the birdsong. "Tell me, what brings you to the Lows?"

The man's face was wrapped in some coarse grey fabric, though a beard poked out of it here and there. He was a huge man, out-gaining Voran by at least a head, and Voran was of the warrior caste. Something about him suggested incredible age, but he moved confidently, like a young man. Voran urgently wanted to make friends with this strange man.

"I am lost. My name is Voran, son of Otchigen of Vasyllia."

The man's grey eyes flashed like the sun reflecting off new snow. "The son of Otchigen? You are far from home, young man. How long have you traveled, then?"

Something in the pit of Voran's stomach twisted. "Only this day. I hunted the white stag."

Voran expected the man to laugh, but instead he unwrapped his face, revealing a smile of recognition. Like the beard, the man's entire face resembled carved stone.

"Ah, a fellow seeker. What good fortune. I am a Pilgrim, young Voran."

Voran could not believe his luck. Pilgrims were unnamed wanderers who traveled all lands searching for the beautiful and the terrible. They were whispered to have a special grace of Adonais. Meeting a Pilgrim in the wild was more valued than catching a questing beast; hosting a pilgrim brought one's family years of prosperity. Many a well-bred housewife would brave open war with her neighbors for the sake of a Pilgrim's visit.

"Good fortune indeed, master! Where do your feet take you this day?" Voran hoped he remembered the correct traditional address to a Pilgrim from his seminary days.

"My feet go where they will, young Voran." The Pilgrim bowed his head, acknowledging the formality gratefully. Voran's shoulders relaxed. "But meeting you perhaps has indicated a surer path. You wish to return to Vasyllia? It will take a week, at least, if you take the usual paths."

Voran's mouth must have dropped open in shock, because the Pilgrim laughed—if harsh rock can be imagined to laugh—and tapped his chin with his stick.

"You meddled with the Powers, young man. No telling what sort of trouble you've gotten yourself into."

"Pilgrim, what do you know of the Sirin?"

The Pilgrim stiffened in suspicion. "Why do you ask? Have you not been chastened enough for your curiosity?"

"Forgive me. It is just...I have seen a Sirin. I have heard her song."

The Pilgrim's eyebrows rose a fraction and his eyes widened a jot, but his body remained still. Voran imagined it took great effort to appear so little moved.

"White stag," the Pilgrim murmured, more to himself than to Voran, "Sirin-song...Is it that time already?" He seemed to make up his mind about something, and now his gaze was firm. "Come, Voran, I will take you to Vasyllia a different way."

Everywhere the Pilgrim went, holloways seemed to carve themselves through the trees. Where Voran saw nothing but trees, the Pilgrim picked out alleys between birches, passages through beeches, and doors through sage-brush. It was like the land belonged to him. As though seeing with new eyes, Voran was inundated with details of the forest he had never before bothered to notice, and he wanted to stop to breathe in the warm birch-smell, to pick out the male sparrow's call from the female's, to run his fingers through rain-soaked juniper for the joy of the sticky drops. But he had to run to keep up with the long strides of the Pilgrim.

"Pilgrim, what was that thing in the sleeping-wood? How did you scare it off?"

The Pilgrim stopped walking, turning to Voran. "That? Oh, nothing but a harbinger." He smiled at something. "Things stir in the deepwoods. Things you Vasylli have not seen, or even heard of, for a very long time."

He continued forward with even more determined tread.

"Voran, tell me something. While traveling, I have heard tales about your father. Are any of them true?"

The anger rose in Voran with the suddenness of nausea.

"Which tales, Pilgrim?" he asked, unable to hide the quiver of anger in his voice. "That he massacred innocent people? Or that he beat my mother, forcing her to run away from Vasyllia in a half-mad state?"

The Pilgrim stopped, abashed.

"Surely *that* is not what is said of Aglaia?"

Voran stopped in mid-stride. The Pilgrim had knowledge of his mother. The possibility made his heart run circles in his chest.

"Pilgrim, do you know what happened to my mother?"

The Pilgrim smiled, but did not answer the question.

"Voran, am I wrong to believe that you have never spoken of these things to anyone? Will you consider it brazen of a Pilgrim to ask your confidence?"

Voran's mouth began speaking even before he gave it permission.

"There is no one I can confess to, Pilgrim. Lebía—my little sister—is still haunted by nightmares. She was only eight years old when we lost both our parents. The Dar is eternally sympathetic, but I don't feel comfortable burdening him with personal worries. His daughter Sabíana, my...intended..." The heat rose in Voran's cheeks. "Well, she is very protective of Lebía, and has a flinty nature. I find it better not to speak of it in her presence."

The Pilgrim smiled knowingly. He pointed forward with his staff, offering Voran to continue speaking while they walked. Voran nodded, and they both walked forward as the carpet of fallen leaves rustled comfortably underfoot.

"Pilgrim, have you heard of the Time of Ordeal?"

"Who has not? Vasyllia's warrior seminary is famed for it. Though I believe my knowledge of it to be several hundred years out of date." He laughed, with a faraway look, as if remembering. Surely he was not *that* old. "Tell me, how many houses are still extant of the original seven?"

"Three remain. All three are segregated, as you know, coming together only for the training and vigils of the Ordeals. The gates of the seminary close, and no one is allowed in or out, not even with messages from family members. The Dar himself has no right to open the gates, except in times of war. The vigils, physical training, and period of intense contemplation are every bit as grueling as the tales have it.

"Eight years ago, I volunteered for the Ordeal of Silence four years before my allotted time. It's a vow that few take, and hardly ever in their sixteenth year, but I sought out the opportunity with pleasure."

"Voran, did you know that some of the oldest legends claim that the successful Ordeal of Silence fulfilled before its time is rewarded with a Sirin's song?"

It explained a great deal. "No, Pilgrim. I did not."

The Pilgrim's smile was knowing. Chills ran down his spine. It was strangely pleasant.

"A week into the ordeal, my mother fell ill. None of the physicians understood it. There were lesions and bruises, and she just withered away. Then she disappeared. No note, no sign of departure, nothing. She just vanished. When I successfully finished the ordeal, the Otchigen I found was half the man he used to be. He had recently returned from a week of searching the wilds, but had found no sign of her. His state grew steadily worse, until I was forced to beg release from my studies, something I hated to do.

"Soon after, Father volunteered for a commission to Karila. There were unfounded rumors of nomad uprisings in far Karila, and it had led to a worsening of tensions between Vasyllia and Karila. He joined the garrison guarding a group of ambassadors who hoped to strengthen Karila's ties to the throne of Vasyllia. I was against Father's going from the start, but the Dar insisted. Said it would do him good."

Through the haze of memory, Voran saw that he and the Pilgrim walked along a more recognizable path than before, and the aspens interspersed with pines hinted that they were coming nearer home.

"You never saw him again," said the Pilgrim.

Voran nodded. He didn't have the heart to speak of the murder of the ambassadors to Karila, or of his father's assumed guilt in their murders.

"Voran, I thank you for your confidence. You may not understand yet why a Pilgrim would be so interested in your family history. I hope, when the trials begin, that you will find some solace in our shared confidence."

Before Voran could answer, he was distracted by a white streak to his left. The stag.

The path turned sharply and led them to a bald patch in the wooded hills, where they entered open sunlight for the first time since leaving the sleeping-wood. The white stag walked toward them in a straight line. He stopped a foot in front of them, and Voran saw that there was a shimmer in the air between them. Voran touched it, and his hand could not pass through. A transparent wall.

"Never mind, old friend," the Pilgrim said to the stag. "We have need of you after all."

The deer raised his head and shook it. Snorting, he pawed the ground with a foreleg. The Pilgrim smiled at Voran.

"He's annoyed with you. He would much rather remain in Vasyllia. Good country, he says, even if a bit on the forgetful side."

Voran was dumbfounded. "Vasyllia is on the other side of that...transparent wall?"

The stag bowed as he had in the clearing, and the gold light from his antlers burst out. Voran raised an arm to his face, but the stag was already gone.

The mustiness of Vasyllia's birches inundated Voran's senses. He and the Pilgrim stood next to a saddle-shaped branch that Voran often slept on during the hot afternoons.

"The white stag is a bearer," the Pilgrim explained, "a sort of... doorway. Between the worlds, you know. But to bear us to Vasyllia, he had to return to the Lows of Aer."

Voran felt no more enlightened than before, but the Pilgrim only rumbled hearty laughter and strode uphill toward Vasyllia.

All of Vasyllia feasted before the gates. Close to the walls, rows of wedge-pavilions marked the families closest to the Dar's regard, all from the third reach. Farther downslope, canvas tents flapped on sturdy frames. First and second-reacher families gathered around makeshift hearths. Heavy pots boiled over with stew. Carts pushed by pantalooned merchants wended their way among the feasters, regardless of social standing. In the midst of it all, a smaller replica of the market day stage had been built, and a story-teller had all the children in stitches, while their parents feigned seriousness, though most couldn't hide their abashed smiles at the ribaldry their children didn't catch.

On any other day, the spectacle would have cheered Voran. He loved a good pageant, as did any Vasylli. To see the entire city together like this, the reaches mingling, was a rare thing. And yet, something was lacking. Somehow, everything about Vasyllia now seemed half-empty, devoid of meaning.

The master bell roared in the palace belfry, announcing the return of the unsuccessful hunting party. Copper bells followed in syncopated chorus, beating in rhythm to the bay of the hunting dogs. Silver bells clamored in the rhythm of a thousand blackbirds.

"Pilgrim," he said, straining to hear himself over the din of the bells, "Will you do my house the honor of staying with us while you visit Vasyllia?"

"Of course, Voran. I thank you for the offer." His voice was more resonant than the bells. For a quick moment, Voran thought that the grey cloak and the stony visage were a kind of mask that the Pilgrim chose to assume for his own purposes, and that his real face was different. But the moment of intuition faded. Voran shook his head, befuddled.

The mountain city loomed before them, many-tiered and many-terraced. Its houses and streets hugged a sloping peak that curved upward like a saber to a pinnacle high above the mists.

Amid the pines and spruces, the city of Vasyllia seemed to have grown from the mountains' bones many ages ago. Towers were extensions of crags. Alleys, bridges, and archways were natural hollows and caves, gently bent to human will.

Something deep within the city compelled Voran. Not the Vasyllia built of wood, cobbled with stone, and planted in earth. No, that was little more than a mask, like the mask of the Pilgrim. The real city lay beneath it. For the first time in his life, Voran sensed there was something living, something vital in the heart of Vasyllia, something no one knew about or even suspected. The hidden Vasyllia whispered to him, though he could not parse out the words.

"You surprise me, young Voran," said the Pilgrim. "How quickly you pierce to the heart of things. Whatever happens, my falcon, do not forget this. Vasyllia is everything. You must never let Vasyllia fall. She is *everything*."

Vasyllia is the Mother of Cities. Nebesta, our first daughter, will forever be jealous of her second place. Karila, the runt of the three city-states, will seek every opportunity to thrust thorns into the side of her mother. But I charge you, my sons, remember this. A true mother always slaves for her children...

From "The Testament of Cassian, Dar of Vasyllia"
(The Sayings: Book II, 15:3-5)

CHAPTER 3

THE MARKET

To Voran's annoyance, the Pilgrim plunged into the middle of the assembled throng of Vasylli. Voran had hoped that he could have the Pilgrim to himself for a time, before the tide of adoration inevitably took him. But Voran's worries were unfounded.

The Pilgrim walked among the people of all reaches, speaking to none and being addressed by none. It was almost as if the people could not quite see him. And yet, everywhere he went, faces brightened and conversations turned boisterous. Even the colors of fabrics seemed brighter after he had passed.

Walking unnoticed among the people, Voran and the Pilgrim reached the gates of Vasyllia. As they did, Voran's heart skipped a beat. He had forgotten that they would have to pass through the first reach.

"Pilgrim, shall we go up another way?" He pointed at one of the smaller gates at a higher elevation. It avoided the first reach entirely.

The Pilgrim looked at Voran, and it seemed that he looked through him.

Voran was ashamed of himself and of Vasyllia, ashamed that

this splendorous city still hid the poor of the first reach in dim alleyways where dogs and children lay side by side in filth.

"Lead as you will, Voran," said the Pilgrim. His eyes seemed to chide Voran, and he felt his face burning. Voran's heart gently inclined away from his desire. To his own surprise, he found himself leading the Pilgrim *into* the first reach, not away from it.

The gates of Vasyllia yawned to accept them. They passed under the arch—two massive beech-trees carved out of marble, leaning toward each other, locked in an embrace of branches and leaves. The refined perfection of the carvings seemed worse than a mockery compared to the squalor of the first reach.

Voran's senses were overcome, as though he were experiencing the first reach truly anew. Smells of horse-dung and freshly baked bread mixed together. The chatter of playing children and the barking of old mongrels joined in a strange cacophony. Most of the houses were hardly more than sticks leaning against each other, with a board for a door. They were not built along any ordered streets like the second reach. Instead, they seemed to be thrown about randomly. Foul-smelling dirt roads meandered between the houses and towering dung heaps, some of which smoldered with fire that never went out.

And yet, behind all that Voran sensed something he never felt in the third reach. Some native vitality belied the filth and poverty. Yes, the suffering around him was obvious. Every street corner was littered with beggars. Some of them fought for territory out in the open, pummeling each other with no care for the glances of others. A few children had a glint in their eyes as they assessed the contents of his pocket. But most of the people here seemed more *real* than in the other reaches. There was something natural and unconstrained in their interactions with each other. It contrasted sharply to the careful conventionality of the merchants, the sour disdain of the nobles, and the constipated piety of some of the priests.

Voran approached the opulence of the third reach with conflicted emotions. From his newfound perspective, he saw his father's house as a sprawling monstrosity, inundated by peach and cherry trees like weeds.

Among them, Lebía danced, arms outspread. The setting sun lit up three singing firebirds on her shoulder and arms.

"Lebía?"

She turned, startled, and the birds flew up at once, giving her a red-gold halo. She smiled, and her smile's warmth was even more astonishing than the firebirds.

Lebía ran up to him and embraced him, her golden curls pouring all over his shoulders.

He picked her up and twirled her as she loved. She laughed, as though she had not a care in the world. Years of tension sloughed off his shoulders like old skin.

"I'm sorry I took so long, swanling."

"Oh, Voran," she said, ignoring his words completely. "I've been trying for *months* to get the firebirds to come down to me. And today, they all came at once, singing. Can you imagine?"

Voran was astounded. What had happened to his sad Lebía?

"Lebía, dear, run and tell cook to prepare something to eat, quickly. We are honored with a Pilgrim's stay tonight."

Lebía was suitably impressed as she assessed the Pilgrim towering behind them in the shadows of the cherries.

"You grace our house, Pilgrim," she said formally, with a touch of uncertainty.

"The honor is mine, little swan," he said with disarming tenderness. "May the blessing of the Heights be forever yours."

Lebía smiled a little, stealing a quick glance at Voran that said, "I am not quite sure what to make of him." Voran inclined his head toward the house. She bowed to the Pilgrim in the formal Vasyllian manner before running into the house, hair streaming behind her like a banner catching the wind.

Voran sat the Pilgrim at the place of honor, in Otchigen's own high-backed oak chair, then bowed to one knee before him, a supplicant in the traditional ceremony of welcome.

"Pilgrim, I greet you for Vasyllia. I greet you in the name of my father Otchigen (may his honor be restored). I greet you on behalf of my sister and myself, the Dar and his family. I beg you to bestow upon us Adonais's grace, given to all who choose to wander the wilds in search of the beautiful and the terrible."

The Pilgrim looked briefly uncomfortable at the mention of Adonais, but he laid two hands on Voran's head and said, "Sometimes the Heights are moved by our fervent supplication, sometimes they are silent for our hidden good. I wish that Voran will find the strength to choose the right way among all ways, though it be the most painful."

A wave of heaviness lifted from Voran's shoulders. He felt younger than he had in years, worn down as he had been by his family's situation. His head was clear and bright as after a full night's sleep. Still, a shadow lurked behind the final words of the Pilgrim's blessing.

Voran and Lebía served the Pilgrim with their own hands while the servant girls stood in the doorway, gawking at the sight. The Pilgrim hardly ate anything, though he constantly thanked them for the morsels he did eat. He enjoyed the drink in greater quantities. Only after he put his horn down for the final time did Voran and Lebía sit down on either side to begin their own meal.

As they ate, the Pilgrim grew more and more somber. By the time Voran and Lebía had finished, he stared at Voran intently with a pained expression. It unnerved Voran, making the space between his shoulder blades itch wildly. He wanted to pelt the Pilgrim with his questions as soon as possible, but convention would not allow it. At table, a Pilgrim spoke first.

"Voran, tell me about Vasyllia's Great Tree."

Voran's ears pricked up at his tone. There was no doubt—the Pilgrim was testing him. Something told him that much would depend on his answer. He tried to feign calmness.

"Well, it's a bit of a misnomer, isn't it? It's hardly even a tree. It's an aspen sapling. But...well, it's on fire. Every year, the priests officiate a ceremony that summons fire from the Heights. It keeps the tree's fire fresh, and the sapling eternally young."

The Pilgrim looked annoyed.

"No, tell me what it *is*."

Something stirred in Voran's memory, an old story his nanny used to tell him.

"It used to be called the Covenant Tree." The details escaped him, no matter how hard he tried. "A seal of Adonais's promise to Vasyllia."

"What promise?" whispered the Pilgrim, his tone urgent.

"A promise of...protection. Yes, a girdle of protection against...oh, Heights, I don't remember."

The Pilgrim sagged into his chair, a look of open despair in his face.

"The stag was right. How forgetful Vasyllia is. I had not realized how forgetful."

Voran slept badly and lay awake before the sun rose. The morning fog promised to dissipate, though the clouds in his mind threatened to remain the whole day. Something must be done about it.

Not bothering to dress, Voran slipped on his boots and wrapped his bare chest with his old travel cloak. Lebía didn't stir, even when he climbed out the window and slid down the carved lintel to the gardens below, to the brook that Otchigen, with the Dar's blessing, had redirected from one of the city's canals. Their own private river.

At least I can thank you for this one good thing, Father, Voran thought.

Throwing off his boots and cloak, he flung himself into the water, bracing for the icy shock. It was immediate and glorious, the sun inside his head bursting apart his huddled thoughts. As he rose again into the cold, he laughed with pure exhilaration.

Afterward, he sat by the river, wrapped in his cloak, which did little to stave off the late autumn chill. The momentary euphoria of the swim had faded, leaving behind nagging unease. The song of the Sirin, which would often tease him after his morning wash, had stopped entirely since his encounter with the stag.

"Early riser, Voran?" The Pilgrim materialized out of nowhere, making Voran's heart attempt a desperate leap out of his chest. Voran laughed, shaking with more than the cold.

"Good morning, Pilgrim." He gestured for the Pilgrim to sit. "I could not sleep. Too many questions."

"Have you considered that you may not understand the answers yet, even if I told you everything? In any case, I am eager this morning to take part in the feasting before the walls. Will you come with me?"

Inwardly, Voran groaned, but he nodded. "It would be my honor."

Though it was early, already many people were huddled around their makeshift hearths in the fields, busy with breakfast. There was a joyful tenseness in the air; Vasyllia had not yet tired of waiting for the success of the hunt. Already a bustling marketplace stood ramshackle around the storytelling stage.

The married women in headscarves with temple rings, the young women with their hair unbound or in the tell-tale single braid—they all regarded Voran and the Pilgrim with smiles that rarely lit their eyes. The men, in tall beaver hats and wide, sweeping coat-sleeves, barely looked at them before passing on to the more important business of the day.

Pipers and fiddlers danced and spun about among the people, sometimes narrowly missing colliding with them, to general comic effect.

Again, that nagging sense that something was missing bothered Voran. It was as though Vasyllia were a woman far past her prime, who still painted her face in the fashion of newly-married youth.

The Pilgrim showed little interest in the usual wares—ceramics, fabrics, trinkets fashioned from wood, some of which sang on their own, some of which moved about in choreographed figures. The chalices of gold did not hold his attention; the woven tapestries may as well have been rags. He walked past the most ornate stalls with hardly a glance, though many of the merchants' wives, impressed with his mien, tried their loudest to attract his attention.

Like hens flapping their wings to attract a cockerel, Voran thought.

The only stall that seemed to interest the Pilgrim was that of an old potter. It was hardly a stall at all, rather a tattered canvas hung over a frame of grey wood. It stood at the farthest edge of the market, surrounded by refuse. The potter, who smelled as bad as his teeth looked, could not even speak from surprise when the Pilgrim approached him.

All of his wares were plain, unglazed, though Voran sensed that they were made with great skill. The Pilgrim seemed to think so as well. He pointed at an urn of perfect proportion, smooth and undecorated. A hand-written rag sported the price: two copper bits. Voran winced at the price. This potter must have no business at all, if he was willing to sell his handiwork for so little.

"May I buy this?"

The potter stuttered something unrecognizable.

"I'm sorry, my brother," said the Pilgrim. "I did not hear you."

The potter's eyes changed. Their dull yellow cleared to white, and something in them sparked. To Voran's surprise, the potter seemed to shed his years before their eyes. He wasn't old at all. He was hardly more than forty.

"From a traveler, I ask nothing but blessing," he said. "Take it with my thanks."

Voran was taken aback. The man spoke in a beautiful accent,

similar to how the old priests spoke. It was a pleasure merely to listen.

"May you be blessed, my brother," said the Pilgrim.

The potter continued to watch after them as they walked back to the center of the market. Shame nagged at Voran, though he couldn't exactly explain why.

The Pilgrim returned to the center of the marketplace, where the tallest hats and the shiniest temple-rings congregated. Approaching a ceramics merchant, he pointed to an urn twice the size of the potter's, glazed and hand-painted with fanciful images of animals and plants interweaving so tightly it made the head spin.

"Ah, you have quite the eye, good sir," simpered the merchant, his five jowls quivering with subservience. "Best Nebesti make, that is."

The Pilgrim raised the decorated urn in his right hand, the potter's simple clay in his left. The crowd stilled. Just before it happened, Voran saw it in his mind's eye, and he had to stop himself from laughing.

"Sudar," said the merchant, using the honorific of respect for a person of indeterminate social class, "may I ask what you intend..."

All the ladies gasped in unison as the Pilgrim dropped both urns to the ground. The Nebesti urn shattered with a beautiful noise. Next to it, the potter's vessel lay as though no one had even touched it.

"And so falls Nebesta," whispered the Pilgrim. His eyes bored into Voran. "But will Vasyllia prove to be as strong as the potter's urn before the coming darkness?"

Voran's stomach churned at the Pilgrim's words, but the Pilgrim merely turned and walked out of the market, accompanied by shocked silence. Voran picked up the potter's urn and turned to pay the merchant.

"Will a silver suffice for your trouble?" Voran asked, abashed.

The merchant glared at him. "Five silver ovals. Not a lead jot less."

Voran chuckled at the merchant's willingness to take advantage of the situation. But he still pulled out only two silvers. He handled them for a moment, looking over their rough edges. These coins were little more than slivers cut from a long bar of grey metal. How strange that they were more cherished in Vasyllia than the life-earned work of an artisan like the poor potter. Shaking his head at his own muddled thoughts, Voran dropped the silvers down in the bulbous palm of the merchant. He rewarded Voran with cursing eyes.

The Pilgrim was already halfway back to the city, his shoulders bent and his step labored. Voran had no trouble gaining on him this time.

"Sudar!" called a voice behind them. It was the potter. "Please," he said, running up to them, "I know you must be a Pilgrim. Forgive me, but...would you honor my house..." He seemed to run out of words, though his hands continued to gesture expressively until he noticed and laughed at himself. Voran had never seen such unguarded simplicity in any man. Everyone he knew seemed to plan every gesture, every word spoken in public. This spontaneity was strangely refreshing.

"Yes, we will come with pleasure," said the Pilgrim.

In the beginning was the Darkness. The Darkness covered the earth. Yet an ember of light there was in the high places. In Vasyllia, upon the mountain, the Harbinger found a people worthy of the Light. He blessed their leader, a man named Lassar, and he made a Covenant with them. As a sign of their calling, he summoned fire from the Heights upon an aspen sapling. As long as the fire burns, as long as the Covenant Tree remains young, Vasyllia remains blessed by the Heights, and the Darkness shall not touch it.

\- From "Lassar the Blessed and the Harbinger"
(Old Tales: Book I)

Chapter 4

At the Potter's

The potter's house stood wedged between two taller buildings—a common mead-house and a smithy. It seemed built of shadows more than wood. But the open door revealed a different picture. A bright hearth illumined a much longer interior than Voran expected. At the far end, the house grew into a two-story loft swarming with small children. Their clamor was far more pleasantly inviting than the sour smell of the mead-house next door. The potter's wife, dressed in simple but clean grey homespun, laughed with her eldest daughter as they cooked something tinged with thyme and mint in the cauldron over the hearth. The potter's many wares adorned every nook and cranny in the long house. Some pots clearly contained stores, but many more overflowed with flowers. Colors in mad profusion burst from unexpected corners—fabrics, blossoms, the bright eyes of a ruddy child. Voran was breathless with unexpected pleasure at the harmonious madness of it all.

The Pilgrim seemed to grow taller and wider as he entered, and his eyes lit up with more than the light of the hearth. He sighed in relief.

"Come, come, my dears," called the potter, clapping his hands as though herding a flock of turkeys. "It is as we hoped. A Pilgrim comes to our home! You will take part in the day's celebration, yes, Pilgrim?"

The Pilgrim laughed—a full-throated guffaw that encircled everyone with affection. Even the hearth seemed to leap.

"What an unexpected joy!" he said. "And I thought no one in Vasyllia remembered this day." Voran wondered what he meant.

The simmering household boiled over, and all the children exploded into movement that looked perfectly rehearsed. Two girls, their braids pinned to the top of their heads, carried an embroidered hand towel to the Pilgrim. A boy of about ten years floated over with a silver basin of water—where did a potter manage to find himself a *silver* basin? —and spilled only a few drops on his way to the Pilgrim. The Pilgrim washed his hands, then lowered his head. The boy's eyes sparkled with delight. He had obviously been hoping for this moment. He threw the remainder of the basin over the Pilgrim's head. The Pilgrim exploded into laughter, and the two girls with the hand towel could hardly keep their hands steady for their own giggling.

The eldest daughter brought a loaf the size of her head, still warm by the smell of it. The eldest son carried a frothing tankard of mead carved in the shape of a mallard. It was exquisite work-manship. The smallest boy—no more than two or three—stood by them with a ceramic cup full of salt. The Pilgrim tore off a piece, dipped it in the ale, then in the salt. He smelled it with his eyes closed, savoring. Then he threw it over everyone's head directly into the hearth. Everyone cheered. Then he downed the tankard, leaving a sip for the boy who brought it. The boy looked like he had been given gold coins for his birthday.

Pleasant gooseflesh tingled Voran's back and neck. He had never seen anything like these rituals. They were rustic, but clearly ancient. How pitiful his own words must have sounded to the Pilgrim when he welcomed him into Otchigen's cold, empty feasting hall.

The potter walked around his children, tucking in a shirt-tail here, fixing a stray hair there. His wife gestured with eloquent hands to two more girls coming down from the loft so insistently that one of them fell before reaching the final rung. The entire family presented itself to the Pilgrim. But instead of bowing before him as Voran had expected, they exploded into a complicated line dance that weaved in and out of a circle of which the Pilgrim was the center. It felt spontaneous, and yet no one stepped on each other's feet. Not even the smallest children. Above the noise of stomping feet, a song rose as if from the depths of the earth. Everyone sang it, even the Pilgrim.

"We greet you, distant traveler!
Rejoice, beloved brother!
You've come from behind the mountain,
You've risen to the high places.
Now bless our grass, our flowers blue,
Our bluebells with your words, your eyes.
Warm our hearts with gentle words,
Look into the heart of these brave children,
Take out the evil spirits from their souls,
Pour into them your living water,
Whose source is locked, and the key is in Evening's hands.
Evening the bright took a walk and lost the keys.
And you have walked the road and found it.
May you bless us, if you will,
for many years, for the long harvests,
for the endless ages of ages!"

Voran found himself inching away from the song and the dance, since he was not party to its mysteries. But the eldest girl took him by the hand and led him into the pattern. To his own surprise, he melded into it without a thought. Something about the steps, the shape of the dance seemed natural, intrinsic, as though his feet already knew what to do. He even found himself singing the song, which they repeated three times.

Finally, they all ended up in a rough circle around the hearth, seated.

"Will you say the incantation, Pilgrim?" asked the potter.

The Pilgrim stood up and raised his hands and began to chant:

"The Evening of the year has come,
And the joys of sun will fade to naught.
Now sleep in earth, our fathers dear,
Kept warm by our remembrance, tears.
We'll give you joy again anon,
When the rising sun sees snow no more."

The potter handed him a bowl filled with oil. The Pilgrim poured it over the fire. It was scented with lavender. Voran breathed in as long as he could, savoring the symphony of herb, cooked fowl, and sour mead.

Now, platters of food passed from one to the next around the circle, and everyone ate with their hands. A large horn full of mead was also shared by all. Voran's head spun from all the constant movement, but his heart was warm and content.

Was he even still in Vasyllia? Nothing in the third reach compared to this simple joy in life. He had thought that the scholars and warriors of the seminary had preserved the mores and traditions of old Vasyllia. But there, everything was formalistic, strict, conventional to a fault. Repeated movements without inner content. Everything in the potter's world was replete with significance.

"Thank you, my friends," said the Pilgrim from his seat, "for celebrating the departed with me. It is fitting. I had thought no one kept the Evening anymore."

He looked at Voran, his eyes probing. Voran felt the flush creep up his cheek.

"Tell me," Voran whispered.

"The Evening, my falcon. It is the old festival of the dead. The remembrance of our departed parents. The send-off of the world into the sleep of winter."

Two of the younger girls giggled at Voran's stupidity. He was surprised to find himself smiling.

"I have never heard of this festival. How many others have I not heard of?"

"There's the Day of Joy," said a boy with a shock of white hair, probably no more than three or four. "Then the Presentation of the Bride, the Awakening of the Ground, the Cleansing of the Harvest, the Summoning of Fire…"

"*That* one I know," said Voran, abashed at the child's precocity.

"There is much that you third-reachers don't notice, I'm afraid, Vohin Voran," said the potter, laughing. "And even more that you've forgotten."

Voran was mortified. The potter had named him, and he had no idea what the potter's name was.

"Sudar, forgive my rudeness. What is your name?"

"I am called Siloán, Vohin Voran. You are welcome at my hearth."

Again, Voran wondered at the purity of the potter's accent. Priest-like, it was. As though speaking the language of Vasyllia had sacred meaning in and of itself.

The conversation weaved in and out of Voran's hearing as he descended into brooding. Shame uncoiled itself inside him. There was so much he didn't know about his own city. So much beauty wasted in the putrid alleyways of the crumbling first reach.

Siloán put a rough hand on Voran's shoulder and looked him in the eye. It lifted the fog from Voran's heart. They conversed. Easily, without constraint. Siloán spoke about things Voran never expected a potter to know—about ancient songs, about the ways of craft that Voran thought long lost, handiwork that required creativity of mind as well as skill of hand.

"You see, Voran…I am sorry, may I call you by your godsname?"

Voran hadn't heard the term "godsname" since he was in school. It was an archaism, a term found more often in the Sayings than in daily conversation.

"Yes, of course, Siloán. It would be my honor."

"I thank you. As I was saying, your bewilderment at the richness of our life here in the first reach is understandable. It is all connected with our general sickness as Vasylli. You must have noticed how the people of our great city prefer cheap, gaudy wares to the beauty of a craft well done."

"Yes," said Voran, thinking of the shattered Nebesti urn. "Things are not made with beauty in mind anymore."

"Have you considered why this is?" The potter seemed eager to share his own theories, so Voran extended an open palm to him, encouraging him to speak on. "Creating something truly beautiful requires labor pains. Vivid as childbearing. Not many willingly choose such a path, especially if every craftsman is encouraged to churn out cheap trinkets by the dozen."

"Yes, I see," said Voran, warming to the topic. "Without the time of labor, there will be no pleasure from the fulfillment."

"You both reason well," said the Pilgrim. "But I want you to think it through to its end. Imagine if every person in the entire city-state avoided these labor pains, as you've called them. Not just craftsmen, but fathers and mothers, priests and elders, Dars and representatives."

"It is like a disease," said Voran, feeling the gaze of the Pilgrim like fire on his cheek. "A disease that would weaken Vasyllia. Not only as a nation. All would become weak in spirit. If not already dead."

"And consider this," said the Pilgrim, his every word carefully enunciated. "What if Vasyllia were faced with an enemy. Not any enemy, but one that lived for an ideal. That was ready to die for it. What if this enemy were a follower of a dark power, servants of another god?"

"We would not stand against them," whispered Voran, his voice heavy. "Not for long."

"Voran, that is what I fear as well," said Siloán. "We are a trivial people if we only come to Temple services because Dar's law closes trade on holy days. A people with dead hearts."

"And so we must do everything we can to reawaken that flame in the heart," said a new voice from the doorway.

The potter beamed at the newcomer. "Otar Gleb! We only needed you to make this evening perfect. Come, come!"

The newcomer was a young priest whom Voran didn't know. He was dressed in a linen cassock with no adornment other than a red embroidered belt. Blond ringlets and short beard with a few white streaks framed a sharp face with exaggerated features. At first glance, he seemed fantastically ugly, especially with a broken nose that covered half his face. But his smile came easily and illumined his pale-blue eyes. When he smiled, he was beautiful.

"Vohin Voran," he said, approaching Voran and taking his forearm in the traditional warrior greeting. "We have not met, but I have long wished to know you. How fitting that it should be this day, and in such illustrious company."

When he saw the Pilgrim, he went a little pale, as though he saw something in him that Voran did not. The Pilgrim smiled in acknowledgement and nodded once.

"By the..." Otar Gleb cleared his throat and chuckled. "What an honor to meet a Pilgrim. Truly you bless this day, when we bring joy to all our dead."

"Vasyllia is blessed while its clerics still zealously labor for the flame in the heart," said the Pilgrim enigmatically.

The conversation around the hearth grew even more boisterous, if that was possible. Voran watched the young priest intently. He was different from most priests he knew. Less concerned with outward appearances. When he spoke to someone, even the smallest child, he looked them in the eye and didn't flinch or allow his eyes to flick away. His smile was always ready, always present in the corner of his eyes, but he only let it blossom fully when he felt joy in himself. Everyone seemed physically drawn to him, despite his ugliness.

"Otar Gleb," said Voran in a rare lull in the conversation, "please forgive my rudeness, but are you a first-reacher?"

"No, Voran. I am a second-reacher. Merchant stock, as it

happens. But with no interest or ability in the fine art of trading. And in any case, you know, I'm sure, that one of our priestly vows is the rejection of reacher status."

Siloán chuckled. It seemed that he and Gleb shared a private jest.

"But now that you mention it," said Gleb, "I find the division into reaches to be a crippling reality for the city, don't you think, Siloán?"

"No, not in the least," said the potter. "Only in our segregation can we hold to the traditions that are so fast disappearing, even in your second reach."

"But the separation limits the reach of your wares, does it not?" said Voran. "Not many third-reachers will buy first-reacher work these days."

In answer, the potter reached behind himself and pulled out an urn, very similar to the one he sold to the Pilgrim. Except it was more beautiful. At first glance, it seemed no more than a simple clay urn. But the longer Voran looked at it, the more perfect it seemed. Its proportions were flawless. Its form and color were unique. The gradations of the natural clay had been manipulated with purpose, but to look as though it were the work of nature. There were even words and figures in between the swirls of clay, invisible to the careless eye.

"Yes, I see you understand," said the potter. "If this urn were to appear in a third-reacher stall at the market, it still would only sell to the discerning eye. And those are rare in any age. Especially our decadent one."

"You do realize that by limiting yourself thus you are depriving your family of comfort and riches?"

"Oh, you third-reachers!" laughed Siloán. "You have so much that your hearts have become small. You can live very well with very little. Sometimes, it is better this way."

Voran wondered if that were really true.

They spent most of the day at Siloán's. Afterward, Voran was morose and unwilling to talk. He meandered through the first reach's dingy streets, wondering at how few trees remained in these levels. The only greenery he saw was the occasional kitchen garden. The Pilgrim took his arm and led him up a staircase leading into the second reach. Just before entering the archway to the clean and orderly streets of the military sector, they stopped at a naked outcrop with a perfect view of the crowd in the plain still feasting in front of the city. From this vantage point, the embroidered designs of the pavilions of the rich took on a life of their own. Here was an embroidered dragon, there a longboat with sail unfurled, even owl eyes staring from butterfly wings. Everywhere the colors danced as the mist from the waterfalls showered the feasters with drops of gold and opal.

"Beautiful, is it not?" The voice behind them was low and musical.

"Good eve, Mirnían," said Voran, feeling oddly abashed. "I had hoped you would be about. I wanted you to meet the Pilgrim in person."

"A Pilgrim in Vasyllia," said Mirnían, his right eyebrow barely rising.

Voran felt like a hump-backed invalid next to Mirnían, though the prince was not much taller than he. Curling gold hair resting on his shoulders, eyes grey as a storm, perfectly straight teeth—Mirnían had everything that Voran did not have, but desired greatly.

"My father the Dar will be pleased to see you, though he is much engaged with matters of state at the moment. I can walk you through the market in the meantime."

"We spent most of the morning there, Mirnían," said Voran.

"Well," said Mirnían as though brushing off a mosquito, "I hardly have time today, in any case. Pilgrim, surely you have tales to tell of the other lands. Yesterday's storyteller was a disaster. Would you honor us on the stage? Tomorrow will be the last triumphal day before the Dar calls off the hunt for the white stag.

Your story may help alleviate the disappointment the city will feel at our famed hunters not finding any trace of it." Mirnían stared at Voran significantly.

"I would like nothing more, Prince Mirnían," said the Pilgrim.

"Excellent. I will send for you at the proper time. You must forgive me, but matters of state, you know."

Voran breathed a sigh of relief at Mirnían's departure.

"Why do you dislike Mirnían?" asked the Pilgrim.

Voran was annoyed at the Pilgrim's astuteness.

"We were very close as children, and soon I am to be his brother. And yet...I don't dislike him, it's only..."

"Tell me, did he take the Ordeal of Silence with you that year, Voran?"

Voran's heart sank. He nodded.

"He did not last, did he?"

"No, he broke after two weeks. But there is no shame in that. It is a very difficult ordeal."

The Pilgrim stared without expression at Voran, until Voran looked down in shame.

"Voran, do you know why the Nebesti urn cracked so spectacularly, while the potter's vessel did not?"

Voran shook his head, not daring to raise it yet.

"It was baked in too hot a fire."

Voran looked up.

"I thought the heat strengthened the clay, Pilgrim."

"The right amount of heat does, just as the right amount of adversity strengthens any relationship between two people. But there is one fire that is always too hot. Do you know what that is?"

Voran did not answer.

"Envy."

They joined the main road of the second reach that led through the open marketplace—now empty of stalls—toward the center of Vasyllia. Ahead of them stood the large central square, at the heart of which stood the Covenant Tree. Pale flames danced over the translucent leaves of the aspen sapling, which stood barely taller than a man. For a moment, Voran thought the fire was low. But that was unlikely. It was months still until the day of the summoning of the fire.

"Pilgrim. Do you think the potter is right? Can we restore the ideal of Vasyllia? Or are we just idealistic dreamers?"

The Pilgrim exhaled a long, wheezy breath, all the while staring at the sapling. Finally, he looked at Voran with heavy eyes.

"Come, I will show you."

The Pilgrim took Voran's arm, his grip like an eagle's talon. A white light enclosed them, rising out of nowhere, and for a moment Voran saw nothing but the light. Then it dimmed, and the aspen burst into wild color. The aspen was surrounded by red and silver fire—firebirds and moonbirds frolicked and sang with the kind of joy one sees in a one-year-old child just awoken from a full night's sleep. Surging waves of purple, red, orange, blue, brown pulsated around the tree—songbirds unable to contain themselves enough to sit on a branch. All their music interweaved as though imagined by a single mind, harmonized from a single melody.

The single melody came from far above the aspen sapling. Three Sirin reigned over their kingdom of lesser birds, flying a distant circuit around Vasyllia. One wept, one laughed, one remained stern and impassive. All three sang, each her own variation of a single melody, each weaving in and out of the other, first a motif of joy, then a shadow of grief, replaced by a long moment of introspection. Then all three sang in unison, and Voran fell on his knees, unable to bear the weight of the music pressing down on him.

All around, Vasylli walked with heads high, backs straight, quiet joy and hidden song evident in each face. Strange flowing robes adorned both men and women. It was as though one of the old Temple frescoes had come to life.

"This is Vasyllia as it used to be, yes?" Voran asked the

Pilgrim, his voice hardly above a whisper. The Pilgrim inclined his head, looking around with an expression Voran couldn't quite define.

As he looked at them, Voran was amazed at the faces of these past Vasylli. Nearly everyone in his own Vasyllia walked with bent shoulders, eyes turned inward, faces full of cares. In *this* Vasyllia, joy burst forth from the eyes of every person. But there was something more. Voran tried to focus above the music of the Sirin, and suddenly he saw.

"Pilgrim! I can see every one of their talents. That man. With his own hands, he will carve the great stone chalices catching the falls, working days and nights without end. When I look at that girl with the long hair, I see an embroidered banner that will be carried in battle, sparking inspiration in the hearts of many warriors. That woman will raise a Dar long to be remembered. That man will raise a temple in a land far away, a land of endless fields of undulating grass. And their hearts! Every person has a flame in their hearts, burning steadily. What is that flame?"

"It is the soul-bond with the Sirin. This is the Vasyllia of the days of the Covenant. Over one thousand years ago. Lassar of Blessed Memory is Dar."

Voran gasped in pleasure. No time was more decorated with legends. No time gave more of the Old Tales and Sayings than the reign of Lassar. But the pleasure was short-lived, as his own Vasyllia returned to his thoughts, so grey and drab compared to this place.

"How much beauty has been lost, Pilgrim. Every person here is a maker, a creator of vast potential. I can see every man, woman, and child shine with beauty, beauty made and beauty lived. Now all we care about is the latest trinket from Karila sold at market."

Voran sat down on the bare earth, hugging his knees. He felt exhausted, emptied, confused. Why did the Pilgrim show him so much? Was something expected of him in return?

"Why did we lose it all, Pilgrim?"

The Pilgrim's half-smile faded as he looked down at Voran.

"Many reasons, my falcon. Chief among them, you forgot your part of the Covenant."

"We have always been taught that the Covenant between Vasyllia and Adonais was merely an instructive tale. A reminder of Vasyllia's greatness, surely, but not literally true. What have we forgotten?"

The light faded as though the sun were obscured by a cloud. Voran looked up at the sky, but there were no clouds in the sky. Yet the darkness deepened. A chill crept up his arms and down his back. He shivered.

"You forgot the Darkness, Voran. It has been so subtle, these centuries. So wise. And now, no one even remembers it. But it lives. Look up, Voran."

He pointed at the sun, looking at it directly, to Voran's amazement. Squinting in expectation, Voran turned to the sun.

It was almost completely gone, a creeping darkness devouring it. The darkness ate and ate, until nothing was left. Voran began to shake with fear.

"It comes, Voran. The Darkness comes."

All around Voran, men and women were running about, hands shielding their faces in fear. Mothers clasped their children, husbands encircled the waists of their wives. They were no longer in the flowing robes of Lassar's time. Voran's heart plunged.

"Yes, Voran," said the Pilgrim. "This omen is not of the vision. It is happening now."

Vasyllia roiled around them. A river of people rushed through the gates back into the city. Guards in the Dar's black livery ran past Voran, trying to restore order.

"Come, Pilgrim, we must go." He took the Pilgrim by the arm, but the big man did not budge. Voran turned back at him, questioning.

"Voran, it begins. So soon, and so much yet unsaid. They move so quickly against us. If you remember anything, remember this. Find the Living Water. They must not find it first."

The prince lay dead, his heart pierced by his own brother's arrow. The wolf and the falcon watched over him.

"Fetch the Living Water," said the wolf.

The falcon flew beyond the thrice-nine lands, into the thrice-tenth kingdom. He found the Living Water under the shade of a young apple tree in the first garden of the world. He poured it over the prince's wounds, and they faded away as though they never were. The prince came to life again...

From "The Tale of the Deathless and the Living Water"
(Old Tales: Book II)

CHAPTER 5

THE STORY

Though the darkness that swallowed the sun soon dissipated, it took the greater part of the day to calm Vasyllia. After ensuring Lebía was well, Voran put on full armor and joined the ranks of his brother-warriors as they attempted to calm the people and prevent any outbursts of public violence. Only a few young men, their blood up, tried to take advantage of the mêlée to settles scores, but they were easily contained.

Voran returned late to find the house asleep. Not bothering to take off his mail, he crumpled in exhaustion at Lebía's side and feel into a deep sleep.

He dreamt that he walked back to the center of Vasyllia, toward the Great Tree. The path widened into the square, paved in large flagstones, all four sides lined with the gabled inns and taverns of the second reach of Vasyllia. The burning aspen seemed small, its flames sputtering.

Walking around the sapling, the Pilgrim caressed its leaves as one caresses a lover before a long separation. His singsong rumble was nearly in unison with the hum of the twin water-falls, which from this vantage point appeared to plunge directly on either side of the aspen, framing it. His words were inaudible, but chant-like. His joy-pierced tones were tinged with grief.

The flames of the tree flared for a moment, then died.

The song of the Sirin flooded the air. Voran's Sirin flew once around the sapling, chanting with the Pilgrim. Voran's chest ached as though his heart were torn out. He was desperate to run to her, to beg her to sing to him, but as is the way with dreams, he was immobile as stone.

Voran awoke to clanging pots and shattering crockery. The house was in an uproar, servants rushing about and whispering nervously to each other.

"Cook, what is all this racket?" Voran asked as he entered the kitchens, still in yesterday's mail.

The cook, thin as a reed—everyone jokingly called her "your lardship" behind her back—did not even stop to look at him.

"Prince Mirnían sits in the high hall with the Pilgrim, breaking his fast. There is to be a city-wide storytelling today. The Dar hopes it will calm the people after yesterday's omen."

"And you did not think to wake me?" Voran growled.

She flashed him a knowing smile and turned the piglets spinning over the hearth. "Lady Lebía said you've not snored so loudly in weeks. It would've been a crime to wake you."

By the time Voran dressed and made his way down to the hall, Mirnían and the Pilgrim were already mounting horses in the courtyard.

"Voran," said Mirnían with a sardonic smile, "so good of you to see us off. I had quite an appetite today. Her lardship tells me there are no more partridges in your cellars, I'm afraid. Do tell her how much I enjoyed them."

Voran cursed inwardly. Partridge was his favorite.

"I will see you at the storytelling, I hope. Don't forget that it's in the main square today. All festivities outside the city walls have been canceled after the omen." Mirnían turned his horse around and rode off. The Pilgrim followed, surrounded by an honor guard of twelve black-cloaked spear-bearers in helms.

As he joined the crowd of all reaches walking to the storytelling, Voran was pleased that he had an opportunity to walk alone. In his worn travel cloak, he easily blended in with the crowd, affording a rare pleasure of hearing the latest rumors.

Most of what he heard was nervous tattle, the people still nagged by yesterday's fear. Voran let those conversations wash over him, seeking a word or phrase that would force his attention. There! The words were innocuous enough on their own, but there was something unnerving about them.

"You don't believe me?" She was a matronly sort, fat from much childbearing. "He *saw* it, I tell you. That's why I'm braving this morning, what after the omen, you know. I want to see it for myself."

"Your husband is always seeing things." The second speaker was an older woman, probably unmarried, at least judging by a bitterness that sounded long-established. "He's as reliable an observer as he is a teller of tall tales. Every time he tells that story about hunting the boar, he adds to the number of his wounds."

"You *never* give him the credit he deserves. You will see. He said it quite clearly. The fire on the aspen is nearly out. And we're nowhere near the day of summoning."

Voran's skin crawled. Perhaps what he had seen was not a dream, but a vision? Had the Pilgrim sung a funeral dirge for the tree?

Straining for the sight of the tree through the houses, Voran pushed forward through the crowd. As he entered the square, he stopped, hardly noticing the grumbling of the people who jostled past him. There was no mistaking it. The fire on the tree was simmering, no more. It looked as though a gust of wind would put it out.

Voran found himself stranded, the square too full for him to push his way closer to the stage at the foot of the tree. The tension stretched around him like a viol string at its snapping point.

"Friends!" Mirnían spoke from the stage, and the crowd's noise lessened. "Some of you have already heard of our unexpected honor. Vasyllia is visited by a Pilgrim."

All around Voran a murmur of appreciation rose. The tension eased palpably, and Voran breathed out with it.

"He has traveled alone for many days, and all for the pleasure of seeing our land. Let us welcome him."

More tension released in the music of their clapping hands. Even Voran, who liked to think himself impervious to mob mentality, felt his heart swelling.

"Yesterday was a dire day, my friends, there can be no doubting it. Though I am loath to say it, the hunt for the white stag has been canceled, and the omen of the darkened sun is enough to chill the heart of the bravest. But lest we think our own misfortunes too great, let us hear of the horrors and wonders of the other lands. I put it to you, dear friends. Shall we let the Pilgrim take the mantle of the storyteller for the day?"

Once again, universal cheers.

The Pilgrim walked forward and assessed the crowd. All cheering stopped as the people shriveled under his gaze. Some even began to mutter in discomfort. An awkward chuckle broke out somewhere, but was cut off immediately. The Pilgrim seemed to be searching for someone or something. His eyes caught Voran's, and Voran heard the Pilgrim's voice clearly in his mind: *I am sorry, my falcon. I am sorry for everything.*

Voran's breath grew labored. A sense of inescapable calamity seized him. He tried to still his breathing, but the more he tried, the tighter his chest constricted. It was painful just to stand there. He needed to escape, to be anywhere but here. But he was hemmed in on all sides.

"I once knew a man who owned a great wealth of cherry trees," the Pilgrim began in a storyteller's sing-song. "His cherries were legendary—they were just sour enough, just sweet enough, just red enough. But one year the cherry orchard produced no fruit at all. Some gardeners blamed the warm weather; others blamed the soil. The rich man was greatly saddened by this.

"He walked through his favorite cherry orchard, amazed at the beauty of the trees. The leaves were the same transparent green they were in early spring; a faint fragrance rose with every breath of wind. They were a sight to behold, but they had no cherries, and it was nearing the end of the picking season.

"And the rich man grew more and more sad at the failure of the orchard. But there was nothing to be done. The ground was expensive; he could afford no fruitless trees. And so, with tears in his eyes, he took an axe and chopped down every tree himself."

The Pilgrim stopped. Slowly at first, then rising like the wind before a thunderstorm, the crowd gave rein to its disappointment. The Vasylli never liked parables, thought Voran. The sense of impending calamity lessened, but it took a great force of will to unclench his fists. There were white marks on his palms where the nails bit.

Mirnían approached the Pilgrim, apparently encouraging him. The Pilgrim's shoulders sagged an inch further with each of Mirnían's words. He seemed a man broken by grief. It was strangely incongruous—the scene was one of festival, with banners fluttering on every windowsill and the people dressed in their finest. And yet, the fire on the tree sputtered.

Mirnían seemed to have won the argument, because the Pilgrim faced the people again with a story on his lips.

The Tale of the Prince and the Raven

Beyond the thrice-nine lands, in the thrice-tenth kingdom, there lived a restless prince. He had everything he could ever want

—riches, health, a beautiful princess as his intended bride. But despite all this, wanderlust ate at him constantly.

So he left behind his love to climb the mountains, to explore the forests, to swim the rivers, seeking to slake the thirst of his restlessness. But nowhere did he find the peace he sought.

One day he stopped to drink from a pure mountain spring. It was a taste of paradise.

"Do you like the water?" croaked a voice behind his back.

It was a withered old man, all tawny beard and hair, twisted and resembling a tree stump more than a person.

"Yes, I do," said the prince. "I do not think I have ever tasted such water."

The creature leered with a leathery, lipless mouth. "Hah! That is nothing. I have water that will make this water taste like sand. Not only will you never thirst again, but your greatest desire will be fulfilled instantly. What do you desire most, young man?"

The prince could not believe his ears. Could this be the end of his quest?

Just then he looked up and saw a great eagle lounging on a spruce branch like a monarch on a throne. What exhilaration there must be in soaring through the infinite sky!

"I wish to fly as the eagle," said the prince.

"A very worthy desire. The Raven can provide that."

The prince had heard of the Raven, a mysterious spirit of the forest, though he supposed it nothing more than a story in the shriveled imagination of a village hag. He remembered the tales he heard in childhood—stories tainted with blood and loss. A creeping fear wrapped itself around his heart, but he laughed it to scorn.

"What do you require in return?" the prince asked.

"Oh, I require nothing. The virtue of my enchantment is such that I will partake, in small measure, of your pleasure."

"Is there nothing else?"

The Raven shook his head, and the trees began to quiver, and the wind moaned like a crying woman.

"So be it," said the prince.

The Raven pulled a carved wooden flask from his dirty robes, and the prince drank. Fear suddenly flashed in dreadful clarity as he saw the face of his beloved in his mind, pale as death. He gasped as his breathing grew more painful. Terror gripped him. He could not breathe. A light stabbed his eyes, and he fell.

It took him a blank eternity to realize he was flying. His feathered arms caressed the waves of wind as they hugged his eagle body. His eyes met the sun's rays, and he did not need to look away. Through his eagle eyes, the sun was a spinning furnace of purple, orange, even green tongues of flame.

A dark streak dimmed the sun for a moment. A swan, feathers black as a mountain's peak at midnight, flapped toward the mountain stream. Her beauty enraged him, impelling him to destroy this usurper of his glory. He screamed and plunged on the unsuspecting swan.

An alien emotion disturbed him. Pity, a frantic desire for mercy. The eagle recognized the prince still inside him, and he unleashed his anger to drown out the vestiges of man. A warm stream of blood poured over his talons. He could smell the swan's life oozing out. Dropping her corpse with disgust, he turned once again to the dancing wheel of fire.

An intense pain clutched his chest. The colors of the sun turned grey and the whirling dance froze; the air cut his lungs like daggers. His arms lost their feathers; pudgy nobs replaced them.

He came to himself near the stream, a man again. He crawled to its edge. There, propped against a boulder, lay his beloved princess. Her face was white with death. He touched her cheek and took her hand. It was slippery; blood streamed down her arm. Her shoulder had the unmistakable imprints of an eagle's talons.

A noxious croak jolted him. On a swinging branch above him, a raven was laughing, its black head nodding insanely. The prince lunged at it, but it flew without effort up to the sun, laughing still. Near the roots of a nearby tree lay the wooden flask, taunting him.

Silence. Then whispers bubbling up like a pot of stew reaching a boil.

"What a horrible story."

"Is that a Karila story? Never heard anything so absurd."

"What a disappointment. They don't make Pilgrims like they used to, it would seem. What tripe."

The whispers rose into a dull groan, the mass of people rocking back and forth like a river in the wake of a longship. Then they parted in the middle. Voran was confused at first, not being able to see, but as the parting reached him, he saw Rogdai and a few other wardens leading a young man, dressed in brown and green woodsman's garb. Voran had a vague memory of the boy— he was a few years his junior in the warrior seminary. A dreamy, odd sort of boy. Not good for battle. What was his name? Tolnían, he remembered. A scout.

He felt cold as he realized what that meant. The chief door warden was leading a simple scout directly to Mirnían in the middle of a storytelling. Voran pushed some very annoyed old people aside and joined the small party approaching the stage. Rogdai saw him and looked as though he wanted to say something cutting, but he nodded curtly and looked forward.

"Rogdai," said Mirnían, simmering with rage. "I hope you have sufficient reason to disrupt the storytelling."

Rogdai bowed silently and moved aside, prompting Tolnían to walk forward.

"My prince," said the young scout in a soft voice barely heard over the crowd's commotion. "Living Water has been found in Vasyllia. They say a blind man has already been healed."

"Rogdai," said Mirnían, no longer trying to keep his anger contained, "you are a fool if you think this sort of rumor was worth stopping the storytelling."

"But, Highness..."

"Don't interrupt me. You know the proper protocol. It

should be the elders in private counsel that gave us this information."

"Mirnían," said Voran, his heart dropping to his heels. "Rogdai is right. The Living Water is never spoken of in the Old Tales without mention of the Raven and his eternal quest to seek out the Living Water. To become the Deathless One."

Just two days ago all that would have seemed little more than childhood silliness to Voran. But no longer.

"The Raven?" Mirnían looked like he couldn't decide whether to laugh or fume in anger. "Deathless ones? Voran, have you gone mad?"

"Whether or not those old stories are historically accurate, they all contain deep truths that we should never ignore. Living Water never appears without—"

"Enough!" cried Mirnían, now red in the face. "Rogdai, you and the scout are to report immediately to the Dar. Voran, go home before you embarrass yourself any further. Is this the sort of behavior befitting the future consort of the Darina Sabíana?"

The words echoed in the square and in the eyes of the crowd surrounding them. Voran was struck dumb. Mirnían had never yet chosen such a public stage to humiliate him. He turned to seek out the Pilgrim on the stage. Maybe the Pilgrim could speak some sense to Mirnían. But there was no one there. The Pilgrim was gone.

Lassar's days are long gone. Four hundred ninety-six years to the day of his death. And again, the darkness preceding his Covenant gathers. It reveals itself in the plague that already rages in the outer reaches of the Three Lands. The Raven escaped Vasyllia. For all I know, he is at the brink of finding Living Water. But no Harbinger has come to give light to my reign. Am I wrong, then, to seek a renewal of covenant with Adonais for my people, though it cost me my very soul?

From "The Apocryphal Diary of Dar Cassían"
(The Sayings, Appendix D:6e)

CHAPTER 6

THE DAR'S DAUGHTER

Sabíana despised high day afternoons. Once a week, it behooved Adonais—or at least the clerics who spoke in his name—to confine all members of the Dar's household to the palace. All anyone wanted was to be outside for as long as possible before the winter, especially since today was a day of story. Instead, they were ordered to dedicate the half-day to the restoration of the Temple holies. Today—a day of deep winter-blue sky, crisp air, and birdsong—Sabíana's sacred work was the restoration of an ancient banner. She tried to remember how many weeks in a row she had slaved over this half-tattered rag. She lost count at seven.

It was a large square banner depicting a Sirin in flight. The style was archaic: the Sirin was flattened, her face oddly twisted toward the viewer. Her woman's head was badly fitted to her eagle body by an almost nonexistent neck; the wings were far too widely outstretched, the talons looked too long with respect to the rest of the body. The face was long gone, and even in the weeks of her work, Sabíana had managed only to finish the eyes.

To her dismay, she saw that one of the eyes was bigger than the other. How had she not noticed it before? She silently groaned.

Two other girls joined her soon after she began, sitting opposite her at the long table brought into her chamber once a week. They sat demurely, not daring to speak, though the stifled smiles warned that soon decorum would fail, and the gossip would begin. Sabíana wondered if she would even have five minutes of silence with her thoughts.

"What a fine figure that Yadovír made at Temple today, did he not?" attempted one of them, a pale girl of thirteen.

"Yado—who? Do you mean that *first-reacher*?" hissed the other, appalled.

Sabíana groaned, audibly this time. The girls' heads snapped back to their work, and she won another few minutes of blessed silence.

Now that her fingers overcame their initial clumsiness to act of their own accord, Sabíana could finally give a little rein to her thoughts. She told herself she would not think of Voran. Immediately his green eyes invaded her mind. They were striking in his pale face, framed by dark, shoulder-length hair. Sabíana ground her teeth in frustration.

He had changed. For days, he had not so much as sent her a note, much less seen her. Not for the first time, the dark thought nibbled at her mind. If she had not pursued him, would Voran have found the courage to seek her out himself? Immediately, she felt guilty and tried to push the thought away. A sickly sweet afterpain remained in her stomach.

"My father told me that the traitor's son got what his father deserved!" The younger girl's face was red with annoyance. Sabíana realized that she had stumbled into the middle of a heated argument.

"Your father is an upstart second-reacher who speaks far more than he should," said the other girl, smirking.

"Silence, both of you," Sabíana said, smacking her palms on the table. Both girls jumped, and the younger immediately melted into tears.

"Enough of that, Malita." Sabíana tried to make her voice

soothing, but it came out raspy. She patted the younger girl's hand. The girl jerked it away. "Tell me, what traitor's son are you talking of?"

Malita flushed and shook her head, continuing to sob.

"Go on, I won't bite you, I promise." *But I may bark some more, if you don't speak quickly.* "Surely you don't mean Vohin Voran, son of Otchigen?"

It was as if the girl's face were brushed over by white paint, then quickly repainted again in dark red.

"Malita, I am ashamed of you, to be spreading rumors. Do you not realize how much Vohin Voran has lost in his life?"

Malita looked up, lips pursed in exasperation. "I am only repeating what everybody knows. Mirnían himself..."

"Do not presume to name the prince without his honorific."

Malita stamped her foot, and the tears flowed anew. The other girl, embarrassed to be the cause of her friend's fit, interjected, though not looking up from her embroidery.

"What Malita was trying to say, Lady Sabíana, is that *Prince* Mirnían was absolutely justified in his public rebuff of Vohin Voran this morning..." The girl's voice tapered off. She gathered the courage to look at Sabíana, but immediately faded back into dumbfounded fear. Sabíana realized her fury must be visible in her face. She would have to work on her composure. Later.

"Public rebuff? What in the Heights do you mean, girl?"

Malita sensed she had a chance to gain ground. "After the storytelling today, my lady. Vohin Voran and Prince Mirnían had a very public confrontation. The prince threatened him."

Sabíana rose abruptly, pushing back the wooden bench so fiercely that it flipped over. Both girls, shoulders tensed and hunched over, looked very attentively at the embroidered clouds above the Sirin's head. Without giving them another thought, Sabíana pulled the door open as hard as she could. It crashed, and the young sentry at the door, a boy of no more than fifteen, jumped half a foot into the air.

"That will teach you to sleep at your post, soldier," she said as she passed him. "Let that be the last time, or your elders will hear of it."

The boy straightened and saluted, fist to chest. Two beads of sweat streaked down his cheek.

Sabíana hid a smile as she hurried down the tapestried hallway. She really should not enjoy rattling the boys so much, but the pleasure never lessened for its frequent repetition.

Her mirth quickly subsided. Mirnían. Arrogant, pathetic weakling! She knew how deeply he still felt his failure at the Ordeal of Silence, and how greatly he resented Voran's success. Was this how low he would stoop to get his revenge?

Past a rounded archway, a wall of icy wind slapped her face before she could descend the stairs hugging the sides of her turret. Perhaps it would be best to avoid the outdoors. Reaching the new rushes strewn on the bare ground below, she turned left through a heavy oak door that creaked with disuse. A curving staircase stood beyond the door, rising to a latticed hallway lined with white stone pillars in the form of trees, with nothing but the clouded sky as a roof. At the end of the open passage stood another wooden door with a carved Sirin in a tree. Her father's private room.

She raised her fist to knock, but stopped. Voices, raised. She put her ear to the door and closed her eyes. Mirnían, his tone plaintive, petulant in his most childish way. Father's answer. Angry. Gooseflesh prickled her neck. Father had not been this angry in a long time. She closed her eyes and held her breath, trying to make out the words. Her father spoke.

"You dare to excuse..." Something muffled, maybe *reason*? "Can't understand. How..." again incomprehensible... "without my knowing?"

Sabíana pushed gently, and the door opened a crack.

"It is not for you to determine, Mirnían!"

"Father, these rumors come from the wilds every five minutes. Do you remember when all of Vasyllia was in a flurry over a rumor about nomadic armies massing in the Steppelands?

When was there ever a nomadic army that threatened anything?”

“Oh, Mirnían. You will not stand there and tell me you see no difference with this situation.”

Silence, tense as the lull before a storm.

“Father, I really don’t see how I should be held responsible for...”

“A Dar is always responsible, you fool!” Father sighed audibly. Sabíana heard more in that sigh than exhaustion. It was old age. “If you will not take responsibility for your lapse in judgment, perhaps you will be kind enough to explain how it is that a future Dar allows himself to publicly berate a future member of his own family?”

“Pah! You don’t actually think Sabíana will go through with it.”

Sabíana pushed the door and advanced on Mirnían. Seeing her, Mirnían’s eyebrows shot up, and he blanched. He retreated three steps and raised his hands in self-defense.

“You idiot, Mirnían! Why is it that I, a *woman*, can see the ramifications of your actions better than you can yourself? Have you stopped to think for even half a second? You know what sort of element likes to feed the rumors about Voran’s family. You have publicly allied yourself with the babblers. You appear weaker than my future husband. Is that a good vantage point for a Dar-to-be?”

Mirnían stiffened. Sabíana had a sharp desire to strike him across the face.

“Enough, Sabíana,” said Dar Antomír, but his voice was gentle. “He has enough to think about without you berating him.” He pulled her toward him, then leaned on her, grimacing with pain. She helped him sit back down.

“Tell her, Mirnían,” he said, wheezing. “That will be punishment enough. And it is time you learned to respect her counsel more. You will have no better counsellor when I am gone.”

Mirnían looked at her as he did so often in childhood. It was a silent cry for help. How often she had seen that face, whenever he was at his wits' end, whenever he knew he couldn't do without her. Poor Mirnían. So talented with people, so generous of heart, so beloved for his beauty and his charm. But just enough wit to know that he lacked the wisdom needed to be Dar. He was once again a little boy in her eyes, face unwashed and eyes wide. She smiled at him, the pity nearly overwhelming her.

"About a month ago," began Mirnían, "I was finishing an inspection of the door wardens. It was late evening. The doors were already shut when a merchant caravan came into sight at the far end of the plateau. It was one of our second-reachers, one of the more prosperous ones, I believe. I ordered the doors open, though it was after the closing horn-call.

"Everything seemed in order. The Karilan wares—the silks in particular—were exquisite, and the merchant reported nothing amiss with the journey. Just when I was about to send them home, the merchant's daughter, a little sprightly thing, probably five or six, took a liking to me. She ran up to me. Told me she had a big secret. She said she saw a hawthorn tree weeping tears of water."

Sabíana failed to understand the significance of the story. Dar Antomír smiled mischievously. "So, you do not know everything, do you, my swan?"

She felt a flush creep up her cheek. "I'm missing the key to the cipher, Father. What does this story have to do with what happened today in the square?"

"Then today," said Mirnían, more boldly, "Tolnían, a young scout, reports that Living Water has been seen in the form of a weeping tree. At least one healing has been recorded."

"Oh, by all the Heights," she whispered in shock. "This is not your fault, Mirnían, but how terrible that you said nothing."

"I don't understand why everyone is so disturbed by this news," complained Mirnían.

"Do you not?" said Sabíana. She shook her head. "Mirnían, what happened after the last appearance of the Living Water?"

Mirnían's whole body sagged and he raised both hands to his

face. They were shaking. "Internecine war between the city-states," he said. "But how was I to know? It was just a little girl's story."

"Enough of that," said Dar Antomír, more firmly. "No time for it. Now, lest someone in Nebesta or Karila decides to start another internecine war, we must act. Mirnían, stay with me and help me see through this mess. Sabíana, I want you to find Voran. Bring him here."

She was grateful. Father always knows what I need, she thought. She walked out without another word.

Sabíana found Voran wandering the streets aimlessly, seeing nothing and no one. He looked thinner than he had in weeks, with dark shadows under his eyes that made their green color shine with an eldritch light. Where were his thoughts? Would he be upset to see her after Mirnían publicly insulted him?

He caught her eye standing across a cobbled street in the second reach amidst the merchant homes and public houses. People walked between them, only pretending not to see the daughter of the Dar and her future intended. It was not normal for them to appear in public together, certainly not like this. Luckily, he hurried across the cobbles to her.

"My love, I'm sorry, I didn't see you there," he said, breathless, though he had not been walking fast. His face was grey and sickly. He took her hand in both of his. They were hot to the touch.

"Voran, what has happened to you? You don't look well."

"Don't mother me yet, dear," he whispered, flashing his usual smile. It was brief, but enough to warm some of her doubts away. "There will be plenty of time for that later."

"Voran, I came from the Dar. He needs to see you now. Will you come?"

A storm cloud passed over his face for a moment, but he

nodded. His eyes glazed over again, and she felt no responding warmth from him when she took his arm.

Sabíana led Voran toward the waterfalls, up a narrow path hugging the headwall of the mountain, overlooking the empty marketplace of the second reach. The path rose gradually until it entered the mountain's wall through a thick curtain of ivy, near the canals flowing from the twin chalices. It was her private way back home, a secret path in a city full of them. She vaguely remembered that her nanny never liked her taking this way. Apparently, there was an old tale about the Raven escaping Vasylli prisons through this passage.

"Sabíana," Voran whispered as they walked through the torch-lit passage within the mountain. "What do you make of all this?"

"I don't know, Voran, I haven't had time to think."

"Did you know the Pilgrim has been staying with us these past nights?"

It explained much of Voran's absence. "No. No one bothered to tell me."

He was silent, though she was sure she could smell his embarrassment in the dim light. Good. It was high time he apologized for neglecting her.

"Do you remember what your nanny used to say about this passage? About the Raven's escape?"

She stifled her annoyance. She would make sure he would apologize later.

"Yes. She would still tell me the tale now, given half a chance."

"You were not at the storytelling, were you?"

She had been expecting something about Mirnían's outburst. She braced herself. "No. I'm sorry, Voran. Mirnían has so little self-control, sometimes."

Voran looked at her with a confused expression. "Oh, that? I had forgotten about it already. No, I mention it because the story the Pilgrim told was about the Raven. One I have never heard before. It's certainly not in the Old Tales."

As if on purpose, a chill wind howled through the passage, dimming the torches. Sabíana's blood chilled.

"Pilgrims don't say anything without good reason," she said.

"Yes, exactly. Just after the story, Tolnían came with news of Living Water. It made me think."

"About the traditional link between the appearance of Living Water and the Raven's eternal quest for immortality?"

"Yes. What if it's true?"

Sabíana guffawed, but stifled her laugh. He actually looked upset.

"Voran, you don't believe those stories are actually true?"

He looked about to continue, but a thought occurred to him and he stopped, dropping Sabíana's arm. He assessed her with cold eyes, the eyes of a stranger. She felt frigid and half-naked before his gaze.

He turned away without saying another word.

"I don't think there is any way of preventing mass pilgrimage to the weeping tree," Mirnían said as Sabíana and Voran entered.

"There's nothing wrong with pilgrimage, my son," said Dar Antomír, faintly disapproving. "I would go myself, had not Wicked Woman Age grabbed me by the left ankle."

The room was tense with expectation. Dar Antomír, never more bent and careworn, insisted that Voran and Mirnían exchange the brotherly kiss. He beamed at them with sanguine eyes, though Sabíana could not help noticing how thin was his white beard—once an avalanche on his chest. They grudgingly embraced, and only the pleasant babble of the Dar's speech managed to ease their tension as they stood around a small table, staring down at a map of Vasyllia.

"There must be military presence, of course," said Mirnían, though he offered his counsel carefully now, as if expecting Sabíana to contradict him immediately. She kept her peace.

"Yes, and more than a few warriors," said the Dar. "Do you see the opportunity, my children? I've long wanted to gauge the response to a strong military show on the outliers, especially those with Nebesti blood ties."

"Have there been any rumors of discontent from that quarter, Father?" asked Sabíana.

He smiled ruefully. "Only Vasylli are simple enough to think that all lands relish to be under the lordship of Vasyllia. The purported place of the weeping tree is very near the Nebesti border. I know Lord Farlaav of Nebesta well, and I do not think he is the opportunistic kind. But the same cannot be said of others in his court. Do not forget Nebesta is traditionally governed by a kind of mass fist-war they call a representative assembly. Nothing like our Dumar. Voran, what do you think?"

Voran seemed mesmerized by something on the map, his concentration so great Sabíana expected the map to go up in flames. He seemed not to have heard the Dar.

"Voran?" she asked, touching his shoulder. He recoiled from her as though her touch were hot iron.

"I'm sorry, my love," he whispered, shocked at himself and probably also at the livid flush she could not hide. "I am not myself."

He looked away from Sabíana, shimmering with barely-repressed energy.

"Highness, I beg you to allow me to lead the pilgrims."

He trembled feverishly, his face white except for a crimson smear on either cheek. A thin sheen of sweat gathered on his hairline.

"I don't think so, Voran," said the Dar, assessing Voran through half-closed lids. "I would be much comforted by your presence at my side, especially now that the Pilgrim has disappeared. Too many dark omens."

Voran did not seem to have heard a single word.

"Highness, my family is indebted to you for everything, I know that. You have given far more generously than I or Lebía have ever deserved. You know I have never asked anything for myself." He paused, seemingly out of breath.

"No, Voran, you have not," said the Dar, his frown deepening.

"I ask it now. I must seek the Living Water. It is not merely for myself. The Pilgrim told me to. For Vasyllia."

Mirnían snickered and rolled his eyes. To her surprise, Sabíana found herself agreeing with her brother's reaction.

"Voran, you are not well," said Mirnían, his voice lathered in sarcasm. Voran did not even acknowledge him. It was not that he ignored him; he seemed not to have heard him at all.

"Highness, I beg you." Voran's voice was no more than a whisper, but it seemed to echo.

Dar Antomír's eyes began to fill with tears. Sabíana knew why. This whole situation was a repetition of Otchigen's ill-fated command of the embassy to Karila. It filled her with dread.

"I sense this is something I cannot prevent. May Adonais bless it."

Voran fell on one knee and bowed his head. Dar Antomír placed his right hand on his head and kept it there for a moment. When he lowered it, Voran couldn't help notice how covered it was with brown spots, how gnarled beyond recognition.

"Go, my child. Choose what warriors you wish. The pilgrimage will set out one week from tomorrow."

Voran stood, bowed, and kissed Sabíana's hand. He looked at her with a fleeting glance that refused to engage her eyes. She had the disconcerting sense that she had slipped into a dream. Everything moved slowly, and the loudest sound in the room was her own heart beating. Voran walked out without waiting for her.

"Father, am I the only one who sees?" Her throat had gone completely dry. "Or have I gone mad? Does no one else see the parallel?"

Dar Antomír would not look at her. "Voran sees a chance to redeem his family's name, Sabíana. Would you deny him that?"

"Father," said Mirnían. "You once assigned a half-mad

Otchigen to the Karila embassy. Now you assign a half-mad Voran to take charge of tens, if not hundreds, of city-folk, right after an omen of the skies. You expect a different result?"

"I hope for one, yes," said the Dar. He sat down again, exhausted. "My children, I fear that dark times are coming. After the omen of the skies, the Pilgrim came to me. Pilgrims are not as other men. They are closer to the Heights, and some barriers of the natural world are but trifles to them. Some of them live for three hundred years or more. So when he came, I listened.

"We spoke of many things, most of which you will know soon enough. He told me a darkness is coming the likes of which Vasyllia has not seen in hundreds of years. He spoke of a plague that would afflict man, beast, tree, blade of grass. He spoke of a fountainhead of healing flowing from a heart of stone."

Sabíana gasped. "A heart of stone. Voran means stone in Old Vasylli."

Dar Antomír smiled and closed his eyes, leaning back into his chair. "You understand, Sabíana. That is why I have hope for Voran."

And yet, the dread in her chest tied itself into knots over and over again, until she feared she would never be able to untie it.

The soul-bond between man and Sirin is unlike any other bond of love. It defies clear explanation, but it is known by its fruits. The soul-bonded man can withstand inordinate pain, can carry burdens which no man can lift, can survive in battles, though he be the lone warrior in the field. But the true nature of the bond is that it removes a man from earthly wants, calling him to desires of eternity. No man, once bonded, will find rest until he has undergone the seven baptisms of fire and climbed to the very Heights of Aer.

From "On the Nature of the Soul-Bond"
(The Sayings, Book XI, 4:1-5)

Chapter 7

Sister of the Pariah

On the third morning of the pilgrimage, the fog glimmered, pregnant with the coming sun. The birth of the sun brought spring warmth in the midst of early winter. A steaming tarn in winter usually meant one thing—dreadful cold—but the children knew before anyone else that this steam was different. It meant warmth. By the time Lebía had made breakfast for Voran, three boys already blattered in the water with their dogs, while the girls, skirts hiked up, stood at the edge, toes longingly nibbling the water. Lebía had a giggling desire to push the girls in, then to jump in herself. Instead, she sat by the porridge to wait for Voran. She would not be welcome among the laughing children, not the daughter of Otchigen, not the sister of Voran. *We are pariahs.*

She began to plait a new set of bark shoes, humming to herself. Already some of the younger children's shoes were wearing down on the hard roads. It was pleasant to do something for them, even if they might not want to accept a gift from her hands because of her association with Otchigen. She would have to think of a way of gifting them without being noticed.

The music she hummed was a new song, she realized. That often happened to her. She would hear snatches of music already formed in her heart. It never seemed strange to her; how could it? She had been hearing music since she was a small child. Only later did she realize its source.

She had seen her first Sirin when she was ten, on a day when her heart-pain at her mother's loss was like a wedge splitting apart an ash log. It was only a glimpse, but she knew it was no accident, because the shards of her heart grafted together and blossomed. After that, whenever the pain threatened to break her, the memory was enough to bring her back to herself.

The Sirin had continued to visit her, though always at a distance. Lebía sensed that the distance was more for her benefit. She had no illusions about the Sirin's love. It was not gentle; it was fierce as fire. More often the Sirin sent her gifts of music.

The tent shivered behind her. Voran pushed through the flap, sodden with sleep. How strange that their roles should be reversed now. He was always the early riser in Vasyllia, but since they had begun the journey, he seemed incapable of getting up with the sun.

"Porridge again, swanling?" He complained, but with enough of a smile to make rejoinder unnecessary.

It was the first time since they left that he called her by his "little name," and it warmed her more than the unseasonable sun. He had been categorically against her going on the pilgrimage. Only the most convincing stubbornness she could muster—never easy for her, especially toward Voran, who was almost a father to her—managed to sway him. He punished her with dour silence for the first day, and only spoke to her in clipped phrases the second.

"I've added dried apples this morning, Voran."

He ate with the relish of a famished wolf. Poor Voran. He had changed so much since the coming of the Pilgrim. He was restless by nature, but this unquiet bordered on manic.

"Voran, what happened with Sabíana?"

Lebía couldn't help noticing that Sabíana had left their house that morning weeping. She was not even there to see them out of the city with Dar Antomír.

"Lebía, why do you ask me such things?" His face was beet-red. "You are too young to understand."

"Am I? Too young to see that you deliberately wounded the woman you claim to love?"

"It was not…" He stopped, breathed, and sagged a bit in the shoulders. "You are right. It was deliberate. I have not been able to put her face out of my mind since then. I do not know why I spoke to her like that."

"Voran, I am not accusing you. I just want to understand. You know I love you."

The creases in his forehead smoothed into his quick, winning smile. "Oh, swanling. Sometimes I forget about the weight of pain on your sixteen years. You want to know the truth?"

Lebía nodded, purposely not looking at him, intent on her fingers plaiting the rough bark. There were a few cuts on them, but only in the uncallused places.

"When I asked Sabíana to marry me, I did it like a madman jumping off a cliff. I never thought she would consider me, not after…"

He closed his eyes and sighed. His usually thick, curly black hair was mangy, hanging in strands around his shoulders. He had not shaved in weeks, but he looked the better for it, his angular features set off pleasantly by the messy chin-beard.

"Swanling, it's a terrible thing, our human nature. We spend all our energies on getting things we never expect to receive, but if by some miracle we receive them, they start to lose their luster very quickly."

"You didn't expect her to say yes?"

"Well, I hoped she would. But then the Dar had to agree as well. I was sure she was being kept for some Lord something-or-other in Nebesta. When he agreed, and blessed our union whole-heartedly, I thought my joy complete. I saw my life then as it would be. Lord Protector to Darina Sabíana, a life of luxury in the palace, the love of a passionate woman whose beauty has no compare in Vasyllia, children on the bear rug before the hearth."

"Sounds like our father's life when we were children."

"Exactly. That was the first thought to give me pause. Then the small, still voice deep inside me. *Not enough*, it said. I still longed for something with no name, or someone whose name I had not yet found. That was the first time I heard the song of the Sirin."

Lebía's heart raced. She thought she was the only one who knew the longing that sometimes comforted, but sometimes emptied.

"Everything changed after that?"

"Not immediately. I was always with Sabíana in the palace, walking the secret cloisters and the summit cherry groves. Those were moments of happiness I had never known. Poor Sabíana. She doesn't know what longing is. She is all fire, all desire, all forward movement."

"Voran, do you love her?"

He stared at his porridge, his eyes never more green. He plucked at his chin-beard.

"I do, Lebía. I always have. I just didn't know there could be a feeling more powerful than the love of a man for a woman."

It took the better part of an hour for the mothers to convince the boys to come out of the tarn to begin the morning leg of their journey. As it was, the crowd of pilgrims usually left far later than was probably necessary, but there were nearly a hundred people on the pilgrimage of all ages, and it seemed some had come more for the change of scenery and the joy of good company than for a religious experience.

Lebía loved watching Voran race back and forth on his black charger every morning, tightening up discipline among the warriors. She was proud of him, even if she laughed at him silently for being a touch pompous in his manner. He had no idea how ridiculous he looked.

That entire day, Lebía walked alone. By the evening, she had grown lonely again, and almost regretted coming. Finally, Voran rode to her and dismounted, handing his reins over to one of the younger warriors. Voran looked eager to speak, his mood lightened by the warmth of the day.

"How much longer, do you think, until we reach it?" Lebía asked.

"Well, the weeping tree is supposed to be not far from the Nebesti border on the side of Vasyllia's lands. Roughly one hundred miles through mostly mountainous terrain. At the rate we're going? Two weeks, maybe more."

"Will we come near Nebesta, the city?"

"No. The Dar's road splits in two at the Nebesti border. We go straight, the road to Nebesta goes left, hugging the border along a narrow valley until you hit the city at the end of the valley. It's beautiful, you know. All wood where Vasyllia is stone. A confluence of two rivers and some of the most gorgeous forests you've ever seen."

"I wish I could see it."

"You can see the border range over there." Voran pointed at a series of jagged peaks that started at their left and reached all the way to a point directly ahead of them. They looked like the rotting teeth of an old man. Fog encircled the tips of the left-most peaks, and something darker than fog swirled there as well.

"Strange," said Voran. "That looks like smoke."

He stared at the column of cloud reaching toward Vasyllia from the Nebesti side. It was pinkish in the late morning sun. Then he shook his head, thoughtful, before turning back to Lebía with a smile.

"Lebía, here I am blabbing away. And you have not yet told me why you so wanted to see the weeping tree."

Their road led straight ahead to a dip between two drum-hills, the left crowned with aspens, the right with birches.

"It's easier for you, Voran. You are an intimate of the Dar. I sit at home. Sometimes the pain of our parents' absence is like a physical illness. There are mornings when I can't rise from bed."

"You hope the Living Water will heal that wound?"

"To be honest, I don't think it will. But yes, I hope."

"There is something else, then?"

She found a barrier between her thoughts and her words. To speak was as hard as to move a boulder covered with moss from a riverbed.

"Voran, there is something very wrong in Vasyllia. The omen merely confirmed it for me."

"Yes, I have begun to feel it as well, swanling."

"It sounds terrible, what I am about to say. It has hurt so much, seeing how everyone was willing to attack our father in his absence, when he couldn't defend his name. With such obvious enjoyment, too. People who allow that cannot be good. Now, I don't even care much for Vasyllia anymore. I'm going on this pilgrimage because I can no longer stay in the city."

Voran looked thoughtful.

"Lebía, I agree with you. But do you know what the Pilgrim told me? He told me Vasyllia was *everything*. He told me I must never let it fall. As if *I* could do anything about it."

The last sentence was said more for himself than for her, she thought.

"Is that why you seek the Living Water?" she asked

"Well, the Pilgrim told me to find it. But there's also something else. In the Dar's chambers, when I saw that the weeping tree is at the top of a tor called Sirin's Peak, I felt a summons as strong as the music ever was."

"You hope to find the Sirin?"

He nodded.

The first of the pilgrims had reached the narrowing pass between the drums, being forced to walk only three or four abreast. Voran and Lebía were still on the downslope of the road, and for a moment the sun hid behind the right drum, only visible in the golden leaves of the birches crowning it. When the sun came up over the trees, it was fire-white, brighter than Lebía had ever seen. It rose with a faint music, as though singing. Then it hit her. The light was not the sun. A Sirin perched on the top of the central birch, bathed in her own light.

Yearning pierced Lebía's heart with a keen, pleasant pain. She knew, in that knowledge that surpasses a movement of thought, being something already formed in the heart, that the Sirin on the mount offered Lebía a choice to meet face to face. No more distant visits, no more hints of music. She could have the soul-bond only read about in tales. She could be consumed in the fire of the Sirin.

She desired it as much as she had desired anything in life. It all welled up inside her—all the injustice, all the pain, all the promises never kept. Had she ever asked for anything for herself? Did she not deserve this consolation more than anyone? No one else even believed in the Sirin.

But then, she looked at Voran, and something inside her balked. He was so unhappy. And he was so incapable of being unhappy. She was used to it. He needed this more than she did.

"Voran, do you see the birches on the top of the hill there?" she said, her voice heavy. "It's a good vantage point, is it not? Would you do me a favor? Go up there and see what waits for us on the other side."

Immediately, the light faded, the music faded, the world faded. Voran's eyes widened and he gasped in pleasure. She knew that now the Sirin sang for him alone. She had made her choice, and the Sirin had accepted it. Voran rode off without looking back. Lebía wept.

If man is to brave the Heights of Aer, to face the Throne of the Most High, he must endure the seven baptisms of fire. The soul-bond is the first baptism of fire. The second is the passage from Earth to the Lows of Aer. The third is the shedding of the skin of the old man. The fourth is the first death. The fifth is the great sacrifice. The sixth is the second death. The seventh...is a mystery.

From "On the Emulation of the Powers"
(The Sayings, Book VII, 7:1-7)

Chapter 8

The Sirin

The song of the Sirin rang out, drowning out the noise of the pilgrims. Everything else faded from Voran's mind. It was even more intense than in the forest the first time. He left his horse in the hands of one of the warriors. He felt it would be somehow blasphemous to encounter a Sirin on horseback.

"Lead them on," he said, not even realizing who it was he was talking to. "I'm going to take a look from the top of that hill."

Voran climbed, slogging through cold mud to a stand of birches leaning upward along the incline of the hill toward the sun. Their exposed roots held the earth like grubby hands. Voran slipped over them, finding the way harder than it looked. As he reached the head of the drum-hill, he cleared the line of trees and entered a small clearing, in the middle of which stood three white birches, taller than the rest, still clad in autumn gold. His Sirin perched on top of the middle tree and sang. Voran found that his cheeks were wet with tears, and his heart sang in unison with the Sirin. Approaching her was nearly impossible, as though ten strong men were pushing back against him with all their force.

He could go no further and went down on his knees, the linen shirt under his mail sweat-soaked and sticking to his skin. The

Sirin no longer chanted, but Voran feared to look at her. She flew down, alighting in front of him, so that her face was directly in line with his. Mastering himself, he forced his eyes to lock with hers. Something inside him shifted. He heard a soft, regular thumping, as of another heart, and a small flame came to life in the center of his chest, radiating warmth to the rest of his body. He heard many musics—joyful, haunting, terrifying—all at the same time, but with no disharmony. He was covered in golden flame, warm and dew-like, and he did not burn. His mind lurched with terror; his heart raced with joy.

"Voran." Even when she spoke, she sang. "I am named Lyna."

Voran could find no words for a long time, content only to look into the abyss of her eyes. It was never easy for him to look into another person's eyes. It was dangerously intimate, and he was squeamish about that kind of intimacy. Looking into her eyes was like staring from a peak at a river at the bottom of a valley, jumping down without closing his eyes, and then plunging into the river, only to find it had no bottom. There was no single word for it.

After a long time, he retreated from her eyes and saw that she had an oval face framed with auburn curls, a mouth that seemed incapable of laughter, an expression of austere sorrow, like a living statue. Under her collarbone, undulating blue-green feathers shimmered down to her golden feet and talons and ended at the black tips of her outstretched wings.

"What a blessed and cursed day this is, Voran." Her wings moved with her speech like human hands. "Sirin and man are joined once more, though it comes at the time of testing."

"Why have you waited so long to greet me, Lyna?" His voice sounded crude compared to the music of her voice, like two rocks tapping each other.

"My falcon, the love of the Sirin is a blazing fire. We cannot force it on anyone. For generations, none have been ready for the soul-bond. It is a glorious thing, but it is heavy, as any true love must be."

Never had confession of love sounded so simply, and yet if the earth gaped and volcanoes erupted around him, he would not have been surprised. After the soul-bond, he felt nothing could ever surprise him again.

"Lyna, can I stay here with you? Must I continue my journey to the Living Water?"

"You do not know what you are saying, my falcon. No love can exist where there is no forward movement. If you stayed here too long with me, you would be consumed. You are not ready for the full bond."

"There is so much I do not understand, Lyna. So many questions. What is happening to Vasyllia? With the Covenant Tree?"

"The tree's fire is fading, Voran."

"Is it the Covenant, Lyna? All we Vasylli remember is hints of old stories."

"They contain much truth, those old stories. The Covenant was a simple thing. Vasyllia was to protect the Outer Lands against all darkness, caring for and nurturing all peoples. In return, Adonais girded them with power. Nothing could touch Vasyllia. The Harbinger summoned the fire that confirmed the Covenant. While the aspen is on fire, the Covenant stood. When he returned, he witnessed the covenant broken. The fire will fade until it is no more."

Voran's heart chilled. The Harbinger. The greatest of Adonais's allies; a name never spoken above a whisper, so great was the reverence attached to it. Did she mean that the Pilgrim was the Harbinger? It would explain his strange powers.

"No one in Vasyllia believes in the Covenant, Lyna. Even I find it hard to fathom with my mind alone."

"Do you wonder, then, that no Vasylli is bound to a Sirin anymore? In the time of Lassar, nearly every Vasylli was bound to a Sirin. Five hundred years later, in the reign of Cassían, less than half were. Now, four hundred years after the death of Cassían, no one seeks the old beauty."

"How could something this important be forgotten, Lyna?"

She was silent for an age. She seemed to be searching for the right words.

"When love grows cold, my falcon, eternal truths darken."

"You are saying that we have not done our part to care for the Outer Lands? But we have enough troubles in our Vasyllia. The separation of the reaches—it is a terrible thing. How can we be held responsible for the welfare of outsiders, if we cannot keep our own house in order?"

Lyna sighed heavily and shook her head. Her curls danced in the wind.

"Your own heart can answer that question, Voran. But there is so much noise there, so much confusion."

"Lyna, you must speak to me as though I were a child. Please, I want to understand. Be patient with me."

"Yes, my falcon, I will try. Recall the image of Lassar's Vasyllia that the Pilgrim showed you. Was there anything unusual about the people you saw?"

"They were more joyful than any people I have ever seen."

"Do you imagine that their Vasyllia had fewer problems than your Vasyllia? You would be a fool if you did. You know your histories. Lassar was a man of war; only after many trials, much blood, did the Harbinger come to him with an offer of Covenant. And yet, the joy in their faces. You saw it. Joy like that comes from only one source. Pain."

Voran nodded, remembering his talks with the potter.

"Yes, pain. Did you not suffer pain during the Ordeal of Silence? Were you not rewarded for that pain a hundred-fold? Does not the artist suffer his creation? Do you not think all those people you saw suffered pain in the making of those works of beauty whose loss you so lamented?"

Voran was surprised that he did not wonder at Lyna's deep knowledge of his thoughts and emotions. Truly the bond they shared was soul-deep.

"Tell me, Voran. What is the most beautiful thing a man can mold and form, though it is not of his own creation?"

How many times had he pondered the same question while sitting half-frozen on the banks of their river of a morning?

"His own life," he said.

"To make his own life beautiful, what must he do?"

It came to him like floodwaters, overwhelming.

"A human being can only become truly human if he lives for others. That way, the way of love, is by necessity the way of pain. Shared pain. Co-suffering."

He felt the dew-flames flare up around him again. A darkness of which he had never been aware lifted from his heart, and he was calm. He could not remember the last time he felt so calm.

"Where do you think Vasyllia received its name?" she asked. "The Vasylli is the one who gives his life for another. You all know it; you all repeat it endlessly. But meaning is lost in endless repetition."

"Vasyllia was named *after* the Covenant," Voran whispered to himself.

"Yes. There are few true Vasylli left, Voran."

"Lyna, what can I do?" He felt small, like a child called to account for his older siblings' misdeeds.

"Seek the weeping tree, my falcon, before it is found by one who has sought it for ages." She shimmered and began to fade. "We must part now, but know that I am always with you, even if you cannot see me. You are unformed yet, Voran, only crude clay in the hands of the potter. There is risk and loss in every meeting, so choose carefully when you seek to see me again. I leave you with hope. The Harbinger walks the earth once more. If he finds true Vasylli, as he did in the time of Lassar, he may reforge the forgotten Covenant. But I fear much pain and loss must transpire before then."

He heard the sound of wind whistling through reeds as Lyna flew up to the sun. She was gone, but her song remained in the flickering flame warming his heart.

When Voran came to himself, it was already late evening. Nowhere did he see any sign of the pilgrims; even their racket, which he thought could be heard for miles, was absent. How long had he been with Lyna? He shivered with cold and rising dread.

Then he remembered how his encounter with the white stag seemed to move him to a different place entirely. The Lows of Aer. Only entered in certain places and times, and always perilous. He looked around in consternation. Truly, this was not a place he recognized. There was no road, only an overgrown path such as a woodsman might use. The peaks of Vasyllia's main range were much closer than they should have been and in *front* of him. In the dim light, it was difficult to make out much.

He must have entered into the Lows of Aer during his encounter with Lyna. Coming out of them, he must have been displaced again. He would have to be more careful about crossing that threshold in the future.

He heard something behind him. A cry or a moan. Could be an animal, but it sounded human. He ran toward it, along a path cresting to a grassy knoll. When he looked over its edge, he gasped.

As far he could see, a beech wood extended to the horizon, rising and falling gently. A mass of people labored through the trees, their number greater than he could count. Some were already rising up the hill to meet him. They were bloody and hobbled. Then he understood the sound. The wailing of grieving women.

Leading them was a tall middle-aged woman leaning on a branch. She saw him about a stone's throw away, stopped, her expression confused, but not frightened. Next to her walked a skeletal girl no more than six years old.

"Matron," Voran called to her. "What is all this? Who are you and what has happened?"

"Are you but the skin of another changer, come to devour what is left?" She threatened with the branch. Her voice was like dried peas rattling in a box. She had a strange accent. Nebesti, probably.

"I do not understand you. I am Vohin Voran, the son of Otchigen of Vasyllia. I bear you no ill will, Matron."

Her eyes seemed to shift somehow, as though she had not fully seen him until now. He felt the flame in his heart surge toward her, and she gasped in surprise. When she could speak again, her voice had more power to it.

"They are all dead and burning, dead and burning. Blood, fire everywhere. Like...living torches..." She shuddered. "Son of Otchigen, we are all that remains of the ancient and glorious city of Nebesta. The Second City is destroyed."

The world is not as it seems. You think there is only the visible world for the living, and the invisible for the dead and the immortal? You are wrong. There are many realms interweaving with each other like the threads in a tapestry. Most are invisible most of the time. But sometimes, some people fall into other realms or encounter the denizens of those places. Some of these Powers are good. Many are not...

From "A Primer on Nebesti Cosmology"
(The Lore of Nebesta, Book I, 3:6-8)

CHAPTER 9

THE FALL

Among the ubiquitous women and children—some walking but most hanging on their mothers—Voran found no men at all. The implication was chilling—whoever did this had killed or captured the men and sent the women forward to spread tales of terror in their wake. Whoever this enemy was, they were cunning beyond Voran's experience.

The woman who spoke to him called herself Adayna, daughter of Farlaav. Once she seemed satisfied Voran was not a "changer"—Voran had no idea what that was—she took him into the mass of refugees, eager to share something, a secret of some kind.

"I managed to save the Voyevoda, my father. But he will not last long."

He was an old man, though his beard was still black with two streaks of white, like a badger-pelt. He lay on a makeshift litter pulled by a horse half as dead as he was. Only his face was visible in the mountain of furs keeping him warm.

"Lord Farlaav," said Voran. "I am Voran, son of Otchigen."

"Voran? I knew your father." He looked suddenly lost, gazing about wildly, hoping to find something to orient him. "Are we near Vasyllia?"

"No, I suspect we are a week or so away. But you need not worry, Vasyllia will care for your people. You have my word. Please, what happened to Nebesta?"

"I do not quite know what to tell you first, Voran. There was no warning. In the weeks leading to this attack, some of our rangers disappeared in the wild. It should have alerted us to our danger.

"It happened in the dead of night, and suddenly most of the city was burning. How they breached the walls I will never know. An army of mounted men, screaming in a foreign tongue I've never heard. Their skill with the arrow is not human. They are like men possessed, with supernatural strength and cruelty. They call themselves Gumiren."

Voran had never heard of them. In the back of his mind he remembered an old rumor, from about ten years ago, that nomad armies were assembling in the far Steppelands. Could this be the result of that muster?

"But even they are not the worst danger," said Lord Farlaav. "In every shadow of the fallen city, unspeakable things lurked—monsters the like I've only read about in stories. I would not have believed it without the witness of my two eyes. Huge wolf-men and bird-creatures and many-headed snakes with wings."

"Lord Farlaav, are you sure? Perhaps in the heat of the—"

Lord Farlaav lifted himself up from the litter with a groan and grabbed Voran's arm, gasping with the effort.

"Listen to me! I saw what I saw. If you do not believe me, there will be nothing to stop him."

"Him? Who?"

"This is not a human enemy we strive against, Voran. The Raven is coming."

The effort was too much, and he collapsed in a dead faint. A pool of red seeped into the furs at his back. Adayna pushed Voran aside and called for help.

Voran's mind reeled, but his instincts took over. He seemed to hover over himself, watching as he ran back and forth, cajoling here, ordering there, pushing, pulling, jostling, and helping along. Within an hour, he and Adayna—she had a new stick and had tied a wolf-fir around her chest with a leather thong, giving her the appearance of a nomadic priestess—led the mass of wounded Nebesti toward Vasyllia. He carried the skeletal girl on his shoulders. She was Farlaav's great-granddaughter. Both of her parents, Adayna's daughter and her husband, had been killed.

For the first day, Adayna spoke little, leaving Voran to his thoughts. He was almost unnaturally calm after his encounter with Lyna, but his mind told him that he was courting disaster for seeming to abandon the pilgrims, even for the sake of these thousands of refugees. Anyone else would be lauded by Vasyllia for saving the remnant of Nebesta. But it was more likely that the son of Otchigen would be imprisoned for abandoning his charge and leaving the pilgrims to an untamed wilderness crawling with creatures from nightmares and an enemy that slaughtered people just to make an impression. The Dar would be right to imprison him.

Worse still, he had lost Lebía. Agonized worry for her gnawed at him—he was sure he would have a red gaping hole in his chest by the time he reached Vasyllia. The desire to turn back and find her was so strong that a few times his feet seemed to turn aside of their own accord. Every time he moved back to the path, he imaged Lebía's corpse riddled with arrows.

Another fear was the realization that the only way he could justify himself before the Dar and Dumar would be to tell them of the Sirin. But that was impossible. No one believed in the Sirin anymore. Actually claiming soul-bond with a legend? Impossible.

Yet he saw no other possible solution. He could not abandon the refugees. Neither could he fathom abandoning the pilgrims. But he had no idea where they were. To make matters worse, the farther he traveled from his encounter with Lyna, the more his sense of loss and yearning deepened. The flame in his heart remained alight, but it did not fill him, only leaving him warm enough to live.

On the second day, Adayna was more inclined to speak. He

was glad of the change. Speaking to himself was becoming tiresome.

"Adayna, does your father still live?"

"He fades, Voran. I hope he will survive to Vasyllia. To see Dar Antomír would ease his passing, I think."

"Tell me, what did you mean when you thought I was a changer?"

She looked at him with the gaze of those who have seen too much to care about social niceties. Voran felt a flush creep up his cheek.

"Did you believe my father's account of the Raven's army of horrors? I saw it myself, Voran, too clearly to doubt. A warrior, seemingly human, who changed shape before my eyes. Where a nomad archer stood one moment, the next lurched a creature with a human body and a lion's head."

Voran said nothing, though the dread inside him deepened.

"Nebesti lore tells of changers, spirits of the abysses who wield the power of transformation. Vasyllia has no such legends?"

"I have never heard of such a thing."

"Nevertheless, it is spoken of. The Raven is the first of these."

"The Raven I know, though many think him merely a cautionary tale." But if the Sirin were real, could not other legends walk the earth as well? Find the Living Water, said Lyna. If the Raven walked the earth, it was clear that he came to Vasyllia to find the Living Water. How would Voran ever convince the Dar of the need to protect the weeping tree from a monster out of stories?

"That carn ahead of us," said Adayna, "the one red with sun-blood. Is that not Vasyllia Mountain?"

"Yes, it is." Voran smiled at her use of the word "carn"—an archaism in the Vasylli language. "A few more days, and your people will find refuge."

"But for how long? Surely you cannot doubt that the Gumiren come for the jewel of the Three Cities?"

There was faint irony in her voice, and Voran recognized

Nebesta's old jealousy at being the Second City. He could not blame her. If what Lyna said about Vasyllia's responsibility to care for all Outer Lands was true, then the Vasylli had much work before them to restore goodwill with Nebesta, Karila, and the lesser cities. Too many years of bad blood. Housing the refugees of fallen Nebesta would be a good start.

Vasyllia Mountain grew by the day, and on the seventh morning they were within sight of the city. Here, the dirt paths they had taken finally merged with the Dar's road. As soon as Voran and Adayna, walking a bowshot ahead of the others, had stepped on the road, something slipped in and out of view at a point where the road dipped down and out of view.

"What was that?" said Adayna, tense with fear.

"Vasylli scouts. Don't be afraid. They are only performing their duties. Now the city will be informed, and we will be met at the gates." Voran's even tone belied his perturbation. Why had the Vasylli scouts allowed themselves to be seen so easily? Were things truly falling apart so badly in Vasyllia that even the scouts couldn't stay off the Dar's road?

By mid-day, they approached Vasyllia, wading through the stubs of reaped wheat, still poking through the half-frozen soil in the fields of harvest that lay before the city. The gates stood open, and three companies of warriors in black were arrayed before them, banners—gold sun on black field—unfurled, spears glistening in the late autumn sun.

"You said we would be met," said Adayna, "but I did not think you meant armed warriors."

Voran walked ahead with Adayna, his hand tight on his pommel. Two mounted guards cantered toward them, both swordsmen. To Voran's disgust, one of them was Rogdai.

They had not spoken since their wager. Rogdai had seemed eager to avoid Voran, and Voran had been happy to oblige.

Rogdai took off his helm.

"Vohin Voran, I charge you in the name of Dumar with abandoning your charge of protecting the pilgrims. You must come with me immediately."

Voran was struck speechless. He had expected at least some banter about his father's wine, at least, before things got unpleasant.

But to be charged by the name of the Dumar, the assembly of the people? That was interesting. The Dar was still on his side, it would seem. That gave Voran a measure of courage.

"Vohin Rogdai, I will come with you as soon as you can give assurances to the daughter of Lord Farlaav, Adayna, that the remnant of Nebesta will be given refuge in Vasyllia."

Rogdai hesitated, then dismounted. He fell on one knee awkwardly before Adayna.

"Forgive me, lady," he said. "Remnant? Is what Vohin Voran says true?"

Adayna stood tall and straight, through Voran sensed her exhaustion.

"It is. We are all that remains of Nebesta, Vohin Rogdai. I cannot speak for our outlying villages, though I fear the worst. I hope Vasyllia will remember her hospitality in this time of need."

Rogdai looked down at the ground, unable to hold her gaze. He seemed embarrassed to continue speaking.

"I am... sorry, my lady. The Dumar has made it clear that all refugees must remain outside the city until further notice."

"Apparently, the Dumar did not inform the first reach, Rogdai," said Voran, pointing to the city.

A mass of first-reachers poured through the gates, bearing tents, blankets, pots, and sundry other daily necessities. They were led by the potter from the marketplace, the one who made the perfect clay urn. Voran was pleased to see Rogdai seething with impotent anger.

"Lady Adayna," said Voran, "the poor of Vasyllia offer you hospitality, even though her leaders have forgotten what the word means. When you have settled your people, I invite you to lodge at my own home. I will speak to the Dar on your behalf, have no worry. Rogdai, the Lord Farlaav of Nebesta is lying wounded among the refugees. Lady Adayna will show you where he lies. Of course, you will want to accompany him to the Dar's palace yourself."

Rogdai looked like he wanted to bind Voran with chains on the spot, but he merely turned to Adayna and bowed his head in agreement.

"Oh," said Voran, as though it were an afterthought, "and please arrange for my father's wine to be served to the Nebesti. They have need of refreshment."

Voran turned away, not waiting for a reply. He felt Rogdai's hatred like a hot poker in his back. As he walked through the ranks of warriors, he expected to be stopped by one of them at any moment. But they let him pass.

As he approached the gates, tents were already springing up like mushrooms after an autumn thunderstorm. Voran saw not a single second or third-reacher among them. Only the poor of Vasyllia had come outside the city to help the Nebesti in their hour of need.

Voran spent most of the day arranging for food and more tents to be sent out to the Nebesti outside the city walls. As he feared, none of the rich wanted anything to do with the refugees. Even in the second reach—many second-reachers themselves had known poverty at some point in their lives—only a few families, most of them from the warrior caste, opened their doors to him.

That evening, he sat in his own kitchens enjoying the last of his father's wine. He had only drunk half the chalice when the pounding on the doors threatened to splinter them.

Her lardship came into the kitchen, her face red with annoyance.

"Voran, it's the palace guard."

Voran smiled and nodded.

Four black-liveried warriors in full armor, led by Rogdai, stood outside the door.

"You will leave your sword here, Vohin Voran," said Rogdai. "Accused traitors are not allowed arms in the palace."

The Monarchia of Vasyllia is first concerned with the care and welfare of its citizens. Therefore, we have found it necessary to form a representative body, the Dumar.

I. Dumar representation will be based upon population density.

II. Twenty will come from the first reach, fifteen from the second, five from the third.

III. Let the reaches choose their own.

IV. The Dumar will assist the Monarchia in an advisory capacity.

V. According to the discretion of the Dar, the Dumar may also legislate certain internal matters.

VI. The Dumar may, in extreme cases of dynastic turmoil, call for a Council of the Reaches to choose a new Dar.

Official edict of Dar Aldermían II, year 734 of the Covenant

CHAPTER 10

THE DUMAR

The heavy double doors of the Chamber of Counsel opened inward to reveal a fresco of the Covenant Tree adorning the entire far wall. Just as the doors opened, sunlight pierced through the colored glass in the windows, and the flames danced on the painted tree. Gooseflesh prickled Voran's arms at the sight. On either side of the rectangular room stood tiered wooden galleries filled to the brim. Every one of the forty representatives of the three reaches of Vasyllia, the full Dumar, looked at him with undisguised hatred. Of course, Voran thought, he had chosen to aid Nebesti over Vasylli. He understood their hatred, but he deplored it. It shocked him how deeply entrenched Vasyllia had become in its insularity.

In each of the four corners of the room stood a great stone likeness of a tree—a birch, an oak, a beech, and an aspen. For a moment, he thought he saw a Sirin in the branches of the birch, but he was mistaken. Even so, the flame in his heart surged, and he felt new strength blooming from his chest.

Dar Antomír sat in a simple throne of white marble under the fresco of the aspen sapling. Mirnían—his face an inscrutable mask —stood before a throne of malachite a step lower than the Dar. Sabíana sat on the Dar's left on a throne of pink granite. She seemed to look at Voran, but as he approached, he realized her eyes were directed at a point beyond his left shoulder. He had hoped she had forgiven him; it appeared he was wrong.

"The Dumar may be seated," said Mirnían. "Chosen speakers of the Dumar, step forward for counsel."

These were two military men, the willowy chief cleric Otar Kalún, and a young courtier Voran did not know. He could smell lavender on him, even from this distance, and his silver cloak shimmered as he moved. Voran disliked him immediately. He knew the type—a social climber who would not hesitate to sell his own grandmother for advancement in the Dumar.

The chosen speakers stood on a step lower than Mirnían and Sabína and faced Voran. At that moment, when even Sabína looked at him with the eyes of a statue, Voran finally realized the full seriousness of his situation.

"Vohin Voran," said Mirnían, "son of Otchigen, the former Voyevoda of Vasyllia, you are charged with dereliction of duty. Before you speak in your defense, know that it was the Dumar's wish that you be clapped in irons upon your return to Vasyllia. Only the Dar's clemency grants you the freedom you now enjoy."

"Something you hardly deserve," hissed Otar Kalún. His pupils were abysses in eyes of pale grey.

Dar Antomír tensed, as if he were about to rebuke the chief cleric. But he did not. Sabína looked down at her hands, cupped on her knees. The tips of her mouth curled down, either in anger or in sorrow. Voran couldn't decide which. He wanted her to look at him again. He was sure it would give him strength. But she did not.

"Highness and Dumar assembled," Voran said, his voice shaking in spite of himself. "Nebesta is fallen. Your scouts doubtless spotted the refugees days ago. What they did not tell you is that the Second City is no more. Every male Nebesti has been slaughtered or captured." He felt anger rising, his voice hardening. "The invader has sent their women and children ahead, doubtless to spread fear and to *burden* Vasyllia with their care."

This last phrase he spat out with contempt. Every face but the Dar's twisted. In an upsurge of emotion, Voran went on the offensive.

"But that is nothing!" Voran's voice echoed. "Nebesta was invaded not merely by an army of men, but by something the Nebesti call changers. Dark creatures, half-man, half-beast, capable of changing physical form to suit their needs. They are led by the Raven."

The hall erupted in noise—laughter, shuffling cambric, frantic whispers, hands wringing sword-hilts. Voran kept his gaze firmly on the Dar's. He saw understanding there and the beginning of fear.

The older military man boomed over the noise. "Highness, must we listen to stories? This man is charged with treason."

"Perhaps Vohin Voran would care to elucidate?" It was the courtier. He did not even try to hide his derision. Voran's gut twisted. This man was wrong, somehow. Voran had a compulsion to run him through with a sword. It was so strong that he had to physically restrain himself.

"Fools," Voran said more quietly, but his voice echoed still. "Are you blind to the dying of the tree? The fire on the aspen sapling is dying, far earlier than its allotted time. Does this bother no one?"

Voran turned slowly to look at the rest of the Dumar. Some faces were paler than when he entered. A few did not return his gaze.

"*We* have caused Nebesta's fall. *We* have broken Covenant with Adonais, and now the fire on the tree will fade, and we will not be able to bring it back. The ancient protection girding Vasyllia will fade, and our city will fall."

"Father, will you do nothing?" Mirnían shook with anger. "This man is charged with abandoning innocent pilgrims in the wild, and he is raving about covenants."

Dar Antomír continued to stare at Voran. Voran returned his gaze, willing himself to be still. He focused on the flame in his heart. It burned strongly. Dar Antomír nodded slightly and seemed to come back to life.

"Peace, my children." He raised his hands and the clamor died. "These are serious things Vohin Voran speaks of. Otar Kalún. Is what Voran says possible? This covenant between Adonais and Vasyllia. Is it anything other than an old story? And if it is, under what circumstances can it be broken?"

"Well," said the cleric, feeble voice dripping with disdain, "in the more recent redactions of the Old Tales there are several obscure references to the Vasylli being a 'High People, chosen by Adonais,' but it would be very difficult to extrapolate any covenant from those few passages. I cannot account for the older collections of tales; they have serious textual inconsistencies. As for the Sayings, there are a few references to a covenant, yes, but the writers of the Sayings seem to assume the reader knows of such a covenant as established fact. They never describe it explicitly."

"Then there is reason to believe that the Covenant exists?" asked Mirnían, his face once more an impassive mask.

"Highness, if I may speak?" said the courtier. He reminded Voran of a snake with his insinuating and effeminate gestures.

"Speak, Sudar Yadovír," said the Dar.

"I have studied the Sayings," said Yadovír. "If one reads them literally, then yes, the Covenant is an established fact. But if so, then we must take every verse in the Sayings as literally true, must we not? In that case, animals can speak with human tongues and Sirin are still flying around in the deepwoods." He laughed, and his neck muscles stuck out obscenely.

Voran had a nagging sense that Yadovír knew more than he should, that he was challenging Voran to make a compromising admission. He had a sensation of panic, like a drowning man with legs cramping in pain. Yadovír continued.

"It makes a great deal more sense to read the sections concerning the Covenant as a metaphor for the mutual love between Adonais and Vasyllia."

"I agree with Yadovír," said Kalún.

"Do you really, Otar Kalún?" Rumbled the younger military man, huge and red-faced and red-bearded. Until that moment, Voran hardly noticed him, he was so silent. "I am not a learned man, but I know that if you start subjecting all the old truths to the test of your own fallen mind, everything collapses."

He looked at Voran and nodded, though his expression was still guarded.

"Dumar," said Voran, heartened by the big warrior's support. "Tell me, did our scouts give us any indication of this enemy that razed great Nebesta in a single night?"

No one answered.

"This is not a normal enemy we face. Surely there have been enough omens, even for your doubts! I have spoken to Lord Farlaav. He is a man known to many of you. He himself told me of the monsters in Nebesta..."

"You do seem to know a great deal, Vohin Voran," said Yadovír. "But why must we submit to your superior knowledge in this? You abandoned your own people in the wild. And you say nothing of that."

Voran felt backed into a corner. He was still sure, somewhere deep within, that Yadovír wanted him to admit to seeing the Sirin, though why, he could not say. As Voran spoke, his own body tried to stop him from speaking. But it was too late to turn back.

"Highness, Dumar assembled, I did not abandon them. On the third day after we left, I encountered a Sirin by the road. She sang to me, and our souls are now bound. But it is a perilous thing—to encounter the Higher Beings. I passed into another place. Another time. When I came to myself, I found myself in a completely different part of Vasyllia, more than twenty miles away from the Dar's road. It was there that I found the refugees. Ask the scouts. They know how far the refugees traveled, and by what woodsmen's roads. I lost the pilgrims, yes. But not through my own volition."

They didn't believe him, Voran saw it immediately. All he

heard was silence, intense as the hum that follows the ring of blade against blade. Mirnían's expression shifted subtly, and Voran thought there was a glimmer of something behind it, maybe yearning. Sabíana now looked straight at Voran's eyes, her cheeks barely touched with pink. When he met her gaze, she did not look away. He found he could not hold her gaze for long.

"Chosen speakers of the Dumar," said Dar Antomír, his voice touched with finality, as though he were condemning a man to death. "Have you anything further to say before I speak in judgment?"

No one answered, and the silence echoed.

"Very well. Vohin Voran, we hereby find you guilty of dereliction of duty. You are exiled from Vasyllia, you and any children you may come to have, until your death, under the pain of public execution."

Voran remained in his own home, a prisoner, for three days. Outside, Vasyllia mustered. The great marketplace of the second reach—clearly visible from the high room in Otchigen's house— was cleared of its ornate booths, and long planks were set on trestles. Women and girls sewed, gathered, and packed provisions on the tables. Men and boys sharpened swords and spears, polished mail, brushed the horsehair tails of the peaked Vasylli helmets. Merchants gathered food in barrels and granaries that were built overnight. Voran sat at the window, his body itching for action.

On the evening of the third day, they came. A swarm of guards, spear-points catching the half-moon's light. Three waiting-women in furs surrounded Sabíana, who stood a head taller than all of them. Ahead of all walked the Dar, erect and proud, giving no sign of his many years. Voran's heart warmed with love at the sight, then frosted over with regret. Would the Dar ever embrace him as a father again?

Voran put on his finest kaftan—sleeveless, the collar and

shoulders tipped with rabbit fir—and tried to brush the dirt off his boots. He left his head uncovered, quickly tied his now shoulder-length hair back into a tail, and rushed to the hearth-hall. The Dar entered alone, his face drawn in anger. He stood in the doorway for a long moment, looking at Voran, waiting for something. Voran bowed his head and dropped to his knees, then fell on his face in a full penitential bow. He remained there.

Nothing happened. The Dar spoke no word, but Voran did not dare move until the Dar released him.

Something metal clanged on the floor. Voran looked up in alarm, thinking the Dar had fallen. The first thing his eye glanced on was the ancient crown wrought by the smiths of Dar Cassían's rein almost five hundred years ago—cloudy silver with white-gold flowers blooming. It was on the ground. The Dar had thrown it down. His eyes were brimming with tears.

"Highness," whispered Voran in shock.

"My son," the Dar said, voice broken by a sob. "How you remind me of your father. He was so sure of himself, so brazen. Until the time for penitence. Then he was a lamb. How I miss him."

Voran stood up and ran forward. He grasped the Dar's outstretched forearms as he began to go down on his own two knees before Voran.

"No, Highness, not before me." Voran's tears rose at the sight of the bent, careworn Dar.

"Voran, you break my heart. If the Pilgrim had not so much as commanded me to send you after the Living Water, I would never have allowed it. Do you not see? If even one of the pilgrims is found dead, you will be cursed with your father's guilt for all time."

Voran mused on his first memory of Antomír. Voran was eight years old at the time and had been sick for weeks. Breathing through his nose had been impossible, and so he had not really slept for days. He was blowing his nose with all the vigor of his warrior blood when Otchigen and the Dar walked into the house after a week's hunt. The Dar, his laughing, dark eyes a better cure than all the horrid-smelling mustard wraps that Mother tried on him, turned to Otchigen.

"He has a nose like a horn," Antomír had said. "Next time, bring him to the hunt. He could prove useful with such a horn." At which point they both laughed until the tears flowed. Voran had loved him intensely from that moment.

"Highness, you must think me touched by madness," Voran whispered. He led the Dar to the high place and returned to pick up the fallen crown. He placed it on the Dar's head—it was colder than ice—and stood to his right on both knees. "You must believe me. I have seen the Sirin. I have spoken to her. I have soul-bonded with her."

A knot of muscle stood out on Dar Antomír's jaw. "Tell me everything, Voran."

And Voran did, beginning with the echoes of the song. He spoke of the white stag, at which the Dar tutted, smiling. He tried to describe the Lows of Aer, which left the Dar pensive. He spoke of the Pilgrim, the Covenant Tree, the Living Water, and the soul-bond with Lyna.

"Lyna?" asked the Dar, his eyes wide with surprise. "She is of the eldest Sirin. Older far than the Covenant, older far than the Three Cities."

Voran's heart leaped in his chest. "You do believe me, Highness."

Dar Antomír sighed with a rueful smile. "Yes, my son. I have seen the Sirin myself, in the deepwoods, many years ago. Sometimes I think I still hear a song, but I can no longer catch the melody." He seemed a hundred years older at that moment. "Nonetheless, no one else will understand. I can grant you no more clemency, Voran. The Dumar is on edge as it is. They want you imprisoned. Some want you publicly flogged. It must be exile for you."

Voran's heart plunged to his ankles.

"Voran, tomorrow Vasyllia's armies go to seek out the enemy

in the open field. You cannot go with them; indeed, I think you might find a knife in your back if you did. But I will give you a chance at restitution. You will follow the trail of the pilgrims you lost. If Adonais wills it, you will find them before any enemy—human or not. Mirnían insists on going with you, though I threatened to have *him* imprisoned for self-will. I will also give you the young warrior who spoke at the council. The red-bearded one, Dubían. He has uncommon strength, though he is gentle as a maiden in peacetime."

"Highness, I do not deserve your..."

"That is right, you do not," said the Dar, with a flash of youthful anger. Then he smiled again. "I do not do this for you. For whatever reason, both the Pilgrim and the Sirin have indicated that *you* must find the Living Water. If you do, and if you see the pilgrims safe to one of the outlying strongholds, I will recall you to Vasyllia. If we live that long.

"Now," he said, standing up and wincing in pain. "You have a much less pleasant task before you. Sabíana has the strength of a she-wolf, but you wounded her deeply, Voran. Put it right."

Sabíana's eyes were a rare dark brown that warned of deep unhappiness. Voran steeled himself against a conversation he would have given years of his life to avoid. She refused to speak first or even to look at him for longer than a second.

"Sabíana, I—"

"Voran, what has possessed you? You have become strange to me. Half-mad with phantasms and omens."

Her every word was a hot knife-thrust.

"This Covenant you seem so intent on," she continued, now jeering. "How do you imagine it happened? Adonais's hand descended from the clouds and signed a parchment with letters of fire?"

"Sabíana, a broken Covenant explains the death of the tree, the omen of the skies, the burning of Nebesta, the invasion..."

"Voran, these are but the aberrations of history. They *happen*. It's our misfortune that they all conspire to happen now, but there's no need to seek for mystical causes. It is unbecoming of you."

"You saw how the Dumar welcomed the refugees, Sabíana. The Covenant commands us to care for the Outer Lands' people as we would for our own. A camp of refugees denied entry into the richest city in the world? What more confirmation do you need?"

"The Covenant is a fairy tale! Yes, in the stories it makes sense, but you cannot apply it literally. Even if we have failed in some sacred duty, what sort of a god punishes his own people only for forgetfulness? Is that our gentle, loving Adonais?"

On some level, Voran agreed with her. But he had already considered the implications of that line of reasoning. If faith in a gentle god had led the Vasylli to neglect the good of others, then perhaps they imagined Adonais to be different than he really was. Perhaps Adonais was a jealous god.

"Has your father told you?"

"Of his plan for you? Yes." She turned away from him and folded herself into her black shawl.

"I suppose you wish me to release you from our promise?"

She turned back to him, her eyes blazing. "I would sooner run you through with your own sword!" She seemed shocked at her own vehemence, but only for a moment. "Why can you not give me your heart, my bright Voran? I have tried so hard to dispel the restlessness that keeps driving you away from me, but you have built a wall around your heart. I can comfort you; I can be your joy. But you must let me."

"Sabíana, you're upset, I understand."

"You understand very little, for all your new-found importance. Why do you keep shutting yourself from me?"

Voran found no words. She was right. He felt deflated, more tired than he had in years.

"What would you have me do?" He asked.

She slowly released the muscles tensing her body like a bowstring. The beauty seemed to seep back into her relaxing curves, the warrior princess transforming into a sinuous black swan. She took his hand and kissed it, caressing it gently.

"It is not for me to tell you what to do," she said.

His stomach lurched, and warm desire groped him. His head began to swim. His heart raced like a deer through the trees. He enfolded her into his embrace—how small and brittle she seemed! For a moment, everything was foolishness—the Raven, the Living Water, the coming war. It was all even mildly amusing. What else mattered except her embrace?

A kind of madness was on him, a savage excitement. The brittle thing in his arms was now not Sabíana, but a thing. He could do anything he wished with her. He kissed her violently. She shuddered for a moment, then melted into it. His hands itched to caress her.

Cutting through the noise of blood rushing in his ears, Voran heard the song of the Sirin, faint, plaintive. In his mind, he saw Lyna as she had met him, wings outstretched in the birches. She shone in a delicate light that sharply framed her feathered outline, but now she wept. The desire faded, and Voran felt a rush of tenderness for Sabíana. He pulled away from her, laughing gently. Sabíana's face was flushed, rosy. She smelled faintly of tuberose. She rested her head on his chest.

"I adore you, my Voran. I've never had so little control over my own heart. Even in your absence, you fill me. I see you even with my eyes shut. All the memories, brilliant as the sun shining through the rain."

For the first time in his life, he felt calm in her presence.

"I thank Adonais for every moment I've shared with you," she said. "You've been carved into my heart, every moment of you. How your eyes soften when you laugh, rare as that is. How your voice sparks when you become inspired with an unexpected idea. How your head droops when you wander in thought. Most of all, I love seeing you forget yourself when faced with a thing of beauty—a wildcat leaping from a boulder or an eagle soaring above the summits. How did I come to be tied to you, Voran?"

"Sabíana, what do you desire most?"

The final traces of her pain were expunged, and she shone from within. It only made the reality of their parting twist deeper into him.

"We are living in such an uncertain time. I hope for safety, permanence, not only for Vasyllia. I feel a need to find a place and root into it. Our future is dark, I know, but I have strength. I can use it if I know your heart is mine, though you are far away from me."

"I am with you always," he said, and thought of Lyna. "When this is all done, I will come back for you, my love."

They remained still for a long time, entwined in each other, content.

A pounding on the door jolted them both.

"Could they not have allowed us at least this evening?" Voran ground his teeth so hard his jaw flared in pain. "I'll teach them..."

Before he reached the door, it flew open. The hallway on the other side bristled with spears. Mirnían stood at the head.

"Sabíana! You and Voran must come now. The flames on the aspen sapling are going out. Otar Kalún has called for the Summoning of Fire to be performed today."

Usually, the many-hued dusk was the most beautiful part of the day. But now the silence of the evening fog oppressed Voran. The orchards were black and white parodies of trees, looking more like sinister old men reaching up with knobby fingers, as though enraged at the gathering gloom. They seemed unnaturally still, almost bewitched into nightmarish sleep. The sight clashed with Sabíana's gentle warmth next to him.

Down the road from the central square in the second reach, their company entered through a rounded archway into the oblong Temple Plain—a clearing in a grove of ancient red-bark pines that ended in a sheer drop thousands of feet deep. At the far end of the Temple, a small circle of aspens, glowing in orange-yellow vesture, stood guard over the altar stone.

A sense of presence inundated Voran, a barely-evident energy, something between sound and light. It was stronger than usual, fed by the tense expectation of the crowd, many of whom were openly weeping. This is like a funeral, he thought, not a supplication.

Voran and Sabíana took their place at the front, near the quivering aspens. Voran turned back to see two files of longhaired youths robed in black, carrying square banners with embroidered images of Dars, Sirin, and High Beings whose names had long ago faded into legend. Passing through the Temple, they cleared a path to the grove of aspens, then stood in two lines with their backs to the crowd on either side. The clerics followed, robed in deep burgundy, the color of recent sorrow. They chanted an ancient lament.

The melody haunted Voran; for a moment, it seemed that the mountain itself sang. The voices weaved into the melody and out of it in an increasingly complex pattern. One moment the rich tenors predominated, then the dark-toned basses, and finally the middle voices rang out, lush as stringed instruments. The voices united in harmony, then fought each other in unexpected dissonance, only to resolve in chords that echoed over the tops of the red-barks. Images flashed through Voran's mind—falling water, shaking branch, and whispering fields of wheat.

Torchlight flickered beyond the stone archway. Ten warriors in mail and crimson robes preceded Dar Antomír. They approached the altar table, solemnly bowed before it, and stood on their knees encircling the aspens, swords drawn and placed into the ground point-down. Dar Antomír met Otar Kalún inside the circle and kissed him three times on the cheeks. Both then bowed to the altar.

The tenors wailed over a drone in the basses, massive as a full spring torrent. The words of the ancient hymn echoed crisply in the cold air.

"O, gentle light of Adonais and his numberless hosts, radiant and glorious. From the rising to the setting of the sun, you illumine the mountains and valleys. Shine out for us wandering in darkness, show us the merciful gaze of morning. O Lord Adonais, we praise and glorify you until the Endless Age."

The crowd joined in with a rumbling noise at once dissonant and moving. Voran felt no longer merely himself, as though the minuscule creature he called "himself" was nothing but a stone in a much larger edifice, a tower reaching with song and flesh and bone to the Heights. He felt small, but also part of something majestic and glorious, a note in a complex harmony that rose to the ears of Adonais himself.

The hymn was twice repeated, ending in a long, groaning note of lamentation. Silence prevailed as Kalún chanted alone in his watery voice. The words were completely unintelligible. Voran's ecstasy crashed to earth. Why must the chief cleric of Vasyllia always be such a terrible celebrant of the mysteries?

When Kalún's mumbling ceased, he turned around to face the people.

"People of Vasyllia," he said. "It is not the day for the Summoning. But our beloved sapling is already fading. Let us all come together in prayer so that we, your priests, may find the inner strength to call down fire from the Heights, as our forefathers did in the days of Lassar the Blessed."

Voran's stomach soured. That wasn't right. It wasn't the priests who had summoned the first fire. Not according to the Old Tales. It was the Harbinger. What was Otar Kalún up to?

The priest led the procession back through the middle of the Temple and out into the main square. In the evening darkness, the mansions of Vasyllia's third reach—all lit with lanterns—were like jewels lit on fire. Above them, the twin waterfalls fell in perfect lines framing the palace, which from this vantage point looked like it floated in the air directly above the sapling. The sapling! Its upper leaves were no longer aflame. The flames that remained in the lower part of the tree were bluish, barely moving.

One gust of winter wind, and the whole tree would go out. Voran was sure of it.

The procession arrived at the tree, and everyone fell silently to their knees. Only Otar Kalún stood, visible to all in the center of the square.

"As you visited our fathers in their darkest time," he intoned, "so heed our request on this day, Adonais, though it is not the day allotted for your grace. Send down fire. Let it illumine our hearts and give life to the eternal tree of Covenant."

The chanting rose again, bleak and stark in the night. Kalún circled the tree, mumbling to himself with arms raised.

A huge gust of wind lashed the Temple from the summit, as if Vasyllia Mountain had opened its maw and begun to blow with all its might. The remaining fire on the tree sputtered and died, as did most of the lanterns in the city. Darkness seemed to pour over the assembled crowd.

Another omen, thought Voran, his hands shaking with more than mere cold.

"People of Vasyllia!" roared a voice in the half-darkness. "Your hearts are nothing but stone. Do you think you can buy the Heights' favor by forcing the hand of the Most High?"

The Pilgrim stood to the right of the aspen, impossibly tall, arms held high. He glowed with a golden light.

"It is not too late, Vasyllia. You can win back the regard of the Heights. Behold! All Nebesta sprawls at your feet, but you do not give her entry. Take her children's care into your hands."

Many moaned with fear, and many more cried out in agreement. But an angry throng surged at the Pilgrim—mostly young men. They dragged him, screaming, stomping, spitting on him as they dragged him back into the Temple, to try to throw him off the edge of the Temple Plain. Voran rushed forward, but there were too many of them. The mass surged, pushing down whatever was in its way, closer and closer to the far end of the Temple.

Two ranks of warriors appeared and rammed the crowd from either side of the Temple, coming into the open space from the darkness of the red-barks, where they had been silently standing guard. Swords drawn, they beat down the mob. They surrounded the bloody Pilgrim and carried him back toward the square. A wall of people surged to block their way, and only when the priests with their oak staffs joined the warriors did the wave crest and fall back toward the archway. The warriors rushed to the third reach, leaving trampled humanity in their wake.

Vasyllia is fallen, thought Voran. It is too late.

Know this, my dears. Our realm is full of doorways. Doorways into other realms. You may have seen them sometimes. A curtain of water falling where there is no waterfall. A metal gate standing in the middle of a field. A pool of water in the middle of a desert. Do not enter them. If you do, you will be taken to a perilous place, the Lows of Aer. If you ever come out again, it will be to a different place entirely! Many are the children who have entered the Lows. Few have come back...

From "A Child's Retelling of the Sirin's Tale"
(Old Tales, Book VI)

Chapter 11

The Changer

The day that Voran and his companions left Vasyllia, it began to rain—a steady, insistent kind of rain that chilled deeper than snow. It never stopped long enough for the three travelers to dry their clothes, and soon they gave up altogether. Saddle sores became an ever-present reality, despite the cold. Voran forgot to take the necessary precautions, for which he silently cursed himself in language he never used in public. Judging by Mirnían's stiffness, Voran was not the only one. Dubían merely sulked. In their mutual discomfort, all remained silent.

Mirnían's guard of ten warriors traveled with them for the entire first day. But they were not trained woodsmen. They were slowing Voran down, and their racket could be heard for miles. After conferring with Dubían and Voran, Mirnían ordered them to return to Vasyllia. Voran knew what Dar Antomír would think about Mirnían's decision. He also knew how little Mirnían cared about that.

It took them three days to reach the place where Voran bonded with Lyna. Voran hoped that he would see her again, though his rational mind told him that was unlikely. There was no change in his inner flame, no surge in his yearning as they approached. If anything, the closer they came, the less he felt anything, as though something were dulling his emotions from without.

"Why can't it make up its mind?" roared Dubían, face red as his beard. "I can understand rain; I can understand fog. I hate both of them, but at least I can understand them. This...this is like sweat. It's not raining, it's sweating!"

Voran pushed his exhausted charger up through a cleft between two tree-crowned hills. When he came to the other side, he hoped to see clear indications of the pilgrims' passage through that region.

"Voran, what is it?" asked Mirnían.

Voran could not understand. There was no sign of the pilgrims. Nothing. Until that moment, their trail—old food-scraps, strips of torn fabric hanging on black hawthorn, trampled earth—was unmistakable. But here, in the place where he last saw them, their trail veered off the road toward a wood, where it vanished.

Mirnían laughed. Dubían looked near to tears. Voran wanted to vent his frustration by hacking down the nearest tree with his sword.

"Well, now what?" said Mirnían pointedly, as though this was all Voran's fault.

"I don't know," Voran said. "It's too late to go on in any case, especially if we're going into those woods. The morning is wiser than the evening." *Or at least I hope so.*

"I knew you would have some sort of inspirational nonsense from the Tales, you fool," burbled Mirnían. He walked off, head down and shoulders slumped. His words stung Voran like the slap of a birch-switch.

As their mounts munched on the last few greens remaining among the ascendant browns, Voran gathered wood for the fire. Like the insistent buzzing of a fly, he felt Mirnían's anger, though the prince pointedly refused to look at him.

In the failing light, swarms of swallows kept him company.

They wheeled low, almost at ground level. It's going to rain, thought Voran. But the sky was already planted with stars, and no cloud obscured their glint. Neither was there any heaviness in the air. And yet, the birds seemed weighed down. There was something chaotic about their flight, nothing elegant about their circles. A few almost flew into each other, and there was none of the usual playfulness in it. Voran shivered with unease.

All three of them took turns trying to light the fire. All three failed. It seemed to break something in Mirnían's resolve. Voran felt a wave of anger slap him a split second before Mirnían spoke.

"Voran, I have long wanted to ask you. You must have thought of this much over the years. Why do *you* think Otchigen murdered all those innocent people in Karila?"

Voran's nails bit into his palm as he balled his fists. What a coward, he thought. Mirnían could find nothing to attack Voran with directly, so he struck in his soft place, in the place that he could not defend.

"You as well, Mirnían?" asked Voran, pushing the nails deeper into his palm, hoping the pain would keep the anger at bay.

Dubían tried to play conciliator. "Never mind what other people think." He glared at Mirnían. "I've always been sure Otchigen was also killed in the wild, only his body was never found."

"I don't know," said Voran. "Somehow, if he were dead, I think I would be more sure of it. No, he's alive, but something prevented him from saving those people. It's not an easy choice to willingly return home only to face judgment."

Mirnían chuckled, clearly understanding Voran's implication, but he said nothing.

"Voran, tell me. What sort of a man was Otchigen?" asked Dubían. "I would be honored to hear it from you. All the seminary rumors smacked of jealousy. He was a great man, and great men are not often liked."

The unexpected kindness of the big man touched Voran.

"Everyone seems to think that my father was the Dar's

enforcer, a man who thought better with his axe than with his head. But they never saw him tell stories. Every evening he would gather us around the hearth. Some evenings it was something from the old tales, sometimes he told us of his youth. I loved it when he spoke of his first meeting with my mother. He had a particular way of speaking. It was almost in song."

Like the Sirin. The thought struck him with unexpected revelation. He had always known it, but in some deep recess of the mind. Truly, there was something otherworldly about Otchigen when he told stories, leaning on one of the carved columns in their hearth-hall, always the same column. He would shed his years as he spoke, and every time he recalled his early days courting Aglaia, she would sit on her bench, rocking herself gently as she sewed something, pretending not to look at him. Her eyes looked different in those moments: they shone with intense color, revealing a wealth of shared remembrance, pride, and something deep, strong, poignant. The memory made Voran think of Sabíana.

Dubían put a hand as big as a cauldron on Voran's shoulder in what he intended as a gentle caress. It nearly bowled Voran over.

"You must miss them very much," whispered Dubían. There were tears in the big man's eyes.

"Yes." The tightness in his chest lessened for a moment, but as it did, the old yearning for Lyna flared up. He missed Lyna even more than he missed his parents, even more than he missed Sabíana. I'm so confused, he thought. Bonding with her was supposed to make the wistful itch disappear. She was supposed to order my inner world. Instead, I'm more lost than I ever was.

The morning was no wiser than the evening. At first light, Voran followed the trail of the pilgrims into the woods. As soon as he stepped into the trees, the trail vanished. But there was something else. Something crackling behind his ears, like a lightning bolt beyond his peripheral vision. Something wrong with the wood. It was not quite *there*.

Mirnían noticed it as soon as he joined Voran, a few minutes later.

"Did you feel that?" he asked. "What is wrong here?"

Dubían was more enlightening in his reaction. "There was a doorway here," he said, with quiet certainty, "into the Lows of Aer."

Voran nodded, while Mirnían shook his head and rolled his eyes.

"What do you mean *was*?" asked Mirnían. "Can these doorways move?"

Dubían smiled, clearly pleased at knowing something Mirnían did not.

"I thought everyone knew. Once entered, a doorway into the Lows shuts forever. Then you are forced to wander in that perilous realm, filled with all manner of strange beasts and people, until either you find another doorway, or you are forcibly taken out of it."

"Do you not hear how ridiculous you sound?" Mirnían turned back to the camp.

"Wait," said Voran. Something stirred inside him. They needed to go forward.

The wood rose ahead of them for a short stretch up a hilltop. At the top of it, the trees ended like a bald patch. The downslope on the other side was a sheer wall of ragged slate. Voran climbed down, finding plenty of footholds to bear him. A few feet away from the ground, he jumped onto ground covered in dead leaves, but his foot slipped, and he realized that what he thought was flat ground was another slope, though not as steep. He fell in a cloud of brown and landed hard, his breath knocked out of him. When the stars stopped dancing in pairs with the dead leaves, he realized that he lay in front of a large cave. Something beckoned to him from inside.

"I've found something," he called to his companions, who were still standing on the hill above him.

It was a natural cavern in the rocky hill, probably a shelter for wolves. Shards of yellow and brown bones seemed to confirm this. To Dubían's great delight, there was dry wood strewn about aplenty. He set about to build a fire, and soon a weak flame sputtered to life.

For the first time in what seemed ages, their stiff hands prickled with warmth.

"Well, this is much better," said Mirnían, flexing his finger over the flames. "The stories have got it all wrong. There is nothing glorious about questing. The only glory I want is a bathhouse, a roaring hearth, and a piglet dripping on a spit."

"You're right," said Voran, warming on the inside. "What would our exploits be called? The aimless wandering of three soaked froglings?"

Dubían threw his head back, opened his cavernous mouth—several teeth were broken or missing—and exploded in a torrent of laughter. It was so unexpected, and yet so natural, that both Voran and Mirnían laughed together with him until the tears flowed.

But they were far away from home in a distant part of Vasyllia, and they were at an impasse. It quickly sapped their mirth. Soon they were silent and tense again. Voran felt the inner stirring again, more intently this time, as if someone were looking at him. He turned around, but there was nothing there. Something was different, though. Was that rock on that ledge before? Voran couldn't remember.

"I wonder how the Pilgrim is doing," said Voran. "He was a big man, but that was quite a mob that attacked him."

"Well, serves him right. What sort of a fool lectures a mob after a failed summoning? What was he thinking?" Mirnían chuckled.

"How can you be so callous? He is a Pilgrim. And he was our

guest. Nothing can excuse that kind of violence. And in the Temple!"

"Oh, Voran. Always such a purist."

"And what about you, *prince*? Always so presentable in public, so careful about your people's needs. But as soon as anyone turns around, you laugh and scoff and throw them all to the ravens. Should you not actually care for your people if you are to make an even passable Dar?"

"How dare you!" Mirnían's face contorted with rage. "You, a traitor's son, a spineless leech who depends on my father for everything. You have the gall to pass judgment on me? I should slit your throat right here."

"Careful, Prince Mirnían," growled Dubían, his hands hovering over his knife-hilt. "You go too far."

"And you!" An angry vein throbbed in Mirnían's temple. "Are you so blind that you take Voran's side in everything? You think Voran saw the Sirin? You actually believe in some forgotten Covenant? Voran made all of it up himself. Apparently, the attention of the Dar's own daughter is not enough."

Voran's hands trembled. He grabbed his knees until his knuckles turned white.

"Men like you pollute the earth, Voran. You sit on rocks and ponder questions with no answers, while Vasyllia crumbles around you. What have you ever accomplished? Everything you touch is blighted, and now even Sabíana withers under your caresses."

Voran struck Mirnían with the back of his hand, then pounced on him and pinned him to the ground. He felt the point of Mirnían's dagger tickling the skin under his right ear. Mirnían's smile was feral. The feel of the metal thrilled and enraged Voran, and he reached for his sword.

Something rustled behind them. A shrieking, frenzied fear crushed Voran to the mud next to Mirnían, face-first. Every muscle froze, but tore at itself in a wild desire to flee. His heart pulsed hysteria with the blood through his body. His mind demanded that he fly from the unknown horror behind them, but his body was locked in place. He could not even speak. Damp with sweat, Voran willed with all the strength he could muster to turn his head out of the muck.

The rock he had noticed before moved of its own accord off its ledge. It fell, struck the ground, bounced, and *changed...*

...into a monstrous creature, over seven feet in height, standing on two rippling, hairy legs. Its arms and chest had the shape of a man's, but larger and covered in a thick tangle of grey fur. Instead of a face, it had the slavering maw of a wolf. Its eyes were the source of the screaming fear. They were the eyes of a demon with pits of emptiness instead of pupils, black like a bottomless abyss. Brown saliva dripped from its fangs. It growled, but it also laughed. Voran's blood felt like ice in his veins.

"I come as bidden, prince," the creature spoke with a guttural bass. "What would you have me do?"

"I... did not..." Mirnían sounded like he had pebbles in his mouth. "What are you?"

"The sound of strife calls to me like fresh blood. Malice sings to my ears like a lamb in death-throes. I am hungry, fair prince. Will you kill the offending wretch, or will you let me?" He pointed at Voran with a twisted black claw.

Mirnían did not answer.

Hissing with excitement, the changer approached Voran. Its eyes, dull yellow with black absence in the center, darted up and down. Its jaws panted with expectation. Black claws twitched as they reached for Voran's eyes. The wolf ears lay flat against its monstrous head.

"Such young blood I have not tasted in centuries," it whispered, then grimaced. "Is that the stink of Sirin on you? Never mind. I am *very* hungry. Your eyes first, my beautiful boy."

It reached for Voran's face. He lay without power, fear choking him. His breath gasped frantically, but his body was in a vise, helpless, as though laid out in a blasphemous sacrifice to this demon.

Something growled behind the beast, and Voran heard a nauseating crunch. The changer howled. It snapped Voran awake, like falling out of a nightmare. The changer was on the floor, scrabbling at something colossal and black. A wolf the size of a bear. Voran felt the flame surge inside him. He drew his sword. Tense and ready, he waited for an opening.

The changer managed to throw off the black wolf and faced Voran. It screamed and it screamed.

"I do not fear you, creature of the Darkness," whispered Voran. He feinted, waited for the changer to defend himself, then plunged the sword into the creature's chest, underneath its arm. The beast *dissolved*. Voran's sword clattered on the rocks. A stench of rotting flesh filled the cave, and a column of black smoke oozed out into the forest, puss-like.

The black wolf shook its head, as if disgusted. It stood up and padded toward the three travelers.

Voran laughed and extended his arms to the huge wolf. It cuddled against him with its huge head like a house cat.

"I was hoping I would see you again," said Voran, smiling. "It seems you have paid off your debt to me handsomely."

The wolf harrumphed. "You have a high opinion of yourself, cub. Your debt to me is now lifelong. Do you even realize what that thing was?" She spoke with a woman's voice. When Voran got over the initial shock of hearing the wolf actually talk, he realized there was something vaguely familiar about the wolf's voice.

"A changer, is it not?" Voran said.

"You say that as though you know what that is. You have no idea."

Voran turned to the others. Their eyes were bigger than their faces, especially Mirnían's, who was clearly having a hard time convincing himself that the talking wolf was a figment of his imagination.

"Cub," said the wolf. "That creature is the least of your problems. The army of the Vasylli has been routed."

"What?" Mirnían snapped out of his stupor. "What do you mean, routed? Impossible!"

"As impossible as wolf-men prowling the woods, my prince?" She turned on Mirnían, snarling. "As impossible as a prince of Vasyllia calling on a creature of the Raven in the anger of his heart?"

Mirnían flushed.

"I don't understand," said Voran. "Mirnían *called* that thing? How? Why?"

Mirnían moaned, answering as if against his will. "I wished your death, Voran. You drove me to such a passion that I lost all self-control. I wanted to kill you with my own hands."

"Why, Mirnían?"

"You really are that thick-headed, aren't you?"

The wolf growled. "Envy, Voran. That creature smelled his envy like a wolf smells blood."

"Wolf!" Dubían visibly trembled. "How do you know that the Vasylli were defeated?"

"Do you doubt the word of Leshaya?" She bared bloody fangs at Dubían.

"No, Leshaya," said Voran, placating. "But tell us nonetheless."

"Come, I will show you. I watched the battle."

"You did nothing to intervene?" asked Mirnían.

"I have little love for Vasyllia," she said and loped out of the cave.

She took them deeper into the woods, to a craggy hill overlooking the tree line. Voran climbed it before the rest. All around he saw nothing but forest, except in one direction. To the west stood a high plateau, a mile away at most. Even from this vantage point, he saw a horrific mound of piled bodies, their mail glinting in the morning sun. The ravens looked like flies swarming a dung-heap. Voran felt sick.

"What happened?" Mirnían stood next to Voran. His face was chalk-white.

"They never had a chance," said Leshaya. "This is a new kind of enemy, like nothing ever seen in these woods. They have no fear. They sidle up to death as if it were a life-long companion. Pain affects them little. But the Vasylli destroyed themselves. They were too arrogant. It was almost laughable. The initial skirmish was bloody, and the invaders took to their heels and ran away. Thinking this was a rout, the Vasylli ran after them with no semblance of order, giving up the high ground. As soon as they entered the deepwood, the marauders turned around and counterattacked. Reinforcements were waiting in the trees. In seconds, they surrounded the Vasylli. It was a calculated move. A trap. They left none alive."

The reality seeped into Voran slowly, like waking to realize a nightmare was real. That was at least three, four thousand lives snuffed out. How many of them were his friends, his cohort elders? He stood staring at the mound of death, trying to make sense of the disaster. If the pilgrims were also dead, the three of them could be the last Vasylli in the forest.

Voran felt a song rise up from the depths of the earth through him and up to the Heights, a dirge from the time of Lassar of Blessed Memory. He sang.

Peace eternal to your servants,
in your bosom, Adonais,
grant this.

Sobs spluttered through the song. When Voran could sing no longer, Mirnían repeated the dirge with his resonant baritone. Dubían wept aloud, his tears streaming down his beard and hissing as they fell on the cold earth. The wind picked up as they sang, harmonizing. Rain dropped on them, slowly and heavily, then clumped into feathery bunches of snow. The trees swayed back and forth, in time with the flow of the dirge. Then all fell silent.

Voran fell on his knees and bowed his head as his tears continued for his fallen brothers, for all the orphaned children, for Vasyllia's dark time.

Do not joke with giants. Their humor can get you killed.

Old Karila proverb

CHAPTER 12

THE WAYSTONE

They followed Leshaya for a week, heading east. The distant shimmer of the last Vasyllian ridge remained on their right for the first few days, then they turned away, and the mountains faded into mist. By the end of the week, the peaks were no longer in sight. This was completely unfamiliar territory for Voran.

They no longer pitched tents, sleeping instead under the stars, wrapped in wools that kept every part of their bodies warm, except their faces. At least once a night, Voran woke from the numb burning of his frozen nose.

Dubían had insisted that he return to warn Vasyllia. Voran could not stop the big man, but he thought him foolish. Mirnían agreed.

"No, there is no wisdom in returning now," Mirnían had said. "There is as much likelihood of you being captured as arriving in Vasyllia in time. And the scouts will have seen the enemy already."

But Dubían would not be deterred. Seeing the back of him brought Voran more grief than he expected. He feared he would never see him again.

On the eighth day after encountering the changer, the mountains lessened into rolling hills. Voran's ears began to pop as they descended. That day, they stopped early, before the sunset. They laid out their food and furs at the shores of a glass-clear lake.

"You might think that the lake is shallow," said Leshaya, "but it is not. Do not be fooled. That is one of the deepest lakes in this part of the world."

"That should be the slogan of our journey," grumbled Mirnían. "*Nothing is as it seems*. Never in my life did I think I would follow a speaking wolf on a journey to a doorway that exists, but only sometimes."

"What choice do we have?" asked Voran. "It seems obvious that the pilgrims entered the Lows of Aer. We have no other trail to follow." And perhaps he would find Lyna. The need to see her pierced even the veil of sleep. He only dreamed of her now.

"You would be wise to practice a little humility, prince of Vasyllia," said Leshaya. "You Vasylli are not equipped to battle the enemy now approaching your city. Try to learn something. It might prove useful."

Mirnían ignored her.

In the morning, the lake was frosted over with thin tendrils of mist.

"There lies our way," Leshaya said, pointing with her muzzle at the mist.

"What, over the lake?" Mirnían said. "It is not frozen yet."

"Not over the lake. Over the mist."

Voran smiled. He felt unusually eager this morning.

Leshaya led the way, and Voran followed. Mirnían, shaking his head and muttering under his breath, came last. As Voran stepped on the mist, it seemed to be hard ground. He waded knee-deep in what looked like milk. No ice, no water. When they all reached the center of the lake, a wind raised the mist around them until they were bathed in it. Something seemed to shift in the shapes just beyond the white. As the mist lifted, a high plain revealed itself ahead of them. Not a stone's throw away lay the strangest thing Voran had ever seen—a slumbering giant's head, the size of a three-story house, bearded, wearing an ancient helmet made of a curious silver-copper metal. It snored. Every time it snored, a cloud of starlings flew up, only to alight back on the helmet as soon as it stopped.

"Everyone is usually so taken with the head, they never notice the waystone," said Leshaya.

She was right. Voran had missed the ragged plinth. It had carved scratches on its face, too dim to be made out from this distance.

"This cannot be real. I am dreaming." Mirnían stood a few steps behind them, his face pale.

Upon closer inspection, the scratches on the waystone were legible, though barely, after what seemed many centuries of erosion.

If left you go, there love awaits
If right you go, there gold awaits
If straight you go, there death awaits

"What wonderful choices!" Mirnían spat on the ground.

"Maybe the head will be more enlightening," said Voran. He picked up a rock the size of his head.

"Voran, what are you...No, stop!" said Leshaya.

Voran hurled the stone at the giant, just as it was breathing in to snore. The stone flew up the giant's nose, and the head jolted awake, then sneezed like a gale. When Voran picked himself up, the head was awake. It looked very annoyed, but there was also something else in its eyes. The kind of amusement a bear might feel when faced with a charging ant.

"Voran, you idiot," whispered Leshaya. Her tail was stuck out straight behind her and her ears were at full alert.

"Well," the head bellowed. "You have my attention, tiny creatures. What do you want with me?"

A sense of the scene's absurdity struck Voran, and he spoke without even thinking.

"Giant, what happened to you? Why does your head continue to live without...well, the rest of you?"

Mirnían looked at Voran as though Voran had mushrooms growing up his nose.

"UGGH!" The giant's groan was like an earthquake. "Always the same stupid question. It's not fair. It's not as though I can, you know, *walk* away from stupid conversations. No. I'm stuck here, forever subject to witticisms and imbecilities."

"Buyan, ignore him. He's but a cub." Leshaya's eyes flashed at Voran.

"Oh, Leshaya, I didn't see you there. You're so small, you know. Can you remove these pimples from my presence, please? I am sleepy."

"Buyan, have you seen or heard anything of Vasylli pilgrims seeking the Living Water?"

One huge eyebrow shot upward.

"Ah! Always seeking information, aren't you, Leshaya? What makes you think that a big oaf like me knows anything in the wide world?"

"You're right," said Voran, turning away. "This is a waste of time. He's obviously half-man...I mean, mad."

"Oh, thank you for that, annoying little person. I may know something of these pilgrims, or I may not. You'll have to take that chance."

"Oh, by all the..." Mirnían looked ready to burst with frustration. "This is too much like a story. I hate it. Listen, whoever you are. What do we have to do to earn the chance at your knowledge?"

"Finally," the giant head sighed with pleased relief. "A little person with a brain slightly larger than a pea. I will tell you whatever you want to hear if you can guess a riddle." It smiled thoughtfully. "I haven't played at riddles in ages. Oooh, this will be fun. Here's the first one:

Above mighty water most often I mount,
Trying the hearts of heroic men.
I peer over cliffs and perilous jaunts,
Sounding the sum of all of my strength.
Don't think I'm a dragon, though indeed I breathe fire,
A thousand sparks, like scales, rise up from my soul.
I weep among welkin, though always keep watch
To help, never hinder, the poor helpless man."

Voran couldn't believe how easy this one was. "Beacon. The answer's *beacon.*"

The eyebrows came down like a drawbridge, and huge rotten teeth tried to chew the lower lip. In its disembodied state, the head found this difficult, which only made it angrier.

"How did you?...Well, never mind. Something harder, then."

"We guessed correctly," said Mirnían. "Now tell us!"

"There are three of you. Three riddles. Each of you answers one. Here's the next:

My place is high perched apart from all favor
To watch all the workings of this worrisome world.
Well covered and cloaked in midnight's dark color,
I sing all the songs my bright cousins dread."

Voran's skin prickled. That was not an accidental riddle.

Mirnían scoffed. "It's *raven,* you overgrown cabbage."

The giant head opened its mouth wide and tried to bite Mirnían.

"The third!" commanded Leshaya. The head smiled daggers at the wolf.

"I'm hopefully well held, lest I harass all my neighbors,
For fierce am I found, oft forcing my way blindly.
I borrow much beauty of all that's about me,
A shimmer and shine amidst the world's show,
Yet I terrify the toughest amidst my great temper.
Having beheld the beginning of all this world's bounty,
I sing its great song on all sides of the world,
Yet sit happily in stillness, in silence of mind."

Voran was stumped. Mirnían's face fell. Leshaya remained tense.

"That's not funny, Buyan." She growled, deep in her throat. The giant head laughed. There was no mistaking the malice in that laugh. Voran's skin crawled all over his body.

"He will not help us," said Leshaya. "We must choose a path on our own."

"Why do I have the nagging sense that you are going to suggest we go straight?" asked Mirnían.

"Because it's the only possible way," said Voran. "Unless you have something else to say, Leshaya?"

"Why can we not turn back?" asked Mirnían.

"There is no way back," said Voran. He did not look back, but he knew that he would find no trace of the mist-covered lake they had just crossed.

"And we can afford the risk of the path leading to our death?" Mirnían nearly shrieked.

The head snored.

"Do you fear death, Mirnían?" asked Voran.

Mirnían screwed up his eyes and pursed his lips. "Voran, you will rue this day." He shouldered his pack with a grunt and walked past the head to the silvery path leading to the horizon. The head snored on. Voran followed.

That entire day, and the next, Mirnían refused to speak to Voran. Leshaya was not much for conversation, either. She spent most of every day hunting. Sometimes she would be gone for hours. Voran's loneliness ate at him.

Soon the trees became smaller and rarer, until they gave way to shrubs and carpets of grass. Everything was bright green from constant moisture, even this late in the year. Their road led into a narrow dale, both walls of which sloped sharply upward and ended with three jagged peaks directly ahead. A narrow pass was barely visible between two of the teeth. The ascent did not look strenuous, but it was late evening by the time they reached the foot of the slope, so they stopped for the night. The rain picked up again by midnight, and with no shelter of trees anywhere for miles, the night was miserable.

In such weather, even Leshaya seemed uncomfortable. Halfway through the night, she crawled toward Voran and lay at his side. He fit himself against her belly. Her warmth suffused his aching joints, banishing much of the cold to the edges of his hands and feet and nose.

"Leshaya," Voran whispered, unable to sleep. "There is something I don't understand about the Lows. When I first hunted the stag, I had no trouble entering through the invisible doorway. I did not even realize I was in the Lows until it was too late. But in order to leave the Lows, the Pilgrim and I had to cross paths with the white stag. The Pilgrim called the stag a "bearer". Why did we not just find another doorway out of the Lows?"

Her words slurred in the haze of the state preceding sleep.

"There are doorways, and there are bearers. Doorways work only in one direction. If you enter, you cannot leave the same way. If you leave, you cannot enter the same way. Bearers, like the white stage, are two-sided doorways, so to speak. They can bear anyone in or out, but only if they are on opposite sides."

"Seems strange, does it not? Why are there such restrictions placed on the Lows?"

Leshaya panted. It took Voran a moment to realize she was laughing at him. "If you do not yet realize the peril of entering the Lows of Aer, I am sure there will be ample opportunity to find out. Silly cub."

In the morning, Voran and Mirnían started the climb. Leshaya was not with them, and Voran assumed she was out hunting again. As they rose, they waded through small waterfalls, not a dry stone to be seen. They snaked the tortuous way up the hill, which became more and more shrouded in rain and mist. By midday, Voran thought they had entered another doorway into a different level of the world, until they stumbled onto two cairns lining the road. The summit-marks.

At that moment, the clouds parted, and the sun warmed their wet backs. Voran turned to look back. The dale stretching behind them was a pure emerald green, sparkling everywhere as the rivulets and waterfalls seemed to be showing off to the sun. It was a stark, gorgeous landscape. For a moment, it seemed that he and Mirnían were the only beings in existence on the earth. Had Adonais himself descended on a horse of fire from the Heights at that moment, Voran would not have been surprised. In such a place, Vasyllia and her trials were somehow absent. Or rather, Vasyllia did not belong in this world at all; this was a different place, a different time.

"Why do so few of the priests ever talk about Adonais in the right way, Mirnían?"

Mirnían seemed to forget his days-long silence. "What do you mean?"

"Do you not see? The curve of that mountain. The thunder of that waterfall."

"Yes, I do." Mirnían smiled for the first time in weeks. "It's almost as if Adonais is here, present in these natural beauties."

"If the chief priest knew him as he claimed to," said Voran, thinking of Kalún's mumbling of the prayers, "he would spend his days singing the wonders of his craft with the best poetry. Not try to call down fire from heaven by his will alone. You know, it's all written down in the Old Tales. The priests in those stories were poets who sang from the tops of hills as the snow pelted their faces."

The fire burned brightly in Voran's chest. He felt Lyna's nearness, but he had no idea how to call her to himself. It was maddening.

Then the sun swaddled itself in fog, and the cold and wet became all too real again.

"Look at this," said Leshaya, barely visible in the fog down the road.

As they approached, a wrought iron gate seemed to form itself out of the tendrils of mist. It was decorated in shapes of strange animals and plants, none of whom Voran had ever seen or even read about in the stories.

"Is this the doorway out of the Lows?" asked Voran.

"Let's find out," said Mirnían and pushed it open. It opened with little resistance. Nothing changed. The downslope remained ahead of them, leading to another valley where trees of changing colors surrounded a village of thatch houses settled along a snaking river, brown with the recent rains. The village looked empty.

They walked through the entire village without meeting another creature, except for the wild rabbits that fled from them in panic.

"Is that...music?" said Mirnían.

Voran heard the unmistakable strumming of a hand-held harp. Then the smells struck him like a fist across the nose—pork, cherries, apple, bacon. Had he gone mad?

Whether real or not, the source of the sound and the smell seemed to be a wooden hut, crookedly constructed, as though it were stuck in an eternal shrug. From this vantage point, the two dark windows only intensified the house's puzzled look.

The front door was open. The music stopped, but the smells were even more intense. A head popped out of the doorway, belonging to a young girl, buxom, red curls messy on her shoulders. Voran felt an uncomfortable lurch in his stomach. She was very beautiful.

"Come in, my lords! Oh, what joy! I hoped to have company this day. Dinner is almost ready."

It was a meal fit for a king. There was soup of a soft, red fish, unexpectedly tangy and salty from an excess of chopped pickled cucumbers. The first course was a white river-fish garnished with mushrooms that burst with juice at every bite. Lightly steamed vegetables— salty with a smoky aftertaste—followed. Finally, the boar—succulent, tender at the first bite. With it came a purple hash of some semi-sweet root, dripping with juice dark as blood. The ale was sweet, tinged with cinnamon and nuts.

Voran ate with relish. Mirnían waited before eating, staring at Voran as though he expected him to transform into yet another legendary creature. When nothing happened, he ate—tentatively at first, then as ravenously as Leshaya, whose slurping could be heard outside the hut, though she sat some ways off, feasting on the boar's entrails.

They remained silent through the entire meal.

Afterward, Voran and Mirnían walked to the brook to wash their hands and faces. The water had a faint smell of old cheese. Leshaya lay asleep near the door, snoring.

"Voran, I can't rest easy," said Mirnían, unexpectedly friendly. "There's something happening here that I do not understand. Something is very wrong."

Voran said nothing, but plunged his entire head into the brown water. It was unpleasantly warm.

"Is it not all a bit convenient?" continued Mirnían. "An entire village abandoned except for one hut with a girl making dinner especially for us? How does she live in this village? How does she support herself?"

Voran laughed. Such mundane details seemed irrelevant in the Lows of Aer.

"And I can see how you stare at her, Voran." There was a hint of a growl in Mirnían's voice. "Do not forget you are promised to another."

"I don't know what you mean," said Voran, lying through his teeth. The girl was beautiful, *too* beautiful in a way, as though some poet had imagined her into existence. Yet he desired her; lust for her pulsed through his body. He was again on the cusp of that madness when nothing matters, when reason falters. He had to have her.

"You are tired, Mirnían. Sleep with your sword by your side. I will take the first watch. If there is even a hint of something untoward, I will call for you."

Voran stood by the river, deep in thought. Heavy clouds roiled in the sky, churned by warm gusts, pregnant with rain. The river gurgled like an over-full stomach. The trees twitched with each gust as though awakened into a bewitched half-life, only to fall back to uneasy sleep. As each gust heaved and died, the air seemed to bloat, giving off the same acrid odor as spoiled milk. Voran sweated under his cloak, but neither the river nor the wind relieved him.

"It's quite full with storm tonight," said the redhead, somehow appearing next to him. She wrapped herself in a thin shawl, her arms crossed over her belly. Her linen shift was unbuttoned at her throat, just enough to reveal the swell of the breast underneath. Voran looked away quickly.

"Strange for this time of year," he said, lamely. His teeth chattered, but not with cold.

"It is that." She sighed and closed her eyes in contentment. Her lips were unnaturally red. Her hand barely grazed his. It was the touch of white-hot iron.

"You are not lonely here, all by yourself?" he asked.

She lowered her eyes. Even in the dark, he could see a flush creep up her cheek. Her lower lip trembled ever so slightly.

"Oh, I am, my lord." She turned away, the picture of demure modesty.

"I hope we have leavened your solitude a little," said Voran, awkwardly fumbling over the words.

She did not answer, instead walking away to an old willow weeping over the river. She sat down on a bed of moss between two outspread roots. She looked up at Voran and smiled, then leaned back against the trunk of the tree and beckoned to him.

He could never afterward recall exactly how it happened. Rather, the memories remained very clear, but as if belonging to someone else. Before he knew what he was doing, he had lain with the girl. After it was done, as the slow realization slithered into him, he lay between the outspread roots embracing her, caressing her. A drowsy slumber enticed him, and he fell asleep.

He dreamed that he saw the girl standing before him, but her face was unrecognizable through a mask of savage hatred. At her feet lay the carcass of some dead animal; a dagger was clenched in her fist. Blood dripped from its tip with insistent regularity. The animal was majestic, its fur spotted with bloody dirt. Its head, twisted grotesquely to the side, sported a pair of antlers still half-luminescent with gold. The white stag.

A wave of nausea throttled him awake. It was still early morning, and his mind felt muddled as if with wine, his limbs like cold fish. A scream of anguish. Mirnían.

Voran sprang to life and reached for his sword. It wasn't there. He ran.

In front of the crooked hut, Mirnían stood on his knees, his face in his hands. He wailed in pain. His arms, hands, neck, everything was flaky-white, gouged with deep sores. Another wave of nausea checked Voran's run. He knew the signs. Leprosy.

Standing over Mirnían, facing Voran, was something that had once been the beautiful red-head, now twisted and gnarled and wrapped in a hairy black cloak. Her curls were gone, replaced with rare wisps of grey. Her eyes were sunken and red, and a toothless leer replaced the former beauty. She leaned on a stone club that bore a sickening resemblance to a pestle, and she cackled, unable to restrain herself, hopping in place.

Voran tried to approach Mirnían, but found he was rooted to the ground. To his left, Leshaya— hackles raised and teeth bared —seemed also unable to move. The hag leered at Voran, as though challenging him to defy her, though he felt no more than a thing in her misshapen hands, to be thrown around and played with before being devoured.

"Oh, how delicious," she cackled. "The sons of Vasyllia are no more than worms writhing in the mud." She twitched her head side-to-side like a deranged crow.

"Voran," Mirnían sounded like an old man. "Whatever you do, do not tell her anything. She tried to seduce me last night, thinking I would be amenable to talk. Keeps asking about our quest. I spurned her. Disgusting hag!" He spit on her. She danced around him, then struck him with the pestle across his face. He fell on the ground, his legs twisted underneath him, but did not cry out.

"Le-per! Le-per! So much for words, princeling."

"You have no power over me, hag," said Mirnían, blood flowing from his mouth as he tried to roll over. "Though you curse me with this leprosy, you will not stop us from completing our journey."

"Well, well. There you are very wrong, princeling. My darling Voran is staying with me, probably for a long time. You see, Voran gave me the power over you all. Gave it willingly, too, the great-hearted warrior. *He* did not spurn me."

Voran vomited. The hag turned to him, crouching, her head cocked sideways.

"You thought you could take your pleasure from my body," she said, "and it would cost you nothing? You do have a high opinion of yourself, Voran, son of Otchigen."

Mirnían's face creased into disgust and fear.

"Voran? Is this true?"

Voran could not meet his eyes, but nodded once, curtly. Sabíana filled his mind, and the regret was like ten swords plunged one after another into his chest.

"What has Sabíana ever done to deserve you as her champion?" Mirnían scraped himself off the ground and crawled to Leshaya. She crouched to the ground and helped him up to her back with her jaws, as though he were no more than a cub. She trembled in fury. Voran could no longer contain himself.

"Yes, I am guilty!" he screamed. "I despise myself for it. Yet I am friend to the Sirin. Lyna loves me, and will intercede for me. She will not forsake you, Mirnían. Do not give up now!"

"What can I do?" Mirnían sounded as old as Dar Antomír. "I don't believe your tales about the Sirin. I don't claim to have heard their song, you madman. Now, I am a leper. The quest lies with you. I have no more strength. Leshaya, take me home to die in peace."

"Yes, yes!" the hag squawked. "Go and die, pointless princeling."

Leshaya looked at Voran, her eyes red and almost human. She looked like she was about to say something, but she only shook her head. In a moment, she and Mirnían were a blur racing back up the mountain.

"As for you, my delicious Voran, I won't kill you yet. You'll do slave duty for a while. And then I'll eat you."

The hag resumed her frenetic dance around Voran, punctuated with several blows from her pestle on his back and legs, just enough to hurt without breaking anything.

"Now, tell me. What were you looking for in the Lows of Aer?"

My beloved is like a cherry tree in the midst of the desert. I delight to sit in his shade. His fruit is a sweet taste on my lips. Take me away with you; let us hurry from this place. The bridal chamber awaits...

From "The Song of the Dar's Beloved" *(The Sayings, Book III, 2:7-9)*

My beloved is like a cherry tree in the midst of the desert. I delight to sit in his shade. His fruit is a sweet taste on my lips. Take me away with you; let us hurry from this place. The bridal chamber awaits…

From "The Song of the Dar's Beloved"
(The Sayings, Book III, 2:7-9)

CHAPTER 13

THE ISLAND

The sweat, mingled with the sting of sea-wind, burned Lebía's eyes. Her fingernails were threatening to pop off with every thrust of her hand into the black soil. The hand-harrow was slowly transforming into lead. Her back reminded her, periodically, that if she did not straighten out soon, she would remain hunched over the ground forever.

It was exhilarating.

She had never felt this alive, this useful. All her life she was served, waited upon, coddled, and worried over. All her life she ached to help others, but her father's assumed guilt branded her, and all Vasyllia shrank from her touch. Here in Ghavan, everyone needed to work, or everyone would starve. She never imagined something as innocent-sounding as preparing the soil for winter would be the hardest work of her life.

"Take a break, dear girl," the voice was firm, despite the age of the speaker. Lebía secretly envied Otar Svetlomír his vigor. Though his nose looked like an old potato, though his eyes had more red in them than white, he labored over the soil longer than anyone else.

"I will not stop while you still work, Otar."

"Oh, I stopped an hour ago, swanling." His smile smoothed

152

out the furrows in his forehead, making him look twenty years younger.

His young smile had been the first thing Lebía saw when the pilgrims arrived on Ghavan Isle. Even now, the events of their coming to this place were as fresh as if they happened yesterday. The disappearance of Voran, the coming of the white stag, the passage into the Lows of Aer, the waiting longboats on the shores of the Great Sea...

"So pensive for a little one," he interrupted her thoughts. "I know the island encourages it, but you must not grow up too fast, Lebía."

"It is not merely the island, Otar," she said.

A howl shattered the air, as though it were made of glass. There was something human in the howl.

"That is no wolf," said Svetlomír, gathering the long hem of robe in his right hand and running off like a ten-year-old boy. Lebía sprinted after him. The entire village already crowded the beach, keeping a healthy distance from an enormous black wolf with nearly human eyes. At its feet lay an emaciated body, milk-white, but spotted with livid red. Lebía gasped and ran to him. It was Mirnían.

"You've grown so much, swanling," said the wolf.

Before Lebía could fully register the fact that a wolf had *spoken* to her, the creature had turned and leaped into the water. Mirnían groaned in pain, and Lebía's attention was snapped away from the she-wolf. Svetlomír picked up Mirnían with no effort at all, he was so wasted away.

"Svetlomír, you are not afraid of the leprosy?" Lebía asked.

"No, little bird." He smiled. "Are you?"

"No," she said, surprised at herself. "Otar, will you do something for me? Let me take care of him. Put him in my home."

Svetlomír's eyebrows momentarily met in the middle, but his expression softened as he looked at her.

"Yes, swanling. That would be a good thing."

Lebía dedicated herself entirely to Mirnían's care. Her presence seemed to ease his pain, her touch to stop the progress of the disease. After only a few days, his emaciated body filled out. Through the petulant lips and the pain etched into the lines around his eyes, Lebía glimpsed something she had never seen in Mirnían—a man of courage and gentleness.

Two weeks later, he awoke for the first time. When he saw her face, he shook his head as though trying to dispel the lingering tendrils of a dream.

"It cannot be," he whispered.

She caressed his head, and he leaned toward her as if she were a hearth-fire. After that moment, he recovered not in days, but in hours. With every one of those hours, to her surprise, Lebía lost another piece of her heart to him. Even when he slept, she sat by him, content merely to stare at him. She pitied him, but it was more complicated than that—something thrilling and joyful, a stirring attraction that went far deeper than physical allure. She sensed his emotions and his pain as though they were her own.

"How did you come here?" asked Mirnían one morning, when he was strong enough to sit up in bed and hold a bowl of soup with his own hands. "You must know that we have been combing the wilds to find you. We thought you were lost, or worse. You've heard about the invasion?"

"Yes, there is talk of little else among the pilgrims."

"What happened to you?"

"When Voran disappeared, chaos erupted among the pilgrims, and none of the warriors—most of whom were barely out of the seminary—wanted to take command. Half of the families clamored to return to Vasyllia, and they would have, if not for the white stag.

"I saw it before the rest, standing still on a hill-top, its antlers sparkling in the sun. It came to me, no one else, and as the people saw it, the noise stopped. Everyone stopped. Everyone stared. It came right up to me and kissed me—that's the only way I can describe it—then moved away into the woods. I felt like it was calling me, so I followed.

"I didn't speak to anyone—who would listen to me, anyway? —I just followed. Soon everyone was following me, even the warriors. We seemed to have passed into another place, because when we walked out of the woods, we were on the shores of a sea. I couldn't see the other end of it.

"Five longboats waited on the shore, and a small group of Vasylli—or so they seemed by their dress, even if it was a little outmoded—greeted us. Otar Svetlomír was at their head, carrying a loaf of bread in an embroidered white towel, with a wooden cup of salt in the middle.

"They welcomed us like family, and before we knew it we were all on the boats. We sailed to a dim dot on the horizon. Ghavan Isle, they call it."

"Are they Vasylli?" asked Mirnían.

"Yes, for the most part. Many came here because they wanted to leave the bustle of Vasyllia for a quiet life. Many of them seemed also to have premonitions of Vasyllia's impending doom, and so left before it was too late."

"But how did they all find it? Were all of them led here like you and the pilgrims?"

"Yes. The call came in different ways for different people. Sometimes they found it as though by accident. Other times creatures—the white stag, a particularly large firebird, or strange chimaeras—appeared to lead them to awaiting boats. The first settlers, it is said, were led here by the Sirin directly."

"Are you not lonely, Lebía?"

"It is a quiet life here, but busy. We live off the land. It is different from what I am accustomed to, but I like it. Though I confess I am lonely in the evenings. I miss Voran a great deal."

Mirnían's face darkened visibly.

"What happened to you two in the wild, Mirnían?" She asked, barely hearing her voice above the thump of her heart.

He looked at the floor for a long time as the last colors of day faded to twilight. She waited.

"We were separated when we entered the Lows of Aer," he

said. He looked at her directly with a gaze that puzzled her, even as it stopped her breath with its coldness. "I do not know where he is."

Two more weeks passed. Lebía rejoiced to see Mirnían turn away from his dour thoughts and look outward. She often sat with him in front of the house overlooking the valley, already dusted with snow. Occasionally, she even noticed a tear on his cheek, but he always tried to cover it with a forced laugh. They spoke about small, trivial things, but their intimacy grew. Still, Lebía doubted he would ever see her as anyone other than the little girl he had played with as a child.

No matter what she did, the leprosy still remained on his body. She prayed constantly to Adonais—"Tell me what I must do to heal him!" —but no illumination was forthcoming. While Mirnían improved, even allowing himself the rare pleasure of walking through the woods, he was not well, and soon it weighed him down again. His leprosy precluded any possibility of mingling with the villagers, which did not in the least help his tendency to brood.

One quiet afternoon about three weeks after Mirnían's arrival, Lebía walked home after a long day of preparing vegetables for the winter. As usual, she walked alone, content to be with her thoughts, allowing the twittering girls that walked out with her to take the paths before her. The smell of fresh snow was a welcome relief after hours of sweat and dirt, though even the sea-air could not completely dissipate the ever-present tang of manure. She hugged her fur as she turned toward the setting sun and home. It shone steadily between the trees, but for a moment Lebía thought it moved sideways. She stopped, curious. The light flashed again, but now it was a second sun. Her heart tripped and ran forward as she realized what that light was. The stag had returned.

She ran into the woods. The trees spoke to her in hushed voices, their language caressing and mellifluous, pointing her toward the stag. The golden light of the antlers faded in and out of view, but she followed it easily. Soon she was deep in a part of the island she had not yet explored, where the spruces and pines grew taller and more sparse, allowing much of the sun to filter through columns of bark. On the sun-side, the trees blazed orange, but their shadow-sides were purple, giving her the strange sensation of being in two places at once. The gold antlers stopped. Their light brightened as she approached. The stag turned to face her. Its eyes were full of opal tears.

Lebía saw the sun and the moon facing each other in a darkling sky, but they were Voran and Mirnían also. She saw Sabíana, but with a different face, one she did not recognize for its sternness and warlike aspect. Now the sun was Sabíana, and it was shrouded in black, yet a fiery ring shone around the blackness. She saw smoke and fog and ruins of stone. She saw pearly bones overgrown with rich flora that pulsed with life. Where did she see all this? Was it in the opal tears of the stag?

She snapped back, as if awakening from a dream. The stag stood bowed on two forelegs before her. She felt a summons from it: mount, it said. At first, she was afraid, but the stag's eyes were reassuring. She mounted.

They soared deep into groves that danced in twilight. Music surrounded them like a subtle fragrance, and now the light from the antlers was blinding white. As they entered a small clearing blanketed with snow, the stag slowed to a trot, then stopped at the banks of a stream that still gurgled, despite the winter. Steam rose from it, deepening the sense of mystery humming around her like a song. A curving wall of spruces leaned over the opposite bank of the stream. The air palpitated with a muted presence. Lebía was reminded of the high days in the Temple. In this stillness, she hardly breathed as the stag crossed the stream.

Lebía dismounted between two spruces and continued into the grove alone, through interlacing needles, up a rough footpath crisscrossed by roots. The path sloped upward, and the roots of the trees formed a natural stairway. At the top of the incline, where the path ended in a slight semicircle, stood three of the largest spruces she had ever seen.

"Welcome, Lebía," sang a voice in the trees. A Sirin with golden hair and wings of different shades of green—all the colors of the forest—smiled at her, then sang.

All the spruces seemed to grow upward a hundred feet, covering the sky and the sun. The branches widened into an embrace that smelled of pine and fresh rain and overturned earth. Lebía collapsed into it, closed her eyes, and felt—for the first time in her life—complete and utter stillness.

"You and I are one now, swanling," whispered the Sirin, though that whisper echoed over the trees and into the waters of the Great Sea. "I am called Aína."

"I have waited for you all my life," whispered Lebía. "I lost you once. You still came."

"Dear girl," Aína laughed like spring rain falling on icicles. "When you sacrificed your own need for Voran's, you became the beloved of the Sirin for all time."

"My new family," said Lebía as the tears brimmed over onto her cheeks. She had never known joy to be so pierced through with longing. And yet, her joy was not complete.

"I know," said Aína, answering her thought. "I can give you this grace, for this day only. If it is your desire, you may heal Mirnían of his leprosy."

Lebía searched her thoughts, and realized she knew exactly what needed to be done. She ran off that very second, her excitement was so sharp.

"But Lebía, take care," said Aína in her wake. "Mirnían has a secret wound that he will seek to hide from you. If he does not reveal it, you will not be able to heal him fully. And if he remains unhealed...Well, suffice it to say that the choices of men can sometimes topple mountains."

Mirnían slept when she returned. She let him rest, barely able to contain her excitement. She boiled water and prepared a poultice whose recipe had suddenly appeared in her mind. When it was ready, she sat outside, wrapped in furs, watching the flakes gather on her feet. She tried—but did not succeed—to not think of the following day. All that she lacked now for her complete happiness was Voran. Surely their paths would cross again soon, she hoped.

For a moment, she remembered Mirnían's strange expression when he spoke of Voran last. Did he know more than he was willing to admit?

The Dar of Vasyllia had three sons, none of whom could find suitable brides. So, he ordered them to shoot arrows into the wind. Wherever their arrows landed, there they would find a wife. The eldest son's arrow landed in the courtyard of the richest merchant's house. His daughter was famed for her beauty. The second son's arrow landed in the garden of the high priest's house. His daughter was famed for her virtue. The third son's arrow landed in a swamp. An old hag lived there, famed for her ugliness. The third son complained, but his father ordered him wed. On the wedding night, disgusted with his bride, he threw her into the hearth-fire to die. But she came out of it with only her hag's skin burned off. Underneath was a beauty that no story can relate, no pen can describe. "You could have had me, fair prince," she said. "If only you had borne my ugliness one night. Now you must seek me beyond the thrice-nine lands, in the thrice-tenth kingdom." And she turned into a swan and flew out the window.

From "The Apples of Youth"
(Old Tales, Book IV)

CHAPTER 14

HEALING

Mirnían awoke. The stink of his own sweat flushed his nostrils, and his gorge rose. He was just about to curse aloud when a cool touch grazed his hand. Sparks ran up his arm, and he gasped in unexpected pleasure. Lebía stood on her knees, her arms on the edge of his bed. She had a small, mischievous smile. That smile. It made him want to laugh like he had not laughed in years. Warmth spread through his chest, and he couldn't stop an idiotic grin from stretching his face from ear to ear.

Was he falling in love with little Lebía?

Lebía was simply dressed in cream and white, her only ornament a golden headband with two filigreed temple rings. Her unruly curls were forced into a braid that ended at the small of her back. Compared to the third-reacher daughters with their damask and stifling embroidery, Lebía's simple adornment enhanced her natural beauty. But there was something else, a self-confidence absent in her usual manner. She was up to something.

"What a pitiful mess I am, Lebía," he whispered.

"Shall I heal you, Mirnían?" Her eyes positively twinkled.

"Yes, please," he said, taking up her teasing manner.

Lebía rose, opened the curtains, and pushed out the groaning storm-shutters. Powdery snow wafted into the room, sparked into gold by the winter sun. For a moment Mirnían thought he was still dreaming, but the blast of icy air soon convinced him otherwise.

Lebía crossed her arms over her chest and looked at him with an expression he had never seen on her face.

"I will heal you, dear one," she said. Chills ran up and down his back. Yes, she was his dear one as well. He just hadn't realized it until that moment. "But you may not like my methods. I've been a kind nurse, but now you need more serious treatment. Do you give your word that you will do all I say, no matter how absurd it may seem to you?"

"Whatever you do or say, my Lebía, I will follow faithfully." If she wanted to continue to play this part, he would happily oblige.

She raised her right eyebrow the tiniest fraction. "We shall see," one eyebrow seemed to whisper to the other. Was this the same Lebía that sat with downcast eyes on a bench with him only yesterday, never speaking until spoken to?

She glided out to the steam room behind the house. Within half an hour, resin-scented steam, tinged with the headiness of oak, filled the room, making him want to breathe in and never stop. When she returned, her cheeks were ruddy with cold, her eyes shone with the pleasure of physical labor, and the sleeves of her linen shift—rolled up to the elbows—revealed skin glistening like a fresh apple.

"You must wash, my dear," she said. "I've prepared the bunches and the bucket. There should be enough steam even for your pampered tastes."

"Lebía," Mirnían said, tilting his head to one side, "you are not serious, are you? I am covered with sores. As much as I would love a steam, I can't."

"You promised," she said, in a way that clearly settled the matter.

Mirnían pushed down his irritation and hauled himself out of bed. It was excruciating, but he managed to keep from swearing.

His feet felt like bloated sausages. He took one step and tripped on something, falling onto sore-gouged knees. He restrained a cry, but only barely. Lebía crouched down to him, his pain reflected in her face, her mask of playfulness dropped. He forced a smile, and she once again put on the chiding, motherly role. Helping him up to his feet, she continued to lecture him.

"I found an old recipe for a poultice that heals leprosy," she said. "Of course, its preparation is a great secret handed down from woman to woman for generations, so you must not ask how it's made. I will treat you with it, but I put a heavy price on it."

"I have already said I will do whatever you ask. Ask it."

"You must promise to marry me."

She looked serious. The game was growing a bit confusing, and a new headache was making him doubt his ability to play along. Still, he would play his part to the last.

"I do hereby pledge to marry you, Lebía, as soon as you heal me."

"We shall see," she said and winked. That wink was the strangest part of the whole charade, and almost convinced Mirnían that he was dreaming everything.

As soon as he entered the steam room, he wanted to jump out. His sores screamed with the heat.

And she wants me to thrash myself with oak? She's crazy.

But he did it. He almost fainted from the pain. The poultice's effect was immediate, however. It cooled his sores at a touch. He even laughed a little.

What other improbable feats could this new Lebía accomplish?

"Lebía," he said, mocking. "You've grown so talented overnight. Are there perhaps some other talents you have found?"

No answer.

"I need a new shirt, Lebía. This one is seeped with disease and sweat. I noticed you put some fresh rushes on the floor. Can you sew me a new shirt from them before I finish here, so I can put on fresh garments, woven by your love?"

The door to the steam room opened, and a scrap of old wood dropped to the floor. A whittling knife followed it.

"What is this?" he asked.

"I will sew you an entire set of new clothes out of the rushes," she said from outside the door, "but only after you carve me a spinning wheel from this scrap of wood."

Mirnían laughed.

He sat in the steam, melting into nothingness, for as long as he could bear it. Then he ran outside, completely naked, and fell into the nearest snowdrift. After his mind reminded him to breathe, he got up and ran back into the house. A linen shirt lay there. As he put it on, he thought he smelled lavender.

Lebía waited for him by the window, absently humming and twirling the end of her braid on her finger. As he came in, she turned and gasped.

"Look," she said, pointing at his arms.

His sores had healed completely. He felt stronger than he had in months.

"Thank you, my love," he said.

Her face blanched at his words. His heart dropped in his chest. *What did I just say?*

He took her shoulders and pulled her into an embrace.

Lebía did not push back.

"I love you too, Mirnían."

She was crying. Mirnían stroked her hair and put his chin on her head, enfolding her completely in himself.

"I feel so safe," she whispered in between the sobs.

"I hope you always will, my love," he said. "So. When shall we marry?"

Beware the man who thinks himself righteous, for he is a liar or a madman.

Seek out the man who knows himself sinful, for in him the light resides.

From "The Wisdom of Lassar the Blessed"
(The Sayings, Book I, 4:20-21)

CHAPTER 15

THE CONSPIRACY

Vasyllia had been shrouded in fog for weeks. It almost seemed alive, a kind of enormous grey snake squeezing the city in its coils until even the air felt unbreathable. Though the air of the Temple was not as restricted, in Otar Kalún's mind it was forever defiled by the violence done to the Pilgrim. Even now, as he tried to bring his unruly heart back to its usual, pleasant, barely noticeable beat, he could not stop the images of blood and mayhem from huddling in on his enforced silence. For the hundredth time this day, he tensed his bone-thin body and breathed out slowly, willing himself into submission to the purity of thought that he had nurtured in himself for many years. Only then did he allow his thoughts to proceed unchecked.

"How could we have allowed this to happen?"

He often spoke aloud in the Temple, though he had never heard an answer. He continued to hope. Surely the day would come that Adonais himself would speak to him?

"Adonais, your house has never been so polluted. How am I to put this to rights? What must I do to make it fitting for your presence again? It is no wonder that we are hemmed in from all sides by the dirty refugees, by disease, by rumors of war. There must be purification. Even if it be by fire."

The words consoled him. How fitting if he, the chief priest of the great, awe-inspiring Adonais, would be the one to purge the filth that had come over his beloved Vasyllia! Who better, after all? He had dedicated his life to the discipline of the purity of the flesh. He had never taken a wife, though the desires for a woman and a family of his own ran hot in him from his youth. It had taken many years of physical effort, even pain, to extirpate those desires. He had even learned to abstain from excessive food and drink.

Nothing could compare with the inner freedom that was the reward of such willful abstinence. Nothing could replace that lightness, that joy he sometimes felt when he realized the dizzying spiritual heights he had scaled. And yet how far he still had to climb.

A muffled roar intruded on the stillness of his heart. It jarred him. Of course. The execution.

"What a disgusting display the Dar has prepared," he said aloud. "And he expects me to attend. No, I will not befoul the person of your holy one, Adonais. Better for me to be here, to contemplate the Heights of Aer and the depths of human depravity."

Better to prepare for the purification.

Yadovír stood in the palace turret only a few paces behind the Dar himself. He could hardly contain his excitement at being selected from among the commoners. Finally, his hard work was paying off. Finally, all the unbearable flattery, all the sneers, all the demeaning service he had to endure in his rise through the Dumar was bearing fruit. The Dar trusted him. By the Heights, he did not know why, but he did not complain.

Unfortunately, such a place of honor meant a very limited view of the execution itself. Princess Sabíana further complicated matters by wearing a gown with such an absurdly high collar that his view was blocked completely. Oh, how he wanted to grab that collar and yank it backward! But no. Civility. Decorum. No doubt he would see plenty more blades cutting through exposed necks in the near future. The thought warmed Yadovír.

His thoughts were interrupted by a harsh, nasal ox-horn. To Yadovír's relief, Sabíana, face pale with contained emotion, turned aside just enough for him to move forward a step. There they were: ten young third-reachers who dared profane the Temple by doing violence to the Pilgrim. Still dressed in all their gold-fringed finery, those noble born sons of sows! The bright future of Vasyllia. A future soon to be decapitated.

Kalún left the Temple, inspired by an unexpected idea. He would ask Yadovír to dine with him tonight. Yes, the man was very common, no doubt, but his determination to gain power bordered on manic. That could be useful. And they had forged a kind of unspoken accord at the trial of Voran, being the only rational voices in a sea of believers in myths and fairy tales.

As he passed the Temple arch, he was accosted by some of the Nebesti refugees. He hated their tap-tapping manner of speech, so lacking in the proper aesthetic. They touched his robes as they passed. As though his clothes had healing powers! Stupid folk superstitions. Kalún would never understand why the Dumar had not insisted on keeping the refugees in camps outside the city.

Their hands, most of them brown with dirt, reached for him. He tried to smile and walk through them as quickly as possible. Every touch caused a rush of cold sweat from the small of his back to his neck, and he began to feel nauseous. There had been several cases of a fatal disease in the city recently. What if these were the carriers?

The ox-horn stopped, its retort lingering in diminishing waves. Ten swords flashed up, then down in a blur. The crowd roared, some with outrage, most with approbation. Yadovír watched Sabíana with rapt fascination. She closed her eyes in horror, but then forced herself to turn around at the last minute. He was close enough now to see her expression. There was no feminine softness there. Her pursed mouth was no more than a thin red line and there were unhealthy spots on her cheeks, but the fear was gone from her eyes. They were fierce, eagle-like. Yadovír was mesmerized.

She turned and caught his eye, and her left eyebrow rose up ever so slightly. Then she smiled, trying to cover her disgust with him, but it was too late. He saw it and was devastated. At that moment, Sabíana became the face of all that was rotten in Vasyllia.

Yadovír walked home alone, heavy with regret, not even bothering to push through the crowd still seething after the execution. His only comfort was imagining all sorts of fantastic ways in which he would someday be able to torment Sabíana.

"Sudar Yadovír!"

He looked up absently, not recognizing the voice. When he saw Kalún, he hurried to the priest, then bowed before him and kissed his hand in the customary greeting.

"You look as if *you* were the one condemned today, Yadovír." The priest chuckled. "Come and dine with me. I think a hearty meal will lift your spirits."

Inwardly, Yadovír groaned at the thought of a meal with a man who chronically starved himself.

"Oh, Otar Kalún, I am honored, honored!" he said, assuming his habitual subservience. He was surprised to see the priest's face frost over with scorn.

"Don't pander to me. It is beneath you. I invite you as an equal. Act as one."

Yadovír's heart skipped a beat, as much from exhilaration as from embarrassment. He had never before been acknowledged as an equal by a third-reacher.

Yadovír was amazed at the interior of Kalún's spacious third-reach house. It was bare. Stone walls, a few wooden tables, some benches, and nothing else, even in the expansive hearth-hall.

"Otar Kalún, you live so simply. I admire that."

Kalún smiled. "My family is among the oldest in Vasyllia. It does not follow, however, that I should live extravagantly. I have always prized abstemiousness over excess. I do not believe in even moderate enjoyment of physical pleasures. I seek something else. Dare I say, something higher?"

Yadovír felt a sharp thrill at the words. There was an intangible quality to the priest's tone that Yadovír knew well. This man was a fanatic. Yadovír had uses for such a man.

"How sad that more do not follow such a path," said Yadovír. "Certainly, the refugees do not."

"How true. Until I saw these Nebesti, I did not know human beings were capable of swallowing so much food at once."

"You will be happy to know that the Dumar is considering keeping the refugees restricted to the first reach. What with the pestilence rearing its head."

"Yes, I am glad to hear it. What is perhaps less encouraging, however, is the Dumar's continued inability to stop the spread of rumor. Have you heard the latest stories about our mysterious invaders?"

"How they flay their victims alive and brutalize their women? Yes, yes, I have heard. Nothing particularly interesting in that, is there? It is a tactic as old as time itself to intimidate an enemy with propaganda. It would not surprise me if a few of the refugees are in the pay of the invader."

"Now *that* is interesting. I had not considered it."

Kalún's formality had begun to soften. Yadovír wanted to rush forward with his characteristic enthusiasm, but this fish needed to be boiled slowly, or it would jump out of the pot.

Kalún served Yadovír with his own hands—there was not a

servant to be seen anywhere—from a heavy iron pot. The red lentil stew proved to be surprisingly filling and very well-seasoned, even to Yadovír's pampered tastes. Heartened by the food and the conversation, Yadovír decided on a tentative attack.

"I was pleased, Otar Kalún, that we agreed on so many points during the trial of Voran. How shocking to find so little intelligence among any of the other counselors."

"Indeed. Now that you mention it, I had intended to speak to you on this matter."

It took all of Yadovír's honed self-possession not to jump in excitement.

"I hope that we understand each other," said Kalún, lowering his voice, though they were the only people in the entire house. "What I say to you must never leave this room. I do not play court games with you. I know that what you are about to hear will be worth a great deal of money if you decide to betray me. I trust you will not do that."

Kalún's eyes bored into him, assessing, then the priest visibly relaxed. Yadovír assumed he passed the test.

"You were present at the execution, yes? What would you say if I suggested that such punishment is not sufficient?"

"What do you mean, Otar?"

"I believe that we are all at fault for the profanation of the Temple. I believe we must all pay the price. In fact, I welcome the invasion of Vasyllia."

Something twisted uncomfortably in Yadovír's gut. This was not how the conversation was supposed to go.

"You cannot mean that."

"I do, Sudar Yadovír, I assure you. There is more. Vasyllia must be purified by fire. I believe Adonais has provided a refining fire in these invaders."

"Otar Kalún, we do not yet know how the Dar's troops fared against them in the open field. Is it not perhaps a bit early to speak of Vasyllia's fall?"

Kalun smiled knowingly. "I have no doubt the Dar's armies

will be routed by the invader. It would not surprise me if Vasyllia itself would be under siege in a matter of days. And I intend to be the hand that wields the invaders as a tool for the purification of our great city."

Yadovír's blood froze. He had been mistaken. Kalún was no mere fanatic; he was a madman.

"Otar, what you suggest is brave, bold. But surely all other measures must be considered before such drastic action?"

Kalún's manner snapped back to formal. The conversation was at an end.

Yadovír hardly remembered how he managed to walk back to his house in the second reach. He stood before his door with its gilded hinges and couldn't bring himself to raise a hand to push it open. He shouldn't be this disappointed. This was just one minor setback amid hundreds in his life. But he couldn't help himself. He was devastated.

The door opened before him, as though of its own volition. Immediately, the scarlet hangings and golden braziers seemed to leap out of the house at his eyes, laughing at him. You can pretend all you like, they mocked, but you'll never be a real noble. You can wear silver in your ears, drip lavender oil into your hair, collect painted chests from Negoda and ceramic tiled stoves from beyond the mountains to your heart's content. Go ahead, hang that ancient Vasylli suit of armor in your bedchamber. Hang ten of them! What does it matter? You'll always remain just outside the reach of real power.

"Yadovír? Are you ill?"

Yadovír was so lost in self-pity, he had actually thought that the doors opened themselves. He didn't even see Otar Gleb there.

"What are you doing in my house? I've had enough of priests for today."

"Ah," whispered Otar Gleb with that crook in his smile that

endeared so many. "You need to sit by the hearth with me, my friend. I've brought mead."

"I don't drink that first-reacher stuff, you know that."

"Today, you do," said Gleb, and dragged Yadovír into the house and slammed the door behind him. Gleb led him through the hallways like an invalid, with a hand as strong as a cohort elder's. He passed all the smaller rooms, making his way to the end of the corridor, into the noble-sized hearth-hall, Yadovír's pride and joy. It had more wall-sized Nebesti embroideries of High Beings than Otchigen's famed collection. It had higher-backed oak chairs than the Dar himself. It even had a chimney, possibly the only one in Vasyllia. But today, it all had a sheen of falsity. Like a doll's house magicked into abnormally large proportions.

But the two cushions on the stone floor, a hearth crackling and sparking, and a low table laden with a tankard of mead? That was perfection.

"How do you always know?" asked Yadovír.

Otar Gleb guffawed into his eagle-beak nose and said nothing, only pushed Yadovír by the shoulders down on the larger of the two velvet-lined cushions. Yadovír wanted to melt into it, to dissolve into nothingness. But there was mead to be had. Gleb knew how much Yadovír missed it. You could only bear so much of the wine of the rich.

"Gleb, what is wrong with your chief priest? Why does he have such a hard time being human?"

"Ahhhh," Gleb shook his head as he exhaled a long, tired breath. "Poor Otar Kalún. Do you know what's wrong with him? He never, not once, allowed himself to sit by the hearth on a cushion to sip the best mead in Vasyllia."

Yadovír laughed, the first unforced laugh of the last month. It was like poison seeping out of a wound. "Is that it? Excessive strictness?"

"No, I'm afraid it's more than that," said Otar Gleb. "Our dear chief priest is a very righteous man. Very correct. Perhaps even holy, if we were to judge by externals alone. But he forgot a subtle truth long ago."

"What's that?"

Gleb half-closed his eyes at Yadovír, assessing. Yadovír's mouth tasted bitter.

"The heart is what matters. That's what Adonais wants. Your heart. If you spend your entire life cleansing yourself of impurity, and yet your heart does not expand in love for those around you... It's like scouring all the rust off a pot. If you don't stop, you'll rub a hole in the iron."

He shook his head again and clicked his tongue. He always did that when pensive. It was one of the things Yadovír loved most about him.

"But I didn't come here to gossip about my betters," said Gleb, smiling again.

"Why did you come?"

Again the slitted eyelids, the fire in the eyes probing behind pale-blond eyelashes.

"Stop it!" The bitterness in Yadovír's mouth turned sour. "You won't convert me. You've tried for as long as I've known you. It hasn't worked yet."

"Fifteen years. But it's never too late, I say." Gleb smiled again, but without his eyes. "I'm not here to convert you. I only want you to know that there are those who love you. Those who wish you would use your gifts...well, for a better purpose."

Yadovír groaned aloud.

"You have an incredible talent, my friend. Can you imagine if you redirected your endless energy to the refugee problem? You could stop this plague that's beginning to ravage the first reach. Not shut them up like rats in a cellar! You could find places for all the Nebesti. Build makeshift homes in the marketplace, for Sirin's sake! Instead you waste yourself, trying to assimilate power that doesn't belong to you. Why? Haven't you forgotten that you're dying?"

"Dying?" Yadovír almost jumped out of his cushion. "What are you talking about? I'm as healthy as a horse!"

"And yet, you're going to die. We all are. Have you forgotten?"

"You priests are so morbid."

"Yadovír, I have a premonition about you."

"Oh dear, not one of your—"

"I'm not joking with you. I don't know how or why. But I sense that you are on a cliff, and there are abysses to either side of you. There may even be another abyss ahead of you. Some difficult choice that you have to make, or not make."

Gleb leaned toward Yadovír and grabbed him by the shoulders.

"Do not doubt, Yadovír, that evil is more than a state of mind. There are dark powers out there willing to use people against their will. Sometimes, all it takes is one compromise."

"Well, then it's too late for me," said Yadovír, brushing it off with a laugh. But the heaviness in his heart was back.

Gleb said nothing, but his eyes filled with tears. "Here," he said, pouring the last of the mead. "May the morning be wiser than the evening, eh?"

The next morning, the entire city was abuzz with news. The rising sun revealed a fresh onrush of refugees, but these were not Other Landers. These were Vasylli, from outlying villages. Every one of them told the same tale—the invaders had destroyed the Dar's army to the last man.

Yadovír did not consider himself a superstitious man, but the timing of this news rattled him. It was too neat that he should refuse the priest's offer on the eve of such a disaster. In any case, this changed everything. If the army was routed, that meant siege. He doubted he would survive such hardships, and he doubted anyone else in Vasyllia would either. They had all grown too fat and content with their lot. Eventually, someone would betray the city to the invaders rather than be reduced to eating horses and rats. Better for everyone if *he* did it than some half-wit second-reacher. Or an insane high priest.

At that thought, he remembered the cozy pleasure of the evening with Otar Gleb. Maybe the fool was right. What was the point of all this rushing about after power, anyway?

Down the street from his house stood the large courtyard of Sudar Kupian, one of the richest merchants in Vasyllia. It could hold at least a hundred people, and often the old man set up trestles full of food for passers-by, just to show off how little it meant to him. Yadovír envied him. Today, a royal crier stood in the middle of the courtyard. Yadovír hurried to hear what the man had to say. He missed the beginning, but came just in time to hear:

"Effective immediately, the Dar has declared martial law. The Dumar's powers are revoked until further notice."

How dare he? He has no right to deprive the people of their voice!

No. Gleb was wrong. If Yadovír did not take control of things, there would be no more Vasyllia soon.

Yadovír ran up the nearest staircase to the third reach. Absently, he noticed that some of the asters were still hanging on the brown ivy. It made him sad, somehow, but he pushed that thought aside.

The many-gabled house of the high priest glared at Yadovír, and the leafless cherry trees seemed to be reaching out toward him in threat. He banged on the doors of Kalun's house until his hands were red and painful. Only then did he hear the squeak of bolts being pulled back. The door opened a fraction, and was about to close again, but Yadovír pushed it open.

"Otar Kalún. You were right. I want to help you. I want to be the instrument of Vasyllia's purging." Otar Gleb's smile faded in his mind's eye. Yadovír felt himself getting sick at his own words.

The door opened. Kalún beamed. Yadovír's hands trembled at

that smile: it was soft and childish, with no trace of guile. This was the face of madness. Yadovír had not seen it before, and for a moment his body clamored at him to flee. Instead, he walked into the tomb-like house, and the door shut behind him.

The lands under the protection of Vasyllia are called "The Three Lands" or "The Three Cities," meaning, of course, Vasyllia, Nebesta, and Karila, with the lands appertaining to them. There are also other smaller principalities that officially owe allegiance to one of the Three Cities, but in fact are largely independent. There is Negoda, an offshoot of Nebesta, which shares the Southern Downs with its Mother City. Tiverna, Bskova, and Charnigal pay tribute to Karila. They make a kind of three-pointed gate to the hilly country that sits at the foot of the Vasylli-Nebesti Mountains. Another five or so cities do not even merit a name, for they stand at the edge of the Steppelands. Only nomads live beyond...

From "A Child's Lesson in Vasylli Geography,"
(Old Tales, Appendix 3c)

CHAPTER 16

THE GUMIREN

The kestrel keened, hung on the air, trembling with ecstasy, then plunged down into the shadows. Sabíana, standing on a palace turret, thought of Voran. Whenever they had walked in the forests or simply sat in silence together, the kestrel had always commanded his attention. He had called it a "windhover." She never really understood why he was so entranced by the small sparrow-hawks. But now, its appearance was enough to make her cry. Again.

For the first three weeks after Voran's exile, Sabíana had rushed about like a madwoman, busying herself in important and unimportant work. She even finished the embroidered Sirin banner. One morning, when the fog seemed ready to smother Vasyllia, she woke up with the realization that she had never been so tired and lonely. She returned to her bed, hoping no one would hear her sobs. She slept the entire day.

That evening, when she woke up, she was refreshed and able to think about Voran without the memory gouging out the remnants of her heart. Until the kestrel.

Once again, the kestrel soared to the clouds, fell backward and caught himself right in front of Sabíana's face. Its mouse-like squeak was almost comical, but she couldn't laugh. Truly, its sleek, mottled shape was beautiful.

It hovered before her, staring at her.

"Go to him, little sparrow-hawk. Tell him to hurry back for me."

The kestrel flew away, and Sabíana saw it ride a wind-gust out over the Covenant Tree—now no more than a normal aspen sapling, naked in the winter cold—into the forests beyond Vasyllia. Perhaps it had understood her. She stared after it as far as she could, until it melted into a dark band of cloud.

Except it was not cloud. It moved toward Vasyllia with supernal speed, and it twitched. She heard them before she realized what they were. The skies crawled—ravens by the thousand circled over Vasyllia, croaking discordantly, calling for the coming of the war to fill their bellies with the flesh of the dead. They remained high above the city, out of bowshot. Sabíana's uneasy apprehension turned into dread.

Then she saw them: shimmering, dancing abysses at the very edge of the plateau. They resolved into a mass of men carrying torches. There were so many of them! Ten thousand strong or more. The enemy was here.

"Come, Sabíana," said the Dar. "I need you at the wall with me."

The Dar, standing outside her chamber door, shimmered in a halo of torchlight. He was surrounded by black-clad warriors in full armor.

"Parley?" she asked.

He nodded once.

She rose and wrapped herself in a wolf-fur before joining her father in the ring of light. It was already dark in the city, and only smoking torches provided illumination—an angry, red glare that bloodied everyone's faces. It all seemed somehow too vivid to be real, the way Sabíana sometimes felt in a dream the moment before awakening.

As they walked—Dar Antomír a few steps ahead of Sabíana—she felt an itch near her left ear. Someone was staring at her. She turned and caught the open glance of the warrior to her immediate left. He blanched and turned away. She recognized him.

"You are Tolnían, yes? The scout who brought us the report about the weeping tree?"

"Yes, Highness," he mumbled in confusion. "Kind of you to remember me."

"How could I forget you? Your tidings were the beginning of all this, were they not?"

The warrior—if he could be called that, for he was no more than a boy—blushed a little.

"Speak your mind, Tolnían. It would give me relief."

"Highness, forgive me. I was only wondering if there is anything I can do to relieve the Dar. I can almost feel the weight of ruling pushing him down."

Sabíana looked ahead at her father, who walked briskly with the head of the company. He betrayed no outward signs of stress.

"You are a bit young to be able to read people so well, Tolnían," she said.

"I never had a childhood, my lady. My mother and father died when I was little. They were ambassadors to Karila."

"Do you mean—"

"Yes, they were among those massacred."

Sabíana was surprised by the calm tone. It was full of warm remembrance, but resigned in a way typical with older men, not youths.

They had reached the turret built into one of the carved trees framing Vasyllia's doors. They climbed onto the platform, and Sabíana's heart grew cold, her limbs heavy, at the sight of the enemy. There was no end to them—torches as far and deep as the eye could see—endless lines across the high plain, into the groves on either side, and all the way down the slopes until they were shrouded in fog. Sabíana nearly despaired. She and the Dar approached the wall, and a banner-bearer raised a large, black banner with the figure of a High Being. Sabíana couldn't remember what sort of being it was. Perhaps someone invoked during wartime.

In the torchlight, details were difficult to distinguish. The invaders were all dressed similarly in loose kaftans cinched at the waist, worn over tight-fitting pants—good riding clothes, Sabíana realized—and no external markings seemed to distinguish the common soldier from the officer. All of them were brown-skinned, squat, well-built, with silky black hair and faces like round bowls. There was some similarity in feature to the Karila, but these had a much more pronounced angle to their eyes. It looks like they're always laughing, thought Sabíana with an unpleasant lurch in her stomach.

One of the largest came forward, surrounded by a guard of archers with bows impossibly long, almost the height of two men standing on each other's shoulders. Surely, they were no more than ceremonial, she thought. But the grim set of the archers' jaws changed her mind. This leader had a silk scarf tied to his fur-lined conical hat, probably to designate importance. He looked up at them and bowed to the waist. He then snapped his fingers, and a large band of shirtless, muscular brutes armed with spears pushed a prisoner forward. He looked familiar. Then she recognized him, and she reeled at the edge of abysmal despair, barely holding on. It was Dubían.

"Father, what does this mean? What about..."

"Hush, my dear," he whispered, his eyes set and firm. "We know nothing. Not yet."

Dubían was bloodied and his face was swollen, his eyes barely visible. The brutes pushed him down to his knees with spear-points. The silk-scarfed leader said something in an undertone to Dubían, and to Sabíana's surprise it sounded like the Vasyllian tongue. How could these mysterious enemies from beyond the Steppelands speak Vasyllia's language? Dubían shook his head, stubbornly looking down. The leader took up a heavy horsewhip and beat him twice. Dubían tilted his head up, though Sabíana still doubted he could actually see much, so battered was his face. She pitied him, but the face she saw in her mind—battered and bruised—was Voran's. Her hands trembled.

"Highness," rasped Dubían. "Forgive me. I have failed in my charge before you. I did not come in time to warn you."

The whip cracked again. The leader angrily muttered something at Dubían.

"Dubían, my son," said Dar Antomír with unexpected vigor, though Sabíana couldn't mistake the slight tremor, "do not fear to speak. Whatever they force you to say, say it. You are not accountable. Adonais forgives, and so do I. Speak."

The leader guffawed and slapped the back of Dubían's head, almost as a friendly encouragement. Sabíana's stomach lurched again dangerously.

"I thank you, Highness." Dubían crouched over in pain, then forced himself to straighten. His eyes were now completely shut. "The Gumiren have one condition. They will allow Vasyllia its peace and continued existence. In return, the Dar must recognize the lordship of the Ghan of Gumir, though as a courtesy he will retain the title of Dar. Every ten years, three of Vasyllia's best young men and three of Vasyllia's best young women will be sent to the capital city of Gumir-atlan, to be given in marriage to the clan-lords and ladies of the Gumiren. An additional tribute of timber, furs, gold, and wine will be levied every few months. Furthermore, a representative of the Ghan will preside at all ruling sessions of the Dar. He will have power to supersede the Dar's command, should the Ghan's wishes contradict those of the Dar."

Dar Antomír suddenly took a spear from one of his retainers and hurled it over the wall. It landed point-first at the feet of the leader. Sabíana gritted her teeth, expecting an immediate reprisal. The leader smiled derisively and spit on the spear.

"Vasyllia rejects your offer, Gumir!" cried the Dar. "We know who you are. Tell your Ghan's masters that we will never treat with them. Our blood and our lives first, you filth!"

The leader smiled no more. The Dar turned away from him and spoke to the wall-guard.

"This is the time of testing, my children. Stand fast, and fear no darkness!"

Sabíana sensed the rising of an invisible cloud of anger from the direction of the Gumiren. The air itself seemed poisoned. The leader rattled off a curt command in a guttural language that sounded like spoons beating each other. He pointed at Dubían. The entire army of Gumiren shrieked—a high-pitched, blood-curdling whooping that sounded more beastly than human. Dubían's guards hurled their spears at their prisoner. His face twitched, but not a sound of pain escaped his lips. He half-fell to the earth, the spear-shafts twisting his body awkwardly.

A shout rose among the Vasylli.

"Rogdai," cried the Dar, "now!"

Sabíana felt the shadows widening around her into dancing spots, and everything started to go dark. The shrieks pursued her into the darkness.

"Princess dear! Little one? Wake UP!"

Sabíana woke, finding it difficult to remember where she was, why she was wherever she was, and even for a brief moment *who* she was. A round, wrinkled face with two apple-red spots on her cheeks was not a foot away from hers. There was something familiar about it.

"Well, my chick. Took you long enough."

"Nanny? What are you doing here? I haven't seen you in ages."

"You were not doing so well. They needed my *special* knowledge."

The old face, wrapped and tied elaborately in the manner of

widows, had hardly a tooth left in it, but still she smiled in that way only the old have, so full of memory. Sabíana imagined how the old woman must be seeing all her selves—the precocious child, the headstrong girl, the Dar's solemn daughter—in a single moment. It unnerved Sabíana, though the sensation was not unpleasant.

"How long have I been sleeping?"

"Sleep? That wasn't sleep, my little one. Three days. They thought you had caught the pestilence."

Everything came flooding back, especially Dubían's broken body lying askew on the muddy ground. Again spots danced before her eyes, and the world swam around her. Enough of this weakness, she said to herself. I am of Cassían's proud line. We have iron in our hearts, and if all others fall to the madness out there beyond the wall, I will not.

The world righted itself, though Nanny still looked worried.

"Poor Dubían," Sabíana whispered. "How terrible to die within sight of home, but never to enter it a last time."

The corners of Nanny's mouth trembled.

"Adonais is good, my little one. You should have seen them! Our Vasylli went war-mad. They stormed those... whatever-they-call-themselves. Those pigs never expected the mad charge. A hundred of our best men. They fell on the enemy's thousands like bees. Dubían they brought back. Yes, it was at great cost. We lost many, but the enemy lost more."

Sabíana swelled with pride, and the tears gathered. She held them back. "How brave Dubían was. He never cried out. Not once! Though the pain must have been terrible. His wounds..."

"Mmmm. Yes. I washed him, you know, ducky. His face. You should have seen his face. Well, I'm sure you will. You were never one to shrink from death."

"How could I? Mother died so young..." Her poor father. How he must be suffering Dubían's loss. "Nanny, how is the Dar?"

The old woman's breathing became erratic, and a sob escaped.

"Oioioi," she keened, "my Dar, my wonderful Dar. He would not be so badly off if Dubían wasn't killed. He can't ask him—"

"About Voran and Mirnían," Sabíana finished for her. "I must see him, Nanny. Get me my housedress. The green one." She swooped into action, every movement of her body pushing the dangerous thoughts about Voran further away from her mind. The old woman, well-versed in the behavior of the Dar's family, stopped chattering and hurried to be useful. She dressed Sabíana calmly, with firm, quick hands. Sabíana was grateful for it.

"No. First show me the fallen warrior," said Sabíana as they left her bedroom. She would not use his name. To name him would be to personalize him. No more. She must become stone.

He lay in a vaulted room with high ceilings. As in the Dumar's council room, decorating each corner of the room was a tree carved of stone. The air shimmered gold from the many candles surrounding his bier, which stood like an altar in the center of the room. Dubían was arrayed in ancient robes over golden scale-mail. The candlelight ricocheted off his helmet and greaves. His red beard looked almost bloody next to his white face, yet he smiled slightly. He looked so young. The few lines that etched his forehead in life were smoothed away by the hand of death.

Sabíana dismissed Nanny. She had a sudden urge to pull aside Dubían's armor, to see the wounds for herself, to understand the nature of their enemy, but his face stopped her. He was so peaceful. Where was Dubían now? Was his spirit still living? Had it flown away somewhere? Why did his body appear still so vigorous, even in death? It looked like he would open his eyes at any moment and sit up to speak to her.

The candles flared, becoming impossibly bright. Their light rose like a wave, no longer gold, but pure, blinding white. Voices, faint and ethereal. The sound of wind whistling through reeds. The voices arranged into harmony, at first simple, then growing in complexity until it was like a river bearing down on her, like the rush of wind through heath, like the pounding of the sea on stones. Sabíana fell to her knees.

Three Sirin sat over the dead warrior's body and sang. The first—her wings green as the forest—cried tears of fiery joy. The second—her wings like living sapphire and amethyst—cried tears of inconsolable pain. The third—her wings dark indigo like twilight—did not cry, her face grave and reverent. They took Dubían's body with their talons and unfurled their wings, raising him gently, rocking him like a mother would a child. The colors of the gem-feathers burned from within, until they were flames engulfing his body. Sabíana's eyes watered with the pain of looking at this light—so much brighter than the sun—and she was forced to turn away. From the corner of her vision, it seemed to her that Dubían opened his eyes and gasped for breath, but when she turned back to look, they were all gone. The world seemed grey and faded in their absence.

Hag: a shape-shifter of dubious loyalties. She may or may not be immortal.

Leshy: a spirit of the forest, Alkonist. Sometimes goes by the name "Lesnik."

Rusalka: the unquiet soul of a drowned girl. Likes to tickle young men to death.

Bukavach: a six-legged amphibious monster with a taste for human flesh.

Vila: also known as "rain maidens." They feed off the powers of others.

The Storyteller: a large cat with an inordinate love for fairy tales. Alkonist.

Alkonist: a general label indicating any creature of authority in the Lows of Aer

From "A Bestiary of Vasyllia"
(Old Tales, Book II)

CHAPTER 17

AN ORDEAL OF STORIES

"Breakfast time, my darling Voran."

It was the girl's voice, not the hag's. He dusted the night's snow off his filthy rag-blanket. When will she tire of this game?

As usual, he was surprised he slept at all. Every night, as he lay down on the brown straw near the outhouse, he hoped he would simply freeze to death. Every morning he woke up, aching and miserable, but very much alive.

This morning, like all mornings, the smells coming from the lopsided hut were obscenely delicious. His eyes confirmed the promise of his nose—the table was littered with thick, buttery pancakes, stuffed chicken and pike, pickled tomatoes and cucumbers. He groaned slightly. The girl—her red hair a gorgeous mess framing her pale beauty—laughed a little as she blushed. He almost laughed himself. She was so obvious in her attempts to force the information out of him.

"All this I prepared for you," she whispered. "You do not know how hurt I am that you never eat. Please, I beg you, join me today. You must be very hungry."

He sat down next to her, compelled by that invisible string

binding him to her will. She took a pancake, doused it in butter, slathered it with red caviar fit to burst, adorned it with dill and parsley. Then she lifted it to his nose. The smell was overwhelming.

Voran turned his face away, though it took a great deal of effort to do so.

"Why do you do this to yourself, Voran? All you have to do is tell me. Simple. A few words. What do you seek in the Lows of Aer? Then all this food is yours. And so much more." She leered at him, and he nearly vomited again.

It took all his remaining strength—little as there was— to croak out his daily answer to her pleas: "I would sooner gnaw on that table than eat what food is on it."

"Get out, pig!" The hag had returned, brandishing a clawed fist. Voran scurried out of the hut—his stomach reluctantly groaning—the hag after him, now wielding the pestle-club. She contented herself to a mere three blows this morning. Must be tiring of me, he thought, and did not know whether to be relieved or afraid.

This was their monotonous routine, their eternal courtship. After withstanding the temptation of food, he experienced a certain reawakening of his heart. He tried to inflame his hatred, hoping it would give him enough resistance to break the hag's power. But the moment he began to gather strength from such thoughts, as if by enchantment his fall with the maiden-hag flashed on his memory, and he stewed in his guilt, trying not to think of Sabíana.

This morning, he was so overwhelmed by despair that he searched for large stones to dash his head against. But the moment that he bent over to pick a particularly jagged rock, total apathy was thrust on him, leaving him powerless. Again, he fumed in impotent anger, and the cycle repeated itself endlessly, until he merely fell over from exhaustion.

That internal war was far worse that the degrading tasks she forced on him—cleaning after her, washing her, dressing her, mending her clothes. Soon, time blurred into a single unending day of drudgery.

"The outhouse needs scrubbing," she growled at him, her hands twitching on the handle of the pestle.

His legs felt more like lumpy rocks than usual, and he rose—too slowly for her tastes, as the pestle-club reminded him—to do her bidding.

To his surprise, Voran heard the unmistakable, and very unexpected, sound of a human voice. A man's voice, apparently speaking nonsense over and over again. Soon some semblance of words reached Voran's ears.

"Broken windows, broken heart
All beyond your feeble art.
Strong you are, but wise are not
If you think to hide your thought
To force that Raven Son to speak
Better drown him in a creek!
Too late! The Lows are here to call
Your naughty actions to account.
If you lose, the cursed goes free,
And his care will come to me."

The speaker was an old man with a curly, matted black beard unevenly streaked with grey. His head was a shock of tangled white bursting from under a woven black cap. His face was remarkably free of wrinkles, his eyes innocent and childlike. He wore a nondescript grey robe, and rough shoes woven from tree bark peeked out from the tattered hem. He held a dark wooden staff with a crooked crossbar on top. As he approached the hag, he placed his hands on the crossbar. A kestrel appeared out of nowhere and sat on his head.

"Oh, there you are, you silly thing," he said, smiling like a child, eyes nearly rolling back into his head in his attempt to look at the kestrel perching on his skullcap.

His behavior was as strange as his appearance. He leaned down and kissed the roots of every tree in the vicinity, as if they were objects of sacred worth, wiping his forehead on the bark of the trunk and jumping up with all his might to reach the leaves, until he ran out of breath. The kestrel held on to his cap the whole time, nonplussed. All the man's movements were punctuated by a clicking of the tongue and an awed murmur, with the occasional hop in place.

The hag stood with her hands on her hips, an expression of half-disgusted indulgence on her face.

"Have you missed me, hag?" he said, as though remembering the reason for his visit.

"Humph," she said.

He walked up to Voran and smelled him, making an exaggerated grimace. He faced the hag and smiled lopsidedly.

"Why are you bothering me again, Tarin?" growled the hag. "I don't want to hear any stories today, especially after the horrific one you sprung on me, for which I paid you a king's ransom."

"Don't lie," he chuckled, "you *loved* that story. But I'm not here to entertain you. I'm afraid you're in a bit of a pickle. You've got the attention of the Authorities. And not for the right reasons. Seems you've annoyed the Alkonist with your mistreatment of this poor specimen."

Voran's heart hammered. He did not quite understand what was happening, but he had heard of the Alkonist. They were Creatures of Aer, High Beings. It seemed they were the ruling authority of the Lows of Aer. Would they take his side over one of their own?

"You have no authority to speak for the Alkonist, Tarin. You're only a man." Voran thought he detected a sliver of fear in the increased shrillness of her voice. "Let them come themselves and speak to me. I dare them."

"Baaaaaah! Do you really?" said one of the trees near the watermill. Except it wasn't a tree at all. It was a giant, covered with matted hair and green moss, with acorns and pinecones sticking out of his long beard. He sniffled like a porcupine. Voran had heard that sniffle before, in the sleeping-wood, what seemed like such an age ago.

"What are *you* doing here?" complained the hag. "Don't you have some travelers to scare with your clapping?"

The giant took an angry step away from the trees and shrank in a second to the size of the grass blades surrounding the hut. "I hate it when that happens," he muttered in a mouse-squeak.

Something laughed in the trees. It was a girlish laugh, uninhibited and slightly insane. She had thick, waving blond hair reaching to her heels. It dripped wet, but still covered her body. Voran was grateful for that, because she was completely naked. She rocked back and forth on an oak-limb, tears of laughter streaming down her face.

"What do you have to laugh about?" complained the former giant, who by now had grown to the height of a tree-stump.

She gasped and fell silent, hands raised to her mouth in mock alarm. It was such an exaggerated gesture, that Voran felt he was watching a very badly-done stage play. The girl broke into laughter again.

"What do you expect, Lesnik?" drawled a bored voice from the roof of the hut. "She is drowned, after all. Can't help herself."

The girl stopped laughing and began to moan, tears of sorrow seamlessly replacing the tears of laughter. The bored voice came from a huge tawny cat with the most cunning eyes Voran had ever seen.

The stump-sized former giant named Lesnik snuffled into his overgrown, mossy beard.

"Hag," said the cat, yawning so hugely that Voran was surprised its jaw remain hinged, "we of the Alkonist have been keeping an eye on you. It seems you're breaking the rules again."

"I haven't done anything illegal," she grumbled.

"Do you know? I never liked liars," said the cat. "I knew you were the worst when we let you into the Lows, but I didn't expect you to be so blatant about it. Yes, we can all appreciate occasionally harassing a human. We all do it! But what you've done with that poor creature is unforgivable. You should know better."

The hag bristled at the cat's manner. "Don't insult me, cat-thing. I demand a trial by ordeal."

Lesnik laughed. It sounded like a pig eating swill. "We thought you would. So we brought the storyteller. It will be an ordeal of story."

"Couldn't I just tickle the human and be done with it?" said the naked girl. To Voran's horror, she had the same expression a wolf might have after being starved for weeks. To his even greater horror, he found himself strangely attracted by that expression. He tried to shake it out of his head.

"Only if the hag wins the ordeal," said Lesnik. "You know the rules."

"An ordeal of story?" The hag groaned. "That's the most idiotic—"

"The ordeal of story is the most ancient ordeal in the world, hag," said Tarin, clicking his tongue. "And who better to judge than the original storyteller?" He bowed to the cat, who graciously acknowledged the compliment. It purred, conceit evident in the fluffing of its tail.

"Perhaps I can tell a story while you decide, hag?" said the cat, its eyes wide and excited. "In a certain kingdom, in a certain land..."

"No!" The hag stomped in frustration. "Your stories are the worst. If I win the ordeal, what do I get in return?"

"You?" said Lesnik, one eyebrow—which was actually a chestnut—raised derisively. "You get nothing. Continued permission to reside here, that is all."

"And if I lose?"

"Tarin takes your slave for himself."

Voran's heart leaped. Tarin was strange, it was true, but anything would be better than bondage to the hag.

"For the benefit of all concerned," the cat drawled, extremely upset at being interrupted, "I will review the ancient rules of the ordeal. Its premise is simple. Two tellers will weave a story of their choosing, and we three Alkonist will decide the winner. We will consider the following criteria: originality, beauty of language, musicality of expression, and truthfulness."

"Truthfulness?" The hag made a sour face. "That's very vague. Very subjective."

No one paid any attention to her.

"Now for the traditional incantation," said the cat.

"Oh, this is too much," said the hag. "I will not say it. It's silly and outdated."

"It will be done in the proper way, or not at all," said Lesnik. He was nearly man-sized again, his voice deepening with the growth.

"Maybe I should just tickle him?" ventured the drowned girl. Everyone ignored her, as though they only tolerated her presence out of necessity. Voran tried not to look at her as her hair waved lazily in the wind.

Tarin drew himself up to his full height, and the kestrel flew up and re-alighted on his shoulder. It looked intently at Voran, as though trying to think something at him. Tarin intoned.

"The art of story is sacred and old,
So, teller, beware, lest your heart be revealed,
For the power of words can turn iron to gold
Or bind fetters as fast as the roots of the elm."

The hag repeated the incantation through gritted teeth. Tarin raised his staff and began to tell his story.

The Tale of the Sirin and the Child

In ages when the earth was untamed and curious as an infant, men were yet a thought in the mind of the Heights. Strange and magnificent creatures inhabited the earth. Wardens of this wild earth were the Sirin, highest of the natural creation, fiercely beautiful and glorious. The Sirin reveled in the delights of mountain and steppe, lake and river, basking in the simple company of the beasts who adored them.

In those days, mankind was created and began to sing their quiet songs. The beasts listened in awe, and man tamed Nature to his gentler hand. But man had yet to meet the Sirin.

A morning bright and fine it was when one of the Sirin beheld a marvelous sight. A giant warrior, mounted on a giant horse, towered over the forest. His mount's shoulder reached the crowns of the trees; its mane flashed like lightning with each shake of its head; the earth trembled with each step. The warrior scowled through a mountainous beard as he spoke aloud to himself, dispersing the hordes of ravens perching on his shoulders.

"Oh, my strength, my curse! Why do I have such power if I find none to test it, none to challenge me? Oh, if only the earth would grow a great ring from its bones, that I might grasp it and turn the earth inside out."

He stopped. In his path lay a rough purse. Hardly giving it a thought, the giant nudged it with his spear, but it would not move. He tried to lift it, yet it was as though rooted to the ground. Intrigued, the giant dismounted, but even his tree-trunk arms could not budge the purse. Pleased by the challenge, he pulled with all his might, and buried himself to the ankles. He pulled again, and buried himself to the knees. He pulled again, and buried himself to his neck.

The Sirin, watching silently, saw a new wonder. A small creature, all softness and grace, approached the trammeled giant. It was a young man, leaning on a stick. He limped as he walked. His beauty pierced the Sirin's heart. The youth reached the purse and lifted it off the ground, as though it weighed no more than a goose feather.

"How is it that you," said the giant, amazed, "a crippled human, can lift what I—mighty as I am—cannot?"

The youth opened the purse and poured its contents to the ground. They were nothing but kernels of wheat.

"The wheat has a great secret, giant. The secret of all power.

In order to flower, it must die. True strength is found in that most humble of acts—the death of one's self for the sake of another."

Years passed. The Sirin often returned to look upon the youth, but never revealed herself to him. Over the years, his crippling illness worsened. His grieving mother would carry his emaciated body to a seat near the window, where he would sit and stare with unnaturally round eyes at the world moving past him, paying him no heed. Every day, when his mother left to work in the fields, he repeated the same prayer.

"I give my legs, my life, to all those who sicken and die on this earth. May my sacrifice prove useful to them."

And his prayer was answered. Every day sick children jumped with renewed vigor, every day the dying found life again. And every day the young man faded a little more.

One morning, the youth heard a loud voice outside his small hut.

"Rise up and greet your guest, young man!"

The young man obeyed, and his limbs knit together, and life flowed through them once again. He came outside to greet a bearded ancient in long robes. He held a bowl carved in the likeness of a mallard. The old man presented it to the youth.

"Drink this," he said. "The bees labored over it in their clover-fields, their strawberry-meadows."

The youth sipped thrice.

"How do you feel, young man?"

"I feel life in me again, as I have not these many years."

"Now dip the bowl in the running waters of the river and drink."

The youth did so.

"How do you feel now?"

"I feel the strength of ten men within me."

Suddenly the old man was there no more. A glorious creature —half-woman, half-eagle— stood before him and sang to him. Thus were the Sirin bound forever to their beloved, and while the bond lasted, the earth gave fruit, the mountains gave pure springs, and the Heights reached down to earth in a harmony of endless song.

"I don't think I've ever heard such utter nonsense," muttered the hag. "You expect to win with *that* story? It's a mishmash of several battered horses. But you knew that already. And who ever heard of a Sirin who could transfigure?"

Tarin winked at her and smiled. "Poetic license."

With a loud harrumph, the hag sat on a tree stump and began her story.

The Curious Princess

You have probably heard the horrible story of the prince and the raven. I hate that story. It ignores all the important details and never considers the Raven's point of view. Well, I'll tell you the true end of that story. As you probably already know, after the Raven had his fun with the prince, the Sirin caught the Raven and imprisoned him in Vasyllia.

The prince came home and—somehow getting over the grief of killing his own beloved—married and had a daughter. She must have inherited some of his restlessness, because she could not be prevailed upon to stay in any one place for more than a few minutes. There was too much to be seen! She would disappear from the palace to wander around the city, the fields, the wild forests. The prince finally had enough of his little girl's wanderlust, and he ordered that she be confined to the palace.

Unfortunately for him, the palace itself was an endless labyrinth of discoveries, especially in the dungeons. There, the mountain itself bled into the palace, and some of the rooms were hardly distinguishable from caves. Most were empty, but some had fascinating treasures—ancient tapestries, old rotted chests with moldy drapery and robes woven with dulling gold, drafty armories with rusted swords and mail from the forgotten days of Lassar. The princess was nearly in constant ecstasies.

But her curiosity was insatiable. Naturally, there was a single door that would not open, no matter how hard she pushed. She could not simply ask someone to open it for her. Soon all other rooms lost their charm. She would come to this old wooden door and sit in front of it, staring.

One evening, she was caught prowling the dungeons and brought to her father. He looked grave, but not angry. He didn't even scold her. Instead, he put her on his lap and petted her hair and spoke softly to her.

"You must not seek beyond that door, my dear. There is great evil there. It must never be let out, or many will die."

Well, so much for the prince's wisdom. Anyone knows that for a child as inquisitive as that, a prohibition is little more than an invitation. But the problem was still all too real: how to open the door? She decided to wait. Despite her impatient curiosity, she knew very well that if she really wanted something, there would always be a way to get it. She was a prince's daughter, after all.

So she waited. Every day she would spend at least an hour in front of the locked door, but no idea presented itself on how to open it. Finally, her patience was rewarded. One late evening, a hunchbacked and very deaf servant carried a bucket of water right up to the forbidden door. She managed to hide before he saw her. To her delight, he pulled out a set of keys bigger than his head and opened the door. To her even greater delight, he walked in and left the door open. She sneaked in behind him.

They entered a long passage that ended in another shut door of heavy black iron, bolted in ten places with locks and mechanisms that made her head spin as the servant deftly worked them open. Another passage followed, faintly illumined by torches, smelling unpleasantly of pitch and tar. This passage ended in a huge stone. Pushing with all his might, the servant managed to budge it enough to open a small enough chink to walk through. She followed.

The room was so dark, she had no trouble hiding. Barely illumined by the torches in the hallway, the old man poured the contents of his bucket into a well in the center of the room, then wiped his forehead with his arm. To her chagrin, he immediately walked out and pushed the stone back into the doorway. Blackness fell. She was shut in.

Eventually, she noticed that there was a thin slit in the wall high above her. As her eyes adjusted to the faint light, she began to look around. It was obviously a dungeon. Old chains lay on the ground and hung from rusty rings on the wall. Then she saw *him* and nearly jumped out of her skin. He was a wretched old man, nary a hair on his head, a wispy white beard barely hanging from a receding chin. There was nothing but skin on his bones. She had never seen such a pathetic creature.

"Water..." he gasped. "Please, give me some of that water."

There was a large bucket next to the well, too far for him to reach. How terrible, she thought. That horrid servant brought in the water just to torture the old man.

"You poor thing," she said. She was, for all her curiosity, rather a soft-hearted girl. "Of course I'll give you some water."

And so she did. At first she was a little put off at how greedily he drank it, bucketful after bucketful. She was a little more unnerved by how his eyes kept getting redder and redder. It's only torchlight, she said to herself. By the fifth bucketful, she was afraid. The bony old man was now a huge, beastly creature with burning eyes. He looked at her with his head cocked to one side. He's going to eat me, she thought, unable to move for sheer terror.

Instead, he hurled himself at the stone door and pounded it to dust. He tore off the second door of iron in one blow. He shattered the third door of wood to splinters.

The Raven turned back once more and looked at the princess. He smiled. It was not a pleasant smile at all. She screamed.

Thus, the Raven escaped his unjust imprisonment and fled Vasyllia to hide and gather his strength for a final, devastating retribution.

"Well, Tarin? Didn't expect me to have a story *that* good in my skirts, did you?"

"Tut, tut." He winked at her. "Our judges have yet to make their choice."

The Alkonist were already conferring under the drowned girl's tree, since it seemed she refused—or was unable— to come down. Voran could not hear what they were saying, or if they were speaking in a human language at all. There were far too many squeaks, burbles, clicks, and whoops for normal speech. Finally, they seemed to agree, though the drowned girl looked morose again. Voran hoped that meant she would *not* be allowed to tickle him to death.

"We judge in favor of Tarin," said the cat. "Hag, you must leave the Lows immediately. Since you seem to like the Raven so much, we suggest you join him. He's in Vasyllia."

Voran froze in place. The Raven was already in Vasyllia? Could that be possible?

The spark in the hag's eyes spewed into angry flames. Starting with a low rumble, she shrieked, louder and louder until Voran thought his ears would burst. Her hair stood on end like a writhing mass of snakes. She pulled a jagged knife out of nowhere and lunged at Voran, arm upraised. She was a mere breath from plunging the knife into his heart, when she jerked backward as though someone threw a rope around her neck and pulled it hard. Voran looked at Tarin, thinking he had done it, but the old man stood a little way off, holding his knit cap to his head, staring up at a lamentation of migrating swans. Lesnik was once more the size of a tree, and one hand was outstretched toward the hag.

"Let me go!" she screamed and thrashed wildly as she began to float above the ground.

"The power of words can turn iron to gold, or bind fetters as fast as the roots of the elm," said the giant Lesnik. "You know the power of incantation, and yet you still defy it. Your kind was always too smart for your own good. Now pay the price."

She began to hiss. Wider and wider grew her eyes, louder and more insistent grew the hissing. A snake's forked tongue darted out of her still human mouth. Voran turned away to find Tarin next to him, looking at him intently.

"What's happening to her?" asked Voran.

"Focus," commanded Tarin. He pulled out an old sword from his robe-skirts. It was only then that Voran noticed the ropy muscle of the man's arm. Tarin was an old warrior; the signs were all there. "Stay alert," he said and gave him the sword.

Voran felt a gust of wind from the direction of the hag. He turned to face her and nearly fell over from the shock. Instead of a hag, he saw two dancing reptilian heads attached to a serpent body as big as a longboat. She flapped two bat-like arms and flew up. One of the heads lunged at him and hot fangs slashed at his neck as he rolled away. Fear paralyzed him. He shook from exhaustion and lack of food. His mind screamed at him—Run! Run! Every joint of the serpent's wings was edged with a claw as long as a dagger. Even her tail was razor-sharp.

She swooped over him, nicking his arm with her tail. The wound bubbled and burned. Tarin grabbed him and pushed him forward with a cry. Voran grasped the old sword and ran at the diving serpent. She evaded his slash and battered him with iron-clawed wings. Again and again he faced her. Again and again she eluded him, punishing him for every miss with another slash of her tail. Soon the ground was black with his blood.

But with every new wound, his old strength, his old freedom clawed its way back, even as his vision began to swim and his arms sagged with fatigue.

The serpent landed as Voran tottered. She slithered toward

him, one of her heads reaching forward ahead of the other, eager to deliver the death-stroke. But the other head would not be outdone. It opened its jaw and buried its fangs in the other head, just as it was about to lunge at Voran. The bitten head jerked and thrashed, beating the ground spasmodically. The other head then lunged at Voran, but now he was prepared. With a quick feint, he lured the head forward, leaning back at the last moment. He hacked once, and the head lolled, still half-attached. He kicked the neck aside and hacked again. The head fell away, spraying turbid blood. The bitten head writhed, then stopped.

Tarin laughed until tears poured down his cheeks. He embraced Voran—heedless of all the blood—and danced around him, holding Voran all the while. He kissed his cheeks three times. The Alkonist were nowhere to be seen.

"Well, the first step is taken, Raven Son. How many more until your chains come clanging off? We shall see, we shall see. Come along now."

"Tarin, how long have I been here?"

"Over a month, my Voran. It's deep winter in Vasyllia. Spring is not far coming."

Voran collapsed into Tarin's arms, his legs giving way under him. His hands trembled, and he could not control them. Tarin held him fast as he carried him to the bank of the river. He washed his wounds tenderly. Barely conscious, Voran felt relief as pleasant as a day-long thirst quenched. His eyelids drooped. As they closed, he saw the kestrel on Tarin's shoulder chattering insistently. Tarin smiled.

"Silly bird. He wants you to know that Sabíana misses you. She told you to hurry back."

The story begins from the grey, from the brown, from the chestnut-colored horse. On the sea, on the ocean, on the island of Varian—a baked bull stands with a pounded onion. In the side of the bull, there's a sharpened knife. Now, pull out the knife. It's time to eat! This is still not the story, but only the pre-story. If anyone listens to my story, he will receive a sable and a marten coat, a beautiful wife, one hundred gold coins for his wedding, and fifty silvers more for the party!

From the traditional pre-story of all tales
(Old Tales, Book I)

CHAPTER 18

THE SORE

Mirnían took his place among the villagers for the first time on the day after his healing, standing among them as their equal in the central square. Otar Svetlomír was the first to embrace him with tears in his eyes, then every other member of the village followed suit. Soft snowflakes fell throughout this almost ritual greeting, steaming on his new skin.

"With the blessing of Otar Svetlomír," said Mirnían, raising his voice for all to hear. "I hereby announce my intention to marry the Lady Lebía, daughter of Otchigen of Vasyllia."

All the old women raised their hands to their mouths and laughed, shedding their years in their joy. The children danced around the couple, chanting their names to the rhythm of their feet.

"Ladies!" cried Otar Svetlomír. "Are you waiting for my invitation? Get on with it!"

Mirnían felt his eyes grow wider as every single woman in the crowd surrounded him and pushed him away from Lebía. The younger ones did it while laughing hysterically. The old women—some without a single tooth in their head—sang:

"Away, away! Avert your eyes,

The sacred distance don't despise
For now's the time the bride must die
To all her past. Cry, nightingale, cry!"

They turned him until his head spun and he fell. At that, they chittered like birds and gave him his space. Then they descended on Lebía like a swarm of bees.

"Cry, nightingale, cry!" They sang. "Cry, nightingale, cry!"

Lebía tossed off her heavy fur. Underneath, she wore a white dress. In the light of the winter sun, she was blinding.

Mirnían had to turn away.

"Oh, my single braid, my single braid!" someone sang with a voice like the last songbird in winter. Mirnían sighed involuntarily. It was Lebía. Where did she learn to sing like *that*?

"Is it time for my braid to be split?" Lebía keened, almost wailing. "Is it time to part from my father's house?"

At that, she tottered and stopped. She looked ready to fall over. Mirnían's heart plunged. Of course. Lebía had not had a father in years.

All the young ladies encircled her, their arms entwined. They picked up her song, and Lebía came back to life.

"It is not time yet, nightingale.
Your braid is single still..."

Two young men picked Mirnían up and hoisted him on their shoulders.

At that, the children cheered.

"Wash, wash!" they called. "Wash away the old life, bring to life the new!"

Two more men picked up Lebía and brought her near to Mirnían.

"Now is the time for the last word," said Otar Svetlomir, chanting. "You will no longer speak until the fateful day. Choose wisely."

"The lady first," said Mirnían, remembering the words of the rite.

Lebía looked at him for a long time. She did not even blink.

Her presence grew inside him until it was too large to fit in his heart, and his heart seemed to grow. Then it was too large for his chest. He was sure he would burst.

"All that I lack now," said Lebía, "is Voran, to make my joy full."

Mirnían's heart froze at the words. At that moment, seemingly for the first time, he remembered that Lebía was Voran's sister, and hatred for him threatened to drown out every other emotion. Something stabbed him under his left arm, like a pinprick.

"My love?" Lebía's shoulders tensed, as though she had read his thoughts. What was wrong with him? Why did he have to kill his own happiness the moment it was born? He forced Voran out of his mind, though a sliver of hatred still pulsed deep within.

"Burn away the old life, my love. You and I will be everything to each other."

She sighed, but seemed content.

"Wash, wash!" cried the children. "Wash away the old life, bright to life the new!"

At that, Mirnían and Lebía were carried to the opposite sides of the village for their ritual bath.

The village feasted deep into the night on trestles set up in the center of the village under a sky plowed with stars. Mirnían and Lebía sat at the high table that was built on top of a mound of earth, but Otar Svetlomír sat between them. He made sure they hardly had a chance to look at each other.

The food was never-ending. As soon as all the fresh trout was devoured, platefuls of boar magically found their way to the tables, followed by venison. Ale flowed more plentifully than mountain springs.

Mirnían had never seen Lebía so happy.

As the village's smith blew the midnight oxhorn, everyone fell silent.

"Behold, the beauty of the bride!" someone called.

The women all keened—a wild, unfettered sound. It sent pleasant chills down Mirnían's back. Something walked up the road toward the square, something huge. It bobbed up and down like a drunk man.

"What in all the Heights?" Mirnían heard himself say.

It was an effigy of a young woman with a long braid, carried on a stick by a boy with red cheeks. It was the size of a house. Ribbons flew from every conceivable place on the effigy, in all colors ever seen by man. Or so it seemed.

"The beauty! The beauty!" All the women keened again.

"What shall we do with the beauty?" asked Otar Svetlomír from his seat.

"Burn away the old! Make way for the new!" cried the women.

The effigy was now in the midst of the feasting crowd, facing Mirnían.

"Who will burn away the old?" Otar Svetlomír stood from his seat. "Who will make way for the new?"

Mirnían looked around, expecting one of the girls to answer. But no one did. Then he realized, with a sinking feeling, that everyone was looking at him.

Oh no, he thought. These village rites are all quaint enough, but they can't make me actually take part. Can they?

Everyone looked at him. No one moved.

Finally, Mirnían turned to look at Lebía. There it was again— that new look. It commanded.

Mirnían sighed and stood up. The crowd erupted into cheers.

A girl ran up to Mirnían, holding a candle. She gave it to him with hands shaking from excitement and cold. He skirted the table and approached the effigy. He shook his head, and smiled.

"I will burn away the old!" he cried, trying to sound enthusiastic. "I will make way for the new!"

He stayed as long as he could at the table after the effigy had burned away. He wanted to feel everyone's joy, but something pricked like a thin dagger under his arm. At first it throbbed, then jabbed. By the time the sun began to come back up, his skin prickled with the same heat that he had while still leprous.

Excusing himself to Lebía and Otar Svetlomír, he slipped into Lebía's house and examined himself in the polished metal hanging on her wall. Facing him were nothing but eyes, deep gouges in a bony face that challenged him angrily. Were those his eyes? They looked more like Voran's half-mad falcon eyes. He shivered, disgusted that he had allowed himself to descend to such a state. He shrugged off his shirt and probed under his left arm. There it was. He turned to see his side in the metal, and his heart plunged.

There was no mistaking it. It was a sore.

And behold, I will show you wonders in that final day. There shall be a black sun, and the moon shall turn to blood. A column of fire will stand in the midst of the congregation of peoples, and the temple of the abomination will fall, stone by stone. And yet not one of them will know it for the work of the Most High. Such is the work of the prince of lies, the great deluder of human hearts.

From "The Prophecy of Llun"
(The Sayings, Book XXIII, 2:4-7)

CHAPTER 19

SABÍANA'S TEST

Sabíana stood rooted to the ground before Dubían's empty bier, unable to muster the strength of will to move.

The Sirin were real.

Everything was now different, and all possibilities must be considered—the Covenant first among them. If the Sirin were real, the Raven might be real, and they would need the help of the Heights against such an enemy. But how does one go about re-forging forgotten covenants? What did Voran say? We must begin by caring for the downtrodden of the Outer Lands.

Freed by this thought, she hurried out of the room. She must make arrangements to care for the refugees. Now that the Dumar was disbanded, she must convince her father to open the first reach and to lift the quarantine, no matter what the risk.

The door to the Dar's chamber was shut, but she barged in as she always did, heedless of the proper form. She shut the door behind her. It thudded.

The Pilgrim faced her from the other side of her father's bed. His eyes were softer than she remembered. He showed no sign of the wounds on his body suffered in the Temple. He looked into her eyes, and she felt like there was someone behind her, so completely did his glance spear through her.

"Sabíana, you have come. That is good." His voice sounded like it came from a great distance, or even out of the deep past. "Your father sleeps, but he will wake soon. He will not see me again. You must tell him I am well, and that I have gone. He will be worried, as he always is."

Sabíana found it difficult to think, much less speak, in his presence. It was like trying to breathe under a waterfall.

"Sabíana, I know you saw the Sirin take Dubían away. I know that you desire to re-forge the Covenant. But it is too late. The Raven is at the gates."

"But why is it too late?" she whispered, the tears gathering in spite of herself. "Surely Adonais can forgive."

The Pilgrim's face dimmed at the mention of Adonais. "There are so few Vasylli left. The fate of Vasyllia now lies on the edge of a knife. I do not know what will happen, though I fear the worst. It is given to me to offer you a choice. Vasyllia's trials do not have to be your burden if you do not wish it. If you come with me, I will take you to a place called Ghavan. There, the Covenant may be re-forged with the remnant of the faithful."

"Pilgrim, I am afraid."

"Yes, Sabíana. I fear as well. Vasyllia is a place far more important than you can ever imagine. If it falls, much that is good and beautiful in the world will wither. Possibly until the Great Undoing."

"I cannot leave Vasyllia, Pilgrim," said Sabíana. "I cannot leave my father."

The Pilgrim smiled, and his face brightened and he became young, his wrinkles smoothing into the face of a beautiful youth, a face that shone white. His robes were gold like the sun.

"You are indomitable, Sabíana. Perhaps I am wrong. Vasyllia may yet survive, with the Black Sun at her head."

He was gone.

"Sabíana?" said the Dar, waking up. "Oh, thank Adonais! I was so worried for you."

"Father, my poor father." She had not seen him this wasted

away. He looked like an old man playing the part of the Dar on one of the market-day spectacles. She wanted with all her heart to cry, to comfort and to be comforted, but she had made the choice. She must be iron and stone.

"Yes, my love." He laughed softly and coughed. "I am at the doorstep, so to speak. I've always wondered if Death was a man or a woman. I suppose I'll find out soon enough."

"Father." Her voice sounded harsh to her ears. "The Pilgrim has gone. He asked to be remembered to you. He leaves us with hope."

"Did he say anything about Voran? About Mirnían?"

Sabíana shook her head.

"I suppose we must continue to hope, even when darkness falls. My dear, you must prepare yourself. Soon you will wear the crown. I do not think I will live out the week. I am so tired."

"Sleep, my dear," she said, feeling strangely motherly toward him. "I am ready. Sleep now. Rest." She did not, could not cry, though it seemed a violation of her nature to prevent it.

Sabíana remained by his bedside all night. She left when the sky was still dark, but a certain tense watchfulness in the air predicted the coming of dawn. Feeling already burdened beyond what was humanly possible, she went outside, hoping against hope that today the fog would lift—though it had choked Vasyllia for weeks —and the sun would rise.

As she left the palace, she stood before the Covenant Tree. It looked cold and pitiful. To think that this had once been a symbol of Vasyllia's dominance over the Other Lands! She recoiled from the view and turned away.

Sabíana closed her eyes and let the mist of the falls soak into her hot cheeks and burning eyelids. She saw, even through closed eyes, two red dots approaching her. She opened her eyes to see two firebirds flying toward one of the basins left especially for them to bathe in. Sabíana always loved to see them wash, rare as that sight was. They alighted on the lip of the basin, but as soon as they touched it, they disappeared in a white light, blinding Sabíana. The light didn't abate, and Sabíana's eyes adjusted slowly. Something many-colored fluttered and cavorted in the basin. The blur resolved, and Sabíana recognized her. She was one of the Sirin at Dubían's bier. The one with the feathers dark as twilight.

The Sirin bathed as a bird would, splashing light around her in defiance of the surrounding murk. The effect was like looking through the window of a dark room at the rising of the sun. Sabíana felt a thin filament weaving between her and the Sirin. The Sirin looked at her with eyes like lightning, opened her mouth, and sang.

The weight of the song crushed Sabíana, as though she were pinned down by the full force of both twin waterfalls. But as it washed over her, it lightened her. The heaviness of her father's sickness, the doubt over Vasyllia's fate, the fear about her own place as future Darina, the pain of losing Voran—all of it fell away from her. She felt re-forged from within, the impurities burned away by the force of the song. The Sirin stopped, and Sabíana felt light enough to fly to the Heights. Barely evident inside her chest was a soft patter, like another heart, and the faint sense of warmth, like a candle flame.

"My name is Feína, my swan. We are now joined until the Undoing."

Sabíana remained silent for utter wonder.

"Sabíana, you chose a difficult path, but I will bear it with you. May it be a lessening of the burden on your heart."

"Feína," she whispered, feeling no bigger than a child. "It is going to be terrible, is it not?"

The Sirin spread out her wings and looked to the horizon. At that moment, the sun came up for the first time in weeks.

Sabíana rushed to the first reach. It had been walled off for quarantine, its only entrance a black iron gate manned by several armed guards. Sabíana stopped for a moment, wondering if what she planned to do was as mad as her rational mind insisted. But reason had no place here, she told herself, and swallowed her revulsion.

"Open the gates," she said.

The guards at the gate hesitated. For a moment, Sabíana was sure they would challenge her. She was in the middle of preparing a withering response when they simply turned, opened the gates, and bowed to her. Sabíana walked in. Immediately, the stench beat her back.

The people were teeming, like rats in a gutter. Dogs and children lay together on the road, covered in sores. Mothers rocked babies that cried for milk from withered breasts. Eyes with no hope looked at her, then looked away again. Flies swarmed. Burial mounds poked up everywhere, like cysts on dry skin. Garbage lay interspersed with the half-rotting carcasses of horses and goats. Some children played near the dead animals, apparently unsupervised.

Many, especially the aged, fell at Sabíana's feet and kissed the hem of her robe. They chattered at her in their own dialect, words interrupted by sobs.

Sabíana's tears gushed, and it took a good deal of self-control to prevent the sobs from shaking her visibly.

What has happened to Vasyllia? How could we have allowed this to happen in our own house?

Just down the lane, a doctor in the pantaloons of the merchant class applied some sort of creamy poultice to the sores of a pregnant woman. His hands were caked with the white cream, and his goat-beard was smeared with all manner of dirt and blood. But he didn't seem to notice. In fact, the dirt only made his hazel eyes shine brighter. They looked like little suns. Sabíana, mesmerized, came to watch what he did. He looked up at her, recognized her, but looked back down at his work without acknowledging her presence. Her momentary wounded pride faded when she saw how pockmarked the young woman was. She was probably no more than twenty, but she looked over fifty.

"What does the poultice do?" Sabíana asked, feeling foolish for having nothing more erudite to say.

"It heals the sores," said the doctor nonchalantly.

"Heals them?" That surprised her. From what she heard of the plague, it had no cure. "But what about the plague?"

"Plague?" He snapped his head at her, his eyes furious. "There is no plague. It is only lack of food, lack of water, and dirt. That is all."

Sabíana's head began to spin. She should have known. The Dumar hadn't quarantined anyone. They had caused "the plague" in the first place.

"Guard!" she called, and four immediately appeared at her side. "You, inform the elders of the warrior seminary that every cohort is to be called to the marketplace this moment. Every merchant table and booth is to be disassembled, and tents for the refugees are to be built from them. You, go to the healers and tell them that the refugees are to be relocated to the second reach, and that they will need care immediately. You, go find the Marshall of the Dumar. He is to be told that there will be a collection of food, living necessities, and medicine from the houses of the third reach, beginning tomorrow morning. You, go to the palace and tell the scribes to await my coming. Warn the criers of city-wide circuits tonight and tomorrow. Why do you still stand here? Go!"

They went, bowing hastily. "Dear Feína," she said silently. "The Pilgrim may have said that remaking the Covenant is beyond our hope, yet I will restore Vasyllia to its honor in spite of it all."

"Highness!" The voice was behind her. She turned to see Rogdai in full armor, save for an uncovered head. "You are summoned to the palace, my lady."

She understood.

"I come," she said, and her voice cracked. As she passed, the soldiers inclined their heads. The whispers accompanied her out of the first reach: "The Black Sun. *Our* Black Sun."

Dar Antomír's eyes blazed with unearthly light as he lay on his deathbed. Sabíana understood it to be the last surge of life before the final dimming. He saw her and smiled, extending a bony hand. She took it—he was still so strong for a dying man—and fought to contain the tears. The light in his eyes was almost blinding.

"Sabíana," he whispered frantically. "Listen to me, listen. I have seen a vision, a final gift. I knew I had few hours left to live, and I begged Adonais as I have never begged before, to tell me something of my sons. For I had no hope left.

"As I lay on my bed in gloom, I was in my chamber no longer. I stood at the edge of a stream fed by a cascade of falls. The river wove into a deep emerald pool, fringed with a dense assortment of birches, osiers, and hollies. Beyond the trees, jagged hills sheltered the pool from all wind. On three sides was the pool thus sheltered, but the fourth was a great tumbling waterfall.

"I walked to the ledge and there was no bottom in sight. I looked once more and saw a different sight—a dry marshlands with many rivers snaking through it. Two men ran across it, pursued by a shapeless darkness. Still a third time I looked, and I saw the Great Sea, interminable to the horizon, and in it lay an island from which grew a white sapling covered in golden leaves.

"Then I stood on the top of the tallest mountain in the world, and the earth was riven at my feet, riven and bleeding. A voice thundered at my right, coming from a pillar of a thousand eyes and a thousand wings, all of fire and light. It spoke these words to me:

"'Behold, this is the place of death and the place of healing. Tell me, Dar of men. Will the water flow?'

"I said to him, 'It will, for without it the world will wither and die.'

"He said, 'It will, but only if the falcon sheds its skin, the swan spreads its wings, the bear forsakes its hunger.'"

At these last words, the fire within Dar Antomír simmered and began to fade.

"Father, not yet, please!"

"Do not grieve for me, my child. Do you not understand?"

"No, father, I do not," her voice subsided to a hoarse whisper.

"The falcon is Voran's blazon, the bear Mirnían's. They are alive. And the swan is you, my love. It is your time now."

His eyes wandered beyond Sabíana, smiling at something he saw there. She looked up to see a dark-haired Sirin, her face wet with tears. Sabíana found her strength returning.

"Taryna," said the dying Dar. "I am ready. Take me with you."

Sabíana walked out of the chamber, hardly conscious of anything except her grief and the need to hold it in, to not give it any quarter. Rogdai stood at the door. One look at her face, and he fell on one knee and took her right hand in his own shaking hands and kissed it. His face was hot to the touch. He looked up at her through his own veil of tears, and said, "Praise be to Darina Sabíana. May your reign be long, and may the holy gaze of Adonais shine upon you."

Kalún had waited in the palace cherry grove for what seemed like hours. He was growing extremely displeased with Yadovír. He had had such high hopes for the young man. But all Yadovír seemed to do was run around, very busy and very solicitous on behalf of the Dar, though with little to show for the work of their conspiracy. With every passing day, the pestilence reached its pox-ridden hand closer to the third reach.

Something rustled in the trees. Yadovír squeezed himself

between two trunks and nearly poked his eyes out on the groping branches.

"You do seem flustered, Sudar Yadovír, if I may be allowed the observation."

Yadovír sighed in obvious exasperation.

"Otar, I know you expected me to arrange matters with greater alacrity. But I do have good news. All is in readiness for a meeting with the Ghan himself."

"This Ghan travels with his own army?" Kalún was hardly a strategist, but it seemed a foolish way to conquer future tribute states. Unless the Ghan never intended to return to his capital city of Gumir-atlan.

"So it would seem, yes." Yadovír did not seem perturbed by it. "At great personal danger to myself, I arranged an exchange of information with their camp. They made it clear that they would welcome us tomorrow night."

"How are we supposed to do that? Walk out of the city and stride over to the enemy side? That should go over very well with the door wardens."

Yadovír ignored the sarcasm. "The Raven's escape, Otar Kalún. You know the old story, yes? Well, it seems at least part of it is true. There *is* a way out of the palace through the dungeons. An old passage into the forest below the city. Not many know of it, and those that do, think that it's been blocked for centuries. But I was curious, so I checked. It is mostly blocked, but after some careful manipulation of the fallen rock, I found that one or two people will be able to squeeze through with a little difficulty."

"How convenient. Can you guarantee our safety?"

Yadovír smiled, and there was a kind of madness in his eyes. "Oh, Otar Kalún, I think we have gone too far to think about safety."

Gamayun, the Dayseer, sits in an ivory tower in the sea of times. Does she sing the future into being, or does she only speak of what she sees? No one knows.

From "The Tale of the Black Sirin"
(Old Tales, Book VII)

Chapter 20

A Narrow Escape

Tall warriors, robed in grey, faces confined behind black iron helms with no eye-slits, held screaming children over vast fire-pits. The mothers, shrieking in despair, all turned to Voran, asking him that most horrible of questions: "Why?" Tortured forms that once were men—now misshapen freaks with empty eye sockets and bald, bloodied pates where their hair was torn off—huddled around him, reaching for him with blackened nails. The ones without eyes saw him the best.

Tarin laughed, and Voran awoke. Voran's upper lip twitched. He snarled and barked at Tarin. His hands groped for a rock with which to beat the old man to the ground. With a start, Voran awoke again.

They were still in the hag's village, though some distance from the carcass of the dead serpent-hag. Voran's wounds throbbed. The skin around them was yellow and gummy. He tried not to look, afraid he would be sick or faint. Tarin sat by the river, arms hugging his knees, looking at nothing. His lips moved noiselessly, repeating something. He turned at Voran and made a face.

"You should wash," he said. "You're quite filthy, you know. A bath of fire would really be best."

"A bath of...what?"

Tarin turned away and began to mumble to himself again.

"Why?" asked Voran. Tarin's expression was unreadable. "Why did you come to save me from her? What am I to you?"

Tarin huffed. "I knew your father well."

Voran fell silent. It was not what he expected, and he was not sure how he felt about it. For so long he had grown used to avoiding thoughts about Otchigen, or when that failed, to hate him until his heart grew numb like an overused muscle. Now, to think of his father in any positive light was uncomfortable.

"It's a strange thing about words, Raven Son," said Tarin. "We talk and talk and talk and never seem to get anywhere. While if you really meant the word, you could make a tree flower."

"I don't know what that means."

Tarin chuckled and continued mumbling to himself happily, patting his head with his hand. His kestrel flew down from a branch above. Tarin made a show of falling to the ground in fear as the kestrel landed on his head, as though it were a dragon with talons bared. Then he turned over and laughed at himself.

What a strange man, thought Voran.

"That dream you just had," said Tarin, "the warriors holding babies over bonfires. It was not a dream, you know."

Voran's heart tripped and started again.

"Vasyllia has fallen?"

"Not quite. I didn't say it was the *present time* that you saw. Just one of possible futures. It seems Gamayun whispered to you in your sleep. She really can be the most pestilent annoyance."

Gamayun? Who in the Heights was Gamayun? Voran was becoming infuriated with the man's lack of useful answers.

"You come here and rescue me," said Voran. "You helped me kill the hag. Now what?"

"Who said she was dead?" Tarin had an impish smile. "The hag is an intimate of the dead lands. Don't count her out yet."

"Will you help me?" Voran felt like punching the crazy old man.

"Will you help yourself?"

Turning to a stone on his left, Tarin kissed it and blessed it with a strange sign. Then he crouched with his ear to the ground, listening intently, until his eyes closed and he began to snore.

"Tarin!"

Tarin opened his eyes and winked.

"What should I do?" Voran felt no older than ten, called to account before the elders of the seminary. Come to think of it, this man could very well have been an elder in his time, if not for his madness.

"Ah, something useful at last," said Tarin, becoming serious. "I know of your search for the weeping tree. I can take you to it. One condition. You must become my slave."

Voran laughed. "You freed me! Now you want me to put on my shackles again?"

"That is my condition."

"And if I refuse? What is to stop me from going to Vasyllia now? As you said, Sabíana waits for me."

Tarin grimaced like a masked jester. He extended his hand and began to count off his fingers. "First, those wounds will kill you soon. Second, you severed your bond with Lyna when you lay with the hag. You won't stand a chance against anything out in the wild. Third, you are still in the Lows of Aer, and I doubt you will find a way back without me. Fourth, Vasyllia is already under siege by the Raven. Fifth, you are an idiot."

Voran bristled, but managed to keep quiet.

"While I offer you a solution to all of those problems, especially the fifth one. You have the word of a storyteller, and tellers never lie. But you must become my slave."

There was no point in having this conversation. Voran was too tired to think, much less construct a rational argument.

"I am leaving in ten minutes," said Tarin. "Come with me or not. Your choice."

. . .

Voran followed Tarin through the village. Beyond a stone hedge marking the edge of the village, the valley continued straight for a day's journey, then crested up into a narrow pass.

Where were they? Were they in the Lows or in the real world? What was the real world, anyway? The thoughts left Voran with bile in the back of his throat.

As they approached the last house of the village, a leaning ruin with a young osier bursting from the roof, Tarin stopped and entered.

"Stay here, slave" he said, leaving Voran no time to come up with any suitable answer.

When Tarin came out, he had a pack in each hand. Tarin laid both packs—one of them felt like it was full of rocks—on Voran's back and took the sword from him.

"You are now my ass," he said, beaming at him proudly. He slapped him on the back, and Voran fell face-first into the mud. Tarin laughed as he walked out of the village. Curses that he didn't even know he knew hissed out of Voran's lips. Tarin seemed not to hear.

It took them most of the day to reach the pass. Beyond, the grayish path switchbacked up into white-capped mountains, taller even than those in Vasyllia.

"We are going there?" Voran pointed at the peaks. "It's the middle of winter. We'll freeze to death, if an avalanche doesn't get us first. And I don't have any clothes other than these rags."

Tarin broke into verse:

"Raven Son, hark now to me.

Twixt faith and mind, what shall it be?

A choice I leave to you to make—

To crawl to doom (a fool, a snake),

Or walk with me. Which shall it be?"

Voran sighed and bowed his head. Tarin clapped him on his shoulder again. This time, Voran stayed on his feet. Tarin seemed pleased by that, judging by the way he hopped in place and hiccupped.

They continued to walk, even after the sun set. Voran expected them to camp for the night, but Tarin kept on walking, head erect and back perfectly straight. Heavy flakes soon swirled around them, but Tarin only sang at them. They seemed to dance to his melody. Voran had always prided himself on his strength, but his endurance was nothing compared to the old warrior's, whose head did not so much as dip during those heavy night hours. Voran soon began to trip over his own feet from fatigue, and once or twice he caught himself falling asleep between steps, only to jerk awake at the pain in his knee as his leg caught the full weight of his body and the two packs.

Just when Voran thought he could go no further, a dark shape loomed directly in front of their path. It was a huge bear, standing on its hind legs. It roared and rushed at them on all fours. Voran cried out in warning, but all that came out was a dry rattle. Tarin didn't seem to see the bear.

At the last possible moment, the bear pulled up short and stood up, waving its arms like a child learning to walk. Tarin raised his own hands and whooped. He chattered and growled at the bear, gesticulating with his hands. The bear...*laughed!*

Tarin embraced the beast and slapped him on the side of the head, and the bear continued on his way. Voran's shuddering limbs refused to listen to him for a time as Tarin—grumbling and whistling all the while—kept walking forward.

This occurred several more times throughout the night, but every time the encounters were never less than horrifying. Finally, the sun inched toward the horizon.

"Well, here we are," said Tarin, stopping in the middle of the road. They had climbed about half the distance up the switch-back path hugging the mountain, and the peak loomed above them, still impossibly far. The sounds of the waking forest bubbled up to Voran's awareness—snakes rustling through dry brush, rabbits running from the cover of one shrub to another, groundhogs pushing up against the fresh blanket of snow covering their holes.

Then Voran saw it. Just off the road was a hole in the ground, gaping at them uninvitingly.

"In you go, slave," said Tarin, waving his arm toward the hole.

"Yes, Lord," said Voran, with a hint of sarcasm that earned him a sound blow across one ear.

"You will learn to keep a civil tongue, my ass."

Voran jumped in head-first, then the world turned upside down and he found himself sitting on prickly, yellow marsh grass. For a moment, his mind thought that he should be falling still, and it spun uncontrollably, until he felt his feet sink into a pool of icy water. He cursed and pushed himself up, and the world righted itself. But something was still wrong. It was too quiet, so quiet that the silence buzzed in his ears.

Someone was watching him, but every time he turned around he saw nothing, not even Tarin. Yet the feeling remained. It grew, until he was sure that an invisible army was staring at him. Far away, dim across the endless marshland surrounding him, Voran thought he saw something swirling and dark.

"Hurry," said Tarin, appearing suddenly at his side. "It seems they knew we were coming."

Now the malice coming from that mass of something dark was palpable, as though Tarin's appearance had enraged a great beast.

"What is it?" gasped Voran as they ran across the dry grass and through shallow pools, turning this way and that to avoid the deeper tarns.

"Raven's horde," Tarin said. "Run!"

Voran's sides felt as though one hundred knives pierced them. His vision grew foggy. His wounds oozed and throbbed, and his feet squelched in clammy water. He tottered. Tarin grabbed his arm and threw it around his shoulders, holding his side with a grip like iron pincers.

"I can't..."

"Just a little farther," Tarin said between heavy breaths.

The long marsh-plain suddenly ended. They stood on the

edge of a precipice plunging thousands of feet down, with nowhere else to go. Voran turned around, and now the swirling cloud was much closer. He thought he could glimpse indistinct shapes in the mist.

"Do not stop, Voran. Forward!" said Tarin.

"Forward? Are you mad, Tarin? What should we do? Fly?"

"If that is necessary, yes."

Voran felt the fear rise like vomit.

No, he said to himself. Enough.

In his mind, a fog seemed to lift. This was another parting of the ways, similar to the waystone. There was no going back, the way forward led to certain death, and yet there was no other way.

I do this for you, Sabíana, he thought with a stab of guilt. Maybe my death will pay my debts.

He stepped forward into the air, expecting the rush of mad pleasure that accompanies a fall and precedes the terror. Tarin followed, laughing, singing.

They walked on air. As they walked, it was not they who descended, but the land underneath them that ascended, almost as if they were climbing. Before Voran's mind registered it, the thick, wet smell of peat slapped his nostrils. He and Tarin stood in another marshy plain. Mountains sheer as glass rose to their left. Only their extreme tips were white; the rest of the slopes were a lush carpet of green. All around was brown-yellow marshland, veined over with meandering rivers of inky blue. Ahead of them was a sight that made his legs, already throbbing with exhaustion, dance with joy. Twisting hearth-fires. There was a village ahead.

Tarin fell on his knees and raised his arms up to the sky.

"Sing unto him, let your voices exclaim!
Bring unto him all your praises and glory,
Honor his name, by its power exult,
For the voice of the Lord thunders over the waters,
For the voice of the King fills with life all the forests,
For the voice of the Father lifts up the high mountains.
Rejoice in his name, all you fighters of darkness,

For his mercy and glory illumine your passes,
For his love and his power destroy all your weakness
We run with all speed to the Lord of the Realms!"

Voran turned to look back at the cliff from which they had descended, and felt the danger fading away. No swirling darkness followed them. Voran laughed, coming back to life with every twitch of his exhausted legs.

"How did we...?" Voran began.

"Sometimes, the earth itself helps us poor ones," said Tarin in an awed whisper.

All around them, grey branches and dead stumps reached up from the muddy earth, giving the land an agonized look. In the riverbeds, glacial water trickled, carving through the land like a blade through clay.

"It's...beautiful." Voran was surprised to hear himself say.

Before Tarin answered, something struck Voran in the back. Sharp, throbbing pain wove through every inch of his body.

It's like I'm milk being churned into butter, he thought.

He fell, cramped over on the grass, the pain rising in waves. He breathed in, but his chest didn't respond. His heart raced. His mind reeled with panic. There had never been anything else but the pain. He had always suffered. He would always suffer. It would never end.

A firm hand took his clenched fingers and forced them open. The hand was warm. Tarin's face looked like it was in a fog, but he smiled. He whispered, and in spite of the noise in Voran's mind, he heard his master.

"Raven Son. Focus on what I am telling you."

The agony twisted Voran as though he were a dishrag.

"Listen! Repeat in your mind, clearly, this one word. Do it, no matter what doubts creep into you head. 'Saddaí, Saddaí.'"

Voran twisted his lips into the right shape, though even that effort racked him with pain. He repeated the word under his breath, softly. The pain receded and his mind cleared. Into the breach in his mind a thousand thoughts barreled through.

That word! What does it mean? What if it's an evil summoning, and Tarin is no more than a creature of the Raven? What have I done? Look at him, that foul beast with his smirk and detestable face. I want to claw that face open. What a pathetic creature I am. Why could I not stand the pain on my own? Stop saying that word. Stop! *There is awful power in it!*

He continued to repeat it stubbornly—Saddaí, Saddaí—until all thoughts ceased. Warmth suffused his body. He stopped twitching. He noticed the sun was shining.

"Raven Son, you did not yield," said Tarin, tears pouring down his face. "As a reward, look. You are healed."

All Voran's wounds had closed, leaving only purple scars.

"Tarin, what in the Heights was that word?"

Tarin lifted Voran by the hand with no apparent effort.

"Perhaps, someday, I will explain it to you. Don't forget it, Raven Son. It may save you again, and not only once."

He looked suddenly thoughtful and perturbed by something.

"What is it?" asked Voran.

"They overreach themselves," he said. "I did not expect such boldness from them yet. Vasyllia must be on the very brink."

In the year of the covenant 845, Dar Mikahil left no male heirs. His only daughter Albiana and his daughter son's Barhuk both claimed the right of inheritance. Rather than choose between them, the Dumar decided to summon a Council of the Reaches to choose a new Dar. On the day before the announcement, Albiana commanded the warriors to imprison the entire Dumar as traitors to the Monarchia. Soon afterward, Barhuk chose a life of solitude and contemplation in a monastery, and no one challenged the rise of the first Darina in the history of Vasyllia.

From "A Child's History of Vasyllia"
(Old Tales, Book I)

CHAPTER 21

COMPLICATIONS

"Highness," said Sabíana's trembling maid—she trembled constantly these days— "the representative of the Dumar has been waiting to be admitted for the last hour."

"Let him wait," said Sabíana, not raising her eyes from her scribbling. They all think too much of themselves, these third-reachers, she thought.

There had been nothing but complaints from the rich ever since she mandated that every citizen of Vasyllia donate their food and clothing stores to the refugees now camped in the second reach. She knew what this man would say to her. More complaints, more bitterness. More insinuations that had she been a *man*, things would not be so dire.

Her nib cracked under her hand. She cursed. She had no more quills. With a reluctant sigh, she looked at her maid.

"Let him in."

To her surprise, it was not Yadovír, whom she expected. It was Elder Pahomy of the warrior seminary. She stiffened. Battle with the old warrior required tact as well as forcefulness.

Elder Pahomy lumbered in, dressed in the black, flowing robes of a cohort father. The traditional dress did little to diminish his significant belly. He bowed formally. She saw his jawline ripple as he rose.

He is as unsure as I am, she thought.

"I did not expect the Dumar to send you, Elder," she said, standing up and approaching him. She lightly took his forearms and reached up to kiss him thrice on the cheeks. His jawline relaxed a little, and his eyes changed from stormy to merely threatening.

"I do not relish the role of errand-boy, Highness," he said, his jowls quivering in irritation.

"I do understand you, Elder." She kept her left hand light on his arm and continued to look him directly in the eyes. "But I promise not to be cross with you, no matter what their nonsense."

"Sabíana," he said, sighing heavily. "May I sit?"

"Of course." She smiled and led him to a chair, which creaked dangerously when he sat down. She remained standing by him. It gratified her perversely to see how uncomfortable that made him.

"Highness, the third reach is very... *unhappy* about your arrangements concerning the refugees," he began.

She sighed very loudly, and he stopped.

"Get to the point, Pahomy."

He flushed briefly and cleared his throat. "It's been three weeks since the siege began, and the weather is only getting colder. They fear a long winter. If their stores are used on these refugees, many will starve."

"And they think I do not know this?"

"Highness, I think it an admirable thing that you do. I do. But necessity sometimes dictates that we become cruel and hard, for the sake of the many. And treachery is a terrible disease to catch during siege-time."

"I know all this, Elder. But if we cannot extend our compassion to our neighbors in the times when that compassion is most needed, we do not deserve to survive this siege."

"In that case, you leave me no choice."

He stood up ponderously and drew himself to his full height. The room seemed to shrink as he stood.

"Highness, the third reach demands, by its ancient right, to convene a Council of the Reaches."

Sabíana felt the blood drain from her face, and spots began to dance before her eyes. The nobles wanted to elect a new Dar. The nobility of Vasyllia had just committed treason.

"Rogdai!" Sabíana called, and immediately the door flew open and the old swordsman strode in and saluted. He looked slightly perturbed at seeing the elder, but only for a moment.

"Rogdai, Elder Pahomy has just informed me that there are traitors in the third reach. Take a full detachment of the palace guard. The elder will lead you to the houses of the conspirators. You are to arrest all of them. Our dungeons have stood too long unused."

The elder looked at her for a long time, then his eyes creased and twinkled. He bowed low and offered her a hesitant hand. She extended hers, and he kissed the tip of her right forefinger.

"Come, Vohin Rogdai," he said and walked out of the room.

Sabíana stood for a long time, smiling. She had taken a tremendous risk, won an important ally, and removed a dangerous infection from the city in one move of the chessboard. It excited her, far more than she expected.

Kalún and Yadovír each held a torch that smelled unpleasantly of burnt lard. The nether regions of the palace, far below even the dungeons, were hardly more than caves. In some of the rooms stalactites dripped water in a maddening, steady rhythm. Every drop made Yadovír want to jump out of his skin. He knew that there was a significant possibility that they were walking into a trap. He was ready to give up and turn back. The darker the caves became, the more the recent stories of the Gumiren's atrocities bubbled up to his conscious mind.

You think you can reason with blood-drinkers? asked his mind. *What sort of madness possesses you to think you can reason with savages?*

"Not much farther now, Otar," he said, more to distract himself than anything.

And yet he recognized that a kind of madness had bitten and infected him. Yadovír wanted power, absolute power, and he was even willing to speak with the Ghan, to give up his own city on the enemy's terms, if only it meant a chance at that power. It was increasingly becoming an irrational urge. The knowledge that he would sell his own family for it no longer bothered him.

"Yadovír." The priest's voice was insufferably calm. "Tell me again why you waited so long to meet with them?"

Yadovír wanted to scream. They had spoken of this already at least five times.

"Winter deepens, Otar. They are Steppe-people. They do not know *real* winters. I waited for them to feel a truly deep Vasylli freeze. It will make them more amenable to our terms."

"Our terms. Yes. Very good." His voice was soft and absent.

Yadovír wondered if the priest was going senile.

They turned past the last bend, and before them the passage was blocked by fallen boulders and dirt. Here, as Yadovír had already found, was a small hole, barely visible even with the torches, through which they should be able, with some difficulty, to push to the other side.

"I am afraid we must leave our torches behind, Otar."

Kalún grumbled under his breath. They left the torches in an old, rusty brazier that clung to the cave wall and plunged into the dark on the other side. The murk was almost substantial, like a hand that groped for their eyes at every step they took.

"Otar," whispered Yadovír, the echoes running ahead of him. "Follow my voice. I know the way from here well enough."

The priest didn't answer, but Yadovír heard his breathing, so he stepped forward into the void. It was far more frightening this time than the last. Every step he took increased the sense that he was approaching something horrid and irrevocable. Maybe it would be best to go back? To just pretend that the way ahead was hopelessly blocked?

"This way, Otar Kalún, follow me. We should come out not far from the enemy camp. Their soldiers have free rein to wander about in search of food or stragglers. If we are accosted, we must not panic. Even it if seems they will kill us, it will be no more than a show of force. The Ghan has ensured our safe passage." Did he really believe that himself?

Yadovír kept one hand on the walls, feeling for the telltale change. The bare walls needed to give way to scattered roots, and only then could they be sure they were near the exit. But they walked for a long time, and Yadovír felt no change. Had they taken a wrong turn? What if they were going deeper into the mountain, and all that awaited them was a dead end and a stone tomb? His temples began to ache with increased pressure, or was that his imagination? Surely they were going deeper into the earth, not closer to the exit.

Otar Kalún persisted in his silence. Finally, Yadovír felt a moist root.

"Not far now, Otar. I did not tell you this before, but the Ghan is eager to meet the chief cleric of Adonais. He said that he expected an interesting conversation."

Otar Kalún merely grunted.

Soon they came out through a small opening, and the icy wind bit Yadovír's face, freezing even the hairs in his nose. Rare, sharp snowflakes did not so much fall as shoot down from the sky like arrows. Below them the mountain sloped down away from the walls of Vasyllia to their left, only a few hundred feet away. There was no path here through the thickly-growing pines. They climbed down with difficulty, slipping on the icy rocks and roots. Mist lay thick around them.

"What's that?" Yadovír pointed ahead of them.

"Torchlight," said Otar Kalún.

"Sixty-five," said Rogdai.

"Sixty-five?" Sabíana could not believe her ears. She had expected ten, maybe fifteen traitors. Sixty-five? A heavy dread settled into the pit of her stomach. This was obviously just the beginning.

She and Rogdai walked through the dungeons, Rogdai naming every one of the conspirators as they passed their door.

"Lord Rudin, his son Nevida…"

Nevida? She thought, alarmed. I grew up with him. He was one of my closest friends. You have no friends, she reminded herself.

"Any clerics, Rogdai?"

"None, my lady. Did you expect any?" He seemed surprised.

She would not speak it aloud, but she feared Otar Kalún had no great love for her. But would he turn traitor?

"I think I have had enough for now. Bring me a written report of their questioning by early tomorrow morning."

Sabíana allowed herself to wander through the lower reaches of the palace on her way back from the dungeons. She found herself in the passage she often walked with Voran whenever they had wanted to be alone. After the bond with Feína, she found it easier to think of him. Her heart did not immediately fold in on itself as though it were trying to hide.

She remembered the moment she first saw Voran as a man, not a boy. He had just successfully finished the Ordeal of Silence, but the only reward he was to receive was the disappearance of his beloved mother, the madness of his father, and the terrible events of the failed Karila embassy.

Voran was only sixteen at the time.

The memory was as clear as though it had happened yesterday.

It was the first sunny morning after nearly a month of rain, and the air was so clear, so washed, that it seemed there was no air at all. Father had relented for once and allowed her to attend the Dar's hours—the one day in the month that the Dar accepted direct petitions from any person in Vasyllia, regardless of reach. Voran was the first to come.

She had not recognized him—he was so serious, so thin. The six months of the Ordeal of Silence lay heavy on him. She knew how much heavier his burden was about to become, and she wanted to leave, to not be forced to endure the pain in his eyes. But she forced herself to stay.

"Voran," her father had said. "I would give my right hand to reward you as you deserve. Instead, I have only pain. The embassy to Karila was attacked. Every single member of the embassy—yes, even the women—were killed. Worse. They were gutted like animals. But..."

Voran's lips were a white line in his face.

"Your father was not among them."

Voran gasped in relief. Then, his face changed. He realized the implication.

"But, Highness," he said, in the voice of a man who had forgotten what is was like to speak. "Surely you don't think..."

Sabíana's heart contracted, but she held still.

"No, Voran. I do not. But others..."

Something happened to Voran's body. It seemed to grow, to become firmer. His face aged before her. His eyes sharpened. They were the eyes of a full-grown warrior on the eve of war.

"Highness, I will do as you command. If it is your desire that I abandon my place at the seminary, I will do so. If you wish me to leave Vasyllia, I will do so. Only I ask one thing. Not for myself. For the memory of the man whom you loved as a brother."

Tears gathered in Sabíana's eyes. She batted her eyes, and the tears fell. She sniffed. Her hands shook.

Dar Antomír wept openly. He nodded. "Ask, Voran."

"Lebía. Make her your ward. I will leave your sight then, and my shame will not reflect on your brightness."

"Scribe!" Dar Antomír cried, and his voice echoed. "Let it be carved in stone."

Voran assumed the military stance.

"From this moment, Vohin Voran and his sister Lebía are declared wards of the Dar. Vohin Voran is relieved from his studies. But he is not to abandon them. Elder Pahomy of the warrior seminary will study with him personally. He will graduate with his cohort in time. Let Dumar confirm the words of the Dar."

In a softer voice, he had said to Voran, "Go, my son. Take whatever time you need to comfort your sister and to arrange your affairs. Our treasuries are at your disposal…"

"No, I must not think of him," she whispered now to the darkness, its cold bringing her back to the present. "Voran must accomplish his quest, or he will never be complete. I do not want half a man as my husband."

A gust of wind blew through the underground passage. The torches flickered and went out, leaving her in complete darkness. Throbbing like a heart, a white light appeared from the depths ahead of her. Strangely drawn by it, Sabíana walked forward. The white light flared, then faded. The torches came back to life.

Her heart pounded with dread.

A bundle lay just ahead of her. Was it her imagination, or did it move?

Terror engulfed her. With shaking hands, she reached down to touch the bundle. It was warm. With a sickening lurch, her heart stopped, then raced with redoubled fury. A body.

She ran back to the dungeons, where Rogdai still paced back and forth, overseeing the questioning of the traitors.

"Rogdai, come with me."

When they reached the bundle, she found it difficult to look at it. She pointed, and watched Rogdai's face, gauging his reaction. Every time she tried to look down at the body, terror crushed her, and she had to close her eyes.

"The face. Uncover it," she said.

He did as he was told. His eyes went round, and he gasped softly. But not with fear. Sabíana forced herself to look down.

A man. So familiar, yet so strange. A face she had never thought to see again. A face so entangled with recent regret, worry, and loss that it was nearly as well known to her as Voran's. But he had changed so much. He was drawn, starved, ashen, his face overgrown with a matted beard, no longer black, but not yet grey. Arms once bristling with the strength of ten men were little more than brown twigs cracked by winter. At her feet lay the erstwhile Voyevoda of Vasyllia, Otchigen. Voran's father.

"Highness," whispered Rogdai. "This is not possible. We are under siege. How does he just *wander* into the palace? There is something very wrong here."

She nodded. "Take him to my chambers, but tell no one. I must think on this."

"Highness, what is there to think about? He *must* have been sent by the enemy."

Thoughts of pity and vengeance tore at her in turn. There was also something else: a sickening unease in the deepest pit of her stomach. She agreed with Rogdai. It was no accident that Otchigen appeared now, of all possible times. So why was she taking him? She had no firm answer herself.

Rogdai laid him in Sabíana's own bed, and she wrapped him in her costliest furs. His breathing, so ragged and rushed, softened. From sickening green, his face took on the pied hue of the hearth-fire. She washed his hands, arms, and feet, marveling at their brittleness. With rose and lavender water, she gently teased out the brambles in his hair and beard. She undressed him and threw the rags into the hearth. She put a royal robe on him. Soon, a vestige of the former nobility began to reveal itself in subtle shades.

"Highness," said Rogdai. "What do you intend to do with him?"

She bristled at the informality, but their shared confidence softened her. "Double the guard at the door, and be there yourself at all times. If this is some ploy by the enemy, we must be ready. But Otchigen was always a well of information. Now, perhaps, more than ever. I know the risk. But I will get it out of him by any means necessary."

He stood straight and gave her the warrior's salute. In his eyes, she saw something exhilarating. *I am their Black Sun,* she thought. *Rogdai is my man, heart and soul.*

Two dancing fire-lights resolved into three, then five, then seven. Seven torches, carried by seven burly Gumiren. The biggest made directly for Yadovír, showing no surprise at meeting him there. The other six surrounded them. Yadovír's heart dropped to his ankles. The leader turned around and indicated that they should follow. Soon, they entered a bustling war camp.

Yadovír was so surprised by what he saw that he nearly forgot to be afraid for a few moments. Campfires surrounded them, some with no people around them, which Yadovír found strange. From all sides, he heard the sound of pounding hammers and harsh words. Logs were dragged back and forth, and he noticed a good number of the Gumiren constructing siege towers fitted with rough, wooden wheels. Yadovír was surprised that the Gumiren were intent on storming the city in winter.

Everywhere, he smelled horseflesh and feces and sour milk. Goats and sheep roamed freely among the men. He was momentarily distracted by the loud braying of a bull, and he turned to look. Immediately, he wished he had not, though he found himself fascinated in spite of himself. Five of the Gumiren lay a bull on its back and held it down as it thrashed. One of them slashed its chest and belly open so quickly, even the bull was surprised. Yadovír expected a spray of blood, but saw nothing. They held the bull until it stopped shuddering. Then they turned it over, and all the blood was collected in wooden basins lying in wait underneath.

"For sausages," said one of the torch-bearers in a surprisingly friendly tone.

"Blood sausages?" Yadovír tried not to sound as revolted as he felt.

"Yes, very good!" said the Gumir.

Several men milked horses. Yadovír was disgusted, but then he realized that by bringing mares, the Gumiren had a nearly limitless supply of milk and cheese on the war path. Grudgingly, he admired their intelligence. He continued to look around, trying to understand these strange enemies better. There were few quarrels, to his surprise. Other than the constant barking out of orders, the predominant noise was laughter. Many sat by campfires joking in their rat-a-tat tongue. Some wrestled goodheartedly with each other as the others cheered. They did not seem like the killing force that had razed Nebesta to the ground.

Then he saw the Vasylli prisoners—all of them men. Hundreds of them, mostly tied back to back and thrown in heaps on the edge of the camp, just far enough from the fires not to freeze to death. It chilled him even as it confused him. What was the use of keeping all these prisoners? The possibilities were frightening, and ruefully he admitted that this was no common enemy. These were experts at total war. Several large mounds of earth lay beyond the prisoners, probably burial mounds for the dead Gumiren who fell when the Vasylli took back Dubían's body. It reminded Yadovír that the Gumiren were still human, for all their prowess in war, and the thought gave him strength.

The leader stopped by the prisoners and said something to the six torchbearers. Two of them seized Yadovír and Kalún and tied them up back to back, pushing them down next to the other prisoners.

"What are you doing?" said Yadovír, heart and mind racing. "We have an arrangement!"

The leader laughed and said something in his tongue. The rest of them laughed and one kicked Yadovír. He fell over and his head landed on a rock.

Otchigen's eyes opened, and their color was Voran's. Sabíana shuddered, but kept quiet. He looked at Sabíana in some confusion, then recognition warmed his eyes.

"You've grown so beautiful, Sabíana," he said, his voice a rasp, nothing like the booming voice that used to be. "But your beauty brings no warmth. How unlike your father you are."

His words were not bitter, but strangely expressionless. It gave no foothold to her anger, which annoyed her.

"What happened to me?" he asked.

"I was going to ask you the same thing, Otchigen. How is it that you appear in the nether regions of the palace in the middle of a siege?"

He struggled to remember, it seemed to her. He shook his head.

"You do not remember?"

He shook his head again. "Did you say Vasyllia is besieged?"

She didn't know what to think. Silence groped from him like heat from a fire, and Sabíana found herself entranced by his still undeniable presence.

"She disappeared," he said, his breath ragged, his eyes glazing over. He seemed half-delirious. "On a day unmatched for brilliance and warmth, she vanished without a trace. My wife, my life-giving spring, my rock. What was I to do? I could not be without her. I left and wandered. Blank, faded years. Memories...bleaker than the wastes of the far downs..."

Sabíana was entranced, drinking in even the silences between his words. No wonder the people loved him, she thought. No wonder my father loves him.

"I never found her," he continued. "Only rumors in lands where untamed forces twist men's minds into shapes of horror. No, I do not want to remember." He panted, and his face was spotted with red. "I heard that she had gone mad, that she was taken by men who would use her for her beauty. I never heard or found anything more. I was half-mad with hunger and grief. I am still mad, I think. Then, nothing. Somehow, I ended up here in your bed. Thank you, Sabíana."

At the unexpected thanks, she felt herself redden. She turned away, eager to be freed of his enticing influence. This was not the playful Otchigen who used to wrestle with her and Mirnían in the tall grass, to the shock of their prim chaperones. This man had suffered, so much was clear, but he was too self-possessed for someone who had descended into madness. There was something indescribably alluring about him. It made Sabíana long to give up her self-control. This man could be an incredible Dar, she thought, then wondered why she had thought it.

She felt nauseous at the thought. He says nothing about the Karila embassy, she reminded herself, forcing herself to be calm. She failed and rushed out of the room in a confusion of scattered thoughts and emotions.

I will come, I will come
I will come to the Dar's City
I will beat down, I will beat down,
With my spears the city's wall!
I will roll out, I will roll out
The barrels from the treasury.
I will gift, I will gift
Them to my father-in-law.
Be kind to me, my father-in-law,,
As is my own dear father...

Vasylli wedding song

CHAPTER 22

THE WEDDING

Nearly two months after the rescue of the pilgrims, the eve of the wedding arrived.

Three aspens stood in the center of the village, alight with lanterns. A life-sized Sirin carved from birchwood adorned the top of the center tree. All of Ghavan Town assembled in a circle around the trees, and steamed breath rose up in tendrils entwining with the smoke from the candles in their hands. The women sang, their joy enough to banish the cold to the outer fringes of the village. But Mirnían shook from miserable cold, and he was ready to fall asleep on his feet from exhaustion.

They had been standing vigil for four hours already, Otar Svetlomír doing his best to keep everyone awake with his dynamic voice and inspired manner of serving. The vigil would last for at least another three hours. Mirnían felt guilty, in spite of all his rational objections to this ancient rite. Every person he looked at was on fire from within. Even the children were still awake, their cheeks pink and their eyes sparkling. As for him, he could barely prevent the snores before they erupted from his throat. He berated himself. *Why can you not stay awake, even for a service performed for the sake of you and your beloved?*

So he stood, and gradually the inner grumbling stilled. Yet he remained apart from the rest, especially Lebía.

Otar Svetlomír approached Lebía and took her by the hand. To the accompaniment of a rhythmical chant in the women's voices, he led her around the trees three times. The children, who had been waiting for this moment for hours, began to ring small handbells handed out before the service. The sound was chaotic and wonderful. Lebía smiled, but tears ran down her cheeks.

Mirnían remained cold, both in body and in heart. He wished with all his strength to include himself in the joy of the village, to foretaste the pleasure of tomorrow's wedding, but his emotions were dull, like a bell cracked from excessive use. The sore under his left arm flared, as though mocking him. Whoever said that all mystical experiences are wishful thinking should be publicly flogged, he thought.

The men erupted into a joyful chant, almost a shout. Lebía returned to her place next to him, and Svetlomír took Mirnían's hand and led him around the trees as well. The bells clanged twice as frantically. One little boy in particular was so red-faced with the exertion of wringing every possible ounce of sound from his bell that Mirnían was afraid he would faint.

Their joy was palpable, obvious. Mirnían could almost smell it, it was so intense. Still it remained outside his reach. He tried to stop himself, but he blamed Voran, as he so often did these days. Surely the hag's curse was still on him in some way, even after Lebía's incredible healing.

"Bless them as you blessed Cassían and Cassiana," intoned Otar Svetlomír, nearly dancing in his ecstasy. "Bless them as you blessed Lassar and Dagana. May their union be a fruitful joining of Heights and earth. May their children bring healing to our land."

"So be it!" exclaimed the women, all of whom were trying to keep a reverently serious expression on their faces, but failing miserably.

"Honor their petitions, Adonais. Hear their requests!"

Lebía gathered her furs and placed them carefully before her, then knelt on them gingerly, trying to avoid the snow with her clothing. She closed her eyes, her mouth moving in quick whispers, her eyebrows trembling. He did not deserve this perfect creature. Mirnían fell on his face before the tree.

"Feel!" he commanded his heart. "Why can you not feel anything?"

Three hours later, he began to feel a slight flutter of longing in his heart. Seven hours, he thought, and only this. It was enough to make him scream in frustration. For the sake of Lebía, he remained silent. The wedding is tomorrow, he reminded himself, you are just nervous. Everything will be well.

Otar Svetlomír raised them up, taking Mirnían's right hand and Lebía's left. He placed a ring of clear quartz on Mirnían's right ring finger. A single pine needle ran the length of the ring. Mirnían realized someone had crafted the ring around the needle. The artistry amazed him. Lebía's ring was smaller, of pink quartz, flecked with pine seeds within like insects captured in amber. It was even more wondrous to behold than his ring.

"The promise of fidelity," said Svetlomír, quiet enough for it to be intended only for the two of them. "Though the temptation be strong, let this night be the pledge of your future faithfulness, for you must wait to perform your duties until after the wedding service."

Lebía blushed, and even Mirnían could not stop a slight smile. Then his sore throbbed, as though the hag stood invisible by his side and prodded him with a white-hot poker.

"Careful around the sore," he said to the boy assigned to help him into the ceremonial wedding garb—an absurdly heavy red-gold kaftan whose tall collar chafed his neck even before he put it on. Mirnían suspected the embroidered sunbursts were sewn with actual gold thread on the doubly layered red velvet.

"What sore?" asked the boy, looking directly at it, but apparently not seeing it.

"Never mind," said Mirnían, fumbling for the boy's name. The boy had already repeated it three times, but Mirnían forgot it every time. It bothered him even more than the boy's apparent blindness or idiocy.

As the boy helped him haul the massive garment onto his shoulders, Mirnían almost screamed with pain. The boy had pushed upward onto the open sore, making fire run up and down Mirnían's side.

"I told you to watch the sore, you idiot!"

The boy looked not at all upset at being called an idiot, but he did regard Mirnían with a look that doubted his sanity. Could the boy really not see it?

Confused by the long vigil and the subsequent lack of sleep, and exhausted by his battle with the kaftan, Mirnían sat down on the long bench against the wall of the main room and closed his eyes. Just for a minute.

He opened his eyes, and saw a vision. Some creature of legend stood before him. Her dress also had a high collar and was also red with gold embroidery of crescent moons and stars. It looked even heavier than his kaftan. Her long sleeves opened at the elbow and trailed to the ground. Her hair was intertwined with a latticework of gold wire and gems that looked like the sun rising over a peak.

"Lebía?" He could do little more than whisper.

She smiled, and the sun itself could hardly compare with the light of joy in her eyes.

In a half-dream state, he stood and took her hand, leading her out through the door into the midwinter sun. A carpet lay before them, made of cut flowers. Where had the villagers found flowers in winter?

The air was still, as though all of created Nature took a long breath before the opening chord to a festal hymn. Villagers stood here and there in loose clumps, every face a red sun surrounded by furs like clouds. Mirnían and Lebía walked by the houses of

Ghavan, their road a river of red amid white. The gentle ascents and descents of the village brought the aspens ever closer.

They spoke no word to each other, though Mirnían could not tear his eyes from her, and almost fell on his face several times. Every time she looked at him, the rosebuds on her cheeks blossomed. Only when they stood before the trees did she meet his gaze, stopping him with a gentle squeeze of her fingers on his hand.

"Mirnían," she whispered, "whatever Voran may have done to you, forgive him for my sake. That is the only gift I ask of my husband on our wedding day."

Mirnían's chest constricted, his breath rasping with difficulty. The sore prickled, taunting.

"Yes," he whispered and smiled. His face felt like deer-hide being stretched on a rack for the tanning.

She had not seen it.

The lambswool blanket was like butter on his skin. The hearth crackled and smelled pleasantly of apples. A drowsy inactivity suffused through his body slowly, groping toward his fingertips, as though he had drunk just the right amount of Otchigen's famous wine. At the heart of his contentment was a lightness in his chest that he had imagined gone from his life forever. And yet...

She had not seen it.

Lebía slept. In his own bed. In *their* own bed. There was a wonderful dreaminess about seeing her there, a kind of mystery to her sleep that warmed him more than any fire or blanket. He could sit here staring at her sleep for countless ages, and not feel the need to move. And yet...

She had not seen it.

Their lovemaking had been awkward and—he had never expected it—absurdly comical. He smiled at the memories, embarrassing and warm. No one knew, no one would ever know —though every lover in history were to write a paean to first love —the strange madness of the wedding night, not without experiencing it firsthand. And yet...

She had not seen it.

Was the sore even there? The pain of it, underlying all his thoughts and emotions, seemed all too real. But how was it possible that only he could see it? He had to remind himself that for all the normality of daily life in Ghavan, the boundary between real and legendary was translucent. That left him with the uncomfortable suggestion that no amount of medicine would heal this last sore. No physical medicine, that is.

A Sirin-song sounded outside the house, urging itself on his attention. He dressed quietly and wrapped himself in his thickest furs. He suspected this conversation would be a long one.

Lebía had told him of the soul-bond with Aína on the same day that she had healed him, but he had not fully believed her until Aína herself appeared, her rebuke evident in her hard eyes. He had never imagined eyes could cut so deeply into his very essence.

Now Aína waited for him by the house, looking over the slight descent toward the middle of the village. The houses were all dark, though the paths between them were still visible in the light of the torches kept alight throughout the night. Each of the braziers holding the torches had been made by a member of the village, and even after so many weeks here, the whimsy of each design—a fish, a horse with wings, a many-headed serpent, a six-winged giant with coals for eyes—continued to amaze Mirnían.

"Did you know that the aspen sapling in Vasyllia is no longer on fire?" Aína said, her voice wafting in from some unspeakable depth of antiquity. He never felt fully *there* when she spoke to him. His wife—how extraordinary to think of her as "wife"— tried to explain it by saying that Aína was only really present for her. For all others, it was like speaking through a transparent door.

"Is there no hope that this place can be a rebirth of Old Vasyllia?" he asked her.

"There is a very great hope of that, Mirnían. *You* stand in the way."

Mirnían laughed dourly. "It's always my fault."

"Mirnían, self-pity is the refuge of the weak. You are not weak."

"Tell me then."

She nodded, her eyes half-lidded, assessing him as she spoke. "Among our sisterhood there is one who is apart from us. She is named Gamayun, the Black Sirin. She alone has never felt the fire of soul-bond, for she is set apart, an oracle. Gamayun sings all possible futures, and Gamayun sings invariably of one thing concerning your future. You will meet Voran again, and soon."

"I can't trust myself not to kill him."

"That is why you still have the leprosy on you, though it slumbers, and that is why you alone prevent Ghavan from becoming the hope of Vasyllia."

He knew it, had known it for a long time, but hearing it from a Sirin gave it the kind of finality that a man condemned to death is sure to feel in the long agony of the blade's descent to his exposed neck.

"Mirnían, your father is dead."

He heard the words, and his body involuntarily tensed in anticipation of the inevitable shock, but nothing came.

"Vasyllia?" He asked, his voice hoarse, his throat bone-dry from the cold.

"She still stands, but is besieged. Her fate is no longer yours. At least not for now."

No. His fate was rooted here, in the fertile earth of Ghavan. The remnant of Vasyllia must flourish. He must find a way to forget Voran. Forgive him? He could not.

"Aína, there is some measure of protection against the Raven here, on this island, is there not?"

She half-nodded. He sighed, relieved of tension he hadn't realized was there.

"However," she said, looking back over the town. "You, Mirnían, are outside that protection while you are marked."

Marked. Would he never be free of some kind of mark? Dar's son, Sabíana's brother, heir to Cassían's throne, beloved of the people...it was tiring. When would he ever be able to be merely Mirnían, to do with himself as he pleased?

"What can I do, Aína?" he asked.

But she was no longer there, if she had been there at all.

"Why do the innocent suffer?" asked Dar Cassían. "Why do the guilty prosper?"
A voice thundered from the heavens.
"When you have given your life to the suffering innocents, then you may ask. Not before."

From "Dar Cassían and His Daughter"
(Old Tales: Book IV)

TRAINING

A thin brushstroke of gold painted the tips of the pines on the horizon, but the marshes were already the deep purple of twilight. Achingly close were the wood-smells, the fire-lights, the meal-sounds of the village ahead of them, and yet Tarin remained in maddening stillness on his knees, head bowed, leaning on his old sword. His stained mantle wrapped around him, he blended into the darkness like a boulder or a barrow. Only the sibilance of his repeated whisper marked him as living.

The change was uncanny—the lunatic had become an old warrior again, a kind of warrior Voran had never encountered. Tarin continued to repeat the word, or words, under his breath. Voran could not catch the meaning, but whatever it was, it seemed to diffuse a vibrant calm, as though Tarin were a pebble dropped into a pond, and his calm presence rippled outward. Voran found himself sharing the stillness, entering into it bodily. It reminded him of singing in a choir, in the way that seasoned chanters seem to be absorbed into each other's sound, unconsciously wringing their voices into a single, multifaceted music.

They had spent the day on the threshold of the village, just near enough for Voran to imagine the villagers hosting a feast in their honor on trestle tables in the village square. He knew it was mad to expect anything of the sort, but it was so long—how many days? Three?—since his last proper meal. Instead, he had to content himself with hearing the sounds of the evening meal, which echoed in the clear air of the marsh-valley.

"YEEEAAAAAAOOOOOOUUUUUUUUUU!!!!"

Voran managed not to jump, but he was sure three grey hairs had sprouted on his head instantaneously from that cry. Tarin crouched to the ground, arms akimbo, neck stretched out. He yowled like a wounded animal. Then he retracted his head into his neck like a rooster, and proceeded to cluck as he waddled back and forth in a figure-eight.

All over the village, storm-shutters slapped back, making the houses look like they opened their eyes. The doors swung open, and the houses yawned. The village stirred from sleep, a wild noise rising toward Voran. The strangeness of it disoriented him. Only when he saw them did he realize what it was—a crowd of children, followed by disapproving parents, many of whom ran after their bare-headed charges, armed with hats.

"Tarin! Tarin!" They all cheered wildly, expectant joy in every face, even in the faces of the disapproving parents.

He clucked and clucked and let himself be enfolded in their mittened hands and arms, until he could no longer contain his own joy. His laugh was so natural, so unforced, that Voran thought he was a completely different man. Despite all Tarin's strange behaviors, this reaction to the children was one Voran never expected.

The wave of children had crested and was about to pull Tarin back into the depths of the village. Voran followed, already tasting meat and mead, his mouth filling with saliva. They had all surged to the edge of the village when Tarin turned, so suddenly that Voran nearly ran into him.

"Ah, Raven Son! I had forgotten about you. You may not enter the village. There is a task I need you to perform. Here."

He pointed to the second pack on Voran's back, the one that

felt like it was filled with stones. Voran opened it. The pack *was* filled with stones.

"These are stones imbued with power," Tarin said in his sing-song storyteller voice, more to the children than to Voran. They all approved, tittering. "Raven Son, you must arrange a perfect cairn here, where you stand. Then wait for me. I will come out to you and give you leave to enter the village."

"You cannot be serious," Voran said, before realizing that silence was probably a better strategy.

Tarin stiffened and fixed Voran with a gaze that promised repeated retribution.

"Children," Tarin said in a voice that brooked no opposition, "go on home. I will come to you soon."

Only after the houses had once again fallen asleep did Tarin release Voran from his gaze.

"Have you forgotten your word?" he whispered through gritted teeth. "You are my slave. My commands are not to be questioned, especially by a well-known lunatic such as you."

Voran breathed deeply, trying not let the sparks come tumbling out of his eyes.

"Cairn," Tarin growled. "Now."

He turned and walked into the village.

It took all of five minutes to construct a cairn of stones. It took all of three quarters of an hour for Tarin to return for his inspection.

"Good. Now put the stones back into the pack."

"But what about their protection?"

Tarin looked genuinely puzzled.

"You had said they were invested with power."

Tarin threw his head back and laughed, his hands on his belly. It was a parody of a laugh. Voran wanted to strike him.

"So I did," Tarin said, wiping his eyes of the tears of laughter. "Well, I lied. Get on with it, then."

Tarin only let Voran into the village after midnight, and by that time he was obviously the worse for wear. Voran didn't look at him, hoping the churning annoyance—so thick he was sure it would eat him before he ever had supper again—would be obvious. He wanted Tarin to apologize, or at the very least, to notice his displeasure. Tarin hardly seemed to notice anything.

As a final insult, Tarin let Voran no further than a mudroom that smelled of old furs, wood, and rats. A plate of bread and dried meat sat next to a clean straw pallet. Voran tried to console himself with the blessed warmth of the room, but it did little good. He silently promised himself that he would not sleep all night. That would show Tarin.

Voran was awoken by a laughing Tarin. The door was open and a nearly midday sun streamed into the mudroom.

"Well, you proved your point, Raven Son," said Tarin, and erupted into his lunatic laugh. The crowd of children cheered and jumped and laughed with him. Voran found his resolve to punish Tarin—for what, he had already forgotten—fading at the sight of the children. In the daylight, they looked much worse than last night. Most of them were stick-thin, the whites of their eyes more like yellows. Some had bellies protruding even through the furs. With a rush of shame, Voran realized that Tarin was probably the only joy this village had experienced in months. And all Voran had thought of all night was his own comfort. He swore and promised to curb his pride better next time.

In the center of the village, Tarin climbed a rickety table that shuddered every time he moved, and he moved constantly. Voran was just about to utter a curse about breaking wood and fallen warriors when he remembered his promise. Grumbling, he moved closer to the assembled throng. It seemed the entire village was present.

"In a certain kingdom, in a certain land," declaimed Tarin with a flourish, the table reeling like a drunken man underneath him. The children all hopped up and down, clapping and screaming their delight at the top of their voices. Even Voran, in spite of himself, felt propelled into the energy of Tarin's speech. For all of his madness, the old goat had a way with words.

The Tale of the Cub's Hunger

It was spring, the time for a new-born bear cub to attempt the hunt for the first time. The cub was, as you might expect, excited and full of energy. He left in the morning, sure he would bring something big home—a badger maybe, or even a buck—but the figure he cut when he returned that evening was not what his mother expected. He was bedraggled, wet, and utterly miserable.

"Well, my boy," she said, "did you bring anything to comfort your old mama?"

"Oh, Mama, it was horrible! Even the squirrels laughed at me. I gave them my best roar, but they threw nuts at me. I came to the river; the fish were lazy, sleepy in the summer sun. Easy picking, I thought. I made my attack, and suddenly they were all gone. One fat porker of a salmon actually jumped out and smacked me in the face with his tail. I saw a perfect berry patch—the berries were so perfect, Mama! —glistening and nearly popping with ripeness. But as soon as I came close I was viciously attacked by a stinkbug. It sprayed me! My eyes are still crying from it."

"My poor boy. So much to learn still. You can't conquer the forest in a day. Try again tomorrow. Be patient and careful, but do not let your poor mama go hungry for a second day."

For four days, the cub caught nothing. On the fourth day, he waddled through a birch glade, his stomach grumbling. Suddenly a finch, all yellow and obnoxious—all of their species have that unfortunate deficiency, I'm afraid—took it into its little brain to torment the cub. Around and around his head it flew, screeching always at the moment it passed his ears —for maximum effect, you understand. Finally, the cub had enough, and he swatted the bird with his paw. His swipe was mortally on target, and the bird fell at his feet, its wings awkward and its neck snapped. The cub looked at the bird and felt a savage kind of pleasure. It was the killing itself. He liked it.

That evening, he brought his mother a rabbit. She praised him, but something about his manner—maybe it was his eyes, she could not tell—frightened her.

After that, he killed more and more, starting with small animals like squirrels, and sometimes even bringing down a mountain goat or two. But the more he hunted, the more he began to kill for the mere pleasure of it. Sometimes he even wounded small animals and left them in the forest to die. The kill dominated his thoughts day and night. His mother saw the macabre series of dead creatures from afar, but she was a wise old bear. She bided her time.

One day, the cub came to her, shaking and crying inconsolably.

"Mama, Mama, I'm so miserable!"

"What is it, my sweet cub?"

"I can't stop killing. The desire for blood is huge inside me. It's so big now, it has nowhere else to go. Maybe I should jump off a cliff, so the forest will be rid of me."

She cradled him in her warm embrace, like she did during his first months underground. He cried and he cried, until he could cry no more. Then she looked deep into his eyes, and he felt the pieces of something broken inside him come together again. Drying his eyes, he went out on the hunt again.

Two squirrels were playing in front of their cave, completely oblivious to the bears' living in the vicinity. The cub felt the now-familiar, groping desire to kill them. He was not even hungry, but he could imagine the warmth of their blood and the feeling of power it gave him.

He looked at them for a long time, then sat on his haunches and bellowed. The squirrels nearly left their bushy tails behind them, so far they jumped, and began to chatter at him angrily from the safety of a high branch, though neither was brave enough to throw anything at him. He laughed at them and turned back inside. It was time to sleep.

"They loved it," said Voran as he and Tarin enjoyed a quiet repast, sitting on the ground, leaning on one of the houses. "I didn't think they would understand it, but they seem to have understood more than I did."

"Does that surprise you?" Tarin's voice was only slightly sarcastic. He seemed younger and in better spirits after the telling.

"How much of that story was intended for my ears?"

"You do think much of yourself, don't you, Raven Son?" Tarin shook his head, apparently genuinely disappointed in Voran. "It was a story of the darkness that lives in the heart of every man, not merely the great Voran, son of Otchigen of Vasyllia."

Voran's face grew hot, and he was grateful for the sound of approaching footsteps. It was a little boy, hardly more than four or five. His face was pockmarked, and there was something wrong behind his eyes. The realization pained Voran more than he expected—the little boy's mind was damaged, probably by some kind of disease.

He approached Voran, not Tarin, which surprised Voran, even as a kind of panic began to itch at him. What does one do with a damaged child? His instinct was to ignore the boy or to shoo him away. Actually speaking to him, interacting with him was more frightening than walking off a precipice in the wild. The boy looked at Voran's shoulder, never at his eyes, but still he shuffled nearer. He had no shoes, only rough leather slippers tied together in a slip-shod manner. It suggested that the boy had an older sibling, but no parents.

"Is he an orphan?" whispered Voran to Tarin, unwilling to look at the boy, feeling the unwelcome revulsion, yet unable to look away.

"Why do you not ask him?"

"He is not?...You know..."

Tarin did not answer. The boy reached out a hand and touched Voran's knee, then smiled, tucking his chin into his neck and leaning back. He moaned a little and began to chortle. The piercing in Voran's heart was now a torrent of fire. With a trembling hand, he reached out to the boy and curled his fingers in, inviting him closer. The boy closed his eyes and shook his head, moaning gently, but he didn't back away. Voran spread out both arms to the boy.

The boy cocked his head to the side, his eyes still closed, and turned sideways while shuffling forward, like a reticent crab. He tapped Voran's knees, as if appraising them. Before Voran realized it, the boy was curled up in his arms, his head on Voran's chest. The boy's breathing stilled and deepened, and soon a faint snuffle rose and fell with the little shoulders. He was asleep.

Voran wept, afraid that his heaving chest would wake the boy.

"His name is Voran, by the way," said Tarin, looking away. "And yes, he is an orphan."

Voran did not think he could feel any guiltier in his life than he did at that moment.

When the tears were spent—though the wound in his heart still throbbed, as he hoped it would throb forever—Voran turned to Tarin. The old madman looked different now, as though the touch of a damaged little child had transformed the entire world for Voran.

"Tarin, this village. These children. What happened to them?"

"*You* happened to them. Vasyllia happened to them. But that is the difficult answer. The simple one is that they were in the path of the Raven's armies. Many of them are Nebesti outliers living near the Vasyllian border. Their men were foolish enough to raise arms against the invaders."

That was why there were so many women and so few men. Voran let the reality seep into him as it irritated his new heart-wound, like fermented potato-brew poured over infected skin.

"Tarin, I must find the Living Water. Finally, I know why I must."

The old warrior smiled and closed his eyes. The wind shifted, bringing a strange, almost spring-like fragrance of budding snowdrops. Was it really so near the end of winter?

"That is good, Voran. It will help you in your training. As for Living Water, you are not ready yet."

Tarin stood up and wiped the brown grass from his robes. He yawned hugely and stretched like a cat, until something popped loud enough for the entire village to hear. Tarin yelped in pain and grabbed his back.

"It is time we were off, Raven Son," he said, straightening out with a grimace. "Don't want to attract anything that might hurt these children. Your smell is ripe, and there are many hounds still seeking."

Voran looked down at the boy, trying to commit every single pockmark on his face to memory. *This is our son, Sabiana, our little Voran. They are all our children.*

Don't look for evil in the dark shadows. Don't look for evil in the night. Look for it in the middle of the day. Beware the demon that wears the skin of those you love.

From "The Tale of the Raven and the Living Water"
(Old Tales, Book II)

Chapter 24

The Raven

Though it seemed like days, the Gumiren kept Yadovír and Kalún tied up for little more than several hours. When the guards came to untie them, they could hardly contain themselves for laughter. It seems this "imprisonment" was intended as little more than a practical joke. Yadovír failed to appreciate the humor.

He and Kalún were led, hands untied, to a flat space cleared of trees, various stumps poking out here and there from the frozen ground. In the center of the clearing lay a long sheet covered in a wooden board. The board was laden with foods of many different shades of brown. Wooden pitchers were filled with some white liquid. A group of Gumiren half-reclined, half-sat around the board, grabbing brown bits of food from common platters with their hands, then wiping them on their long, brown, fur-lined coats. By the designs on their hat-sashes, it seemed these were the elite. The Ghan himself, an enormous man with a rare beard and almost feral cunning hiding behind his eyes, sat at the head. His face creased into a smile, and he looked like he would explode any minute into a torrent of laughter.

The Ghan saw them and half-bowed, still sitting, indicating

places on his left. For a moment, Kalún looked unwilling to debase himself at such a table, but to Yadovír's relief he sat down, leaving the seat nearer the Ghan for Yadovír. Yadovír didn't speak at first, thinking perhaps it would be considered rude to speak to the Ghan with no invitation. Kalún stared down at the food with a white face, and seemed intent on saying nothing at all.

"You no offend?" said the Ghan, laughing in his eyes. "Men have little jest at you." He laughed loudly, his rounded belly bouncing up and down. "Eat! We make *horse* for you. Eat."

They were given a plate of brown meat cut into small pieces. Yadovír was sure he would be ill if he ate any of this food, but the Ghan's emphasis on the word "horse" made it clear they were being given a great honor. Yadovír took a large piece and tried to swallow it without chewing. It was not horrible, even faintly seasoned with a spice he didn't quite recognize.

"Saffor, yes?" The Ghan frowned as one of the others corrected him. "Ah, yes. *Saffron.* Your people do not know this, I think."

"It is very good, thank you," said Yadovír, not sure what honorific to use.

"Ghan speak now, yes?" said the Ghan. "My name—Magai. Ghan Magai. You, I know. Priest Kalún and common man Yadovír. You have offer for us, yes?"

Yadovír nodded, pleased things were progressing so quickly.

"Wait," the Ghan laid a meaty hand on Yadovír's shoulder. The reek of body odor was the last thing Yadovír expected of the Ghan, and he blanched from it. "You no tell me yet. I *guess.*"

Yadovír inclined his head, hoping no one noticed his fervent desire to vomit.

"You have secret way into city, yes? No need tower and—how say? —*elaborate* attack? Yes?" The Ghan seemed very pleased at his extensive knowledge of the Vasyllian tongue.

"Yes, Ghan, you are right."

The Ghan clapped once and said, "Ha!" All the other

Gumiren lifted their small wooden cups in salute. It soon became clear that Yadovír and Kalún were expected to do the same. But no one drank yet, to Yadovír's relief. He could only imagine what sort of abomination these savages drank.

"But I ask you," said the Ghan, a little crease appearing between his eyes, "Why we go your way? Why, when we already destroy all city in this land. Why use secret way, when we can use *our way*?"

Yadovír took a deep breath. This was the moment. The power was within reach now.

"It would be easier for all concerned, great one. You would not have to weather this winter, a winter our wise men predict will be terrible. You will lose fewer men, and Vasyllia—a beautiful city with riches you can scarcely dream of—will be yours with little destruction. Is it not better to have a strong city as tributary, instead of burnt ruins? You have seen how tenacious the Vasylli are when pressed to the wall."

The Ghan did not seem appreciative of that reminder. "Gumiren always destroy city if city no surrender. Always!" He frowned grotesquely, like a mask, and the whole assemblage tensed.

"It is a very wise policy, Ghan Magai. I understand your wisdom. You discourage rebellion, and you reward those willing to submit without a fight. Am I correct?"

The Ghan smiled again. "You clever man. I like you. Yes, you correct understand. But still, you no answer. Why work I with you? Why trust I a traitor to his own people?"

Yadovír's heart raced briefly at that reminder, but he persevered. "It is a time of confusion, Ghan. The Dar is dead."

This provoked an unexpected round of whispers, until the Ghan slapped a grimy hand on his thigh, cutting off the sound instantly. He nodded at Yadovír to continue.

"The future Darina is not yet crowned, and already there are people in the city who would stand against her rule. There are several conspiracies, and the people grow testy. There is no better time for your armies to come in secretly, kill the warriors, and secure the city for the Gumiren."

"What say dark one?" The Ghan nodded at Kalún.

Kalún looked up with a dreamy stare, as though surprised to be called upon. He looked like his mind was addled. Yadovír feared this would be the end of their short conspiracy.

"I am the high priest of Adonais, Ghan Magai," Kalún said with quiet firmness. "It is my belief that you are sent by my god, an instrument for our correction. I humbly beg you to grant us peace under your wisdom."

Yadovír breathed out, amazed at the tact from Kalún. The Ghan was also surprised, but far from pleased, as though he had read some secret intention behind the spoken words.

"Dark one. You—no good. You have—how say?—*deceit* in your heart. Yadovír, we have no agree if dark one remains."

Yadovír's mouth dried up in an instant. If they did not agree soon, neither he nor Kalún would be offered the luxury of returning to the prisoners. There was death in the eyes of all the Gumiren.

Sabíana stopped before entering her chamber, her heart leaping like a fish snatching at flies on the surface of a lake. She tried every exercise she knew to calm the heart and still the breathing, but nothing seemed to work. Worse yet, her complete inability to control her emotions at the mere thought of Otchigen lit a spark of panic deep in her stomach, and if she did nothing, soon it would be a conflagration. She pushed the door and entered.

Otchigen lay in her bed, sleeping as before. Even asleep, his allure caught at her and tried to pull her in, a fish-lure sparkling in the sun just above the surface of the water. *Let him be Dar*. Not quite pushing the thought away, Sabíana poked at the fire in the hearth to give her hands something to do.

Then she sat down in the great chair by the fire, looking at Otchigen. The knife hidden in her palm was a steadying weight.

When Otchigen awoke, his eyes were still watery with sleep. He smiled a little, though now it seemed a hollow mockery of his former joy, which had rivaled the twin waterfalls for its enthrallment with life.

"So. What do you intend to do with me?" he asked, lightly mocking.

"I have not yet decided."

"I don't expect a hero's welcome. There must be much about my disappearance that looks suspicious. I want to explain it to the Dar. Will you let me?"

Sabíana was surprised at the question, not immediately realizing that of course Otchigen could not possibly have known of the Dar's death.

"Dar Antomír is dead."

Something twitched in Otchigen's face, something *underneath* his face.

"You will have to answer to me now," she continued, trying to push down her revulsion. "I should have you put before the judgment of the Martial Voice. That would be the proper thing to do. But we shall see. You can speak to me for the time being."

"Ah, I see. I am being fattened for the slaughter."

"Perhaps. Or perhaps what Vasyllia needs is forgiveness. But you are useful in either case. I can have you executed as a traitor. It would be easy to tie the current invasion to your personal treachery. That would excite the warriors. Or I can publicly pardon you, appealing to the compassion of your fellows. You would then lead them in war against the enemy."

"You want to know what happened in Karila," he said. It wasn't a question.

"Yes. Spare no detail. The full truth, if you please."

He smiled sardonically, as if questioning the existence of truth at all.

"Nothing could be simpler, Sabíana. There was no real reason for a man of my rank to go on a routine embassy to Karila. But the Dar and I both agreed it would be good for me to leave Vasyllia for a time after Aglaia's disappearance. There was not supposed to be any trouble. Before we ever reached Karila, in the lower Downs of Nebesta, we were attacked by a band of marauders. I thought they were Karila, but they were darker of skin and spoke an unfamiliar language. I suppose they were from beyond the Lowlands, maybe even the Steppes."

"Beyond the Steppes," said Sabíana. "Sounds like the Gumiren."

"The ones besieging Vasyllia." Otchigen laughed at the realization. "In that case you could very easily tie my supposed treachery with this invasion." He descended into thought, the light going out of his eyes in a moment.

"Go on, Otchigen."

"Whoever they were, they were the most bloodthirsty warriors I have ever encountered. They drank the blood of their horses instead of water. I saw it with my own eyes. They killed every member of the embassy, expect for me. I was necessary, they said, to warn the others of their coming. I think they intended me as a scare tactic, so they began to do unspeakable things to the ambassadors, even after their deaths. I will not describe it. Suffice it to say that had I not been Voyevoda, had I not seen death and torture firsthand, I would have done as they wanted and run screaming for the hills, whipping up the populace with the nameless fear.

"But I did not. As they left me alive, I considered it an uncommon gift from Adonais. I would go searching for my Aglaia, I thought. She was supposed to have been seen near Karila, so I sought her trail. I should have returned home; I know that now. I could have warned Vasyllia. But I wanted to find her. Instead, they found me again and brought me to their great secret, their true inspiration."

"The Raven."

Otchigen was taken aback at this. His smile was now

venomous. "You know much more than I expected," he said with a voice not quite his own. Terror ran up and down her back like mice. She clenched her hidden knife so tightly, she was sure it would draw her own blood.

"Yes, I saw him," continued Otchigen. "Well, not *him*, exactly. His vessel. That is what they called it, I think. It seems the Raven has a habit of possessing human bodies, though this vessel was hardly human by then. The Raven had consumed most of him already."

He stopped, the memory apparently too painful.

"The rest is rather dim. The only other thing you might be interested to hear is that I *did* find one of my family out there. I saw Voran."

Evidently, whatever valiant effort she mustered to prevent her face from reflecting the mad dance of her heart failed miserably. Otchigen's snigger was more than malicious, it was nearly feral.

"Oh, yes. Happily living with a certain red-haired farmer's daughter in the wilds. She was very fetching, if I say so myself."

Sabíana saw it. Voran entwined in lust with another woman. Hatred rose up from her depths with the sudden ferocity of a winter blizzard. She looked at Otchigen and spots danced before her eyes. She nearly fainted.

There was bestial hunger in the face of Otchigen.

"Why, Sabíana, you look upset. You did not set your hopes on Voran, did you?"

All pretense had been dropped. This was not Otchigen, but some *thing* wearing him like a winter coat. And yet, that frightened her less than the visions of pain and blood that danced in her head—all of them variations on the theme of killing Voran.

"Oh, you could kill Voran easily, Sabíana. I know you would like that. For me, it would be a simple thing to arrange. I could do that for you."

Her vision swam; her thoughts moved like stale molasses. Everything about this seemed dream-like in its simultaneous vividness and indistinctness. Small details took on ridiculous clarity—the ashes fell by the hearth in a floral pattern, the blood pumped through Otchigen's temple like a wriggling worm, she had a speck of dirt under her third left fingernail. The room looked like it was underwater.

"All you have to do is desire it with all the force of your will. I will make it happen. Go ahead."

Sabíana tried to look away, but couldn't. Voran lay on the flagstones at her feet. His eyes were closed; he seemed to be in great pain, his skin pasty and splotched with red in several places; his shirt was open just enough to allow for a quick knife-thrust to the heart.

"Imagine that you are plunging that knife you hold in your hand into Voran's heart."

She gasped, sure that he couldn't possibly have seen the concealed knife.

"How did you know?" she began, her voice sounding groggy, half-drunk to her own ears.

"That you were ready to use that thing on me? You are not as subtle as you imagine, Sabíana."

Though her mind recoiled from it, the desire to plunge the knife into Voran's exposed chest uncoiled itself like an adder inside her chest, an adder that had slept her whole life, waiting for this moment. She knew Voran was not actually there, that this was some kind of phantasm conjured by her imagination or by the power that possessed Otchigen's body. But it no longer mattered. She wanted to kill Voran, and the desire was warm and sweet like too much wine.

"Just do it," he whispered. "I offer you your heart's desire. Go ahead. Take the knife, stab him, plunge the knife in."

An ever-shrinking part of her still felt intense revulsion, but it was too late. Her hand moved up of its own accord, the knife coming out of its concealment like unfolding fangs. Voran's chest moved up and down steadily with his breath. She thought she could see the thumping of his heart through his ribcage.

"Just a little stab. So little effort, but the pleasure is great, I promise you. Go on."

"NO!" She screamed and hurled the blade into the hearth. Immediately, Voran dissolved, and the light in the room went dark. Only a glimmer remained among the smoldering logs. Sabíana faced the savage fear weighing on her and willed herself to stare at Otchigen, though she knew he was Otchigen no longer.

The creature was shadowy and black, all darkness and chaos spread out like huge wings, and its eyes burned darker than the darkest black. It did not speak so much as groan like falling boulders. She did not need anyone to tell her that this was the Raven.

"Too late, Sabíana. You've let me in."

The Raven embraced her with wings of shadow and death, and Sabíana choked under their weight and the pressure of the malice bearing down on her.

The door flew open with a crash, and a winged fury of dark blue feathers and ice-grey eyes flew into the room. Faintly Sabíana heard the music of wind whistling through reeds. Time ceased for Sabíana. All that remained was the song—wailing, keening, bursting with ancient power. Feína sang, and each note was a barrage of fire-arrows, a forest of spears, a field of slashing blades. Her wings were a rushing wind of fire, hurtling the song at the Raven. He shrieked in agony and hatred and released Sabíana. It felt like the snapping of twine, and Sabíana fell back.

But Feína was only one Sirin. Despite her song, despite his pain, his wings moved ever closer, choking her. Feína battled on with voice and talon, trying to gouge out the eyes of black flame, but he repulsed her. Her song faltered, faded, and stopped. Her fire turned into shadow. The Raven growled over his two fallen adversaries. Sabíana closed her eyes, ready for death.

A light brighter than the sun shattered the gloom of the Raven, forcing Sabíana's eyes open. Its edges were red and white flame, curling and twisting like living creatures. The Raven burned from within, and his agony shone out of his eyes like a beacon on a foggy night. A magnificent rose of light and fire swelled and blossomed from inside him, until he was completely engulfed in a writhing pyre that smelled of crushed rose petals. The Raven screamed and dissipated into a foul, swarming mist burned up in the rising fire of the hearth. Soon all that remained was the rose of fire.

"Do not fear, my own Sabíana. Look up."

Sabíana recognized Feína's voice, but it was different. What she saw was impossible. Feína was still a Sirin, but a Sirin of flame that filled the entire room with her warmth and soft fragrance. Her every fraction cascaded with kaleidoscopic light, her eyes so effulgent that Sabíana couldn't look at them directly for more than a few seconds. But somehow Feína seemed more truly a Sirin than ever before.

"Dear Feína, you saved my life! What happened to you?"

"I...Oh, by the Heights! How wonderful!" Her voice was as bracing as the sound of morning trumpets on a cold, clear day of winter. "Sabíana. You saved *me*. I can see...so much. My Lord, how wrong have we all been!"

"What is the matter? What do you see?"

Feína's eyes bored into Sabíana. The flame that she had ignited in Sabíana's heart fluttered and flared. Sabíana wanted to embrace Feína for a mad second, before she remembered Feína was fire. She laughed.

"I cannot put it in words yet, my Sabíana. But know this. What you did by resisting the Raven may have changed the fate of Vasyllia. It may have been a pebble. But sometimes, sometimes pebbles start avalanches."

There is still hope for Vasyllia. Sabíana nearly collapsed into tears before bracing herself again. I am stone. I am steel.

"I will come to you again soon. Soon."

A great wheel of fire began to spin about Feína, faster and faster until Sabíana had to look away. Even with her eyes shut, the wheel danced purple and green before her. When she opened her eyes, she was again alone in her warm room, but the sweetness of Feína's fragrance still wafted in the air, cleansing any vestige of the Raven's presence. It was only then that she noticed the body of Otchigen near the hearth. He was wasted and drawn, nearly a skeleton, but his dead face was once again his own, and it was finally peaceful.

The Ghan was tense, rubbing his hands together, and Yadovír noticed with disgust that they were nearly black with grease. He also noticed that of all the people at the table, the Ghan alone used a knife to cut his own meat. It lay on a plate next to Yadovír, its handle slippery with the grease from the Ghan's hand.

Yadovír grabbed the knife. Falling on Kalún, he plunged the knife right into the cleric's neck, through the silky hairs of his beard. The expression on the priest's face was one of complete surprise. A horrible gurgle seeped from his throat, and he fell over, dead. His eyes were still wide from astonishment. Yadovír crumpled over to the ground and vomited.

All of the Gumiren stood, hands on the defensive, shoulders tense and ready for attack. Only the Ghan remained seated, not having moved an inch. He took Yadovír by the shoulders, and pulled him back to the table. His eyes were cold and inscrutable.

"You no common man, Yadovír. You make good Gumir. Is sad for me."

"Sad?" wheezed Yadovír. His face was still warm with the priest's blood, making him want to retch again and again. "Why sad? I have done a terrible thing for you. I have killed the chief priest of Adonais. Do you not understand what that means?"

"Ghan no fool, Yadovír. I know."

"Ghan Magai." Yadovír collected whatever little was left of his self-control and forced his shuddering body to stay still. "Will you agree to my proposal? Do we have a deal?"

"Yes, *Ghan* agree."

The emphasis on his title was unmistakable and significant, but Yadovír decided to ignore it.

He sighed, and his whole body sagged with relief. He even began to laugh a little, not yet fully aware of what he had done, though that knowledge stood off in the shadows like a silent predator. The Ghan, however, continued to stare at him with hollow eyes. This was not how Yadovír expected them to seal a bargain.

"Should we not drink to our bargain?" Yadovír smiled, but the utter lack of response from any of the Gumiren chilled him. Then he noticed that the Ghan no longer looked at him, but a little behind him. Confused, he turned around.

It was a feathery, shriveled creature that would have been pitiful, if not for the eyes. They were black, but somehow they glowed with fire—not orange-red, but utterly dark. At that moment, Yadovír understood and despaired. With the desperation came a cold kind of acceptance that stopped the hammering of his heart and began to slow the blood flowing through him. So, this was why the Gumiren seemed to know everything in advance, he thought.

"You are the Raven," said Yadovír, his voice husky and not his own.

"Ah, a clever one." The voice was a bestial cackle, something between the wheeze of a sick child and the bark of a dog. "Well, you must have something you wish to tell me if you have gone through all this trouble." The Raven looked with disgust at the corpse of the priest. "But do hurry. You cannot imagine how hungry I am."

The words nearly stopped Yadovír's heart cold, but he forced himself to clear his throat. "I can be useful to you, Raven. I know the ins and outs of the city, and I am well studied in Vasyllian lore. I am an indefatigable worker, and..." As his mind blanked, he felt himself reeling from panic.

"You can be useful, yes. I agree. I do not think it will be conceding too much to tell you that I have been disappointed in a line of attack I was sure would work. No matter. You provide me with a different opportunity. I am sure you will be happy to oblige. Yes, my little rat?"

The Raven extended outward in flame and fury. The eyes turned yellow with a pit of black fire; the back expanded into billows of brown smoke like jagged raven wings. A clawed arm whipped out and picked up Yadovír by the scruff—a bird of prey dangling a rat before swallowing it. A foul stench filled his nose, and he began to dry heave.

"I accept your bargain," said the Raven.

Yadovír fainted into the stench and blood and smoke, pursued into the darkness by the face of Kalún and his surprised eyes.

When Yadovír awoke, he was in his own room back in Vasyllia, shaking in a pool of his own sweat. A rotting stink permeated the room. He tried to find the source of the smell—perhaps a mouse had died in the walls? —then realized that he was the source. The stench came from inside him.

Elder Pahomy chewed his lip; Rogdai shook his head as his eyebrows furrowed deep into his head, threatening to dig into the soft matter underneath. They both avoided looking at her, instead inspecting every possible detail of the map laid out on the table in her private chambers. Sabíana's impatience loomed over them all like a twisting snake's head, poised to strike at the first sign of the prey's lapse in attention.

"Well, my lords? I ask you again? Is it as bad as I think it is?"

Finally, Elder Pahomy answered. "It is worse, my lady. We do not have the force to dislodge this siege, and our stores are already thinning. The imprisonment of the traitors, though necessary, is vastly unpopular among the people with influence in Vasyllia."

"Not merely that," said Rogdai, scratching the back of his head, his eyes wide. "The Gumiren have built siege towers of amazing complexity. They could use them at any moment, even in winter, but now they have stopped. There is nothing stirring their camp. Silence. Enough to drive us to madness."

"Or they simply wait for us to destroy ourselves from within," said Sabíana and sighed. She had come to rely a great deal on the opinions of only two men. It was a dangerous trust she placed on them. *I have no choice,* she reminded herself through the pain of her ever-clenched jaw.

"There is one option we have not yet considered," said Rogdai, though he did not look confident in his own idea. "Escape."

"Are you mad?" Elder Pahomy looked personally offended at the suggestion.

"Why not? I see two possibilities—one, a spear thrust through the enemies..."

"You would sacrifice most of our fighting force to do that," growled Elder Pahomy, his jowls quivering with anger, "and it may not even work then. We do not know the full number of this enemy."

"Or we may cross over the summit and flee over the back of the mountain."

Sabíana gasped, then felt the blush creep up. There was an ancient, traditional taboo about climbing Mount Vasyllia, though now that she thought of it, she could not call to mind a single good reason for it.

"Why not?" she asked, directing her gaze at Elder Pahomy.

He sighed. "Old superstitions die hard, I suppose."

She smiled at him. "For my part, I think crossing the summit in winter would be inviting disaster. How many of us would survive? And where would we go? For all we know, even Karila is destroyed."

"If that is our people's only chance of survival," said Rogdai, "why not set out farther east, toward the Steppelands? Or West, to the deserts and beyond."

"I do not know why," she said, "but I have a strong feeling

that Vasyllia must not be abandoned to this enemy. It is stronger than a mere sense; it is almost a compulsion."

"I agree with you, Highness," said Elder Pahomy, and for the first time she heard respect in his voice.

The door slammed open, and in flew a mass of silver robes billowing about a thin figure hidden somewhere in their midst. It fell at the feet of Sabíana. Rogdai lifted it, none too gently. It was Yadovír.

"Oh, my lady," he finally said. "It's...unspeakable. Otar Kalún's body has been found at the gates of Vasyllia. It's rumored that he was murdered by the Gumiren for trying to strike a deal with them to save his own skin."

A novice came into the monastery. He knocked on the door, begging for admittance. The abbot came to the door, looked at him, and shut the door in his face. The next day, the novice was still there, begging for admittance. The abbot came to the door, looked at him, and shut the door in his face. On the third day, the same happened. And the fourth. And the fifth. On the tenth, the abbot came to the door, looked at him, and opened the door. The novice entered.

From "The Paterikon of the Great Coenobium"
(The Sayings, Book III, 4:8-11)

CHAPTER 25

THE WARRIOR OF THE WORD

A week of traveling the marshes satisfied even Voran's appreciation for their beauties. He and Tarin now seemed to be beyond the knowledge of any people whatsoever. The only inhabitants of these lands were the many animals—rabbits, foxes, wolves, deer, and elk with antlers like young trees. None of these paid Voran any attention, but every one of them met Tarin personally, a friend returned from long travels. The wolves in particular greeted him with high-pitched yelps, no more than friendly dogs to all appearances, though if Voran was foolish enough to extend a hand too close to any of them, the fangs were quick to flash. Tarin enjoyed them immensely, loping on all fours with them, his tongue lolling out absurdly.

They still walked day and night, but Voran grew accustomed to gathering enough strength during their short morning rests to last him the whole day. Despite the poverty of the village, Tarin didn't refuse their gifts of food. It was enough to feed an army. Voran understood: refusing such gifts, given freely, would have been worse than stealing from starving children. Such was the hospitality of Vasyllia as it used to be.

How far have we fallen, thought Voran with a pang.

Though Voran now bore four packs instead of two—*two* were filled with rocks as punishment for his insubordination—Tarin allowed him to carry the sword, and leaning on it provided some support. Secretly, Voran was grateful to Tarin. The hag's ravages had left Voran rail-thin and weak, and though he was not gaining much flesh, his muscles grew wiry like a horse's.

It was a sword like its master—not much to look at, old, tarnished, but impossible to break. Unlike every sword made in Vasyllian smithies these days, it had no fanciful decorations, no etchings on the blade, no jewels on the hilt. Only one strange sign —something between a flame and a feather, or maybe some amalgamation of both—was stamped in the place where the thumb gripped, as though it were a reminder of something.

"Lord Tarin," said Voran as they made an unusual stop in the early evening. "This mark on the hilt. Does it mean anything?"

At first Voran was sure Tarin would answer as the lunatic, but it seemed Tarin had a last-minute change of heart. "Have you heard of the Warriors of the Word?" he asked in a voice remarkable only for its normality.

Something warm and pleasant stirred in Voran's memory. The piney smell of morning fog. The thrill of hiding all night in the burial grounds. The sting of young nettles on hands and ankles, and the white spots on the skin that burned and burned. Morning sprints through dewey fields, the wet rising up the leg with every step.

"Of course," said Voran, smiling in spite of himself. "Every boy pretends to be a Warrior of the Word in childhood. The games are quite elaborate, and the stories are always the most colorful and strange."

"They are not stories," said Tarin.

"You are a Warrior of the Word?" Voran laughed, thinking Tarin was again playing the madman, but Tarin remained still and serious, until Voran's laugh subsided awkwardly. "You can't be. They're legendary, like the sleeping-woods and the..." Voran felt himself turning red.

Tarin smiled, and it was warm, like a father's. "Yes, it does take some time to come to terms with the legendary, I'll grant you that. There are few of us left. None in Vasyllia. We were established by Lassar at the very beginning, you know, but always have we been consigned to the shadows. Those youths who show enough spirit are whisked away for the training at night, and though their parents know, everyone else is told stories of sudden illness and early death. You would be surprised at how many graves in old Vasyllia are empty."

"Why the secrecy?"

"Because of the nature of evil, Voran."

Tarin busied himself about making a fire, and Voran knew now was not the time to continue speaking, though he buzzed with excitement at having a childhood dream come true. He hurried to be useful, gathering dry moss and twigs for the kindling, but Tarin immediately threw out most of it as unsuitable.

"Get me some dry birch-bark," Tarin said as he pulled out an old flint and a char-cloth from a tinderbox of wrought iron, garishly decorated in a flowing script that Voran couldn't read.

After the fire had caught, Tarin began to dig in one of the packs. He pulled out two chipped earthenware bowls and placed them on the ground. Reaching into a pouch on his belt, he pulled out a brown rag, much-used, unrolled it, and took some dried leaves with his thumb and forefingers, rubbing under his nose. Even from across the fire, Voran could smell the earthy smokiness. Tea.

Voran never had a better cup of tea, not for the rest of his life.

"I suppose, since you've gotten me to say so much, you may as well try your luck with more questions, Raven Son." Tarin's eyes smiled, though his face remained serious. He cupped the bowl in dirty hands, resting his elbows on his knees, seeming to absorb the tea's warmth with his whole body. Voran hastened to do the same. It seeped lazy comfort into his aching body.

"You said that the nature of the Warriors of the Word has something to do with the nature of evil."

"Yes." Tarin looked annoyed. "Is that a question?"

"The sign on the sword. What does it mean?" asked Voran, strangely afraid of speaking it aloud.

"Have you heard of transfiguration, Raven Son?"

Voran must have had a remarkably stupid expression, because Tarin winced. "Perhaps that is not a good place to start. We should start with the least important, and work our way inward, like a cockle shell."

Voran had not the faintest idea of what a cockle was, but he knew it would be counterproductive to ask.

"Let me start by asking *you* a question, Raven Son. Why do you think that you were attacked in the marshes after we crossed from the Lows, while nothing happened to me?"

"You obviously have power, Tarin. I do not."

Tarin nodded and chuckled. "Well, that is part of it, yes. But my kind of power never frightened the Raven and his beasts very much. No, you were attacked because you are still stained. What you did with the hag bound you to her. Yes, some of the chains loosened when you killed her, but you are not free of her curse."

"But it felt like every link of that chain burst apart when I spoke that word you gave me." A sudden insight flashed on him, and he felt foolish. "Is *that* the word that your kind is named for?"

"Well, not quite, but if we don't get into the details, yes. When you were attacked in the marshlands, you called a great power to your aid by the invocation of the name. A power even greater than...well, perhaps now's not the time to talk about that."

"Greater than what? The Sirin?"

Tarin had a pained expression, the kind a parent has when their child no longer believes in childish fancies.

"Yes, certainly greater than the Sirin. It was a taste of the power with which the Warriors of the Word are invested. But if you were to neglect yourself, if another ruse of the darkness—like the red-head in the village—were to ensnare you, you would be in great danger. They know your weak point, and now you should expect to see buxom young women throwing themselves at you in every village. I doubt you'll be able to keep chaste for long."

Voran felt disappointed, for he had hoped that his deliverance from the hag had been immediate and complete. Now it seemed it would take a deal of labor to wean himself from her continued influence. He should have known.

"Never mind," said Tarin, eyes closed as he smelled the tea. "I will help you with that. If you are willing to suffer through my training, anything is possible. The power to which we submit is an old power, a wild power, one that makes and harmonizes out of nothing in perpetuity. Not the soft, gentle divinity you Vasylli are used to worshipping in the Temple."

"You speak as the Sirin do—" Voran stopped in mid-thought. "Of course! The Sirin. They also thrive in a similar power, one equally destructive and loving. Do we even know Adonais, whom we claim to worship? Have we become so comfortable with a loving, endearing father figure that we stopped considering his unbridled power?" With chagrin, he realized by Tarin's rapt expression that he had spoken these thoughts aloud. "But what am I saying? What do I know about all this?"

To Voran's increased embarrassment, Tarin laughed out loud, making no effort to conceal his enjoyment.

"Oh, Raven Son. How close you come to wisdom, without even realizing what you are saying. If only you could see the whole truth!"

"Why not tell me?"

"Because you wouldn't believe me. You may even want to do something drastic. You may even want to kill me."

The conversation was not going as Voran had hoped. For the first time since the hag's village, Voran feared Tarin.

"If that is true," countered Voran, "then how can I know whether to trust you?

"Indeed, my falcon," Tarin said, chuckling. "You have hit on it exactly. How indeed?"

What a terrible lack of an answer, thought Voran.

The silence surrounding them deepened, until even the crackling of the bonfire faded. Gently, with no jarring effect, Voran's heart inclined to the calm surrounding Tarin like his own breath. Unbidden came the word to his lips—*Saddai*—and he whispered it, feeling the stillness reach out to him and envelop him, until the very act of questioning seemed spurious. How long they sat thus, minutes or hours, Voran never could recall. It was one of the most wondrous moments of his life.

"You begin to understand, Raven Son. Good. I hoped you would."

"Lord Tarin, it has no words, what I experienced," said Voran, breathless with wonder. "It was as if the most thunderous harmony and piercing silence mingled into one. Time raced and stopped altogether, all at a still point. It was as if I actually experienced truth personally, and yet I know nothing at all. How can I explain it? If the power of the sea could be contained in a drop of water, if the limitless potential of words could be expressed in a single thought. An infinite multiplicity in a single entity. Is it I who even speak? I don't recognize my own voice."

"What you experienced is but a splinter in the Great Tree, so to speak."

Like a sunset, the nameless experience faded, but it left behind a twilight magic.

"What else was it like, Raven Son?" Tarin's eagerness was child-like.

"It was like being on fire."

Tarin slapped his knee loudly, his smile creasing every possible inch of his face.

"Yes! You asked about the sign on the sword? It is the wing of a Sirin that has undergone the baptism of flame. It is said that, to scale the Heights of Aer, one must be baptized in fire seven times..."

Tarin grew thoughtful, and his recent inspiration seemed to run out. There was much Voran did not understand, but it seemed he would have to content himself with waiting for now. Nevertheless, he decided to try one more question.

"Why do you call me Raven Son?"

Tarin, torn from his train of thought, looked irritated. "The question of your name is not mine to answer. You will know soon enough." He stood up and began to pack. "Time we were off. Not so far now."

"Are we so close to the weeping tree?" asked Voran.

Tarin stopped, sighed heavily, and stretched himself to his full height.

"Raven Son. You must give up all thoughts of finding Living Water. You are not ready. You need to be trained. When you are ready, we will both seek it."

An avalanche of fury burst from Voran's chest. "Vasyllia is on the brink. You said it yourself. Why do we dawdle? We do not have the time!"

"You do not direct the flow of events in the world, Voran. There is a greater power than you at work here. If you go now, you will be eaten alive in minutes. Have you heard nothing of what I have said? The hag's curse still stinks on you. Do I need to remind you of the five reasons for your slavery, especially the fifth one?"

The morning sun revealed a change in the landscape. In the distance towered a line of cedars—incongruous amid the bare trees and low shrubs—standing as if sentinels over an ancient borderline.

"That is the extreme end of ancient Vasyllia," said Tarin. He hoisted his single pack and turned toward the cedars.

They reached the treeline by midday. The cedars were even more impressive in proximity, standing so near each other that the other side was barely visible, even through the trunks. There was something shimmery on the other side, as though they looked into a pool of water, not a landscape.

"That is a doorway, yes? We are entering the Lows again?"

Tarin winked at Voran and chattered like a chickadee.

As they passed through the trees, they were plunged into complete darkness. Voran could only see Tarin's outline in the shadows the trees cast. On the other side, to his disappointment, Voran saw nothing but a fallow, brown field. Drab elms, shorn of leaf, surrounded the field. Nestled under a particularly large elm, still within the shadow of the sentinel trees, three greyish wooden shacks slouched.

They appeared hardly standing, almost ready to fall over at a whisper of wind. Sloping thatch roofs, brown and ancient, bleary windows framed in dirty, cracked carvings—these were the only adornments, if they could be called that. They seemed to have been thrown together on a whim, not built according to plan. Voran's heart sank at the thought of living in such a place. Tarin, on the contrary, seemed genuinely excited, and even broke into verse again.

"I know you marvel at this land,
This paradise, my palace grand.
Does not its splendor catch the eye?
Do not its many towers high,
Replete with every earthly need
Surpass all legends that you read?"

He spread his arms out like a child presenting a favorite toy to a new friend. He actually seemed to believe in his own description of this eyesore as a palace.

The inside of Tarin's shack was as the external appearance would suggest—four walls, a rough pallet in the corner, the straw brown and pungent with neglect, a bench, a small table. On the windowsill stood several clay jars with twigs sticking out in odd assortments. Tarin diligently watered the twigs, as if they were exquisite roses. Voran half expected them to sprout on the spot, but nothing happened.

Voran's own shack was much the same, except without the twigs, for which Tarin apologized: "You have no garden, Raven Son. You have yet to earn it."

The brief tour completed, Tarin sighed and seemed to brace himself for something unpleasant. Walking to a sort of courtyard of mud between the three huts, he drove his staff into the soft ground. Turning to Voran, he said, "Raven Son. If you have any idea of what is good for you, you will water this tree"—he indicated the staff—"every morning, until it flowers. Today, since we've traveled long and you are tired, your work will be easy. Come."

He led Voran behind the largest shack, where Voran saw a large metal tool that looked like the lower jaw of some huge animal, with rusted metal teeth pointing up. It had a harness that looked fitted for an ox. Voran's heart sank.

"The land is not fit for sowing," said Tarin, his hands on his hips as he looked over the field with an expression of distaste. "I have not harrowed it in years. Hundreds of rocks in the soil, I'm sure. So. Strap the harrow on your back, since we do not have a proper ox, and you, as we already know, are my ass. Collect all the rocks and pile them up on the left side of the field."

Voran laughed. Tarin's face frosted over, turning white as his eyes grew larger. He drew his sword.

Voran stopped laughing.

"Raven Son," said Tarin calmly. "It would be wise for you to consider even the most ridiculous things that I say as indispensable. May my words be sacred scripture for you."

He turned back to his hut. "Oh, one more thing. You are never to enter my palace without abasing yourself before it, face to the ground, and saying in a loud voice, 'I, who am wretched, beg leave to enter.' Those words, please, slave. You may not rest or enter your own rooms without my permission.

As Tarin turned, Voran tried his best to burn Tarin to the ground with his eyes. But nothing happened.

The sun had crested by the time Voran began. The harrow was old, and its teeth were worn down. Sometimes it didn't pick up stones at all, just nudged them for a few feet, then gave up with a groan. Voran had to work every inch of the field with his hands, digging into the sandy soil until his fingers hit stone, then digging them out, then repeating it all again.

Soon he gave up the harrow entirely, and just crawled up and down the field, digging up stones.

The sweat poured down him and his chest burned from the inside. Worse than the fatigue was the mind-numbing boredom that accompanied such work. He imagined all the different ways he would make Tarin suffer. Soon his irritation extended to stones, trees, shacks, everything. All his thoughts became a long drawn-out grumble.

After digging up all the stones, he carried them to the left side of the field. Some of the stones were almost as large as he was. These he could not raise, but only push inch by inch to the edge of the field. Voran soon realized that he had lost much more strength than he had thought. Maybe Tarin was right. Maybe a stick-thin former warrior with no endurance wasn't the best choice to find the Living Water.

As he placed the last stone on the pile—now taller than he was—he sat on the earth and closed his eyes. A thought flitted through his mind: Tarin told him he could not rest without permission.

"AAAAAASSSSSSSSSS!"

Too late.

"Raven Son, you blithering idiot! Why did you put the stones on that side of the field? I expressly told you to put them on the *right* side of the field."

He stood with one arm cocked on his hips, like an irritated mother.

"But...you said..."

Tarin shushed him.

"Did anyone give the idiot leave to speak?" He addressed the shacks directly, then cupped his hands to his ears, as if listening for their response. "No? I didn't think so. Go, fool. Carry the stones across to the other side."

"But Tarin…"

"Don't dare to call me by my name. What? Don't you have an ounce of shame? I am your lord, so call me so. Now take the stones away, and put them in their proper place. You'll never finish at this pace."

Voran sized Tarin up, thinking it was time to teach the old man a lesson. Tarin merely laughed.

"You don't want to try it, boy. Believe me."

For the next few hours, Voran carried all the stones to the other side of the field.

The next day, Tarin told Voran to return the stones back to the left side. The day after that, he told Voran to put the stones back in the soil.

"What?" said Voran, his fists balling up of their own accord.

"You heard me," said Tarin, as calmly as a corpse.

The day after that, Tarin told Voran to dig the stones up again and pile them up on the left side of the field.

"The left?" asked Voran. "You're sure?"

Tarin grinned at him stupidly and crowed.

Voran dug up the stones and piled them up again. Without even realizing it, he fell asleep while placing the last rock on the heap, still standing.

"UPUPUPUPUPUPUPUP!!!!"

Voran jumped in the air, and all the rocks fell on him, nearly burying him alive before he managed to roll aside.

Tarin was dancing around the field, smacking a wooden spoon on a frying pan. Every time he had to take a breath, he stopped and hopped in place three times, as though that would help him inhale more air. Then he danced again, smacking and screaming "UPUPUPUPUPUPUPUP!!!" at the top of his lungs.

It was pitch black outside. Still night.

"Raven Son! Who sleeps during the day? Get up and working!"

"Day, lord? It's the middle of the night."

"What? Look! There's the sun!"

He pointed at the thinnest moon Voran had ever seen, just rising over the tips of the sentinel trees.

"Oh, yes," said Voran, mustering as much sarcasm as he could. "How foolish of me. There's the sun."

Tarin cocked his head at him like a curious bird. "Sun? You're confused, my dear boy. That's hardly enough sliver even for a moon! I think you've gone a little soft in the head."

Tarin patted Voran on the head as though Voran were a sick dog. His expression was the kind reserved for children who insist to their parents that their imaginary unicorn friend is real.

The next day after that—the fourth day after their arrival—Tarin didn't bother Voran at all. That worried Voran more than any of the other nonsense. He approached Tarin's hut, fearing that he had forgotten something, and that he would be punished with another round of tiring absurdity. Falling on his knees before the door, he spoke through cracked lips, "My lord. I, who am wretched, beg leave to enter."

"You may enter." Tarin's face showed only composed calm. "Raven Son, did I not make myself clear to you? Why did you put all the stones in a heap? What a waste of time. Did you not understand that you had to plant them all and water them?"

That's it. The old goat's gone crazy.

"Raven Son," said Tarin with a face that suggested that the half-wit he was speaking to may have dangerous tendencies. "Do I have to use a stick on you, or will you do as you are told?"

Voran went. Though he was starved and every muscle in his body shuddered with overwork, he did as he was told. The sun rose, bathing even the lifeless tract around him with unexpected colors—hazy purples, dark reds, and oranges in the field, blue tones in the bark of the trees.

Voran had been wrong about this place. It *was* beautiful here.

As he worked, a compulsion to sing tickled at him. Soon he could hold it back no longer. He bellowed all the old sowing songs that his third-reacher education had given him. As he did, he understood them perhaps for the first time in his life. How he wished, at that moment, that he had become friends with Siloán the potter earlier. His first-reacher sowing songs must be even better.

The earth itself seemed to respond to his song, seeming more willing to accept even such lifeless seeds as he was offering it. He began to notice birdsong, tentative at first, then stronger as he worked. Somewhere very far away, he heard the music of wind whistling through reeds. Lyna was close, though still she could not approach him, it seemed.

As Voran worked, a calm seemed to rise up from the earth and hug him. He laughed.

He thought he finally understood what Tarin was doing. It was probably a trial that every young Warrior of the Word had to undergo at the early stages of training. A kind of breaking down of the self, so that the master could rebuild the student in his own image. A true warrior. Voran realized, with something like surprise, that he actually *wanted* Tarin to continue the nonsense. He'd never felt more free, more truly himself, in his life.

"Lyna, wait for me," Voran said to himself. "Sabíana, don't forget me. I will come back, and whatever the cost, I will bring back Living Water."

Eventually, Voran planted all the stones at equal intervals and watered them from a moldy bucket that threatened to fall apart at any moment.

After he finished, Voran walked on stiff legs toward the staff in the middle of their small court of huts. No longer thinking lightly of the absurd task, he diligently watered the "tree," leaving no spot of earth dry. So intent was he on his work, that he didn't notice Tarin standing behind him until he spoke.

"Voran, you may rest now." Tarin's eyes, full of tears, glimmered in the morning sun.

"Thank you, my lord, for a most interesting few days," whispered Voran, hardly able to keep his eyes open as he half-walked, half-dragged himself to his dirty straw pallet, which for one night at least was the most luxurious bed of his life.

Do you never wonder about the power of the earth? Earthquakes, avalanches, lightning strikes, deluges...It is great indeed, is it not? But do not think it is accidental. There is a race of beings that manipulates the power of the earth. And they want to be worshiped.

From "The Wisdom of Lassar the Blessed"
(The Sayings: Book I, 7:4-6)

CHAPTER 26

CONTAGION

Even in winter, life on Ghavan was loud. For Mirnían, it began with the morning bell, whose tongue he could feel beating the inside of his right temple. Lebía never heard it, but in her condition, it was entirely natural—or so he was told —to sleep through anything until ungodly hours of late morning. Then the storm-shutters slapped open, one after the other, as goodwives and their daughters and daughters-in-law traded the latest gossip from house to house. How they could have gathered so much information in the dead of night, Mirnían had no idea. Nor did he particularly wish to find out. Then the call to prayer, nearly as insistent as the morning bell. Then the endless chatter of men and women at work around the village, which was too small to provide any modicum of peace or privacy.

After a month of married life, Mirnían had found that there was really only one place where he could be comfortably alone. This morning, as Lebía lay next to him, one hand instinctively protecting her belly, the other thrown across her eyes in a position Mirnían found uncomfortable even to look at, he felt an especial need of that place.

It was the work of a few minutes to dress and be out of doors. Luckily, not many of the villagers were up yet this morning, so the going was quiet. He gritted his teeth as he passed the house of the baker and his wife—she was always very solicitous about Lebía's health, and the word-for-word repetition of their daily conversation grated beyond endurance—but they were either busy or sleeping in. As soon as he passed, he rushed along an uphill path, then down an incline to the rocky beach. Every step on the old snow crunched. He was sure that someone would accost him with yet another pointless conversation. But no. Before he knew it, he was in the thickest part of a pine grove.

The pines leaned down a little over his head, as if bowing in greeting. He didn't mind the noise *they* made—as opposed to the women in the village—though here the trees were a little too quiet. Most of all he preferred the noise of the sea, its gentle and constant complaint about something so old it had long forgotten what it was.

Finally, the deaf stillness of the forest gave way to the suggestion, then the echo, then the sea itself—slate-grey near the beach, then deepening to black farther out. He had never imagined water could look so black. There was a mystery and a beauty to it, one he never thought he would appreciate in a color always associated with the darkness in stories. He sat on his knees on the last stone before the water. The water tried to reach him, but lazily, as if it never got enough sleep, despite the endless nights of winter. He agreed with the water, once again wondering how it was possible to constantly want more sleep in a season when ten hours a night was not considered over-much.

Such trifling half-thoughts took up all his time at the sea, doing what they were supposed to. Everything would fade into the soft complaints of the sea and his mind—the disaster of Vasyllia, the unhappiness of Sabíana, the death of Dar Antomír, the fear that gnawed at him as Lebía's paleness daily tried to match the new-fallen snow for whiteness. She was transformed by what she carried within her. The mystery was too deep for him to fathom, and more often than not he felt isolated from that almost sacred reality of the child inside her.

There goes the bell again, he mused as the sound reached him like the sun through a heavy fog. He continued to stare over the water, hoping to glimpse a rare otter, or even a pair of them entwined by their paws, as they did for hours, even as they slept. The ringing continued, still a haze in his mind, until he snapped to attention, like falling out of a dream. That was not merely a bell. Its insistence, it regularity, its color—that was an alarm.

Lebía lay on the floor of the bakery, covered with blankets up to her chin, though her right hand lay atop the covers. It was so pale, it was nearly blue. Her lips *were* blue, and the skin around her eyes was splotchy, though that could have been the light of the fire in the oven. But it was not all this that poured terror like ice water down Mirnían's throat, but the complete lack of expression on her face. She looked dead.

"...knew something like this would happen, I did." The baker's wife had been chattering on for minutes now, but he heard little until that moment. "Weak blood. Nothing to worry yourself about too much, my dear boy. Now, mind you, I don't think we have enough stores of game to toughen her blood back up."

"What? What are you saying?" Mirnían croaked, his throat dry and gummy.

The baker's wife was a round woman just the far side of middle-aged, though her skin was smooth and her quick smile showed the lasting vestiges of a former beauty, of a sort. Bits of grey-flecked hair kept getting entangled in her temple rings. She seemed ashamed of it, and would retie the scarf every few minutes, no matter what the conversation.

"And you, a future Dar? Silly. It's normal when a woman expects a baby. The baby takes all of mother's best blood. Lebía should be all right, my boy. If we can find enough meat, that is."

Mirnían was confused by the constant talk of meat and blood.

He was sure that Lebía was in the first stages of leprosy, but he didn't dare speak it aloud.

I've done it, he thought. *Everything I touch gets infected and dies.*

"There isn't enough meat for her in the village," said the baker, who was a passable leech as well, though where a Vasylli first-reacher would learn such things, Mirnían couldn't imagine. They were still talking about meat, to Mirnían's annoyance, but the repetition of the theme began to suggest to his limping mind that perhaps it was important.

"Is that all it is?" he asked, incredulous. "She needs more meat?"

"I see no other reason for concern," said the baker's wife. "She has been overworking herself, yes, but now it seems the baby and her body will force her to rest and sleep. It is well that she lives here, not in some mountain city where no one cares for anyone else." She harrumphed. "The entire village will take care of our swanling."

He had no doubt they would, and it relieved him. But something else—a thought, or the beginnings of a thought—added excitement to the relief, something that he almost felt guilty about.

"Matron," he said to the baker's wife, "will you be kind enough to take charge of Lebía's care for a day or two? I have determined to go hunting."

"But there is no meat to be had on the island. Not after all that feasting," protested the baker.

"I know," he said, hoping the excitement now flaring inside him like the fire-light over the mountains would not show in his face. "I intend to try the mainland."

Mirnían had come so close with a few of the arrows, but the deer escaped him. One of the arrows even had the slightest dab of red gore, tipped with a fluff of downy fur. Always at the last possible moment, it ran, as though it were prescient. A few times Mirnían nearly screamed in frustration, but he must not. No need to scare anything that might not have caught scent of him yet. Though he had been hunting for three days, enough of his original excitement remained to keep him going forward at full-tilt.

It was not merely deer he was after. Seeing Lebía in that state, pale as death, finally suggested to him a horrible truth—if he was still marked by leprosy, however latent, he was a threat to her and to their child. He needed to find healing. He needed to finish the quest for the Living Water, and quickly. How, he had no idea. But a strange kind of sureness was on him; a buzzing excitement that suggested the possibility of merely crossing the next ridge and finding another waystone, this one with a much more helpful direction. In the meantime, he hunted in vain.

He didn't know the part of the world where he hunted. The trees were mossier, somehow more sinister and older than at home or on the island. Even the sounds were foreign. The trees creaked in the wrong tune, the needles of the conifers were the wrong length and far too sharp, the smells were old and dank, as though the trees didn't breathe in this part of the world. Then a creeping certainty—he was being watched—tickled at the back of his neck and needled at the pit of his stomach. Shadows became hidden beasts waiting for the pounce.

Something immensely bright flew over his head and landed in the forest ahead. It was round and burning, like a sun fallen from the sky. He couldn't hear the force of impact, but then he noticed that sound itself seemed to cease. He drew his sword and crouched forward, half-crawling, using his other hand to find the quietest path. Smoke filtered through the trees, but it did not burn his eyes. It was pungent, like the scented resin burned in the Temple, and it seemed to contain flashes of light, like small bolts of lightning, within it.

Mirnían saw that an entire section of forest had been annihilated, though there was no fire except for a few smoldering logs at the edge of the cleared circle. In the middle stood a monolith of stone, or at least so it seemed at first. Then the smoke cleared enough for a full moon to shine milky-blue, illuminating not a stone, but a giant warrior.

He was the height of a tree, the width of a house. His mail was golden-red, reaching down to his knees. His helmet was peaked and open-faced; its horsehair flowed down to mingle with his own hair like molten gold. The ear-covers were gilt serpents of iron that seemed ready to burst out of the iron and bite the giant's neck. His eyes glowed, and his features were smooth like marble and beautiful like an iceberg. He held a tear-drop shield bearing the same twisting serpent as on his helmet, and the sword in his right hand was taller than a full-grown man. Flames of dark red played around his body, and Mirnían was reminded of the circle of fire around the darkened sun he had seen in Vasyllia, what seemed so many years ago.

"Your light has dimmed of late, Mirnían, scion of Vasyllia." The giant's voice was surprisingly gentle, though it echoed. Mirnían had no doubt that this was the giant's whisper, and that he could tear down trees with a shout.

"I have been watching you for some time. This sedate, quiet life you have chosen. It does you no good. When my brother saw you last, you glowed with black fire. Now your sister is alight, and you are in wane."

Mirnían, without realizing it, had cast aside his sword somewhere and stood at the foot of the giant, feeling for all the world like a two-year-old being scolded by his mother.

"Who are you?" he managed to whisper.

"I am the serpent of fire, the old power of the earth, the ancient lore long forgotten. You may call me Zmei."

"What would you have of me, Zmei?"

The giant smiled, though his sun-eyes remained beyond all emotion.

"That is the right question, future Dar. I would have you

healed. I would have you empowered. I would have you take your rightful place as Dar of Vasyllia."

Mirnían scoffed. "You must be so old that you do not know of the Raven. Soon there will be no Vasyllia to rule."

The giant laughed, and the earth rose and fell like a wave, throwing Voran down to the scorched grass. "The Raven? Do not make me laugh. A doddering fool who cannot understand that his time to die came centuries ago. A leech whose power derives from the power of others. He is nothing, a mere phantasm."

"If you are so powerful, why is he ascendant?"

The laughter stopped, and the world seemed to hang in the balance, waiting for Zmei to pronounce judgment on it.

"It was not my time yet." He rumbled, his fire dimming a fraction.

Mirnían snickered, then wondered at himself. When had he become so comfortable with the dark and legendary?

"I have never heard of you, Zmei," he said, sneering. "You are not spoken of in the legends."

"I predate the legends, Mirnían," he said. "I was here before any Covenant, before any Adonais, before any Lassar. My power is not like theirs. It is the power of the earth itself."

"You lie, giant. No power existed before Adonais."

The giant's half-smile returned. "Oh, is that so? Tell me, wise one. Why has that sore under your arm not healed, for all the power of the Sirin and their precious Adonais?"

"Are you baiting me? It is leprosy. Leprosy cannot be healed."

In answer, the giant thrust his sword into the ground, shaking the trees as though they were mere bushes, and reached down with his finger. Mirnían wanted to run away screaming, but he held his place and didn't flinch, sensing that this was some sort of test. The fires licking the edge of Zmei's finger touched Mirnían, and his entire body flared with pain for a moment, then it faded. Something was different about him, though his senses were confused about it. He touched the place where his sore had been, and his touch revealed nothing but smooth skin. A wave of exhilaration rose up inside Mirnían.

"Very well, Zmei, you have my attention. But I know how this works. You require something of me in return for your generosity. What must I sacrifice?"

The giant smiled, and there was something fatherly in his expression.

"Ah, you poor child. The world has used you ill. But the *earth* will not. I require nothing. It is enough for me to see you rise in power, and to know that my gift began it."

"I don't believe you."

"Do as you will, Mirnían," said Zmei, chuckling. "Only know that if you seek to use my power, the only power that made you whole, you must always force events to turn in your own favor. Never wait for things to happen. *Forge* events. I happen to know that your steps are directed to a place of great moment. The Sirin was right in one thing—you will face your old enemy, Voran. And he is being trained in another power, a power not as old as mine, a power that revels in weakness and submission. You must exert your control, your will over him. If you do, you will have access to his power, which is not insignificant. That is the road to Vasyllia."

The image of Voran standing on his knees as the hag danced around him flashed in Mirnían's memory. A rush of hatred rose up with his gorge, and he nearly vomited from its fury.

"My pleasure, Zmei," he said, and a savage excitement took him by the throat until he laughed from the sheer thrill of it. "It is the duty of any future Dar to ensure all traitors receive their just reward. Lead on, Zmei. I will follow you to the very edge of the world."

The giant rumbled in laughter. "As a matter of fact, that is exactly where we are going."

The fire licking around his edges consumed him until he was a nearly circular ball of red flames, dark as blood. Something seethed within the circle, and it resolved into a sinuous neck attached to a scaly body with a humped back, the legs long like a horse's and covered in piebald scales. It had horse-like hooves and tufted ears that were too big for its head, a strange amalgam of a lizard and a horse, but not in the least awkward-looking. Its mane and tail were flame, and yet they were solid things that you could hold.

"Mount," said Zmei, "if you have the stomach for it."

The world spun in all directions, with Zmei as the eye in a storm. When Mirnían closed his eyes, he felt no movement, but as soon as he opened them, he felt sick. Mountains formed around him like piles of newly-churned butter, craggy ridges of hard grey-brown rock with hardly any plant life. As they hardened and ceased their strange, undulating dance, Mirnían breathed in, and felt the sparseness of the air. It left him giddy.

The giant stood next to him, looking over the dips and rises of the crags. They stood before a tall conical peak, probably the highest point of the ridge.

"There it is," said Zmei, pointing at the tip of the peak.

Mirnían saw nothing of importance. "What am I looking at?"

Zmei sighed. "I had thought that maybe..." He shook his head. "The weeping tree is on the tip of that conical rock. You cannot see it; neither can I. But it is there. Just not in this Realm; it is in the Mids of Aer. Very soon Voran will find a way to it. We will help him find it."

"Why can you not find it yourself, if your power is so great?" Mirnían was beginning to doubt his strange new friend.

"You have much to learn about the world, young pup," said Zmei, no longer smiling. "Try to pay attention."

With that, he spun into his serpent-horse form again and disappeared in a storm of fire and thunder. Mirnían sat down in the sparse shelter of a twisted pine, and closed his eyes to sleep.

There will come a time when the glory that is Vasyllia will fade. Much knowledge will be lost. Much wisdom. Much beauty. But we, the Warriors of the Word, will preserve it. In time, one will come who will have to restore it all.

A private letter from Vohin Elían to Dar Martinían, year 643 of the Covenant

Chapter 27

Black Turnips

Voran faced Sabíana, but she refused to look at him. For all his desire, he could not approach her. She sat at the edge of a still, oval pool, ringed on all sides by holly trees and osiers, their silver bark luminescent. She sang, and she and the song were somehow one. As her fingers plaited her black hair, they seemed to be plaiting music as well, the melody intertwining in and out of itself. Then she looked at him, and her eyes were all wrong. They were blue and cold, and too narrowly set together. Then her nose shifted slightly in her face, and green sprouted in her hair like fast-growing moss. She smiled, and her canines were long and sharp. The ground gaped at Voran's feet, and he fell awake.

The terror was a foreign thing in his chest, a parasite feeding on him from within. Just a dream, he reminded himself. Just a dream.

This was the third night that the drowned girl, one of the three Alkonist who ruled in his favor against the hag, intruded on his dreams of Sabíana. Now, Voran no longer doubted she had done it intentionally. Every night, she seemed to be digging deeper into him, provoking, and today the unpleasant stir of lust for her was intense, yearning for release.

He threw aside his wool coverlet, stale with sweat, and ran out into the winter night with no shirt or boots. The biting cold, quickly turning to fire on his skin, was effective at purging the desire that she kept feeding him at night.

"You must be dying here, Voran," said a girl's voice, husky in a sultry way. The drowned girl, naked in spite of the cold, sat in the branches of a nearby oak. Her hair still waved as if she were underwater. The darkness did more than enough to hide the details of her nakedness, but Voran still squirmed. The unpleasant stirring was not going away this time.

"Why do you torture me?" he whispered, not wanting to awake his master. "I want no part of your games. I remember very well what you wanted to do with me. Tickling, was it?"

"Oh, it would have been such fun, I promise." Her laugh was lunatic. As if to taunt him, the moon decided to pick that moment to show its nearly full face.

"For you, I have no doubt. But I imagine I know what happens to the men whom you... tickle."

"Really, Voran, you are so morbid. Not everything in the world is out to kill you or eat you, you know. I can't help it if I am desirable to such as you."

He guffawed, though his stomach still churned from the thoughts he was trying to beat back from his conscious mind— images of white flesh and red lips.

"What do you want?" He spat in her direction. The spittle froze before it reached the ground.

"I want what you want. The right thing to happen. I want you to go on your quest, to find the weeping tree, to heal Vasyllia, and to live happily ever after."

"No, you do not. You want something else."

"Why do you men always think every woman desires them? Could I not want something simply because it is the right thing to do?"

She sounded sincere enough, but the moon did not provide enough light to test the truth of her eyes.

"What are you suggesting?" he asked.

"I am a bearer through the levels, like the white stag. I can take you to the weeping tree in a heartbeat."

"How?"

"Well," she looked away like a demure maid, and he thought she blushed, "I am not a beast you can simply ride. I am a creature of love and passion. You would have to bed me, properly. That is my only way of passage."

Voran laughed. "I knew there would be a fee."

She slapped the branch like a petulant three-year-old. "It's not my fault. I'm a rusalka. It's what I am. I merely give you a choice to fulfill your vocation."

"You offer me a way back to my love by taking it from me?"

She tossed her hair back in a parody of an elegant lady's gesture. "I am basically a goddess, anyway, Voran. Your princess can't hold it against you if you are bedded by a goddess."

He shook his head, smiling in spite of himself. He didn't like to admit it, but it was a tempting offer.

"Go away," he said. "If I need you, I will call for you."

"That is really all I wanted from you, dear little thing. Was that so hard?"

She was gone, and the place where she had been was nothing more than an oddly shaped branch illumined by the moon into the semblance of human shape. Had he dreamed it all? He returned to bed and was asleep again in moments, this time dreamless.

"Up, up, you ass!"

The daily wakeup call was more joyful this morning, to Voran's surprise. Gold dust was suspended above his head, caught by the sun's ray, turning softly as if dancing to an unheard tune.

"Come, Raven Son. Look what you've done!"

Normally, Voran would have cringed at his words, expecting a fresh round of pointless work. But the joy in them—a child's undiluted outpouring—was obvious. Voran heard thumping outside. It seemed Tarin was dancing in the snow.

Then Voran saw the reason for Tarin's excitement, and all tiredness fell from him like molting skin. The field—despite the snow, despite the cold, despite the stones—was covered in strong, green shoots reaching up to Tarin's knees. Turnips. Voran laughed, and Tarin laughed with him.

For the first time since they arrived almost a month ago, Voran had a day of rest. Tarin himself harvested the black turnips—each as big as a melon—and stored them in the third shack. He sang and screeched a litany of birdcalls and growls and whines and whistles, as if practicing his varied knowledge of animal languages.

Then he fell silent for hours, a silence almost impossible to bear. Not that it was empty. On the contrary, there was too much uncomfortable presence in the silence, as though Tarin was bracing for something wonderful or terrible that would happen very soon. Voran hoped that meant they would be leaving soon. He had no desire to force the issue with Tarin, especially since his only way of leaving the Lows seemed to be a half-crazy drowned girl with improper designs on him.

That evening, the smoke rising from Tarin's small roof-hole was scented with pine. Voran's heart gamboled like a child. They were having tea again. Perhaps this was a sign of important conversations to come. The invitation came as soon as the sun went down.

Tarin's table was laden with two old radishes and a black turnip, still steaming from the boil—a veritable feast. The same two earthenware bowls were already filled with resin-thick black tea. Voran's mouth watered.

"A good day today, Raven Son. An occasion. And we have been working hard. A bit of a chat will do us both some good.

Don't let the bow get too stretched, you know? It might crack, and then what good would all the arrows be?"

Voran chuckled. It was exactly the kind of thing Dar Antomír used to say in the old days.

"But I can answer your first question even before you ask it. No, it is not yet time for us to seek the weeping tree."

Voran's heart sank, along with all the pleasant sensations of the previous moments. The turnip turned hard; the radish was peppery; the tea faded to ash in his mouth. A storm threatened somewhere in the back of his head, but it was still distant enough for him to remain calm. For now.

"There was something that made me wonder," said Voran. "The Alkonist. They are higher beings than both humans and Sirin, yes? But they seem just as susceptible to vice. If they are higher, should they not be also... more virtuous?"

Tarin's expression soured, as though his tea was too tart. "That is a very simple way of imaging the world, Raven Son. It sounds like you see the hierarchy of the world's levels as a great ladder, the earth on the bottom and the Heights of Aer on top, with Adonais's throne somewhere in the clouds."

Voran wisely kept silent, though the invitation to comment was there. Tarin looked pleased.

"The world is not like that, Voran. It is difficult to find a good analogy, but I imagine it is something like this. When you peel an onion, eventually you reach the smallest layer and the golden middle, yes? Well, imagine that instead of getting smaller, the onion gets bigger every time you peal a layer."

"The middle would be infinitely great," said Voran, unable to contain his eagerness. Tarin looked as though he were considering boxing his ears.

"Yes, precisely. The earth is the outer layer of the onion, and only to the external appearance is it the largest layer. Every deeper layer is more complex and greater. But it does not end there. Each layer is not whole, but porous, like a good cheese, and the layers of reality in those places fold in on each other."

"That is why there are doorways to the other levels, such as the Lows, yes?"

Tarin nodded. "As for the Alkonist and the Lows of Aer, although technically speaking the Lows *are* higher up, that only means that there are fewer places for evil to hide. Earth is a realm of shadow. Evil hides better here than in the Lows, but that does not mean there is less evil in the Lows. Does that answer your question?"

Voran nodded. "But inspires new ones, of course." He smiled sheepishly, and Tarin laughed, giving Voran enough encouragement to ask again.

"When I walked with the Pilgrim, I was able to cover great distances of space and, I think, time, by crossing the boundary between the earth and the Lows on the white stag. Is it possible to cross the boundary when the bearer is on the same side as you are?"

"Crossing the layers on a bearer is extremely dangerous, Voran. Effectively, you are ripping a new hole in the barrier between the worlds. Every time you do that, you give access to the evil things that seek the shelter of earth's shadows. Even the most powerful use such means only sparingly. And no, bearing only works if the two are on opposite sides of reality. I do not know why. I think it is a natural defense mechanism, something to discourage easy passage to and fro."

Voran was amazed at his master's volubility. He hurried to press his advantage. Who knew when he would be so chatty again?

"The Raven," said Voran. "I want to know what his power is. Why is he so dangerous?"

Tarin harrumphed with a rueful smile. "If only more would ask that question, Voran. Things would be much better in the world. Recall the story of the bear cub that I told the children. The hunger for killing that seemed to possess it, turning it into a monster? That is an effective illustration of the Raven's power. He is endless, ravenous hunger—for self-ness, for acquisition of power over others, for pleasures. He eats everything in his path. If there were nothing left in the world, he would end up eating himself.

"Do you remember when I mentioned transfiguration?"

Voran nodded.

"I told you only a part of the story. It is true that humans and Sirin can ascend all the way to the Heights of Aer through the seven baptisms of fire. The other orders of creation also have that privilege. Through every baptism, they transfigure, losing more and more of the old, and becoming gradually something new. But true transfiguration is a painful process that can take entire lifetimes."

He stopped, then began to whisper, his eyes screwed up in concentration, as he had a silent conversation with himself. After coming to a decision—punctuated by a vigorous nodding of his head and a hard slap on his knee—he hugged himself, crossed one leg over another, and looked at a point somewhere to the right and above Voran's head.

"Have you heard of the concept of universal harmony? No? No, I don't suppose philosophy is much taught in the seminary these days. Pity. Anyway..." he coughed twice and breathed sharply in through the nose. "The world, as intended by the Lord of the Realms, is like music. Every voice—that is, every reasoning creature—must sing its assigned part for the song to sound well. That may sound limiting, as though the notes that determine the fate of the world have already been written, but that is not quite the truth. There is a great deal of room for improvisation, as long as harmony is maintained throughout. Thus, the low voices must not break the flow of the high, so that each moment is a beautiful chord. Do you understand so far?"

"Yes, and I think I can see where you are going with this."

"I doubt that," said Tarin, grinning widely before assuming his previous faraway expression. "Try to imagine that one of the voices improvised wildly, beyond the scope of the harmony. What would result?"

"The music would be jarring and ugly."

"Precisely. Now, what if not one voice, but many would simultaneously break the harmony to seek their own melodies."

"The noise would be horrible."

"Perhaps. Or, if they were very talented and attuned to each other, they could make a new, strange, different music. Do you see?"

"Yes, I think so."

"Well, something like this happened. Transfiguration is a gift given from the Heights to those who ascend. But some creatures were weary of waiting, and tried to ascend themselves. They found ways of changing their physical form, thereby gaining some of the higher realms by stealth, not by virtue."

"Like the changers of Nebesti lore, yes? The stone I saw turn into a wolf-man in the forest."

"You encountered one of *those* and lived to tell the tale? You are strangely lucky, Voran. Yes, the changers are lower orders of such creatures. Their masters were originally High Beings who willingly combined their natures into a single being, shedding their personal existence to become an amalgamated High Being of tremendous power. This chimaera then stormed the Heights of Aer with an army of changers, intending to seize control of the Realms."

"The Raven," Voran whispered, his skin prickly and cold.

"Yes, that is one of its names. This abomination appeared lordly and beautiful, and many other beings were tempted to follow him. But the Heights' retribution was swift and terrible. The changers and the Raven were stripped of their original forms, which they had shed so lightly, and they were left as beings of pure will. The now formless ones realized the agony of being formless, the agony of infinite desire, infinite will without the power of fulfilling infinite desire, of bringing that will into action.

"They wandered as their hunger increased. The Raven gathered them to himself, having found a way to allay the hunger temporarily. Whenever a creature of the lower orders—human,

Sirin, Alkonist, Mujestva, Vila, Serpent, or many others—was tempted to follow the Raven and his horde, the formless ones found a way to possess their forms. But their hunger was so great that they quickly devoured every form they assumed, and still their hunger grew. That is the Raven's power."

"But what would possibly tempt anyone to follow such a monster?"

"His cunning is old, and he lies very well. He is a master of gathering power to himself, and he often allows his allies the fulfillment of their most cherished desires and dreams before he devours them. And he is a chimaera. He enjoys wearing the form of a creature of Light. It is his most effective weapon. He can afford to give much to his followers, even things that are initially good, because he inevitably devours all his children."

"That is why he seeks the weeping tree, is it not?" asked Voran, the terror growing. "Living Water is a healer. He thinks it will give him a permanent form."

"So the legends say. Permanent and immortal form, yes."

Voran jumped up and threw the cup of tea to the earth, shattering it.

"Then why do you persist in keeping me here? If the Raven finds the Living Water, it is not merely Vasyllia that will fall, it is everything! All the Realms!"

Tarin remained immobile and calm, though his voice sharpened to a knife's edge. "Have you not considered, dear boy, that because of your *association* with the hag, the Raven might be trying to use *you* to find the Living Water?"

All of Voran's bluster evaporated in an instant, as cherished hope after cherished hope collapsed in a heap near the shards of earthenware at his feet.

"You have declared the kind of war that takes no prisoners," said Tarin. "And you are not ready to fight it. If you were to be found alone by the enemy, you would not be destroyed, no. You would succumb to the Raven. You would become his creature in a heartbeat. If you do not believe me now, I fear you will soon enough. You need a guide, a master, until the moment when you can so guard your thoughts and inner movements of the heart that not even a stray intention will escape that can aid the enemy."

"Is that why you call me Raven Son?" Voran asked, his voice hardly more than a whimper.

Tarin fell on his knees before the standing Voran and extended his arms outward—the traditional gesture of a supplicant. Amazement gripped Voran at the sight.

"Voran, my son," he said, and his voice broke. "Do you not know that when I took you from the hag, I took upon myself your suffering, your pain? I feel everything you do. Every doubt that pains you, every wound that ails you pierces me as though it were my own. I call you Raven Son because that is what you must never become. Raven, the color deeper than black, is a color for the fallen sons, not the sons of light."

Voran couldn't halt his own tears. He leaned down to embrace the old warrior, feeling something he never thought he would feel again—pain and sorrow and joy like fire. He had found another father.

Tarin tensed like a bowstring at its breaking point.

"Voran, did you hear that?"

It was faint, but unmistakable. Something growled outside Tarin's window.

Trust in the Heights with all your heart; lean not on your own understanding.

The wisdom of men is madness with the Heights; the wisdom of the divine is inscrutable to mortals.

Above all things, guard the ways to your heart and sow its pathways with divine seeds, so that the thoughts of your heart sprout the wisdom of faith.

In the vale of the dark shadows, seek the guiding star of trust in the Most High.

From "The Wisdom of Lassar the Blessed"
(The Sayings, Book I, 15:4-9)

CHAPTER 28

THE FUNERAL

Sabíana was swathed in furs and warmed somewhat by the braziers in each corner of the stone gazebo. Built near the altar of the Grove of Mysteries, it was almost completely concealed from the view of the people in the Temple. She had been here, trying to contemplate in peace, for the whole night.

One of the guards hiding behind the redbarks sneezed. Elder Pahomy, standing by her side, sighed in exasperation.

So much for the secret guard, thought Sabíana with a smile.

She had been against it, fearing that any public display of protection, however secretive, would only play into the conspirators' hands. She wanted to show her people that she feared nothing, that there was nothing to fear. But the unexpected treachery of Kalún convinced her to listen to Elder Pahomy's suggestions. Twenty of the best seminary men, fully armed, hid among the trees.

"Elder Pahomy," she said, turning to him. She was sick of trying to concentrate. It was useless. "Tell me. Do *you* think Yadovír was complicit in Kalún's treachery?"

"Yes, I do, Highness."

She sighed.

"You do see what a position I'm in, don't you?"

Elder Pahomy spread his arms out in an apologetic gesture. "I do, Highness."

She was momentarily annoyed by his prescience.

"Speak it out for me," she said curtly.

"Yadovír claims to have tried to save Kalún from the Gumiren. It's made him into a bit of a hero with exactly the kind of people who are most sympathetic with the traitors. If you imprison Yadovír..."

"I could have a full-blown rebellion on my hands." She sighed again, then felt disgusted with herself for it. "He's an odd one, that Yadovír. Do you remember how my father invited him to the palace to witness the execution? Well, I caught him staring at me with the strangest look. Adoration, but contempt also. It unnerved me. Caused me to shudder physically. He noticed, and his face changed so quickly into open malice and hatred that I was afraid for my life, for a second."

"He wouldn't have dared to do anything. Not with all the—"

"Of course not, Elder. That's not what I mean. But I think him capable of exactly the sort of treachery that got Kalún killed. Only he wouldn't die. Too good with words."

Elder Pahomy said nothing. His expression gave nothing away either. To her own surprise, she was grateful for it. She didn't need someone to coddle her. She needed to be decisive. On her own.

"Do you know?" She smiled at him. "I think I need the spectacle of this funeral as much as the people do."

Elder Pahomy smiled. It was a gentle, fatherly smile, a rare gift from the old warrior. She felt warm. *Now I'm ready,* she thought.

Soon the Temple began to fill with people. They were silent, even sullen, though nearly everyone seemed to find comfort in the serene beauty of the redbarks and the whispering intimacy of the aspens, still orange-clad despite full winter.

The great bells exploded in cacophony, all of them ringing at once, the kind of peal usually reserved for weddings and the births of new children to the Dar. She hoped it would raise a dormant half-hope in the hearts of those assembled. The very rocks seemed to sing aloud in welcome to the bodies of the last great men of Vasyllia. Clerics robed in purple trimmed with gold—vestments crafted in the likeness of ancient Vasylli armor—entered the Temple in rows and began to sing. The hymn was fierce and olden, in a dialect not spoken any more save in certain Temple ceremonies. The curious martens and foxes amid the trees stopped and harked to the song, laden with the grace of the ages. Behind them came the coffin-bearers—lightning-white against the profusion of dark furs worn by the people. Then, the singing and the ringing ceased in a single thunderous chord that threatened to topple all the assembled to the ground with its force, just as the two bodies were placed on a bier in the midst of the Temple.

The master bell tolled its velvety call forty times. Sabíana saw the bell in her mind, an ancient relic of old Vasyllia, made in a time when the art of pouring great bells was not lost. It was adorned with reliefs of legendary beasts too old to be named, with deeds of heroes raised to the rank of demigods, some of whom were still remembered in the songs of blind Bayan, Dar Antomír's ancient verse-weaver who still lived in a high chamber in the palace.

The final toll rang, then continued to pass through the crowd like a rising tide. Sabíana followed it, surrounded by her guard, many of whose tears streamed down their beards. She took her place by the bier, and the clerics surrounded her and the bier before beginning the lament. Sabíana felt the blood rush to her face as the bass voices among the priests took the drone, deepening the sound of the singing into eternity. She wanted to weep with the men, but forced her face to remain as stone.

Acolytes lit and scented censers, and the smoke rose to accompany the chant offered on behalf of the fallen Voyevoda of Vasyllia and the greatest Dar of their time. Slowly, with each new hymn sung by the weeping warriors and the priests, the nightmare of Otchigen's fate, though not fading completely from memory, molded itself into a hopeful longing for his eternal rest. If any man deserved to find lasting peace, it was he, for he had suffered the ultimate ignominy and pain.

Soon all the people, their voices cracking in the cold, the steam from their speaking merging with the smoke of the censers, joined in the final lament.

Peace eternal to your servants
In your halls, O Adonais
Grant this.

Sabíana took a torch from one of the warriors and lit the biers herself. She paused, savoring the hunger of the flames, forcing the spectacle to imprint itself on the back of her eyes. This is what will happen to us if we do not prevail, she thought.

She turned to look at the people. Seeing them made her realize how right she had been to burn these two—inseparable in life, as in death—in the same ceremony. It was as she hoped. There was a calm acceptance of the burden of what it meant to live—to carry on the work that others, so much greater than we, have started, but not finished. I can mold this, she said to herself.

"My people, go in peace!" Sabíana said in almost a whisper, but her voice carried well. "Rejoice as is meet for the passing of our father Dar Antomír, but be mindful of our constant danger. Sleep not the sleep of the unprepared. Any day the call to battle will sound, and though it be in the dead of night, may your sword-hands be not found empty."

As if on cue, the bells accompanied her last word with a thunderous ovation. Many eyes glimmered, ever so slightly, with hope that had been dead only hours before.

"Highness," said Rogdai a bit behind her. A loud thump indicated he had fallen on one knee. He was doing that a lot more these days, and every day a more worshipful look came over his face as he watched her. Poor man. She turned and nodded to him, half-smiling the graciousness she didn't feel in her heart.

"There is something I believe you would like to see," he said, his voice slightly tremulous. But it wasn't fear in his voice, not this time.

Yadovír saw Sabíana take Rogdai's arm and walk back to the palace. Even now, there was a fresh pain from the wound she had inflicted on him. A small part of him still wished that he could tell her everything in the hope of seeing her eyes light up with hope. It was only a small part of him, though, and it was drowned out by the hatred that glowed like white metal in his chest. That part of him was disgusted to see how many of the warriors had been moved by the funeral and were now obviously Sabíana's men. Many of them now worshiped the ground she walked on.

"Don't worry, my rat," a slithery voice sounded in his head. "Let them have their moment. It will not be long now."

Rogdai led Sabíana to one of the many open-air cloisters of the upper level of the palace. The snow was eldritch under the nearly full moon. In the center of the cloister, adorned with the remnant of trailing vines and asters still in bloom, stood one of the palace's many small bell towers. It was built over an enclosed pool of spring water blessed by the Sirin, as the tales told. It was also said, Sabíana remembered, that this particular tower's bells quietly rang on their own some mornings, beating melodies that no bell ringer knew any more.

They entered the white chamber of the spring through a low, crumbling doorway. The room was covered in a series of panels, framed in gold. Each panel contained an ancient fresco of a king, a queen, an ascetic, a saint, or a hero. They all wore the flowing robes of Lassar's time, painted in a flat, abstract style with exaggerated poses and over-large eyes. The colors of the robes were still bright. Sabíana realized they must have been made of crushed precious stones--the most expensive kind of paint, used only on the most sacred icons. Some of the panels were so old that the faces looked intentionally rubbed out.

Perhaps they had been, it occurred to her. Nothing was impossible any more.

Even in winter, the spring was not frozen. She knelt before the pool and dipped her face in the water three times, then took the silver flagon and drank.

"In here, my lady," said Rogdai, indicating a blank wall behind the pool.

"There is nothing there, Rogdai," she said, confused.

"That is what I thought as well," he said.

She followed. As it turned out, there was a faint outline in the wall—a low doorway hidden by age and cracked mortar. She was sure no one had opened it in generations. Rogdai took a candle from the many stands in the chamber and pushed at the door, which creaked as it lurched open.

Ahead was a stairway leading down into another chamber, apparently hewn from the mountain itself. Rogdai walked in first and raised the candle, and golden light bounced off the walls. Sabíana had the feeling that she breathed gold. The walls were gilded in more panels containing even brighter and more ornate icons. These were all of hermits, notable for their floor-length beards and hair-shirts. Some of them were completely naked—the ultimate sign of renunciation of decadence. Sabíana remembered from her studies that this kind of chapel was common in the outliers. In Vasyllia, icons of kings and queens were preferred to those of ascetic men and women of the wilds.

There was a low table at the end of the semi-circular altar, and the back wall was covered in florid text, the gold paint as bright as though the brush were applied only yesterday.

"This place must be hundreds of years old," Sabíana whispered.

Rogdai was on his knees, his head bent. She began to read the text aloud.

"Thus saith the Most High King, the Unknown Father, the Artist of the High and the Low. I will make my covenant with Lassar of the Vasylli, to be binding on his children, and his chil-

dren's children until the final fading. Upon this people I appoint a sacred duty—to protect and ward the Three Cities, with all lands appertaining to them, or to die in their sworn duty.

"For duty faithfully rendered, great shall be the measure of my recompense. I shall make this race glorious among men, and the grace of my power shall flow through them as a river of Living Water. For failure in duty bound, terrible shall be the wrath of my reckoning. Their seed shall be wiped from the earth, and they shall be cursed to the darkness eternal.

"Yet if they endure the war that never ends, they shall have peace in a place of sanctuary beyond the endless ages."

"O Adonais," whispered Sabíana, trembling. "How foolish have we been."

Around the text, smaller icons of great kings of old were rendered in astonishing detail, barely tarnished with age. It struck her that if the figures came out from the walls and spoke to her, she would not be surprised. For the first time in her life, the Covenant, Adonais, and all of the old stories were no longer fairy tales, but had become painful reality.

"You feel it too, do you not, Rogdai? The terrible abyss of time in those words, especially when read aloud. We forget so easily..." A thought struck her. "We must read this aloud at my coronation. We must pledge, as a people, to renew our commitment to the Covenant. We must seek for the last help we have left."

And then she knew what she must do, and she began to weep.

The warrior came to the edge of the forest. There, in a clearing, he saw the hut standing on chicken feet. "Hut, hut! Turn with your back to the forest, with your front to me." It turned. He stepped forward, but stopped in fear. A river of fire appeared between him and the hut. The hag stood at the doorway, leering at him. "I can give you what you want!" she cackled. "But you'll have to brave the baptism of fire."

The warrior jumped in...

"The Tale of Alienna the Wise and the Deathless One"
(Old Tales, Book II)

CHAPTER 29

THE RIVER OF FIRE

The stars were snuffed out like candles. The field was shrouded in black. The other shacks were simply not there. Outside Tarin's window, it was so dark that it looked as though someone had painted the windows black. The growling continued—regular, insistent, ravenous. Voran's hands shook.

"How?" whispered Tarin. "They could not have found this place. It is protected. It is beyond their knowledge."

Voran knew how. Tarin had said it: "You must so guard your thoughts and inner movements of the heart that not even a stray intention will escape that can aid the enemy." Apparently, even considering the drowned girl's offer was enough to open a chink in the ancient protection.

"I did it," Voran said. "The drowned girl, the Alkonist, she offered me a way out of the Lows." Tarin's eyes grew wide. "I did not accept it, but neither did I curse her out of my hearing. I may have even considered the possibility."

Tarin breathed out heavily. "Perhaps. But she is an insignificant power, a thing the other Alkonist endure only because they must. She could not have done this...unless..." Something dawned on him, and he seemed even more afraid, if that were possible. "Oh, my dear Voran, I hope not..."

"What, my lord? Tell me, please."

"There are powers of the earth...strange, shadowy powers with ever-shifting allegiances. They have no love for men. They have long remained dormant, but if they have awoken, it could only mean..."

Tarin took Voran's forearms in his hands—an ancient gesture of kinship in war—and his eyes were frightening. They were the eyes of a man ready to die.

"Listen to me, Voran. The only way that the Raven's horde could have found me is if the boundaries between worlds are tottering. That could only happen if Vasyllia is on the verge of falling to the Raven." Voran must have looked more confused than usual, because Tarin smiled in spite of his fear. "Yes, my boy, Vasyllia is far more important than you realize. It hides a secret that may determine the fate of all the Realms, not just this one. Promise me, my boy. No matter what happens, you must not let Vasyllia perish. Even if it has already fallen, you must win it back. At whatever cost!"

His eyes were on fire now, and Voran was truly afraid for the first time in his life. His restlessness, his desire to quest, his wish to make a name in the world—all that vanished. He knew, with the conviction of someone on the doorstep of death, that he was not ready to face the Raven and his darkness.

"I promise, my lord."

"I am no longer your lord, Voran. You are a free man. Though you are so unprepared, so unprepared."

Once again, Tarin had a mumbled conversation with himself. Something knocked at the door, a soft knock, not threatening at all. It chilled Voran to the marrow. Tarin's eyes were full of tears.

"I have been cruel to you, Voran, but it was done with a pure intention, I hope you realize. And it has not been enough. I am throwing you to the Powers, and I do not know if you will survive. But if you do not, we will all die."

He fell on his knees and began scrabbling at the hard earth of the shack. For a moment, Voran wondered if madness had finally struck Tarin, but the old man looked up after his fingers had grabbed something, and he smiled his usual, impish grin. He scratched out a wooden trap door, pulled on it, and the trap screeched open.

"This place is protected, as I said. The line of sentinel spruces is a line of power, and the rest of my land is encircled by a river of fire—both are a deep magic from the days of Founding. If the Raven's horde has truly passed it or avoided it somehow, then there is no hope. More likely, they are casting illusion at us from the other side. In any case, you must chance it. At the end of this passage, you will come out on the banks of the river of fire. You must not hesitate even a moment—jump in. It will be excruciating, yes. You may be consumed by it. But we have no more time to prepare. The battle has come to us."

Before Voran could say anything, Tarin pushed a sheathed sword, bundled in fresh black fabric and tied with a new belt of black leather, into his hands and nearly threw him into the passage.

"Go, before it is too late."

The knock on the door repeated, still soft and not remotely threatening.

"That is good," said Tarin, smiling. "It suggests they are not actually here yet. You may have time. Run!"

The darkness in the passage was so thick that Voran was sure it would simply eat him before he could pass through. The silence was so complete that it thundered in his ears. His heart did its best to try to jump through his chest. He exhaled until there was no breath left, then inhaled a long, pure breath, and began to repeat the word in his mind.

"Saddaí. Saddaí."

There was no change in light, but suddenly he realized that his hearing was enough to tell him exactly where to go, how long the passage was, and how fast he could run without falling or crashing into anything. This must be how a bat sees, he thought. He wrapped himself in the black fabric—which turned out to be a full cassock with fine bone clasps all the way down the front—strapped on his sword underneath it, and ran forward, the loose edges of the garment flapping behind him.

It seemed a long time, but the air eventually changed, becoming cold and fresh. The passage sloped sharply up, and before he knew it, he stood outside on the banks of a small river that flowed contentedly as though it were the middle of summer. It took him a moment to realize that this must be what Tarin had called the river of fire, but it looked merely river-ish.

"It took you long enough, my sweet," said the drowned girl from above him. She landed on him like a cat, and her claws were just as sharp. Her arms and her hair engulfed him. He tried to push her off, but she was inhumanly strong. As he thrashed, he tripped on something and was on the ground. They rolled back and forth violently, and Voran felt her nails tickling him. They were cold as iron.

At first he laughed, it was so absurd. But it soon grew unpleasant. She laughed and laughed and continued to tickle until the nails dug into his skin, and the pain was searing. He found it harder and harder to breathe. The stars danced before his eyes for a moment, and he felt himself go under, but then she sprang off him.

"That was a foretaste," she said in her girlish voice, dusting off her arms with her fingers, again parodying a typical gesture of a courtly woman. "I can kill you quickly, or I can do it slowly. It depends on my mood. Now you know."

Voran reached for his sword, but it was not there. She held it, still sheathed on its belt, though it seemed to disgust her, like an old cheese gone green.

"None of that, Voran. Last chance. Take my offer, bed me properly, and I will take you to the weeping tree."

"You lie, as I should have known. You are in the Lows of Aer with me. Of that, I have no doubt." He felt the soreness under his arms. His hand came away bloody, and it disgusted him more than the sight of blood ever had before. "You cannot bear me over the barrier unless you are on the other side."

"How clever you are." She looked disappointed. "Never mind. I can still get my pleasure by force." She lunged at him with the speed of a lynx, but he had no desire to stay and fight. He merely stepped a few paces back and fell into the water. The girl recoiled from the splash with a shriek. Voran, not stopping to think, splashed her as hard as he could before she could get away. The water caught fire on her hair, and in a moment, she was a blazing inferno, running away into the darkness. Her wail cut into him almost as painfully as her nails had.

Voran was in pure, clear water, but somehow it was also fire, though nothing like the usual red-orange flame. Each little eddy was also a translucent tongue of fire, and he was covered in them. At first, the flames were dew-like—soft and cooling and thicker than water. Then the pain seeped in as the flames reached through his clothes into his skin. He threw off the new cassock—it somehow remained untouched by the fire—and hurled it to the shore. It landed next to his sword.

He fought down the rush of panic, held his breath, and forced himself to submerge completely. It was excruciating, as Tarin had said. As he washed, he burned. As he took off the thick layers of mud and sweat, layers of skin sloughed off as well. Soon the pain was a scream in his ears, but he forced himself not to come up. He continued washing himself, continued mouthing the word—*Saddai, Saddai*—until even the scars from the serpent-hag came off in purplish clumps.

He stood up, bracing for the cold air, and waded out of the river. The water should have frozen on his skin the moment he broke, but the flames continued to dance over his body, though they no longer hurt very much. With a flash of embarrassed fear, he touched his head and chin. No, his shoulder-length hair was still there, only smoother and silkier, as was his still young beard. He sighed in relief.

He wrapped himself in the new cassock. It was clean. He had last been clean months ago. That moment, a short moment of exhilarated pleasure, was one of the longest of his life, one he would remember again and again for many long years. The fabric was thick and well-woven, excellent for cold weather, though he wished he had his old travel gear from Vasyllia to go atop it. As it was, his training with Tarin had hardened his body against cold in a way he did not think possible. All Vasylli prided themselves on their ability to bear cold, but his capacity to endure it now was far greater than the hardiest Vasylli.

There was something else that was different as well. As he realized what it was, he almost wept for the sheer joy of it—the soft palpitation in his chest, as of another heart.

Lyna had come back, and with her came the dawn. She sat on a low bough of a bent-over oak, its bark green with moss. Behind her head, the sun rose between two distant hills, giving Lyna a halo of gold. At first, he couldn't see her face. When his eyes got accustomed to the light, he saw she was smiling.

"Lyna, how I longed to see you."

"Oh, my falcon. My poor falcon. You cannot imagine the pain I felt when you broke our bond. It can be remade, if you wish it. But it will be painful as nothing else."

Voran laughed dourly. "Today, that seems appropriate."

"First, you must hurry. Tarin has crossed the line of sentinel trees to distract the Raven's creatures, so that you could escape. I do not know how long he has left."

As soon as Voran passed the line of spruces, the swirling darkness was on him, and invisible bonds stronger than steel pinned him in place. His senses sharpened, so that every movement of his pinioned arms was a cacophony of pain. At first, he saw nothing but murk, but the shadows resolved like fading smoke around a prostrate figure on his knees, bloodied hands clasping a hoary head, face planted firmly into his thighs. Voran refused to believe this was Tarin. Over him towered a hideous monster—a leonyn over seven feet tall, his head and face a horrible amalgam of feline and human, with only the worst qualities of both. He bared brown fangs and roared as he beat Tarin with a monstrous leather whip, edged with many tails.

Voran could not move. His frustration reached a boil, and he screamed out his defiance at the mass of formless creatures swirling in the darkness around the leonyn and Tarin. The lion-thing turned to look at Voran—its eyes were black shards of the void swirling around them—and smiled.

"Ah. The hag's lover." The leonyn's voice was incongruously gentle. "Well met at last. How typical of your kind to hide in the stinking marshes. Quite a warrior you are."

Tarin looked up. His face was battered, but his eyes still had the old fire. He assessed Voran for a heartbeat and seemed content with what he saw. With a groan, he got up. The leonyn stepped back in surprise.

"The old goat has some strength left," the creature said and hissed, skin stretched back over his gums, revealing all of his fangs in challenge.

Tarin paid him no attention. He assumed the stance of the storyteller and cried out, as if in challenge, "How do you feel, young man?" The leonyn beat him again, but Tarin only flinched at it, as if it hurt no more than a mosquito's bite.

Voran remembered the ordeal with the hag, when Tarin told the story of the healing of the crippled young man by the Sirin. To his amazement, Voran did feel an increase of strength, as though the river of fire had newly forged him.

"I feel the strength of ten men within me," Voran said, echoing the words of the young man in the story.

Tarin laughed with tears in his eyes, and the leonyn stepped back in fear. Into the blackness flew Lyna, her eyes glowing golden fire. She fluttered overhead like a falcon readying to dive. Voran shrugged off the power holding him pinioned as if it were string. He unsheathed his sword. His heart beat like a hammer on new steel, and his sword responded. It turned red with heat, then lightning-white, as if it were itself furious at the attack of the Raven's creatures.

From a deep recess of his heart, something flowed out like fresh wine bursting out of its cask. He began to sing, and to his heart's leaping joy, Lyna sang in harmony with him—a hymn he did not know, yet it flowed unimpeded from his lips.

I arise today
Through the love of the Heights.
Light of sun, radiance of moon,
Splendor of fire, speed of lightning,
Swiftness of wind, depth of sea,
Strength of earth, firmness of rock.
I arise today
Through his strength to protect me
From snares of the darkness,
From tempting of pleasures,
From everyone who wishes me ill,
Both far and near, alone, among many.
I summon today
All these Powers to keep me
Against every cruel and malevolent power,
Against every thought that kills body and soul,
Against poison and burning,
Against drowning and wounding.
I arise today
Through a mighty strength—
The power of the unspeakable word.
May the grace of the Heights
Sustain us forever.

He rushed sword-first in a wild attack, completely careless of life and pain. The leonyn unfurled like a banner into ash and black smoke, though his black eyes still burned in the storm of the formless ones. Voran flew at the seething wall, and his white brand cleaved a furrow in it. The sun's light streamed in like water, and the slit expanded outward, pressing in on the host of creatures until Voran, Tarin, and Lyna stood in the sunny marshland, and before them spun a column of blackness swirling in rage, reaching higher than the clouds.

A flash like a thousand bolts of lightning struck the mass of the Darkness. Voran fell on his face from the force of it, barely able to look up. Something mountainous looked down on him and spoke in a voice like a thousand trumpets in unison.

"I come as summoned, Son of Otchigen."

It was a giant in the form of a man of light and fire. His eyes were suns, his teeth were moons. Six tapered wings of gold, lapis, emerald, ruby, silver, and topaz flickered in constant movement about his body. He had four faces turned in each direction—a man of searing beauty, an eagle, a lion, and a Sirin. As monstrous as such a creature should be, Voran could hardly keep from worshipping him right there on the field of battle, so beautiful he was. In his outstretched right hand, he held a sword of fire that was at once the sharpest metal and the hottest flame. In his left was a war hammer the size of a small mountain.

The giant attacked the column of darkness, and everywhere he walked, the earth opened and fire burst forth. Fissures in the ground yawned open, and winds swirled from every direction, visible winds like molten gold and silver. Voran realized they were not winds at all, but living creatures. They pushed the mass of the Raven's creatures inexorably down into the earth. The formless ones wailed and burned and cursed, but they could not withstand the attack. Voran's entire body shook from fear and exhilaration, and he fell into a stupor.

Voran came to himself as silence once more reigned on the marshlands. He feared to look up, feared the Power he had summoned. He wished he could just crawl under a rock and wait until everything went back to normal again.

"Voran," said Lyna next to him. "It is time."

Groaning within, Voran stood up and faced the giant, who towered over the place where the Raven's horde had been. The great rents in the earth were healed, and the marshes looked as though nothing strange had happened at all.

"I am Athíel of the Palymi," said the Power in a voice that could rip stone apart. "I have heard much of you from my brother. He has hopes for you."

"Brother?" Voran's voice sounded like the squeak of an insect.

Athíel smiled, and it was like lightning. "Yes, the Harbinger. Do you wish to have your bond with Lyna restored?"

"I do," said Voran, with slightly more power in his voice.

"Know this. The Palymi come as summoned by the great hymn of the Powers, but I can help you no more. You have gained much strength from your time with Tarin, but you must never forget that such strength is nothing against the Raven. You can only prevail as the true Vasylli have ever prevailed. Nurture the flame in your heart, cultivate your bond with Lyna. That bond is the lifeblood of good in this world. And take heart, dear one. Your path will be dark, and in the Heart of the World you will face the crumbling of everything you ever believed in. In that time, listen to the song in your heart."

Athíel raised his sword of flame and pierced Voran through the chest. Voran fell, his mind shrieking with the pain. It was as though his body had been unmade completely, then put together again, piece by piece. When his eyes could see again, he saw a foul green-brown vapor seeping out of the wound in his chest. It hissed in the crisp air until it ran out. The wound closed on itself, leaving a hairline scar down the length of his chest bone.

Athíel was gone. The song of the Sirin was inside him again in thunderous harmony, and his inner fire blazed. Lyna flew above him, hovering on her jewel-wings, crying tears that landed on his face and steamed.

"When will I see you again, my Lyna?"

"I do not know, my falcon. Gamayun can see no further than this moment. I fear for you and for Vasyllia. I do not know how this will end."

"I will seek you after I find the weeping tree. Much will be determined there, I think. Will you come to me then?"

"I am with you always," she said, and was gone.

The palace of Vasyllia has seven towers. The tallest of them is closed off to all, locked away, the key in the keeping of a select few. For that is the home of the treasure of Vasyllia, the bard of the Dar. Every Dar has had his own chosen bard. The last, and most brilliant of all, was blind Bayan, who outlived two Dars and died on the eve of the great battle for Vasyllia.

"A Child's History of Vasyllia," chapter 21

CHAPTER 30

BAYAN'S LAST SONG

On the morning of the coronation, Rogdai was turned aside from his already mounting responsibilities by a very annoying boy. At first, he could not for the life of him recognize who the boy was and what his position in the household was intended to be. The boy was not particularly illuminating, waiting to be told to speak before offering any useful information on his own.

"Go on, boy," Rogdai said, exasperated, rushing through the halls of the palace as everyone else seemed to be going the other way. "Tell me your charge."

"It is my master. He begs a word with the Lady. He says it is very urgent."

Rogdai almost growled at him. "*Who* is your master, boy?"

The boy's eyes were as big as trenchers. "Bbbb..." he stammered.

"Well?"

"Bayan. The bard."

Oh, by all that is holy in the Heights, he thought. What horrid timing.

"He will have to see me, I'm afraid," Rogdai said. "The Lady has been in the Temple since midnight, preparing for her coronation."

The boy nodded and rushed forward, almost as though he were escaping Rogdai, not leading him. For that speed, Rogdai disliked the boy a little less.

The old bard was dying. It was the smell that made it most obvious—something like stale bread and rotten fruit mixed with sweat. He knew that smell well enough from seeing both his parents die.

"Vohin Rogdai," Bayan croaked, his white eyes uncannily fastened to Rogdai's face. "The Darina will not see me?"

"She is at her coronation, my lord," said Rogdai, his voice soft in spite of his irritation. Bayan commanded respect, even in the worst of times.

"You will have to tell it to her, then. I was visited by a song this morning. It has not happened in decades."

Rogdai understood. Writing a song was one thing, but being visited by one was another. This was an oracle. He bent to his knees and leaned on the deathbed, so the old man did not have to strain.

"I will not play it for you, for my fingers are stiffer than old roots. But I will sing the words."

Rogdai's heart leaped to hear the clarity of the old man's bass, so unexpected after hearing his croaking speech. It was almost as though someone else sang through Bayan's body, using it as an instrument. But as the words sank into his conscious mind, his heart did an about face and plunged into his heels for sheer terror. Bayan sang a prophecy of defeat.

The smoke! It blinds and frightens.
The shouts! They're all around.
The flaming stones are falling,
But the shouts don't lose their sound.

The Lords—impotent, silent—

Lie crumbled in the smoke.
The shouts increase their fury
At Dark's death-dealing stroke.

You cannot see their faces,
  For darkest is that hour
  When skies light up in fury
  At chaos' gath'ring power.

While Raven in his glory
  Declines to show his face,
  The wise hear in the shouting
  His rotting, fallen grace.

The time for words is over
  For Light hangs by a thread.
  Will no one stop the shouting?
  Will no one stir the dead?

Rogdai walked like a dead man back to the walls of Vasyllia. Bayan's words thundered through Rogdai's consciousness as he joined the throngs headed for the Temple, feeling like a corpse carried by a swift tide. He could not tell Sabíana this prophecy. Not in her hour of glory.

Sabíana closed her eyes and reveled, for the last time, in being merely Sabíana, daughter of the Dar, intended of Voran, sister to Mirnían, Black Swan of her people. She opened her eyes, and now and forever she would be the Black Sun, the Darina of the dark time of Vasyllia. Swathed in a brown fur, Sabíana walked out from her gazebo slowly, with bowed head, not daring to look up yet. She stopped before the throne and turned to the assembled crowds, so full that some were even standing on the lowest boughs of the redbarks. Falling to her knees, she touched her forehead to the bare ground and raised herself up again. She repeated her obeisance three times before turning to the Grove of Mysteries.

The new chief priest, Otar Gleb, stood in front of the grove by the ceremonial throne—an unadorned chair intended to remind the future Darina of the need for humility in the wielding of power. He was a surprisingly young man with a joyful face, if somewhat ugly. His hair was blond and curling at the ends that rested on his shoulders. His eyes were deep and kind, so different from Kalún's wells of contempt. He placed his right hand on Sabíana's forehead as he half-chanted, half-cried in a sharp, high tenor, "Woman! Why do you approach the sacred grove?"

"To abase myself before the mercy of Adonais and to confirm his will in the choice of a new Darina." Her voice sounded weak to her own ears, young and scared.

"Why do you, a humble slave, dare to take this duty upon yourself?"

"By the right of blood..." She paused, hoping she had memorized the words correctly. "...and by the humble desire of my people do I approach. I, a worthless thrall, do myself neither desire nor deserve such honor, such a dreadful duty."

"How do the people answer this claim?" His voice rang out regally, and she was jealous of it. "Are they in one mind and one mouth of accord?"

"Yea!" echoed through the Temple, truly as if it were one, many-faceted voice.

The priest indicated that Sabíana should kneel.

"I confirm, as mouth and warden of the will of Adonais, your claim, slave Sabíana, daughter of Antomír, to the Monarchia of Vasyllia. Forget not that you are a servant of your people, the slave of a higher Dar. Rule in remembrance of the ancient Covenant that our forefathers made with Adonais."

How empty that sounds, she thought. It reminded her of how difficult it would be to awaken in the people any understanding that the Covenant needed to be upheld as a reality, not merely as a beautiful idea.

One of the clerics held a gilded malachite box. The chief priest opened it carefully, pulling out a silver crown of ancient make. It was wrought in the shape of a flowering wreath, rising to a single peak above the forehead, like Mount Vasyllia. In the midst of the silver peak shone an emblazoned red-gold sun. Sabíana stood up, kissed the sun, then sat on the throne, still facing the Grove of Mysteries. He placed it on her head.

"Adonais, with your glory crown her..."

"So be it!" cried the priests.

"...with your invincible grasp wield her scepter..."

"So be it!" cried the clerics and the royal court.

"...with your omniscient providence guide her judgment."

"So be it! So be it! So be it!" cried all the people.

Four of the priests lifted the throne with Sabíana on it to face the people. She felt the emotions they had all held back suddenly overwhelm her. Instead of cringing, her heart held firm, and she took the energy of their worry, their tiredness, their pain, and forged it inside herself into pure joy that streamed out of her to the tips of her fingers. She felt afire, re-forged, new. She smiled.

Everyone prostrated in the snow. Many faces were white with awe, even terror. She raised her hands to bless them, when frightened cries and gasps rose among the people.

"The crown! It flowers!"

Unprompted, many voices began to chant, "So be it! So be it!"

Sabíana threw off her fur, and her cream and gold underdress shone like lightning. Under the fur, she was girt with a sword. She unsheathed it and raised it high.

"Words? What use are they now?" Her voice rang even louder

than the priest's, and her heart rang with it. "Hope? What hope can you expect, my people?"

Her eyes teared up from the icy air, but she held her body firm. The steam floated from her body like an aureole. She felt the fire of the flowering crown on her head. She was half-mad with exhilaration.

"Death awaits the sleeping, death spares not the upright. It is death's time, my people."

The fear was everywhere, in every pair of eyes now, but still they hung on her words, hungry for more.

"Come, death, I say! Come, so we can spit on you. We are not your slaves. We serve life, and we defy you! Sword-fisted, helm-crested, we take life and we impose it on you!"

All through the crowd, swords were unsheathed and held aloft. They scattered the feeble light of the sun hidden in fog and the fires of the lanterns.

"We are a high people. We are the hammer of Adonais, the axe of the Heights. We are the wardens of the Three Cities. Arise with me, raise your swords and your hearts, set them alight, blaze forth the anger of the righteous!"

The sea of people seethed. Old men, boys, warriors, even priests raised weapons. Their eyes were alit with the war-wind.

"But dare I say the righteous?" She moderated her voice, allowing it to soften, as though she doubted her own words. "Are we not perhaps become fallen, diminished by long laziness and selfishness? Do we dare to take up arms in the name of Adonais if we have broken Covenant with him?"

Not a single voice, not even a whisper disturbed the silence of the frosty air.

"Hark now to the word of your Darina! I have found proof of the Covenant's existence. I have read words carved by our fathers into the face of the mountain, words that cannot be unsaid. Hearken to the words of Adonais, my people!"

It looked like a wave struck the people's backs, so quickly did they fall down on their faces. All the armed men thrust their swords into the ground before abasing themselves. Sabíana did the same, but she only knelt, her gaze intent on the people she hoped to move to an act of insane heroism.

The herald read out the words that Sabíana had first read only a day before. Even now, after copying it for herself and hearing it reread many times, the words pierced with their power. It was not incantation or magic. The words had the power of making. These kinds of words were spoken by the deity that created them all. Sabíana was either committing terrible blasphemy, or she was reforging a lost Covenant. She did not know which it was, but she had cast the stones, and it was too late.

After the herald finished, murmurs rose like the first rustling of wind that promised rain. Here and there she heard expressions of agreement. She searched for any sign of defiance, but all she saw was the adoration.

"Now is the time, my people. Now we must renew the Covenant with Adonais. But I cannot do it for you. We must all agree to it; we must all renew the Covenant within our hearts. Vasylli! Pledge yourselves to the will of your Darina, the will of Adonais!"

"So be it! So be it!"

The cries were reluctant at first, hesitant, but the sound rose like a fire. Soon the mountain shook with the repeated cries. Still, even now she saw that some held back. The fire of the flowering crown dimmed, and by the lessened light in the eyes of the people, Sabíana knew that the sign had faded. It left her aching and empty. She gathered the reserves of her strength.

"So be it! We will be his people again, and may he guide our death-stroke against the foul enemy outside the walls!"

The terrible understanding dawned in the eyes of many. They understood.

"Sing with me, my children!" She stood up. "We go to war."

The warriors surrounding her bellowed the opening chords of the ancient call to war, and the women and children in the Temple joined them. Even the clerics sang, tuning into the single harmony like a bag-pipe warming up. Over their combined voices, Sabíana unfettered her own, and it flew above the choir like a hawk catching a warm gust.

> *The Heights resound with thunder;*
> *The mountains sing aloud.*
> *Our people burn with anger*
> *At the enemies' gathering cloud.*

> *We gird our arms with iron;*
> *We bind our tongues with prayer.*
> *Our children and our loved ones*
> *We leave to Sirin's care.*

> *O Adonais, hear us,*
> *Defend us as we cry:*
> *"Annihilate this Darkness,*
> *And give us strength to die."*
> *Lord! Give us strength to die!*

The fog outside the city glowed yellow, swirling with loathing, challenging any who would come. Arrayed like rows of candles ready to be lit, Rogdai's men tensed for the charge behind the great doors. A moment before, the gates throbbed with the violence of the drums; now the air echoed with silence. Rogdai held his breath, trying to calm the thump of his heart. Any moment now the call to charge would sound. As mad as he knew it was, and probably fatal, he was infected with war-wind, and his finger itched to feel the cramp of a sword-hand after hours of battle.

All around him, the men stood with jaws set and swords out, so still they could have been statues. His heart burst with pride at their form. Only the banner-bearers betrayed any of their eagerness, but they were all boys still in the seminary. Rogdai recognized Tolnían, the young scout who had started everything with his report about the tree that wept Living Water. He impressed Rogdai more than the other boys. There was no bravado in his manner, only calm determination that belied his tender years.

"Ho there, boy!" called Rogdai at Tolnían. "I believe I see your nanny over there. Hide, or she'll uncover your secret. What are you, ten?"

Tolnían didn't even flinch as he answered. "Vohin Rogdai, before this is over, we *will* be arming ten-year-olds."

Rogdai laughed, because it was necessary, not because he was amused.

Tolnían's hand-woven banner—a Sirin in flight, talons bared —caught even the sickly glare of the foggy sun, sowing light on the warriors. Rogdai felt a semblance of hope rising. He turned to look back at the palace. He imagined he could see Darina Sabíana even at this distance, raising her hand. Something gleamed in the highest turret of the palace, and the braying, glorious cacophony of trumpets exploded around them.

The doors groaned. Rogdai screamed white-steaming anger as his men rushed out into the high fields around the city. All of his brothers strained—he could sense it as his own strain—for that fearful first blow of steel against steel, that entry into the whorl of war. He sang, and his brothers took up his song, an old ballad of death and glory.

They were answered with silence. Out and out they poured through the open doors, but no enemy came to greet them.

Something hissed and crackled around Rogdai. A wall of malice rose up from the very earth, it seemed. The fog swirled, as if some huge, invisible finger was mixing a poison to choke all who approached. The hissing grew louder. Rogdai realized it came from above. Swarms of ravens plunged down in a blinding attack, a black wave of talon and beak. Just ahead of him, the fog suddenly resolved itself into thousands upon thousands of

Gumiren. But then they all changed, as though their human forms were cloaks to be cast off before battle. He faced an army of monsters.

Most were chimaeras combining human and animal features in the most grotesque parody of creation—leonyns, wolf-men, bull-men. Huge snakes seethed everywhere. Some walked on short legs, and some were no more than worms with mouths that unfurled outward to reveal rows of dagger fangs. Everywhere, growls replaced the calls of men.

"What in the Heights is going on?" Only decades-long discipline stopped Rogdai from running away, screaming.

"It is the Raven, Vohin Rogdai," said Tolnían next to him. All that was visible of his fear was a slight paleness in his cheeks. "The Darina was right. Only Adonais can help us now."

"Well, I am not going back, crying for my nanny, boy," said Rogdai, punching himself on the chest to knock his sense back into his body. "Vasylli! For our Darina! For the Black Sun!"

"The Black Sun!" The lines caught the chant like a wooden ball and passed it on, until the field rang with it.

There was no time to form ranks: the monsters were among them, biting and clawing. Before charging, Rogdai looked back to see how Tolnían fared, and laughed to see him mumbling some prayer under his breath.

"Careful, boy, it will take steel, not words, to survive today."

"I am not interested in surviving. I am interested in the annihilation of this Darkness." He smiled, but it was a warm smile, a smile of farewell.

Then, Rogdai was in the midst of it, and the war-wind took him. Even through the haze of red, Rogdai saw that the monsters were aiming for the banners, as though the embroidered High Beings were a source of power. The Vasylli would not long survive without the hope that the banners held out to them.

One by one, the ranks of spear-men protecting the banners were mowed down by the rising enemy. One by one, the banners near Rogdai tottered and fell, and with each one the growls of the creatures seemed to grow more vicious. As they fell, the light they scattered faded, and Rogdai felt the terror rising with each downed banner. Some of the boys fled in screaming fear. They were easy prey for the ravens, who wheeled above, ready to swarm on anyone who ran.

A ring of spearmen directly in front of Rogdai disappeared like smoke. Before he realized it, he engaged a reeking lion-thing over seven feet tall, with two or three more at its heels. They pushed Rogdai back into Tolnían, and his strength proved nothing against them. Cursing aloud, he tripped on a rock and felt the sinews of his ankle tear. What a pathetic way to die, he thought.

But the creatures reeled from a new, ferocious attack. Tolnían had thrust the point of the banner into the earth and attacked the enemy like a one-man avalanche. Every stroke was perfectly directed, striking some vital part of the monsters now cringing from him. He hacked and slashed and parried with incredible skill, not a hint of fear in the way he held himself. The creatures shrieked with mad terror at his calm and deadly assault. They ran, falling over friend and foe alike. All around them the Vasylli, embolden by Tolnían's courage, shouted and charged.

The banner-bearers that remained alive—and they were few—labored to raise all the fallen banners by lodging them in earth as Tolnían did. Once again, the images of ancient Powers rose over the battle-scarred slope. Some boys even began to climb the trees to lift the banners higher, to try to catch the sparse rays of sunlight. Rogdai was amazed—the ravens did not touch them, as if their resurgent courage somehow gave them added protection.

The battle raged. More and more creatures rushed at them from the mists below, constantly replenishing their losses. Rogdai saw many men simply crumple to the ground in pain, though they faced no enemy. Snakes hidden by creeping mists were everywhere. Rogdai himself was surrounded by a mass of snake carcasses, since they were the only creatures he could still fight off, unable as he was to stand on his torn ankle.

Then he heard the great bell, and his heart sang. Its velvet peal poured fresh strength into the men around him, and they redoubled their fury, pushing the monsters back into the churning mists. Someone picked Rogdai up and supported his weight. It was Tolnían. Together they pursued the enemy to the churning fog on the edge of the killing field.

Something bright flashed deep within the fog, and the mists dissipated with a breath of wind. Not a single monster remained in sight. All the way down the slopes, beyond the plateau surrounding Vasyllia, boulders and earth and grass were covered in the bodies of fallen Vasylli—many too young to be called men. Their dead faces were bone-white in the sun, expressionless and calm. Rogdai wondered if their spirits had found better habitations in the Heights. As he stared at them, the momentary ardor of victory cooled.

"Where are they?"

Not a single mangled corpse—or any trace at all—remained of the monsters that had appeared from hell and apparently returned there. And there was no sign of any Gumiren anywhere. Rogdai wondered if this was victory, or a prelude to something far worse.

I have seen evil. I have felt it in my blood and in my bones. I have been it. And I survived. But after it all ended, after I paid the ultimate price, the question still remains. Did the Raven control my actions without my will? Or did I willingly let him into my body?

Unsigned note found among the personal effects of the Karila embassy

CHAPTER 31

THE LAST BATTLE

"You are mad!" Yadovír shrieked, sick with nervous excitement. His clerk had just burst in on him, announcing the victory of the Vasylli warriors over the enemy. Yadovír was so shocked, he even forgot to hold the lavender-scented kerchief to his nose, as he did ceaselessly now, only to have the stench of the Raven inundate him again. He raised his now-skeletal white hand back to his nose, and stamped his foot, whining.

"You lie, you gullible fool. How can that be? The day is not even far gone, and already we are victorious? Impossible. You lie! Get out. I do not want to see you anymore. Out!"

Yadovír was aware that to others he now cut a rather pathetic figure, always shuddering, muttering to himself, and holding his scented kerchief to his nose, but his mind was as keen as ever, and he took special pleasure in storing hatred for every slight—perceived or otherwise, it didn't matter—for the right moment.

"Ha! It seems they have done it," he said aloud after the clerk left him. "Now what will you do?"

The appearance of solitude belied the obvious presence—unseen, but sensed by creeping skin, foul stench, and slithering voice that was and was not in Yadovír's head.

"It is unbecoming of such a noble heart to stoop to foolishness, my rat."

The Raven's tone oozed malice and calm. Yadovír's momentary excitement shattered, and the voice laughed, almost in spite of itself.

"My very own fool," he hissed. There was even a kind of unctuous tenderness in the voice. "Your people truly are fools if they think to have won any victory."

"Fools that somehow managed to beat off your creatures."

Yadovír felt a chill of displeasure from the presence.

"Yesss. There was perhaps a moment or two of unexpected bravery there. But no matter. It just makes your part in all this a bit more urgent, nothing more."

"You have c-c-come to d-demand payment, h-have you?" Yadovír's assumed bravado was completely betrayed by the unfamiliar stammer, which had begun to decorate his speech at the most inopportune moments.

"Y-y-yes, I h-h-have," the voice mimicked with half-suppressed laughter.

"Will you leave me alone then, after I have done your dirty work?"

"What? No demands that I install you in a position of power over those you hate? No pathetic attempts to wrest terms from the jaws of the pitiless Raven?"

"I don't n-n-need you for that," Yadovír said.

"Oh, I see. You rely on my munificence to keep you alive as a boon for your treachery, and then you plan to take advantage of the ensuing commotion to murder your enemies in their beds, is that it?"

Yadovír stamped his foot again in frustration. The Raven laughed inside his head.

"Do not worry, you will get all you wish for in that quarter. But you can give up any puerile hope of my ever leaving you alone. You are my favorite plaything."

Yadovír almost gagged at the feathery touch on his arm.

"What do you want of me?" Yadovír nearly screamed.

"What do *I* want? I want you to be happy. I want you to feel the pleasure of vengeance, my rat. Not to wait and wait and wait. When all this is done, you can punish Sabíana in whatever twisted way your strange mind desires. Now go. The Gumiren are waiting for you. They have already cleared the blocked passage. Open the hidden way into the city."

"But how will I protect myself? I don't want to be known as the man who betrayed his people."

"Of course, how noble of you! I have a very special idea on that score. Come, my stupid little one. I will explain everything on the way."

Sabíana rushed into the palace proper, surrounded by her generals. Contrary to her own common sense, she had summoned the Dumar, reinstating their privileges, hoping the victory would rally the representatives to her. Her sense told her that there was little chance of that. She battled a heavy dread, fearing that everything she had just witnessed—all the monsters, the carnage—was all a play, a farce to distract her from something else, something she could sense with every cell of her body, but could not see. She tried to maintain the appearance of confidence.

Her heavy wolf fur chafed at her neck, and she wished she could cast away the heavy curved sword she wore at her side. She had chosen her clothing for a purpose. She needed to be an avatar of victory, as far as the warriors were concerned. She strove to maintain that illusion for as long as possible.

"We must not become drunk over this victory, my lords. True, our men have outdone themselves today. We must reform and defend the city against any further attack. It seems we have the upper hand now, and perhaps we can even send out sorties into the forest to harry the Gumiren." Wherever they are, she thought, but did not say.

"Darina, is it wise to entrust so much of this to the Dumar?" rumbled Elder Pahomy by her side. "They have hardly deserved much trust of late."

"They dare not rebel now, not with this success in the..."

She was cut off by a wheezing intake of her own breath. They had entered the Chamber of Counsel. The room was a lurid mess of bloodied bodies. Every member of the former Dumar lay dead or dying, stabbed many times. The floor glistened with blood. Some still moaned. Only one among them was still lucid—Yadovír, who was also wounded, though not fatally. He wept uncontrollably, his voice like a serrated knife.

"Darina Sabíana, we are undone! Do not believe anything of what you have seen or heard. We have not triumphed. It was all a ruse of the Raven. One of the clerics did this, possessed by our ancient enemy. I barely escaped with my own life before I stopped him."

Yadovír pointed at the body of a young priest holding a long knife, red to the handle. He lay open-eyed in the shocked surprise of death.

"One of our prized clerics," screamed Yadovír.

Sabíana shook like a leaf in a gale and found no voice to answer Yadovír. Her knees no longer supported her; she fell and the shuddering grabbed her violently. Her mind was a protracted scream of pain; her eyes lost their focus, and she felt foam rise to her mouth. Against her will, a moan slithered out of her, and even to her own ears, the sound of her teeth chattering was pitiful and horrifying.

Two of her guards knelt by her, trying to do something to relieve her, but they had no idea what to do. Finally, the convulsion stopped. Her eyes remained cloudy and unfocused, and she couldn't speak except to moan without words.

Yadovír stopped weeping as if he had become another person in the blink of an eye. Cold terror gripped Sabíana; Yadovír seemed to grow in her eyes, as if a shadow spread out behind him like a raven's wings. His eyes were black fire, and he commanded with the power of a legion.

"Come," he said with a voice not his own. "We must see to the order of Vasyllia."

To her shock, everyone did as he commanded, crumbling to a will that seemed to be outside him, yet inside him as well. Her two guards picked her up and dragged her. All she could do was moan.

Rogdai limped back to the city, leaning on Tolnían. By now, most of the warriors had returned, leaving the wounded on the field of battle. An eerie uncertainty hung about the air like smoke, and most of the warriors were intent on the palace, hoping for some word from the Black Sun. Tolnían still clutched the banner as if his life depended on it.

"That was quite a thing, my boy," said Rogdai, shaking his head in disbelief. "I did not know they still made warriors like you."

"I never made it through the first year of warrior seminary," said Tolnían and laughed.

Rogdai struck Tolnían playfully on the back of his head, as if to stop him from becoming too tall in his own estimation.

Rogdai couldn't concentrate his vision through the throbbing pain. Everything slowed down through his eyes, and objects didn't focus unless he looked at them with careful intention. But when he did, they became somehow too real, and he had to look away again. When he heard the marrow-chilling cries coming from the palace, he looked up at one of the turrets to see the pale figure of a skeletal Yadovír holding his hands out. Then the terrible focus came, and the horrifying reality struck him.

Yadovír's hands were covered in blood.

Sabíana was next to him, but she was unrecognizable—white and hardly standing, supported by two of her black-robed guards. They looked like the bringers of death.

"People of Vasyllia," roared Yadovír. "Fell deeds have been done. The Dumar has been infiltrated by treachery. Every last one of your beloved councilors lies in his own blood. I alone escaped by a miracle. Who could have done such a deed? The Gumiren, you say? No. One of our own people has perpetrated this atrocity. One of those sworn to protect us, to minister, care, and watch over our lives with benediction is a traitor. One of our priests has sold himself to the enemy, for I know not what price. His knife it was that brought death's swift bite to our own people. A priest! We are betrayed by one of our own!"

Yadovír foamed at the mouth. A young priest, one of those who had just fought at the wall, stepped forward to protest, but his words stopped short. Silence filled the open courtyard where he stood. The priest, fair as a spring lily, was alone, ringed by warriors who looked at him in disgust. His eyes rolled back, and he rattled at the back of his throat. A sword's point thrust through his chest, and Rogdai, red with fury that he did not realize was there until this moment, held the sword.

"Death to all traitors of Vasyllia!"

Rogdai's cry was taken up all around him. Swords were unsheathed yet again. He was the first among them, charging at any priest he could find. Some were in mail and fought back, but none could withstand his fury. He no longer felt the pain of his ankle, rushing back and forth, stabbing and slashing and hacking. When three bodies lay at his feet, he pursued the fleeing priests. He ran into homes, broke down doors, overturned tables and ripped off curtains to find the cowering traitors. The shock and pain he saw in their eyes only fed his hatred. He spit on them as he skewered them.

When he had run out of priests to kill, he stopped to look around, finally noticing that his right leg could no longer support his weight. The streets were spattered with red, and everywhere the open eyes of the dead clerics stared at him from dead pates. There were even a few dead women—wives, sisters, daughters—who had tried to appeal with their bodies to the mercy of the sword. There was one in particular, a girl hardly out of her childhood. There were tears on her dead face.

It was that detail, not the blood and carnage, that thrust into his mind the realization of what he had done. He tore at his hair and screamed.

Tolnían, still clutching the banner, ran from the scene of carnage back to the gates of Vasyllia. He had tried to fend off Rogdai himself, but he could not, and nearly everyone else had followed in Rogdai's madness. Vaguely, he hoped that some of the still-returning warriors might help him. As he turned a corner, he ran into a wall of men. They were not Vasylli.

The Gumiren surrounded him, silent as hunting cats. They crawled out of every street, every shadow in the city. Tolnían thrust the point of the banner into a crack between two flagstones, drew his sword, and sang a challenge. The banner fluttered slightly, showering Tolnían with dappled sunlight. The enemy advanced.

As they attacked, he lost sense of his own arm. It flailed back and forth, striking everywhere with deadly accuracy. Like being possessed by a High Being, he thought. Two of them were at his feet. Another three came down in two strokes.

When he came to, ten mangled figures lay before him. He stopped to breathe, and iron pierced his left side. He fell and his eyesight began to dim. All he saw was five curved blades above his head, rising with the war-shriek of the Gumiren. They waited for the command to hack him to pieces.

Suddenly, light streamed from his banner, striking them like spear-thrusts. They screamed and retreated from him. Leaving him alone, they walked around him, not daring to approach the image of the Sirin in flight. They passed by and continued toward the palace. Tolnían succumbed and fell unconscious.

The despair that followed Rogdai's madness choked him. At that moment, when the last hope shriveled within him, Gumiren warriors—hundreds, thousands of them—entered the courtyard, and with them came smoke and fire.

The war-wind abandoned Rogdai. He hardly tried to ward off the avalanche of curved blades rising high against him. He fell. He saw his brother-warriors around him fall like wheat cut down by a scythe. All of them—dead or wounded.

Within minutes, not a single armed Vasylli stood against the invaders. Rogdai, blood pouring from three wounds, lay on the ground, trying to rise only with a left arm. His right arm lay near him, hacked off by the Gumir who stood over him now with death in his eyes.

A loud retort of an ox-horn stopped the Gumiren, as though they were one man.

Yadovír, white as death, stood next to Sabíana, looking down on Rogdai and the rest of Vasyllia as though he had just given birth to a stillborn child.

I have long wondered what the fate of humanity is. We have a spark inside, fed by our soul-bond with the Sirin. And it leaves us forever restless, searching for something. But for what? I have heard that some holy men have experienced a change, a transfiguration into something higher, something stranger. Perhaps we have to shed this body of flesh for a body of fire. Perhaps the flame in our heart must engulf us whole. Perhaps only afire can we stand before the throne of the Most High and hear our ultimate fate...

From the personal archive of Dar Lassar the Blessed

CHAPTER 32

THE STAFF IN BLOOM

Voran laid Tarin down by the staff that still had not flowered. Tarin's face was white, but his arms were streaked with blood, and his breathing was labored and heavy. Voran could not believe that the man who had projected such physical strength for so long could simply wither like a rose struck by an early frost. It hurt Voran, more than the river of fire, more than the sword of the Palymi. It did not help that after the war-wind had passed, it left Voran exhausted, his strength sapped.

Tarin opened his eyes, and still he did not groan or give any other indication of the pain he must be feeling. His young eyes—still such young eyes—were plaintive.

"Where were you when I suffered?" he exclaimed.

Voran leaned back, shocked and struck dumb. Then he realized Tarin was not speaking to him.

"I am your faithful, loving slave." Tarin's voice was stoic, lacking any hint of self-pity. "Why did you wait so long to send deliverance in my hour of need?"

The silence that followed was immense and terrible. But then, the voice. The ineffable voice.

"I was waiting, Tarin, by your side. I wished to see your greater victory, to grant you the greater reward."

Tarin laughed and wept at the same time.

"Tarin," whispered Voran. "Was that...Adonais?"

The look in Tarin's eyes was strange. Voran didn't understand it. He had never seen it before.

"No, Voran. Not Adonais." He began to cough, and could say no more. The voice spoke again, soft and yet terrifying.

"Come to me, Tarin. I have need of your counsel."

Tarin burst into flame—a bluish, warm flame that consumed his frail body. But it left behind something greater, an ageless warrior with sad eyes and dark hair. Completely alight, the transfigured Tarin stood up and bowed to Voran.

"Voran," said Tarin in a high tenor, without the grating heaviness of his usual intonation. "There is much you must still learn. I fear that when you learn the truth about Vasyllia, about the Raven, and about Adonais, you will find no more strength to go on. In that moment, remember me. I have lived my life in the shadows, never thanked by anyone for what I do. And yet, we Warriors of the Word have buttressed the walls that hold up the worlds."

Voran said nothing. Pain pressed his heart, and his mind refused to think.

"One gift I leave you," said Tarin. "There is a path behind the third shack that leads out into the plains. Follow it. When you reach the end, an old friend will be there. Till we meet again, my friend. Oh, and congratulations on your first three baptisms of fire."

He smiled, and Voran was alone.

The staff was covered in small pink blossoms that smelled of orange. Voran laughed, but his joy was a shard of metal in his heart.

It was as Tarin had said. The path—curiously untouched by snow—was a purple shadow between snowbanks gilded by the early morning. It sloped upward toward a rise, atop which tall grass waved awkwardly, encumbered by the snow at its feet. During his time with Tarin, Voran had never so much as left the enclosure with the three huts, much less ventured to see the view from atop the rise.

It was finally his, as he had dreamed of for so many weeks—freedom. He could go anywhere, do anything—a strangely frightening thought.

He looked around, unwilling to go anywhere. Not yet. For all of the drabness of the huts, this was a beautiful place. In the distance, the mountains peeked out above the line of sentinel trees. All around him, the land rolled up and down like gentle waves, mostly clad in white, but with occasional flashes of color—red berries hanging on for dear life, a sprig of purple heather anticipating spring, the pink flowers of the staff-tree.

I could stay here, he thought. I could weather the storm here. No one would seek to find me.

It was a comforting thought, so unusual for a life filled with ranging, training, weeks on the march. Tarin was right. If Vasyllia was to fall, what could he possibly do to stop it, much less bring some dreamy vision of old Vasyllia back to life?

His conscious mind offered him the traditional riposte—will you stand by while the world burns? Yes, he said. If I learned anything from my master, it is that one man's efforts may avail much, but not everything. It is too late to seek the Living Water, too late to seek pardon from my exile.

But what about Lebía? His stomach lurched in warning, and his heart tugged in rebuke. He had not thought of Lebía in so long. What had happened to her? To the pilgrims? Were they safe?

Then a picture flashed on his mind. Otchigen, with his familiar, thick braid and tightly curling black beard. He lay by the hearth in the sleeping embrace of three hunter-borzoi. Lebía, a newborn child, lay cradled on his thick forearm, her own arms extended at impossible angles, like an archer nocking an arrow, her mouth open, a wheezing half-snore rising up and down with the roll of Otchigen's great body. Aglaia stood in the doorway, wrapped up against the cold, stopping for a moment before going out to pick the last of the rowan berries before winter. Her eyes were filled with tears, in spite of her laughing eyes. He remembered the immensity of the peace, the contentment of the scene, and some of its old grace still remained in his heart.

He ran into his shack to gather the barest of necessities. Somehow, he knew that the journey would not be a long one. Last of all, he took Tarin's old travel cloak and wrapped himself in it. Perhaps, he thought, someday I can find respite in the life of a Pilgrim? He chuckled.

"Not likely," he said aloud, his thumb tracing the comforting outline of his sword-hilt.

Voran reached the top of the rise. The view was a continuation of the same landscape surrounding the three shacks, save for a clear path, which led directly to a trellised doorway covered in green ivy. Voran laughed. Even for the Lows of Aer, this doorway was comically obvious. Maybe this was Tarin's final joke? It was as though his old master were saying, "I know, Raven Son, you are quite the idiot, but I have made it easy for you."

Voran ran forward, not even slowing to pass through the doorway. The already-familiar sensation of displacement and temporary confusion quickly faded. He stood on a wide plain, the thinness of the air indicating high elevation, and just ahead of him was the waystone, and not a stone's throw beyond it—the giant head, still snoring as the flocks of starlings flew up and down, as regular as heartbeats.

Voran was thrown to the ground by something huge. A huge dark thing was atop him, its snout wet against his face. It licked him.

"I'm happy to see you too, Leshaya," spluttered Voran as he labored to find enough space to breathe.

She growled. "You are such an idiot, Voran." Her body quivered with mixed excitement, anger, and joy. He understood her completely.

"Tarin had said I would find a friend. I hoped it would be you."

"That old goat. Do you know how long I waited for the two of you? Where is he?"

It was strange. In the excitement of seeing Leshaya again, he had momentarily forgotten everything. Now the world came crashing through the walls he had put up around himself, and all of a sudden breathing the very air seemed dangerous.

"They found him, Leshaya. He's gone. Transfigured."

Leshaya's ears went back in pure animal fear, and she bared her fangs.

"It is time, then," she growled. "There is something you must know about our friend, the giant head of Buyan. He is the father of a race of giants who wield immense earth-power. They've been asleep for a long time. But they have returned."

Voran nodded, remembering Tarin's warning.

"He wants to make a deal. He says he knows where the weeping tree is, and he is willing to show us the way."

"For a price, naturally."

"I imagine so. Come."

The head was awake, its stillness more unnerving that the bluster it showed the last time they met. It raised its eyebrows ponderously, and Voran took it as the only sign of greeting the land-bound giant could still express.

"Well met, son of Otchigen. It is unfortunate that you did not inform me of your exalted bloodline the last time we met. I may have arranged things a little differently for you."

"We don't have time to play riddles this time, Buyan," said Voran. "To be frank, I have no desire to treat with you. I would much rather seek my own path."

"Are you sure about that, my boy?" asked the giant head, almost growling. "Have you looked at the waystone?"

Voran did. The writing was different.

If left you go, there death awaits
If right you go, there death awaits

If straight you go, there death awaits
If back you go, there death awaits

Voran became aware of a brooding sense of menace bearing down on him from all sides. He had a strong desire to turn around, but his heart told him that if he did, he would be dead in seconds.

"Is this another riddle?" Voran challenged Buyan, his hand on his sword.

The giant head laughed. The sound ripped several shrubs in the vicinity out of the ground with their roots still intact.

"I am quite sick of lying here in the ground, tied by the Powers. It is time for me to come out. My sons are awakening. Zmei is already abroad."

The sun hid behind clouds over Voran's head. He looked up, and it was not a cloud, but a giant in full armor, a spear in his right hand, his teardrop shield taller than the walls of Vasyllia. He inclined his head at Voran, but his face was backlit by the light of the sun surrounding his head like a parody of a halo. It called to mind the omen of the darkened sun.

"Why would I ever want to help you, Buyan? Do you not come from the same fallen line as the Raven?"

"Do not insult us," bellowed the other giant, Zmei. "Our power is not his borrowed power. We are the power of the earth. Ancient, eternal, self-sufficient. We owe allegiance to no one but ourselves."

"Our power is mighty," continued Buyan's head. "But it has been chained, contained for too long. You will restore that power, and in payment, we will give you Vasyllia, for you to refashion in whatever way you see fit."

For a moment, Voran saw the vision of the Pilgrim, the Vasyllia of old where every person was animated by a burning soul-bond. Could they truly have the power to give him Vasyllia? He could restore its ancient splendor. He was sure he could. But at what cost?

"I am but a humble warrior," said Voran. "I don't seek to play a role in the games of the Powers. I only want to find my family. Leave me be."

Buyan raised an eyebrow. "Your family? We can arrange that." He smiled, and his old, rotting teeth stank.

Like a bolt of lightning, Zmei's spear flew over Voran's head. Voran ducked. It hit with a sickening thud, and not into the ground. Voran trembled, not wanting to look at what he knew he would see, but forced his eyes to look at Leshaya.

She was pinned to the ground, so completely that she had no leverage even to push herself up, like a butterfly pinned to a piece of parchment. Something about her began to change, shift, like ripples on water. Her wolf form lessened, faded, turned in on itself, lost its color. Voran became ill and vomited violently. She was not Leshaya. She was his mother.

"You did not know?" said Buyan, all innocence and good humor. "Yes, Aglaia was transformed by my power all those years ago. It was a mercy. She was on the verge of death, were you not, my dear?"

"Why do you do this?!" Voran pulled out his sword and tensed, ready to fling himself at both giants.

"To make a point, you fool," said Zmei, moving just enough to let Voran see his face—beautiful, yet cold as chiseled stone. "We have no love for the Raven, and the Raven fears us. It is time for us to reclaim ownership of the earth. Your supposed master, the Power you call Adonais, has abandoned you. The Covenant, such as it was, is broken. We offer you everything that he gave you, and more. All we need is Living Water."

"*You* need Living Water as well, little man," said Buyan, looking significantly at Aglaia. "Better hurry, or you won't be able to heal her."

Voran looked at Aglaia. Her hair was whiter than he remembered, but otherwise no different than his memory of her, except for the paleness of her face and the look of absolute terror in her eyes. They rolled into the back of her head, and she fainted, though she did not fall, stuck as she was by the spear through her chest. Voran's terror swallowed him, and his hands shook uncontrollably.

But something in his mind nagged him. It was something that he should have noticed a long time ago. The Raven had great power; these ancient giants claimed to have even greater power. But the Raven had not even seemed to make the attempt to seek out Living Water, going straight to Vasyllia, as if that were his only goal. And Buyan claimed to know the location of the weeping tree. So why did the giants not take it for themselves? There were reports of at least one person being healed by the tree. Unless....

"You cannot find the weeping tree without me."

Buyan's face darkened visibly. "It is the nature of our power. A bargain, sealed ages ago with the Powers. We would rule the earth, but we abandoned our right to travel the other realms."

"But you know of a doorway?"

"Yes," said Zmei.

It explained much. People could cross over into the other realms. Some, a few, obviously had, and they were healed by the Living Water. But the giants could not.

Voran looked at Aglaia's limp body, at the blood choking her clothing, and he went on his knees to touch her face. It was still warm.

"I will come back for you, Mother," he whispered.

An icy breeze pushed Voran's hair across his face, coming from the right. Not a bowshot away, Voran saw a hole in the fabric of reality, a shimmering gap. On the other side, mountains stood tall, and atop one of them was a tree, made black by the setting sun behind it. Before stopping to even think, Voran ran to it and jumped through.

O tombs, you tombs,
Our eternal homes!
Long may we live,
But your doors we must face.
Our bodies belong
In our mother, the earth.
To be given to the soil,
To be eaten by worms.
But our souls will wander
Each to his own place...

Old Nebesti funeral dirge

Chapter 33

THE RAVEN'S CHOICE

Horrible cries surrounded Sabíana, exploding into her confused consciousness and fading to nothing in strange waves. Dimly she glimpsed blasts of flame and smoke belching from rents in the earth. Not yet fully recovered from her fit, she saw everything with varying focus, through a fog. She couldn't form her thoughts into complete patterns; the words gathered together only to hit an obstruction like a wall inside her head, and she gave up, exhausted from the effort. But through it all, she heard the sound of wind whistling through reeds. Sabíana felt the nearness of Feína, the terror receded a little, and her mind began to clear. But her limbs were still stone-dead.

Feína sang quietly. All the noises of war, the screams, the madness faded away, replaced by the blossoming rose-fire of the Sirin of flame. Sabíana's thoughts gathered in her mind like raindrops falling into each other down a windowpane. The pain was still there, but now it was bearable.

"My Sabíana," said Feína. "I cannot bear to see you like this."

The voice was in Sabíana's mind, as was the vision of the Sirin of fire. In her mind, Sabíana found it possible to answer.

"Feína, I do not know if I can bear my burden much longer. Please, lighten it for me."

"I cannot, my swan. It is beyond my power."

"Dear Feína, I think I could bear it if I understood what is happening. Why do I not just die and leave this pain behind? Why do I linger?"

"If that is what you wish, Sabíana, you can lay down your life right now. You are given that choice. But if you die, the last spark of light in Vasyllia dies with you. The Raven's victory will be complete."

"So I must remain and suffer on? How can that possibly benefit anyone?"

"Your suffering is not without purpose, my bright swan. Your remaining in Vasyllia is a challenge to the Raven that cannot fail to bear fruit. Ever the Sons of the Swan will be a thorn in his side. And perhaps, if things go as Lyna hopes, you will be the source of his downfall."

Sabíana understood the reference to Voran. He was alive, and he still strove on his quest. His image warmed her heart, and the song of the Sirin rang out, stoking her inner fire until it blazed. She understood.

Her presence in Vasyllia was necessary. The Raven would not touch her; she was Cassían's line, and he needed legitimacy if he was to maintain any sort of power other than the rule of the fist. She must slowly heal, slowly become an image of endurance and hope for true Vasylli. Perhaps Adonais would see her sacrifice and would re-forge the lost Covenant.

Sabíana regained full consciousness at Yadovír's side as the smoke began to clear. Near her, the young chief priest Otar Gleb lay on the stones, bloodied, but still alive. Yadovír seemed to be protecting him, or keeping him for his own use later. Gleb nodded at her once and raised his hand, blessing her. She felt new strength rush into her.

The Gumiren had herded all the people of the city to every open square and courtyard in Vasyllia. The faces she could see seemed barely human; nearly all had succumbed to brutish terror and hatred. Only a few still had the same light in their eyes that she had ignited at the coronation.

Yadovír twitched and his face pulled into a focused expression, listening intently. Looking at Sabíana, he seemed for a moment to lose confidence, as if he noticed some change in her, some addition of power. He must have decided it was nothing, because he turned away from her and faced the crowds. He spoke not in his own voice, but in one augmented by several others, so it seemed a host declaiming from a single mouth.

"High people of Vasyllia! You have fought valiantly, but not to victory. I, the Mouth of the Raven, now declare your doom. The women and children may all live, provided every one of them gives up the worship of Adonais and spits on the Covenant. You warriors must pledge your swords to the Raven and swear to do his bidding in all things. Refuse, and the beasts whom you defeated not an hour ago will gladly feast on your unarmored bodies. Warriors! How say you? If yea, raise your right hands in solemn oath.

It took a long time, but eventually nearly every warrior did so. Sabíana's balance tottered, and her shakes began again. Somehow, she stopped herself and forced herself to watch on.

"Warriors of Adonais you were," said Yadovír, sneering. "Warriors of the Raven you become. But first, a test. Desecrate the Temple of Adonais, and you will live. Refuse, and your women and children will die before your eyes."

Now everyone was frozen in indecision. Sabíana understood them. It was one thing to denounce Adonais with the lips and to secretly worship in one's heart and home. It was another thing to raise a hand against his Temple.

Yadovír leered like an old man of millennial cunning, gesturing to the Gumiren with an arm that was made more terrible by a suggestion of a wing-shadow behind him. The Gumiren built a pyre around the Covenant Tree and lit it. Sabíana felt the terror of the blasphemy like it was a living presence next to her. The Gumiren then gathered all the women and children like cattle and pulled the babies from the arms of their mothers. They held them over the fire. Unmoved by the screams, they stood still as cold stone, ready at Yadovír's command to hurl the shrieking children into the fire, even as they reached for their mothers in uncomprehending terror. Sabíana thought her heart would rip apart from the strain.

None of the warriors hesitated any longer. Given torches and axes by the Gumiren, they rushed through the reaches like a swarm of fire-ants and vented all their fear and frustration on the trees of the Temple. Red-barks were torn asunder, burned, hacked to pieces. The Grove of Mysteries was mutilated, and Sabíana felt the death of each tree as though a child of hers were killed before her eyes. The low wall surrounding the temple was broken stone by stone with meticulous malice. The altar table was hurled off the edge of the cliff. The lanterns were shattered, and with their undying flames the Temple burned, and the conflagration rose up to the Heights, joining the blasphemous sacrifice of the Great Tree. Sabíana closed her eyes and willed the tears to come, to unburden the heaviness of her heart, but they would not.

With an effort, she forced her eyes open again. She needed to see this horror to its end. The warriors who still refused to join the Raven were jostled toward the gates of the city. Many of them bowed before the burning Temple as they passed it, heedless of the sharp points wedged into their backs. At that small act of bravery, Sabíana's tears came—slow and deliberate.

Many women and children followed their men, desiring no other fate than to join their loved ones in death. Most of the others who remained huddled away from them in fear. The crowd of faithful ones stopped at the open doors leading out of Vasyllia, and all turned back to Yadovír to hear the final pronouncement. His voice became impossibly loud, so that Sabíana was sure they heard every word.

"People of the Raven, denounce your allegiance to Adonais!"

Now there was no hesitation.

"We reject him!"

"Behold your queen." He raised Sabíana roughly with a single hand, and she felt no more dignified than a sack of potatoes. Many faces blanched and lost all remaining hope when they saw her. *I must look as bad as I feel*, she thought.

"Behold your Black Sun!" Yadovír screeched. "May her reign be long and blessed!"

"Long live Darina Sabíana!" they all cried. Some of the women wailed and moaned.

Sabíana wanted with all her power to at least raise a hand to them, to acknowledge that she was with them in spirit, but no part of her body moved.

"Death to the traitors!" Yadovír jabbed his right forefinger toward the people at the gates. "Go, and meet your just reward!"

Sabíana watched as the condemned walked out of the city, showing not the slightest sign of fear. At first quietly, then with greater intensity, they all began to sing. Even in the high turret of the palace in the third reach, Sabíana heard them clearly.

O Adonais, hear us,
Defend us, as we cry:
"Annihilate this Darkness,
And give us strength to die."

Lord, give them strength to die, Sabíana thought.

No sooner had all of them left the city than a white light washed over them. A radiant Sirin appeared over each person—a lamentation of thousands of Sirin in flight and full-throated song —bemoaning the fall of Vasyllia with voices that cut Sabíana with their agonizing beauty. Taking each of the faithful by the arms, including the many wounded still lying on the field of battle, the Sirin flew up into the light of the sun. Their song faded, but the song in Sabíana's heart rose to a great fury. She tested her limbs, and to her exhilaration, the smallest finger of her right hand twitched. The iron of her courage poured back into her heart. She could do this. She would be their hope.

Have you seen the hands of a healer?
Are they rough?
No.
Are they dirty?
No.
What are they like?
Like the sun reflected in water...

Karila nursery chant

CHAPTER 34

HEALER

Voran stood at the top of the world. He had crossed more than a single boundary. This was not the Lows of Aer; this was something deeper. Clouds were scattered below him, as though he were set here by a Power of Aer to herd them. Most of the clouds sat barely higher than a great moon-shaped tarn far below his feet, nestled among the crags that divided Vasyllia from Nebesta. The tarn was lined at one end with bunched conifers that looked like bristles on a hair-brush from this distance. Where he stood, there was hardly any vegetation, except for a few pines gnarled by the constant wind. The rest was grey-brown stone and snow, though there was strangely little white for this depth of winter.

Then there was the black hawthorn.

The young hawthorn, frothing with white flowers, stood on the tip of a conical rock, its roots trailing downward along the stone until their tips dug into great cracks. Its thorns were like iron nails, but each dripped opalescent water onto the rock. The drops rolled individually down the stone, slowly, carefully, as though they were looking for the right path down, until they followed the roots through the cracks into the earth. There were no clouds above them, Voran checked. The tree wept.

Though Voran's panic and fear beat at his heart like hammers, he froze in wonder at the sight. The hawthorn sang. It was nothing like the song of the Sirin; it was far more ancient and alien, and it revealed to Voran a depth of natural power that he never could have imagined. He had no doubt this tree was capable of healing the sick, and much more than that.

Something thwacked in the thin air and whistled. Voran's left shoulder jerked back at a violent angle, and when he looked down, it had sprouted an arrow. He tried to move, but the pain was like his shoulder ripping apart. He was pinned to a tree.

Voran turned his head, trying to gather his thoughts in the maelstrom of pain and panic. Mirnían came out of a shelter of a crag, a set expression on his face. Mirnían pulled the bowstring back to his cheek and waited. His hands trembled slightly, and his face had gone white. He shook his head and closed his eyes for a moment, then tensed and loosed. The arrow grazed Voran's left arm, tearing the flesh. Its whistle lingered in the sparse air.

Voran caught Mirnían's eye and nodded, then dropped his head. He waited for the next arrow, sure that this time a marksman as good as Mirnían would not miss. He couldn't help but feel intense sadness that it had come to this, but to his surprise, he didn't blame Mirnían. He breathed out and was strangely calm.

Mirnían's breathing was loud enough for Voran to hear. "No," whispered Mirnían, his breathing turning ragged, "No, it can't be."

Voran looked up to see Mirnían ripping off his tunic with hands shaking so violently that he remained fully clothed despite all his efforts to disrobe. Finally, he managed to pull part of a sleeve off. His chest was leprous, and it stank, even at this distance. Mirnían's eyes were wild. He raised his hands, and they were riddled with sores. He showed them to Voran like a frightened child.

"They are back," he said, his eyes nearly all whites. "They are back."

He ran toward the hawthorn and scrabbled up the rock, but it was slick with the tree's tears, and he kept falling down. Finally, he reached the lowest thorns with one hand as he clung to the stone face with the other. He grabbed and screamed with pain, let go, and fell head over heels to the ground, where he lay, twitching spasmodically and sobbing. His hands were torn where he had grabbed at the weeping thorns. The hawthorn had not healed him.

Voran could no longer bear it. Gritting his teeth, he pulled the arrow out of his shoulder and nearly passed out from the pain. He forced his mind to ignore it, even as his head began to spin and his limbs wanted desperately to give up the fight. Somehow, he made it to Mirnían's side, and dropped to his knees next to him.

Mirnían no longer struggled; he merely sobbed, looking like a wounded animal more than a human being. He raised both hands to his face in a half-hearted gesture of protection. Voran put his good arm under Mirnían's neck and hugged him close to his body. He wept again—he was weeping far too much lately.

"Look at us," he said to Mirnían through the racking sobs. "Is this what we wanted? How did it come to this, my brother?"

Mirnían's eyes were wide with shock. "You will not kill me?" The question was full of disappointment, as though he had given up on life and wished that Voran would be brave enough to end it for him, since he couldn't do it himself.

Voran's body shook from his anger. Not letting go of Mirnían, holding him with the same gentle care as a mother gives to a newborn, he looked up at the cloudless sky and screamed his defiance.

"Where are you, Adonais?!" Voran's voice echoed, broken by the sobs. "Mirnían has served you with his life. He has sacrificed everything to follow my mad lead. How could you have allowed it to come to this? You have all-power. What Vasylli has given more of himself, lost more of himself, gained more of himself in your service? Will you curse your own child?"

"You're asking the wrong questions, my boy," said a familiar voice. Standing under the shadow of the hawthorn was the Pilgrim, even older than Voran remembered him, leaning on his staff now for support, not merely show. The setting sun above his head hung blood red, barely touching the tips of the hawthorn. "Why do you expect the Heights to intervene for you whenever you need saving?"

"How many times has Adonais already intervened?" said Voran, forcing his voice to remain contained, though it trembled from the effort. "How many times have I been guided precisely to the place I need to be, at the appointed time? Even after I turned away from him, he found me a deliverer. Tarin died for me. Why all the extraordinary care for me, and this disregard for Mirnían? I do not deserve any of it!"

The Pilgrim smiled. "No, you do not."

"I do not hold Mirnían responsible for shooting me." said Voran. "I deserve much worse at his hands. I *should* be dead."

Mirnían's expression was unreadable, but he had stopped crying.

"I call on Adonais," cried Voran. "Let him answer. Why do I, the guilty one, enjoy his patronage, while the one who has suffered the most remains cursed by leprosy?"

The Pilgrim raised his arms and grew, larger and larger until the very sky seemed to rest on his head. His grey cloak thrust back, he exploded into the radiance of a thousand suns. His knee-length chainmail was woven of light itself, kaleidoscopic, yet purely and utterly white. His eyes were as twin beacons, and his face was beyond youth or old age. His helmet-plume was a billowing flame; his hair was fluid gold on his massive shoulders. Joy poured out of him, joy like the first cry of a newborn, like the first star after a week-long snowstorm.

"I am the Harbinger, brother to Athíel of the Palymi. I am the mouth of the Most High. I am the light behind the dawn. I am the fire that burns the setting sun. I am the one who witnessed the covenant between Lassar and the Heights. Do not call on Adonais. Speak to me, if you dare."

For a moment, Voran thought that the Harbinger spoke the name Adonais with distaste. But how could that be?

"I am a servant of the Heights," whispered Voran, forcing himself to look at the giant of light. "I am nothing. Yet has not this man, this prince of Vasyllia, done enough to deserve more than this?"

"Do you doubt that all he has suffered is part of a design?"

"Design? What design can there be? Adonais has abandoned us, and old Powers are coming back to take the earth for themselves."

"Voran. Consider the past days. You cannot fail to come to this conclusion. You four—Voran, Mirnían, Lebía, Sabíana—have been *led*. By me and by the white stag and by others, all along paths thorny and painful. You ask why? If I told you the full truth, you would not believe me. You must come to it yourself. The answer to all that your questioning heart desires is at the heart of Vasyllia."

"The one place that I cannot reach."

"You *must* reach it. Do not forget. Vasyllia is *everything*. Even if she falls, you must go back. Search for its heart. At the heart lie all the answers."

The Harbinger's light flared like a huge furnace and spun faster and faster, until the white light was a huge pillar, reaching up far beyond the sun, ending on Voran and Mirnían, blood pouring from both their wounds. The rest of the world was a colorless darkness; only they two were illumined in color and light. Then the Harbinger disappeared, and time seemed to begin anew. The sun descended behind the flowers and thorns of the weeping tree, turning the tears red as blood falling from spear-tips.

"And so it is the two of us at the end, Mirnían," said Voran, smiling. "As it should be."

He stood up awkwardly, nearly fainting again, and unsheathed his sword. His left hand limp and throbbing with fire, he somehow leveraged himself with his right, sword in hand, and clambered up the rock, foot by foot, until he lay under the shadow of the branches. Breathing with difficulty, he rose to his knees and touched the pale flowers, grazed his fingers over the thorns. It was so beautiful. His tears returned, and he spat in disgust at himself.

"No one should have to make this choice," he whispered. "Forgive me, Mother."

He breathed in, braced himself, and hacked at the thin trunk with his sword.

"What are you doing?" shrieked Mirnían.

Voran struck again and again like a man possessed, his eyes blurry with the flow of tears, his hands unsteady from the pain.

"No one should have access to so much power," he said.

He saw Aglaia's stricken body in his mind, and he despaired.

The sword finally broke through the trunk, and Voran pushed the hawthorn down the far side of the cliff. It fell out of sight. A fountain of fragrant water blossomed from the raw, jagged stump and immediately began to ebb. Voran had a sudden compulsion to drink the water before it disappeared completely. He caught a little in his hands. It sparkled in his cupped palms, multifaceted like a fluid diamond. He drank.

The waves of hot pain receded into the back of Mirnían's awareness. He was tired, so tired that he could easily fall asleep on the bare rock. Now that it was over, now that Voran had single-handedly destroyed Vasyllia and dashed all their hopes, there was little left to do except die. But he remembered Lebía; he remembered their coming child; he remembered the life in Ghavan, and somehow he knew he would press on.

Voran had stopped weeping. He looked at Mirnían with eyes that seemed centuries older, eyes so green that they seemed almost mad. Voran slipped off the top of the rock, holding on to the stone with his left arm and balancing with his right.

His left arm?

"Voran, your arm!"

Voran looked confused for a moment, then looked down at his shoulder. The black fabric was clotted with blood. Voran poked his fingers into the rip made by the two arrows, and his face turned white.

"Mirnían, I am healed."

Mirnían's heart raced. He thought he understood what had happened. He got up, groaned from the pain, and hobbled to Voran, feeling more an old man than a youth of twenty-two years. He took Voran's right hand in both his own.

"No, Voran," he said, strangely elated. "You are not healed. You are the healer."

Mirnían placed Voran's right palm on his own exposed chest, and his entire body felt as though it were burned with hot irons. He screamed, but held on to Voran's wrist as if his life depended on it. It lasted a long time, but then the pain went out, like a fire extinguished by a gust of wind.

Mirnían knew that he was healed—this time completely—but to see that truth reflected in Voran's expression was glorious. Voran looked like a gleeful boy, making his wiry, sparse beard seem a storyteller's disguise. His strong features softened into a smile so full of joy, Mirnían realized he did not know the meaning of the word until he saw it in Voran's face.

"Voran," he said, unsure of the words, "I—"

"No, Mirnían," said Voran, more calm and in control than Mirnían had ever seen him. "All that is past. There is a great deal of work left to be done. A great deal of hardship to be overcome. It would be easier to overcome it all together, as family."

Mirnían felt as though an old version of himself died in that moment, and a new Mirnían arose in his place, a Mirnían who did not merely act the part of the solicitous leader, as he so often used to do in Vasyllia. At that moment, Mirnían felt ready to contain all of Vasyllia in his heart. It occurred to him that his father must have felt the same way every day of his life.

"There is something you should know, Voran. I married Lebía, and we are expecting..."

Voran grabbed him and raised him off the ground. At first, Mirnían thought that finally Voran's temper had the better of him, but there was nothing but warmth in his embrace, and then Voran laughed. It echoed over the mountains.

"My little swanling picked *you*?" He chortled.

Mirnían felt himself blush violently, something he could not remember ever doing in his life. It was very strange for their roles to be so reversed, but there was something liberating in it. He returned Voran's embrace.

"It is time, my brother. We must go," said Voran, staring over Mirnían's shoulder, his eyes illuminated by a golden light. Mirnían turned to see a majestic stag, his fur completely white, his antlers sparkling gold. It wasn't entirely *there*. It shimmered, as though it were in water.

"Will you consent to bear us to the waystone, old friend?" asked Voran.

The white stag lowered its head.

As Voran stood before the waystone, he laughed.

It was the last thing either of the giants expected, and their expressions soured.

Voran turned his back to both of them and ran to Aglaia. Even with his new strength, even with the healing flowing through him, stoked by the Sirin's flame, he was afraid to touch her. The spear point was deep in the ground, passing through her chest completely.

"Mirnían, help me," he said.

Mirnían's face was a fierce shade of green, but he came. Together, they snapped the haft of the spear in two and gently pulled her body up, until she was free of it. She gasped in pain as the blood gushed. Mirnían held his hand to his mouth, looking ready to vomit at any moment.

Voran closed his eyes and began to mouth the word—*Saddai, Saddai.* He placed both hands on the gaping wound and breathed out deeply. He reached for Tarin's stillness, deeper and deeper within, then gently nudged at his heart-flame. Aglaia's breathing was ragged, then she moaned. Voran looked down at his hands, and the blood still flowed over them.

"She is not healing," whispered Mirnían.

Voran plunged deeper within, and forced his accelerating heart to still again into the pleasant rhythm and presence of the word. He forced all thoughts to cease. When there was nothing but the word in his heart, he submitted. *Let it be as it must.*

A soft light throbbed from his hands, and Aglaia was bathed in it. Her eyes opened, wide and surprised, and she gently gasped.

"Oh," she sighed and smiled. She looked at Voran chidingly. "I think now you have paid off your debt to me, my son." Not only was there no wound on her, but her clothing was clean and untouched—a rich overdress of gold brocade, covered in jewels, like something out of an ancient tapestry. Mirnían chortled.

"That was a bit much, no?" He raised one eyebrow at Voran, and Voran shrugged his shoulders and shook his head.

Aglaia closed her eyes and fell into a deep sleep instantly, her wrinkles smoothing away to reveal the same face Voran remembered so well. Only her white hair told of her actual age.

"What have you done?" thundered Buyan. Zmei assumed a fighting stance. "Where is the Living Water?"

"It is gone. I destroyed the tree. Whatever power it left me is now gone in the healing."

Zmei roared and charged the three of them. Mirnían reached for his bow.

"No, Mirnían," whispered Voran, unfazed by the giant. "Wait."

Voran raised both his hands. Zmei jerked back in fear, as

though someone threw fire at his face. His sword out, he backed away.

"Very fine," he growled. "But do not think that trick will work for longer than a day. You shine with the power now, but it will fade. You think you have come out the winner in this game? You fool. Every darkness, every shadow, every power in this world and all the others will hunt you from this moment forward. You thought the Raven was a problem. You do not know what you have unleashed on yourself. You will see me again, soon enough."

Voran unsheathed his sword and saluted, as he would at the training field in the warrior seminary.

"I look forward to that day, Zmei." He bowed low, to his waist. When he looked up, Buyan snored, and Zmei was nowhere to be seen.

There is one thing you must never forget. No matter how evil the times, no matter how dire the calamity, if there is but one person on earth who makes Covenant with Adonais, then the world will not fall. The dawn will come after the dark night, though it lasts for centuries.

From "The Testament of Cassían, Dar of Vasyllia"
(The Sayings: Book II, 21:30)

CHAPTER 35

COVENANT

Lebía stood, as she did every morning, on the banks of the sea, waiting for Mirnían to return. For more than a year, she had seen nothing. After the baby had been born, she came with the little bundle in her arms, that simultaneous source of pain and joy, terror and courage that taught her, for the first time in her life, that she had no idea what it meant to love.

The baby gurgled something profoundly wise, and she found herself enthralled by him. Already he smiled when she looked at him, opening a toothless mouth wide and cackling in joy. *If only he would sleep a little more at night.*

When he had finished his oration, she looked up again and saw something. It was probably nothing; probably yet another trick of the light, another game of the early spring sun. Already all around her Nature was just waking to life; only she remained cold with the winter of her heart.

Then she recognized them—longboat sails. She watched in mute astonishment as two, then five, then ten, then twenty boats came into view, all of them bearing the standard of old Vasyllia—a Sirin in flight enclosed within a fiery sun.

"I will not expect it," she said aloud. "It is not my husband. He is gone from me."

Still, her heart pined and agonized and shuddered in fear. Soon the first boat came close enough for her to see the passengers at the helm. Mirnían and an older woman, hooded, stood together. She looked directly at Lebía. The wind caught and threw back the hood, revealing a face Lebía never expected to see again in her life. The face of her mother. Lebía burst into tears and lifted little Antomír above her head.

The moments of waiting were each an exuberant eternity. Lebía imagined asking them every question hoarded over months and years, felt every prick of pain and swell of joy she could have ever conceived, all in a few moments. And yet, the boats seemed to do no more than stand on the water.

Now, she was in Mirnían's arms, limp from tears of joy. Aglaia held little Antomír. She seemed a favorite of his already, and he babbled to her with all the seriousness of his three months. Mirnían could not contain himself at the sight; he tried to enclose all of them in his arms at once. Behind Mirnían, the twenty boats were filled with Vasylli.

"Who are they?" Lebía asked in wonder at their tear-streaked faces.

"They are all that remain of the true Vasylli," said Aglaia, "rescued by the Sirin from the Raven."

"We have little room on Ghavan," said Otar Svetlomír behind them, approaching Aglaia with open arms. "But we will make more."

Aglaia embraced him as an old friend, then seemed to recollect herself and fell on her knees, begging for his blessing. He put his hand on her head and pulled her close, and they sobbed together.

All of Ghavan met the refugees with cheering and wonder. Some found brothers, children, friends among them, and the dead eyes of those who had seen the Raven began to flutter with new life. Immediately, Mirnían took control of the situation and ordered that trestles be set in the center of the village, and that a great feast be prepared for the faithful Vasylli. But no sooner did he command than Lebía heard a surge of the song of the Sirin in her heart. Aína whispered to her, and only she could hear.

"Vasyllia!" exclaimed Lebía more loudly than she ever had in her life, feeling foolish and elated all at once. Everyone hushed and looked at her in surprise. "This is not the only joy for Ghavan. Come, my dear family, I must show you Vasyllia's hope."

She rushed out of the square into the woods, pulling Mirnían's hand to follow. Aglaia came, still discussing great things with little Antomír. The villagers, somewhat confused, followed a little hesitantly. They walked for what seemed like hours, but the early spring cold dissipated with their brisk pace. Finally, they reached a spruce grove, stately in silence. Hidden within the trees was a tiny white aspen, gently pulsating with light.

"Is that what I think it is?" Mirnían's eyes wide with wonder. He turned to see Lebía smiling at him proudly. "How did you know?"

"The hope of Vasyllia," whispered Otar Svetlomír. He fell on his knees before the sapling.

"We must replant it in the center of the village," said Mirnían.

"I do not know, my love," said Lebía. "It seems somehow disrespectful, no?"

"I mean to honor it, swanling. Were we not punished enough for hoarding our treasures in Vasyllia? Let us bring the tree to a place where all can see it and be filled with hope."

Filled with sudden inspiration, Mirnían walked up to the sapling and reached for the roots.

"Be gentle with it," whispered Lebía.

"I will be gentle with both of my new treasures, always."

Lebía blushed a little, like a white rose tipped with red.

Mirnían gently took the trunk near the base, and to his amazement the roots disentangled themselves from the ground and wrapped themselves around his hand.

"The blessing of the Heights is on you, Dar Mirnían," said Otar Svetlomír, his eyes brilliant in the white light.

They planted the tree in the center of the village. The roots took the earth by themselves, just as they had taken Mirnían's hand.

Lebía hesitantly touched the quivering branches of the white sapling. They thrummed with life, and she gasped in pleasure, like a child might when touching something unexpectedly cold. Suddenly, the tree grew before their eyes. Within seconds, it was a full tree, adorned with golden leaves still half-folded. The white light rose until it was hard to look at the tree directly.

"Look!" said a girl in the crowd, pointing upward.

The sky above them shimmered with red gold. Hundreds of firebirds circled the tree. A single pin-prick opened in the sky above the firebirds, and a light descended on the tree, until it seemed to burn with fire. Then Lebía realized it was no illusion. The white aspen was on fire.

Mirnían embraced Lebía. She nestled under his chin, that most comfortable of places, where she fit perfectly.

"I have so many questions, my love," she said. "But one will suffice for now. How is Voran?"

Mirnían pulled away from her and put his hands on her shoulders to look intently into her eyes.

"How did you know?" he asked.

She smiled. "We have always been bound unlike other people. I feel him like he is part of me."

Mirnían nodded, understanding. "He is well, as well as can be expected." He huffed, at a loss for words. "I do not even know where to begin."

"Where is he now?"

"He is going to Vasyllia. Sabíana waits for him, you know."

Lebía smiled. "Did he find what he sought?"

"No. He seeks still. I think he will seek always. If things were dangerous before, now they are far worse. Thank the Heights, this place is safe. No other place in the world is safe anymore."

On the next morning, before the sun rose, Lebía came one last time to the shores of the Great Sea, to take leave of that part of her life—the long wait for Mirnían—forever. She was surprised to see Aglaia standing there as well, looking out over the water.

"Mother? You are up early."

"Wolves don't sleep as humans do. They need much less." She grinned. Lebía gasped.

"*You* were the wolf that brought Mirnían? You brought me my happiness. That was you!"

"Yes, my swanling. And now, I must leave you again."

Lebía started to protest, but Aglaia silenced her with a glance, as though no time had passed at all since Lebía was a five-year-old girl. Lebía even giggled nervously.

"My poor boy needs someone," said Aglaia. "Voran has taken the healing of many on himself. But he is still so young, so inexperienced."

"Dear mother," Lebía smiled wryly. "What can an old woman do to help the greatest warrior of our age?"

"Ha!" The grin on Aglaia's face was uncomfortably wolfish. "He is nothing without me." She winked, and suddenly a wolf the size of a bear stood next to Lebía. Lebía laughed in her shock and clapped her hands like a little girl.

"Voran thinks I am a helpless old woman. He will learn to value his mother more in the future."

She leapt into the water without a backward glance. Lebía stood there, watching her turn into a black dot. In an instant that seemed to stop time itself, the rays of the sun streamed out between two distant peaks. Everything the sun touched danced with life. Lebía realized with a start that Antomír would be awake already, and poor Mirnían would have no idea what to do with a screaming baby. She turned around, hiked her skirts up, and ran back to Ghavan.

THE SONG OF THE SIRIN

THE RUSTED BLADE

A PREQUEL NOVELLA TO
THE SONG OF THE SIRIN

Chapter 1

The Warrior's Pentagon

Dust on the air rose in cloudlets from the sandy ground. It was fine, slightly sweet on Otchigen's tongue. The silence stretched, tense with the expectation of cheering. A single drop of sweat labored down Otchigen's craggy forehead. Forcing his hand not to brush it away—a warrior does not pay attention to such things—he crouched to the sand. Caressing it, he let it run through his fingers, gentler even than the soft touch of his wife. He closed his eyes and drank it all in. Ecstasy bloomed inside him.

Today was the final mock battle in the warriors' seminary of Vasyllia.

Otchigen, chief warrior of Vasyllia, Mother of Cities, stood up in the middle of the fighters' pentagon, letting the sight of it sink into his bones. The amphitheater seats of carved marble surrounding the pentagon were empty, still half-dark in morning shadow. In the distance rose the three striped and four star-embossed domes crowning the seven towers of the palace. They sparkled like burnished red gold in the summer sun.

It was the sparkle that caused his eyes to water. Yes, it was definitely the sparkle.

Further still, towering over all, the twin falls of Vasyllia plunged down either side of Vasyllia Mountain's summit, where the summer snow glistened, too intense to look at for long. Against the faint hum of the waterfalls, a single birdcall broke into the tedium of repeated sound. As though waiting for it, a choir of birds joined in, and the rest of the silence shattered around Otchigen. At that exact moment, the sun rose over the tip of the amphitheater, warming the back of Otchigen's head.

He laughed at the absurd perfection of it. This was a morning fitting for a demonstration of his young warriors' prowess.

Otchigen turned toward the sun and the deliberately missing fourth wall of the fighting pit. To fighter and viewer alike, that gap in the wall revealed all Vasyllia's three reaches extending down and outward from the heights to the long plateau before the city, cleaved by the Vasyllia River. To call it a city was to ignore the brilliance of it. The mountain itself—crags, groves, waterfall—had been molded into the service of man. Stone cliffs had been made into windowed halls. Arched bridges were carved to span canals, fed from the waters of the twin falls. Groves of wild pine had been tamed into parks and terraces, and now cherries and peaches grew between kitchen gardens set apart from each other by cobbled streets.

Let all the other cities bow in awe and wonder before the Mother of Cities, he thought.

To his left, the iron-barred central gate to the pentagon creaked open. The sandy dust blew outward, as though the seminary were a living thing breathing its warriors out into the world. Karakul walked out of the seminary and into the pit. Otchigen smiled ruefully and shook his head.

Or perhaps not. He might be champion this year. A Karilan. And a foundling to boot.

Karakul hesitated only a moment when he saw that the pentagon wasn't empty, but his angled features relaxed with the cheerful recognition that so flew in the face of the decorum of third-reach Vasyllia.

"My lord Otchigen! You are awake early."

"As are you, Karakul. But that doesn't surprise me."

Karakul blushed. It occurred to Otchigen that if a fair-skinned Vasylli's flush was like a rose suddenly blossoming against snow, then this Karilan reddened like wine poured into a brown clay cup. He had never grown out of seeing their round-bowl faces, flattened noses, and almond eyes as anything but exotic. Certainly not beautiful. But this morning, there was something fascinating about Karakul. He seemed a blood brother to the early sun, the sand underfoot, the hewn marble of the amphitheater and palace. He had their natural joy and strength. And it made him beautiful.

"Well, my mountain eagle," said Otchigen, clapping Karakul on the shoulder. He was pleased to feel the firmness of the muscle under the linen practice shirt. "The amassed greatness of the Vasylli will be cheering against you. It will be like nothing you've ever felt before. Greater men than you have crumbled under it."

Karakul chuckled and shook his head.

"Do you know what my name means in Karilan?" Karakul looked at Otchigen with eyes that caught the sun and shone unexpectedly green. "*Cursed slave.* A name given by my mother."

"I didn't know that," said Otchigen. "A strange gift she gave you. No wonder you wanted to leave Karila."

"No, lord. It was the best gift she could have given." Karakul stared at the falls thoughtfully, as though his mother was somewhere beyond Vasyllia Mountain.

There was no sarcasm in his tone. Otchigen, for the first time in as long as he could remember, had no ready response. It unnerved him.

Karakul looked away from the falls and smiled again.

"Oh, don't worry, lord. I'm going to pound that Vasylli lordling into the sand."

Two hours later, the amphitheater seating was packed with restive young warriors—each sitting with his own cohort, in the cohort's colors. The effect was as though some High Being had covered the amphitheater with six heraldic banners—red, cerulean, gold, purple, green, and gold-fringed black. The banners seethed, as though each hid a nest of hornets just waking up to the short, brilliant mountain summer of Vasyllia. Otchigen knew that as soon as the oxhorn blared, the hornets would be up and in a frenzy.

Those same hornets seemed to have woken up in his gut.

To distract himself, he looked at the first cohort in their gold-fringed black. The "Dar's Swords," they called themselves. Surely his son Voran would be there already.

Gold-haired youth after gold-haired youth avoided Otchigen's probing glance. As always, it made Otchigen simmer. He knew he cut an impressive figure with his blacksmith shoulders and the sharp contrast of his wiry black beard, thick as bear hide, with the white braid flowing down his back to his hips. The air of placid domesticity hiding a seething ferocity. It unsettled the boys, as well it should. Rare was the warrior who took it as a challenge, even rarer the man who recognized it as the first step to a warm friendship, reserved for the very few.

Come to think of it, Karakul was the last to acquire his friendship since... he couldn't even remember when.

Voran had never even try to win his father's friendship. He was too remote, too lost in his reveries, his constant inner search for... something.

Why wasn't Voran the one facing Karakul on the mock battle field? That would have been truly fitting.

Then Otchigen remembered. How could he have forgotten? With a twinge of fear tugging at his stomach, Otchigen pushed the thought aside. He had been forgetting things more and more lately.

Voran, Otchigen's only son, had been walled in the far keep of the warrior seminary for two weeks now. The so-called Ordeal of Silence. Otchigen scoffed audibly, he couldn't help himself. The Ordeal of Silence—the storytellers insisted it was the oldest and most difficult of all the warrior ordeals—was rarely practiced any more. Certainly not by 16-year old boys, no matter which reach they hailed from. No noble third-reacher ever allowed his son to attempt it. More often than not it was a second-reacher merchant-son or the rare first-reacher who took the challenge—and then, only because it promised advancement to the third reach. None of them ever made it, of course.

Come to think of it, no one had successfully completed the Ordeal of Silence for at least a hundred years.

And now not only Voran, but the Dar's own son, Prince Mirnían, had decided to brave the silence at the same time.

Otchigen almost wished that Voran had done it to prove himself to his father. Even a defiant call for attention would be welcome. But Otchigen knew that Voran did it for his own reasons, with no thought for Otchigen. Even less thought for Aglaia, his own mother, who would have gladly strewn his road to the ordeal with strawberry blossoms.

Otchigen caught himself actually growling. With an effort, he relaxed the two bunched masses of muscle on either side of his neck. *Flow like water*, he told himself, feeling the strain leech off his body down to the nervously tapping heels of his worn boots.

Mirnían, he knew, did it because he envied Voran. And for what? Did he think mooning about the forests, sleeping under the stars, communing with the winds was the measure of manhood? In Vasyllia? The Mother of Cities? Her warriors were the envy of all fighting men the world over.

The mass of hornets heaved the banners in anticipation.

Otchigen snapped into his war-awareness. The rustle of the distant falls, the creaking of gloved hand on sword-hilt, the wistful moan of a moon-bird—it all washed over him individually and as a symphony of sound. The sharp smell of sweat tickled his nostrils. The rust-fringed door from the seminary halls groaned open. It was time.

Two young warriors walked out side by side. One was resplendent in gilded scale mail over a red shirt, reaching down to the knees of wildly striped breeches of green, gold, and purple. Nevida, the son of Rudin, chief bootlicker of the third reach. Even though he wore his helmet already, the nose guard a gaudy caricature of a horse's muzzle, Otchigen still noted the glint of gold on his ear.

The idiot was already wearing his champion's earring.

Otchigen's smile warmed him to the pit of his stomach. He felt, more than saw, the cohort elders who sat near him shrink unconsciously away from that smile.

Keep the beast within, he chided himself.

Karakul, walking a bit behind Nevida, wore a tail of white horsehair in the peak of his helm. Like all Karilans, he wore no eye guard or nose guard, just a simple conical metal cap. Nor was his armor anything more than simple chain mail over leather and linen. Not a single stripe decorated his stained grey breeches, the same ones he wore to every practice bout. His boots were service-able. Nothing more.

Then he drew his sword, and all of Nevida's glitz faded as though the sun were covered in a sudden storm cloud. It was an ancient relic of Karila—a double-edged stabbing sword with a metal guard wrought into flowing shapes of waves and tongues of fire so fine, it looked as though it were grown from a tree, not pounded out of crude metal. The edges caught the morning sun and seemed to sing with it.

At the sight of the blade, half of the cohorts hissed. Of the rest, most remained restive, while only a few allowed themselves to cheer. Karakul had done so much to prove himself, and still most Vasylli couldn't forgive him for being an Otherlander.

In a flash of insight, Otchigen realized how much Karakul had trusted him by revealing the meaning of his name. One whiff of the truth, and the entire amphitheater would pelt him with his mother's gift.

Why couldn't you be my son, Karakul?

The guilt only prickled at him as the oxhorns blared. Already, the two combatants were beginning the dance of blades—each choosing a preliminary position based on their relative height, speed, and size. Nevida's stance was an insult in itself—it was a guard against axemen, most of whom were too short to earn the right of bearing a sword.

Karakul was nearly a head taller than Nevida.

For his own part, Karakul took a proper stance—one of humility before a swordmaster. But there was a hint of something about the shape of his sword-arm's sweep... at first, Otchigen couldn't place it.

With a plunge of tingling excitement, Otchigen realized that Karakul was setting Nevida up for a mighty fall.

The fighters danced.

Otchigen, in his war-awareness, missed the sweep and spectacle of the fight—the thing that made the boys in the stands alternately groan and cry out. Like a drunkard who had avoided ale for a week, he thirsted for those nearly invisible details that spoke the true language of the dance—the war dance of hand, foot, elbow, and hip.

Nevida flicked his left hand—a dagger had appeared there as if from nowhere—in a languid attempt at undercutting Karakul's sword arm. Karakul's right knee pushed, relaxed, flexed, then tensed. Otchigen gasped as he saw the move before it even came— a stag-like leap away from Nevida. But he still managed to nick Nevida's left ear with a vicious slash that the Vasylli had never expected. A spray of blood adorned the sand. Karakul leaned back, but the tension in his hip—Otchigen had seen the same anticipation in the body of a Karilan dancer at market day once— proved he was about to leap forward. As Nevida lunged, sure that he had caught Karakul off balance, Karakul spun out of his range of motion, sweeping his blade down as he landed. It sliced down the back side of Nevida's right shoulder.

The Vasylli lordling's blade clattered to the sand, raising a puff of dust.

The fight was over.

The entire city seemed to fall silent.

But something was wrong. No matter what the boys thought about Karakul, the mastery he displayed should outweigh any pettiness. He was their brother after all, even if an Otherlander. Where was the cheering?

Otchigen turned his head around toward the palace.

His heart stopped for a moment. Prince Mirnían stood in the royal box—a turret like an eyrie overlooking the fighters' pentagon. It was carved out of a single block of marble in the shape of an outspreading crown of oak. Like a flower in bloom, the seat of the Dar crowned the top of the tree. Mirnían, with his pale green face and stooping demeanor, looked like a blight on that tree's perfection.

Otchigen silently chided himself for the thought. But the prince looked terrible. His usual grace—the kind that equally attracted the admiration of women and men—was marred. As though a perfectly-shaped peach-colored rose had a single brown petal curling in on itself in the center of the bud, ruining the whole picture.

Metal rang against metal. For a moment, Otchigen was confused, and his head spun as he tried to orient his bulk relative to the new, wrong noise. It was in the pentagon. Nevida had picked up his sword and had attacked Karakul again. Karakul reeled, clearly taken aback.

Nevida had not only broken every rule of decency. He had trampled on the code of the warrior seminary.

And no one protested. Most were taken with the sudden appearance of Mirnían, while a few clearly approved of Nevida's act.

With a stab of guilt and fear in his gut, Otchigen realized...

If Mirnían is here, where is Voran?

But he hadn't any time to follow that thought. He got up, the muscles in his legs tense, even quivering. He raised his right hand and drew breath to call a halt to the fight.

A fleshy hand, with only a vestige of former strength, squeezed his right shoulder.

Elder Pahomy, his five chins quivering, stood at Otchigen's right. He was a full head taller than Otchigen. Coupled with his immense girth, he was a sight that could shake the bravest warrior. The cohort elder shook his head. *Later,* his angry eyes seemed to say. Otchigen wasn't sure who would be the recipient of the elder's wrath—he himself, Nevida, or the entire third reach.

Otchigen's head darted back in the direction of the fight. For a shade of a moment, Karakul met Otchigen's glance. The eyes burned with joy. He wanted the dance to continue.

"Very well," said Otchigen to Elder Pahomy. "It's on *your* head, though."

"Do not crown a winner before his time," said Elder Pahomy. His voice was strained with the effort to keep down his anger.

For a brief moment, Otchigen remembered Pahomy in his youth—a lithe, deer-like fighter whose dance was deadlier than a snake's bite. What had happened to him? What had happened to all of them? With a sigh, Otchigen turned back to the fight that had been marred for him. Short of actually killing an opponent— an offense that would result in immediate execution, like a rabid dog being put down—Nevida could not have committed a worse crime in the eyes of the seminary. There was nothing noble in the continuation of such a battle, no matter how much Karakul seemed to thirst for it. It was a dirty thing.

This will taint all of us.

It was an unworthy thought, but like the lingering aftertaste of spoilt milk, Otchigen failed to purge it.

Nevida seemed to be winning now. He attacked with blinding speed, so fast that Otchigen could no longer anticipate his motions from the cues of his body. A lunge—Karakul bled from his arm. A perfect feint, disengage, slash, undercut—Karakul bled from two more places. A charge, then a leap back, then a punishing swipe on an overcommitted Karakul—the tide of the battle had turned the other way.

Otchigen forced himself to concentrate. Yes. Now he saw it. Although Karakul was bleeding from several livid gashes in both arms and in his left leg, his face was still as a pool of rainwater on a spring morning. More importantly, he still held his blade.

The peace seemed to radiate down into his fingers, which firmed with every second back into controlled grasps, into his elbows, which flowed like water again, unimpeded by jutting stones. And then his feet—they were hart's feet.

Nevida's mask of triumph slipped. In the shuddering of his weight-bearing leg, in the stripe of wet across his temples, in the barely-noticeable lowering of his blade's tip—he was terrified of Karakul.

Bad idea, idiot.

Karakul had seen it.

Then came Nevida's mistake. He overextended himself slightly. It was enough.

Otchigen held his breath in awe as Karakul, in spite of his wounds, counterattacked. In three quick slashes, he had Nevida on his heels. Otchigen had never seen such mastery with a blade. It wasn't taught. Karakul seemed possessed by a power of Aer.

Nevida's blade fell with a double clatter. It had broken in two. For a moment, Otchigen marveled at Karakul's powerful blow. But a twist in his stomach made him reconsider. No, nothing Karakul did would have broken Nevida's blade. It was an omen.

The ultimate dishonor. An omen of Adonais's divine displeasure.

The amphitheater groaned in mixed excitement and horror.

Nevida, at that moment, collapsed into a heap of flesh and tears. It was pitiful. It was shameful. It could not be borne.

"Get up, you filth!" cried Otchigen. "Get up! You shame your people with your self-pity! Up! Get up!"

The roar of the waterfalls rose in volume. Rose. Rose. Rose. It was a thunder in his ears. He could almost feel the spray on his face.

Otchigen came back to himself, what seemed only a moment later.

Nevida's bloodied face lay in sand at Otchigen's feet. Blood dripped from Otchigen's lacerated knuckles. Somehow, he had ended up in the middle of the pentagon. How had he gotten there? Why was there blood on his hands?

Karakul's touch was like a summer thunderstorm that broke the heat into shards of hail.

"Lord, not this. Not this," he said, pulling him away.

Had he just beaten one of the boys?

He looked up in horror. All those eyes. They looked at him.

Mirnían was there too, in the pentagon. How had he gotten there so quickly?

With a look of both hatred and understanding, Mirnían turned away from Otchigen.

Mirnían stooped to help the shuddering Nevida up to his feet, who was still blubbering, spluttering something incomprehensible through a bloody mouth. Mirnían hushed him with a look and a hand around the shoulder. The prince's greenish tinge was gone, replaced by that forceful glance that could sway even the strongest heart. With a final look and a shake of the head, Mirnían turned Nevida toward the seminary and walked away.

CHAPTER 2

THE COLD HEARTH

Otchigen's heart beat so slowly that it seemed barely able to keep him alive. He lumbered through the palace forecourt—another pentagon, but this one larger, stone-flagged, filled with tight knots of brightly-dressed courtiers and black-robed cohort elders gathered higgledy-piggledy in a constant half-dance. They reminded Otchigen of marionettes on a storyteller's stage. It took an effort of will for him *not* to think they were all looking at him, or at least whispering about him. To distract himself, he tried to imagine the feast in the Dar's hall going on without him.

There would be long tables, garlanded and bedecked in towering creations almost too fanciful to eat—baked pies made to look like leaping stags, filled with twelve layers of delicacies like swan, saffron-spiced boar, perch, pike, even mountain goat. The aromas of the cinnamon-tinged mead tickled his memory. Maybe there would even be braggot from Karila to commemorate Karakul's victory. Just thinking of its sour-sweet taste made the back of his tongue curdle with anticipation.

And he would miss it all.

Though the food was only a small part of it. What he would miss most was the stirring warmth in the chest as the singing began after the fourth or fifth goblet, an invisible golden thread uniting all the men under the Dar's roof into a single unit, a brotherhood, a family. It was a feeling no less intense than the love between him and Aglaia.

Or at least their love as it had been only a few years before.

But that way lay confusion and darkness. Better to think of the grainy consistency of the granite flagstones under his feet.

For some reason, the wrought iron of the palace gates commanded his attention. Something about them was different today. Perhaps it was the heaviness of their black sheen, which seemed a bright, happy color compared to the numbness in his chest. Or maybe some mystery hid in the leaf-work interwoven with fine abstractions of sea beasts, mountain eagles, and fanciful chimaeras. There was one creature in particular—a raven in flight with a man's face and a beak instead of a nose—that allured and revolted him at the same time.

He tore his eyes away and almost tripped over the guards at the gates. They didn't turn to look at him, though their lowered face guards could have hidden any sarcastic expression well enough.

It was his imagination, surely. But he'd thought that he had heard a kind of music when he contemplated that raven-figure. A sinuous, alluring dance music, something that might be played on a viol, accompanied by a drum with a steadily increasing beat. A music that, once it took hold of you, would make you dance until you fell from exhaustion, and even then, it might force you to dance on.

Why in the Heights did I think of that?

He was hardly a musical man. That was his elfin daughter Lebía's area of interest.

Again, the thought whispered in his ear, nibbling at it like a rat in a cellar: "*You are going mad, Otchigen.*"

He hardly looked up from the rest of the cobblestoned road, trudging from the palace to his family's ancestral home. It crowned the highest mound of the third reach of Vasyllia. He felt, more than saw, the looming shapes of two- and three-story wooden mansions, each with windows and eaves carved no less fancifully than the gates of the palace. Even when the houses stood long distances away from the main road that wound through the hanging gardens of the third reach, he felt them as though the windows were eyes, each pair more judgmental than the next.

With disgust at his own morbidness, he forced himself to consider the one constant in his life. His hearth. The ancient symbol of married love. Yes, it *was* true that in recent months Aglaia had not been herself and had let the orderliness of the house slip a bit. One day it might be dinner offered half an hour later than usual. Just last week, she had forgotten to give him his cup of smoky tea before the storytelling at the hearth on the night of Temple. That had annoyed him, but he had not let it show. Not too much. Or the day Voran was to start the Ordeal of Silence, a day when he had made it clear that every room should shine in cleanliness. The state of the dinner table that evening was... well, Aglaia did complain of a headache that evening.

Come to think of it, she had been complaining of aches and pains for a long time now. Fah! She was always prey to such fancies. Otchigen was sure that if she wanted it strongly enough, she would be well in a day. One good night of sleep, one day of leaving things to the servants, not controlling their every move, one day in the fresh mountain air—she would be good as new, he knew it.

He approached the cherry groves that surrounded his estate. The trees were blushing and frothing with white flowers edged in pink. The closer he came, the more their subtle, sweet fragrance wove itself into the ever-present smell of mountain pine and the freshness of the falls, closer here than in the palace. Every once in a while, teasing like a lover, the smoke from his kitchen topped it all. The smells suffused him with peace, even more than usual. He thought he heard the clanging of cutlery and the creaking of the spit—partridge, perhaps, or maybe even game hens with that berry wine sauce he loved so much.

He nearly ran through the terraced back garden, where the tomatoes were only just beginning to flower, and the trailing cucumbers were already reaching their tendrils around the wooden stakes placed in the loamy earth. Oh, how he wanted to bite that first ripe tomato, to salt it, to drink it down with sour ale. But they were still green and puny. He would have to content himself with the goblet of wine that Aglaia would surely have ready for him. She knew he would be tired. She had probably not heard of his... mistake... in the pentagon. But she was sure to feel his distress from afar. She always did on such days, when nothing went as it should, when the perfection of the day's order collapsed in chaos around him.

The door to the house was locked.

That was strange. Surely Aglaia, or any of the servants for that matter, would have known that he preferred to come home the back way. It was an unspoken rule that everyone abided by.

They're not expecting me home for at least another hour. Yes, that must be it.

He beat on the door with his fist.

Nothing happened.

He beat again, more loudly this time.

Something crashed far inside, then he heard the unmistakable voice of Her Lardship Verina—the best cook in Vasyllia, who, contrary to all expectations and, indeed, her own nickname, was skinny as a stalk of barley. Her voice barked, more strident than usual, growing louder with every second.

Surely Her Lardship won't open the door herself. What are the maids and manservants for, then?

It *was* Her Lardship who opened the door. Her face, which was red from anger, flashed white when she saw him. Normally, that sort of quick shift in her face would have made him laugh, but his anger was beyond simmering now. It was all he could do to keep his voice calm.

"My dear Verina, what in Adonais's holy name are you doing opening the back door?"

She spluttered, her mouth opened, but nothing but a croak came out.

Otchigen's mouth twisted into a knot that matched the two larger ones forming in his shoulders.

"What is going on? Something's wrong, isn't it?"

"Wrong?" Her voice came back, but it cracked as it did. "No more than usual. Not since..."

"Is my lady taken to her bed *again*?"

A strange expression flitted across Her Lardship's face. Otchigen didn't recognize it. It may have been... sorrow? She was never anything but determined and single-mindedly unswerving. What was going on in his own house?

"This is ridiculous." He said it more for himself than the cook, and felt abashed immediately. He stepped past her into the damp, pleasant coolness of the wine cellar. "Well, I'll deal with it later. Come, since you're here, you must take a flagon of my father's best. Today is a day for celebration." His heart pinched at the memory of Nevida's bloody face. He winced. "A celebration. We have a new champion at the seminary. And do you know who, Verina? Karakul! I told you, didn't I? I told you he'd be the one..." He turned around, but Her Lardship wasn't following him. She still stood at the doorway, staring at him with an expression he couldn't see because of the sunlight behind her. "Are you even listening to me, Verina?"

"Are you listening to yourself? You're chattering like a fifteen-year-old girl. Are you even aware of what's going on in your house?" That tone he knew. Chilling disapproval. He knew how to deal with it.

"Yes, yes, Verina, you've always been the expert on all things *outside* the kitchen as well as within it. But what you couldn't possibly—"

She actually interrupted him. "Don't use that tone with me. Not today. Not when your lady...*your lady!*"

She burst into tears and ran past him back into the kitchen.

"Verina, the wine!" Surely, she was overreacting. He had seen Aglaia that morning before he left. She was a bit pale, yes, but she hadn't slept well. All easy enough to explain. "Never mind. I'll get it myself."

In rising anger, Otchigen walked through the open doorway into the long hearth-hall, the center of the house, and in many ways the center of his heart. Here, he lounged every evening in a specially-made rocking chair carved from birch. Here he had rocked Lebía to sleep every night when she was a small thing that hardly fit across his forearm. Here he told tales every Temple night as the hearth-fire played with the shadows thrown back by the carved pillars holding up the lofts of the second story, making every shadow into a monster or a hero or a Sirin in flight.

The hearth was cold. The wood was frosted over with day-old ash. There was dust on the columns.

The servants had not lit the hearth since last night.

That was the final straw.

CHAPTER 3

A STRONG WOMAN

Aglaia lay in their shared bed, which was raised above the ground on four posts—a rare innovation among the Vasylli. She was in her night-shift of pale linen, propped up with what looked like every single pillow in the house. Her hair wasn't done. It flowed down her shoulders in an oily mess, framing her face. She did look worse than this morning. The livid spots on her cheek hadn't been there before.

She turned her dark eyes at him. They had nothing of sickness in them. Only the stubborn patience of a wife who is about to listen to a litany of complaints from a peevish husband.

Every time. Every time he recognized that she knew what was coming. Every time his heart prompted him to calm himself, to let things be. But no. Every time, the fire in his chest got the better of him.

How dare she look at me like that? Doesn't she know? Doesn't she understand the stresses of life as a Voyevoda, the right hand of the Dar?

He needed no preamble. Her eyes let him know that she had already conducted the preliminary part of the conversation in her own thoughts.

"Do I ask so much of you, my love?" Though he was sure of

the answer, he didn't stop to hear it. "Am I one of those boorish third-reacher husbands who expect their wives to be in the kitchen with the cooks at all hours of the day, who demand things to be done on a schedule, who never let their wives outside the sewing room? I am a generous husband. A loving husband. Am I not?"

"You are, my husband." There was hardly a pause in the middle of that phase, so he wasn't sure if she was agreeing with him or merely admitting the fact of their marriage. It pricked him and goaded him on.

"You know what an important day this is. Not for me only. It's not my comfort I'm talking about here. It's the day. On this day, of all days, was it so hard to ask the servants to bring the house at least to some semblance of order?"

"Otchigen, they were with me all morning. And I didn't expect you for another—"

"You know well enough you wouldn't have managed to get it all ready in time. You needed the entire morning to bring things merely back to normal! And what if I had brought back someone from the seminary with me?"

"You're right, my love. It's my fault. I—"

"I only want a few things, you know that. How many times..." He sighed as his heart constricted in a vise. They began so many of their arguments like this. It was almost pointless to continue. But the thorn pricking him wouldn't allow him to stop. "You know how I am after a day at the seminary. I only want a few things. A bit of food. A warm hearth. A door that isn't shut and locked against its master as though he were a common thief." The memory of the cellar door being locked only stoked the fire in his chest. If only his hearth was half as large as that fire...

"Is that true, Verina?" asked Aglaia placidly, her manner unruffled, as it always was during their arguments. Verina almost crawled from the doorway where she had been standing, half-concealed.

"Yes, lady. It's my fault."

"Can we please have this conversation without any servants?" Otchigen's voice rose in pitch with every word, until he was almost barking the last word.

Aglaia's eyes went round, and she breathed deeply. He knew that reaction as well. This was not going to be a good conversation.

When Verina and the maid had gone, Otchigen began pacing back and forth, kicking up the fresh rushes on the floor as he went. With the corner of his eyes, he noticed an unfamiliar brass basin by her bed, filled with some kind of liquid. He turned around and didn't give it another thought. Finally, when the fire inside him was like a lightning bolt, he turned to her, looming over her.

"Don't you love me? I give my life to you. I am always ready to give you anything you need. I've always tried to anticipate your needs even before you see them yourself. Have you forgotten the second-day dress?" It was their own private joke. Whenever he felt particularly generous or wanted to help around the house, he would ask her to wear the dress she wore the day after their wedding. It was a dress spectacularly unsuited to any housework. She could hardly move in it, it had so much gold thread in it. He would ceremoniously seat her on his own rocking chair, bring her tea, and rub her feet. "Well? You haven't had a chance to put it on in the last few months? Is that it?"

She almost rolled her eyes, but stopped herself. He was too far ahead of himself to react.

"All I ask is a few things, you know that. On this day, of all days, could you not have—"

"Otchigen, my love." The accent on the word "love" was filled with years upon years of long-suffering. It made him even more angry. "I am not well. It's worse today. Verina even—"

"Aglaia, you are such a strong woman. Cannot you just..." He wanted to say it aloud. Something prevented him.

Aglaia's brows were drawn together and she hunched over

slightly, her eyes inward and distant. Otchigen immediately felt guilty.

"I'm sorry, my love. You know I want the best for you, yes? I've already had the best doctors, the Dar's own leech. You know they say that there's nothing wrong with your body. All you need is—"

"Don't tell me what I need." Her voice cracked like a whip. His heart plunged at the emotion behind her words. There was something foreign there. Had they really grown so far apart?

"I only want..."

"It's not about what you want, Otchigen. If you think I'm inventing an illness for my own feminine reasons—you'd be mad to think it—but go ahead and say it." The accent on the word "feminine" dripped with irony. He could hardly recognize his wife in that tone.

He wanted to say it. Terribly. Every muscle in his body clenched in his desire to say it.

He did not say it.

"Otchigen, what will it take for you to believe your own wife? I am very ill."

He sighed, but said nothing. He sat on the bed, but felt her recoil from him.

The silence grew between them like a rent in the earth that formed after an earthquake. She seemed to be struggling with something. Nodding suddenly, as though she had reached some fateful decision, she began to undo the clasps of her linen shift.

"What are you doing?" Otchigen jumped up with the swiftness of his younger self. "I don't want to..."

Her look silenced him. Usually, that look had an edge of irony that could diffuse all his bluster. But it wasn't there today.

She continued undoing her shift and revealed the upper part of her chest. It had reddish spots, almost lesions, on it. Then she raised her sleeves. The same strange lesions marked both arms all the way to the elbow.

So now she had taken to burning herself with hot irons? Was this some kind of ancient, heathen healing practice?

"Is it like those... what are they? Mustard wraps?" he asked, not able to keep the disdain from his voice.

Something in her eyes died. That was the only way he could explain it to himself. And he realized what a blunder he had made.

"My love, I didn't realize—"

"No," she said, in an expression of such profound despair that he wanted to claw his own eyes out. "You haven't realized much of anything these past..."

She let it fade away. Then she turned away from him, hugging herself.

He reached a hand to her, wanting to caress her, to take her in his arms, to kiss her, to promise her everything would be well, that they were one person, not two, that they could weather any storm...

But he didn't.

He turned away from her, sighed, and walked out of the room.

He stopped, his body shivering in the aftermath of the fire in his chest, and stared at the still-cold hearth-hall. The bear-head carvings that joined the vaulted roof to the columns snarled at him with a hint of laughter. The hole in the ceiling, which some idiot artist in his grandfather's employ had decided should look like the sun, looked more like an accusing eye. He had never understood the artist's intention. There were rays painted in cracking gold and vermillion extending outward from the opening. But the effect was never achieved, because the house was built in such a way that the mountain headwall prevented the sun from ever shining from that direction.

Another failure for a moribund house, he thought.

The servants scurried all over the room—either like rats or like beetles, he couldn't decide which—picking up bits of refuse, dusting the corners, trying to light some kind of fire in the hearth, which for the life of it wouldn't light. As soon as the fire in his chest went out, every fiber of his body's muscles felt leaden. He lurched toward his rocking chair, holding on to its back for a moment, considering whether to sit or not.

The fire in his chest having faded, as it always did, it left behind a gaping abyss that ached to be filled with anything. But nothing would fit in it. It was hungry, insatiable. Excuses for his behavior welled up in his mind, but they tumbled into the abyss in his chest and disappeared, leaving only heaviness in his limbs and numbness in his mind.

He sat down with a groan. The chair creaked, as though complaining of his bulk. One of the servants brought the flagon of wine he had brought up from the cellars himself, placing it on the four-legged table that sat just at his right elbow, perfect for plates of food and cups to be reached easily, without any exertion.

Wine? Now? Have all the servants lost their minds?

With a barely-suppressed roar, he hurled the table, the flagon, and the wine across the room. It shattered as brilliantly in the light of the sputtering hearth as a shower of falling stars on a clear winter night.

The servant, sobbing quietly, ran away.

Otchigen didn't even have the energy to call her back to clean up his mess.

What a mess he had made.

Aglaia was sick. Very sick. He should have known it. Why had he persisted in his stupidity? Why had he thought it was just a plea for attention or a feminine fancy or... something? He didn't seem to know which way was up anymore. His thoughts rattled in his mind like rabid dogs in a cage, heedless of the wounds they received every time they threw their bodies against the bars. He wanted to sleep. He wanted to forget.

But the abyss in his chest kept eating and eating, leaving behind nothing but the guilt, the heaviness.

He didn't even rock the chair, staying still as death. He had acted. Look where that had gotten him. She was sick; she needed rest. He had probably exhausted her to her limit. Oh, why was he such a thick-skulled fool? His own darling wife! His own beloved lady!

He moaned.

A slight creak across the hall roused him. It wasn't the servants. It was someone trying not to be seen.

"Is that you, Lebía?" he whispered, as he would to a skittish deer that he wanted to feed from his hand.

A shadow twitched across the hall, between two of the central pillars. The bears holding those columns didn't sneer. They seemed to be mourning. The crouched-over shadow rocked back and forth, softly crying.

"My girl, please, come here. Come to me." Otchigen rose so clumsily that the rocking chair fell backward and clattered on the ground, overturning another table with a candlestick on it, adding to the general racket.

The shadow jumped in terror and ran away. Otchigen had just enough time to see the disheveled head of his eight-year-old daughter as she fled from her own father, as though he were a monster.

"Lebía, I'm your father! Come back here at once."

There was no answer. Only a door opening and slamming shut somewhere on the other side of the house.

Otchigen, like a marionette with its strings suddenly sheared, fell in a heap against the wall. A tapestry twisted uncomfortably behind him. He turned around to see the mounted figure of a Vasylli warrior baring steel at a writhing serpent under his piebald steed's upraised hoof.

"I have always sought to be that warrior," he said to himself aloud. "The ideal of manly virtue. To allow the idea of Vasyllia to be reflected, however poorly, in my efforts. But have I stooped to the serpent's level today?"

"My Lord Otchigen!"

It was an unfamiliar voice, at least at first. Otchigen had never heard it in the comfort of his own home. As he turned to find the speaker, he placed the voice. It was Rogdai, one of the wardens of the main gates of Vasyllia. A bearded swordsman, head uncovered, his black and gold livery smeared with grease and badly wrinkled. At Otchigen's look, his face twisted into an abashed sneer, the kind of subservient, insinuating look that Otchigen deplored. He knew Rodgai's type. Never one to do anything more than the minimum of what was expected of him. Not a true warrior, he.

"Yes?" Otchigen asked, feeling the stiffness of his no longer young body. "What is it?"

"The Dar requests your presence. There's been an embassy from Karila. Something about an omen. And an army of nomads amassing in the Steppelands."

CHAPTER 4

THE RUSTED BLADE

O tchigen didn't bother to change. He was already in his ceremonial best, though his clothes seemed to have gone through the same ordeal his soul had undergone during this past day. The golden embroidery of suns and moons and stars on the pale grey silk looked more like faded copper wire. He considered putting on a cloak edged in the ermine of his office but, even in the evening, the heat was oppressive, as though the air itself had fled to the wine cellars to wait for night.

As he walked out his front entrance, he was struck dumb by the sunset. The summer sky was streaked with bands of clouds that darkened in color from pale orange to wine-red the farther they rose from the far line of peaks which served Vasyllia instead of a horizon. The air just above him pulsed with darkness, as though a great beast were pushing down toward the mountain ridges, waiting for night to overwhelm Vasyllia. Only the flickering flames on the Covenant Tree, barely visible in the Temple Plain far below him in the first reach, sought to push that darkness back. But the white flames on the aspen sapling were low. Soon it would be the time for the annual Summoning of Fire, when the priests invoked fire from the Heights as pledge of the continuation of the Covenant between the creator Adonais and Vasyllia. Until then, it seemed that Vasyllia was vulnerable.

"My Lord Otchigen? Shall we?" Rogdai waited amid the flowering cherries, his face indistinct in the evening murk.

You wait on my convenience, soldier, not the other way around. Otchigen's thought was almost accompanied by a growl, but he managed to stop it in time. The sunset, as though in concert with his darkening mood, lost its luster. It was nothing more than a few clouds in a darkling sky. Nothing ominous. Nothing to wonder at.

To Otchigen's surprise, Rogdai led him through the palace, past the Dar's personal tower, to the Chamber of Counsel. It was unusual for the Dar to use that room without the Dumar, the forty self-important representatives of the three reaches of Vasyllia, in attendance. But surely the Dumar would not need to be summoned for a report from an ambassador. Especially from Karila.

At that thought, his face flushed with embarrassment. How could he still think so little of Karila? Especially after it had given Vasyllia a champion for the ages?

Dim and colorless was the fresco of the Covenant Tree on the far wall, meeting the ceiling at a sharp peak. No light filtered through the multi-colored glass windows. The only light in the room came from three braziers near the thrones at the far end of the hall. Dark shadows cavorted along the empty galleries of dark-stained wood where the Dumar usually sat in attendance. The Dar's throne of white marble was strangely empty. For a moment, Otchigen even stopped walking, fearing that he had been led into some sort of a trap. But his good sense came back when he saw that Dar Antomír sat on the lower seat of malachite, usually reserved for Prince Mirnían.

So, this was a very informal meeting, after all. Why had Rogdai suggested it was so urgent?

Then Otchigen came close enough to see the Dar's face, and he redoubled his pace.

Dar Antomír looked as though he had aged ten years in a day. He was no young man at sixty-seven years of age, but he had always been youthful. One of those who age early but then don't change in appearance for the next forty or fifty years. He had always had a back like an iron pike, the corded muscles in his neck hinting at what must be a warrior's body, even in his twilight years. But what had always astounded newcomers were his eyes. They were almost ice blue, though soft and gentle, and they laughed even when his overly bushy brows met in the middle of his forehead. They were not so much young as ageless. It was no wonder that some of the first-reachers actually believed that he would live forever, ushering Vasyllia into a legendary golden age.

But now, his eyes had actually changed color. Or rather, they seemed to have lost the blue. They were grey, made all the drabber by the sharp red of the several spots in the whites of his eyes. Though he sat with his back propped against hard stone, he stooped. This was a different man.

What could have wrought such a change overnight?

"Ah, my dear friend. Good to see that you... are yourself again."

The Dar's voice strained barely perceptibly. Where was the usual spark of joy at seeing Otchigen? Where was the implicit endless well of shared memories of camaraderie and warrior intimacy?

With a plunge of his heart into his gut, Otchigen realized that his misdeed at the testing of the warriors was probably at least partially at fault for the Dar's distress. But surely not for the sudden aging?

At the foot of the dais stood a nondescript man in a dark kaftan cinched with a multi-colored woven rope. He turned his head only toward Otchigen. The same round face, flat features, and angled eyes that Karakul boasted, but with a full, dark beard streaked with white. His eyes were nothing like Karakul's brilliant hazel. These were brown like slabs of dusty stone. In fact, everything about him was almost calculated to mislead the eye into thinking that he was not worth anyone's notice.

"My sword and my heart are yours, Highness," said Otchigen formally, surprised at the hoarseness of his voice. He fell to his right knee and bowed his chin to his chest. "Though unworthy, I crave the Dar's love and honor his call."

"We can talk about your unworthiness later," said a different voice from the half-darkness to the Dar's right. It was reedy and nasal. With a gurgle of disgust in the pit of his stomach, Otchigen recognized the willowy and dark-bearded figure of Kalun, the chief priest of Adonais. Obsessed with external piety, condescending in his manner even to the Dar, he was possibly Otchigen's least favorite person in Vasyllia. After Nevida, that is.

"Not now, Otar Kalun," said Antomír with a brief flash of his usual liveliness. "I need Otchigen's council. You are here as a courtesy, and to witness."

The cleric's face darkened visibly, even in the smoky light of the braziers. Otchigen chortled into his nose, just loud enough to be heard. Kalun pretended not to hear a thing, though the flush of crimson across his high cheekbones was evidence enough of his excellent hearing.

"Otchigen!" the Dar snapped into his military-command voice. Otchigen responded instinctively by freezing in place and slapping his hand on the hilt of his longsword. "This is Sagynduk. Our father appointed him Special Envoy to Vasyllia from the Karilans."

"Your father?" Otchigen goggled. The man didn't look older than forty. But to be of Dar Mirolov's reign... He would have to be eighty years old at least. What was going on here? There was something he wasn't being told. "Highness. Am I to understand that all Karilans enjoy such blessed longevity?"

Antomír barked a laugh, and in that brief moment, he was himself again. But anxiety reasserted itself in the body of his friend almost instantly.

"No, my dear friend. I did say *Special* Envoy, did I not?"

The emphasis was significant, though at first Otchigen was flummoxed by it. Something he was supposed to remember, something important. Something secret and dangerous.

Then it came back to him. Immediately, he felt the blood drain from his face.

"Has it been stolen then?" his voice was hushed, but more from strain than the lack of it. "Vohin Rodgai said something about nomad armies in the Steppes?"

"No, it has not been stolen," said the man named Sagynduk in a thick Karila accent. His voice was even younger than his body and higher pitched than Otchigen expected. Resonant. Like a horn to Antomír's deep bell-like bass. "Much worse. It has rusted through."

Otchigen's eyelids opened wide involuntarily. With a rush of excitement, he tasted the war-wind. How good it would be to face an enemy again. It had been too long. With a deep breath, he focused into his war-awareness.

"Special Envoy to Vasyllia"—the name was a bit of a joke, though the person himself was anything but. He never came to Vasyllia, never left Karila. No one in Karila even knew what he did, though the ruling council of Karila honored him even more than the noble families, even more than the families of clerics and healers, who were especially honored in Karila above all other cities. He was the keeper of the greatest bond between Karila and Vasyllia. In fact, it was probably the only thing that kept Karila from consummating its ever-present desire for independence from the hegemony of Vasyllia.

This bond was a sword—ancient, long-bladed in the Vasylli manner, and in all respects perfect. Legends held that it was given to Lassar, unifier of the Three Cities and blessed ally of the Harbinger, by that High Being on the occasion of the swearing of Covenant between Vasyllia and the Heights of Aer. Vasyllia received proof of the Covenant in the form of the flaming sapling whose fire never died, ever fed by the annual Summoning of Fire from the Heights. Karila received the Blade of Covenant, and it was said that while the blade remained in Karila, untouched, no war would touch Karila.

And so it had been.

If the blade had rusted, it could mean that Karila would try to separate itself from the Brotherhood of Cities. And that meant war between Vasyllia and Karila. Otchigen's excitement cooled when he realized that if that were to happen, Karakul would certainly fight against Vasyllia. They might even meet in open battle. Otchigen's enthusiasm for the war-wind died down considerably at that thought.

"So the blade is of human provenance after all," said Kalun in a voice as though he were trying to hide a guilty pleasure. "So much for the legends."

Sagynduk spat at the cleric's foot. Everyone froze in shock, even the Dar.

"Blasphemy, even from the mouth of a man called Otar, is still blasphemy."

Kalun's entire body seemed ready to lunge at the diminutive Karilan.

"Sagynduk, perhaps you have—" began the Dar.

"I am old, Highness. And now I smell the dung of my years. No time for... ceremony." He gave the last word all the disdain his slight figure could muster. "Far has Vasyllia fallen indeed, if her Father-Otar does not recall the prophecy of the Harbinger to the Karila.

> *'Bright is the blade, and sharp the edge*
> *Of love and honor between souls.*
> *But rusted blade shall be the sign*
> *That Covenant's last hour tolls.'"*

Otchigen had never heard that particular prophecy. He doubted that it was written down in *The Sayings* at all. Kalun's bemused face seemed to confirm his suspicion.

"I do not doubt your word, Sagynduk," said the Dar carefully. "But my friend Otchigen may. And I rely on his wisdom, sometimes more than on my own."

The rest remained unsaid. Otchigen knew that the Dar placed some sort of vast hope on his shoulders.

If only he knew what to say.

"Sagynduk...Forgive me, I do not know the proper honorific..."

Sagynduk looked ready to spit again, and his eyes blazed. Otchigen was reminded of Karakul's inner fire, and he decided that he liked this strange man. Spitting and all.

"Who am I to doubt the word of an Envoy, of one on whom the Harbinger's word lies heavily," Otchigen said, with an attempt at the pattern of speech that Karakul had tried to teach him once. The way a commoner might speak to a priest. It was the highest honor he could offer to the strange man.

Sagynduk's mouth twitched briefly. It was the only indication that he smiled. Otchigen considered it enough encouragement to go on.

"Your coming to the Mother of Cities cannot sit easily on your back. Not with your burden, never to be lain down. Tell me, is it the rusted blade alone that troubles your peace, or did I hear rumors of war? A nomad army in the Steppes?"

He couldn't help that a note of incredulity crept into the last sentence. The mere suggestion that any nomad chieftain could ever stop fighting his own family members long enough to actually gather a war party, much less an army, was laughably ridiculous.

Sagynduk looked into Otchigen's eyes for a long time. As he did, his own blazing eyes softened, and something like pity seemed to simmer deep inside them. Otchigen began to twitch under their long scrutiny.

"It would be unheard-of, I agree. But the rumors persist. Not a week passes that a merchant does not return to Karila with half his wares stolen, dark stories of armies massing among uniting clans. But that may be nothing more than gossip. What I do know is that the Ruling Council of the Seven, I tell you this in all confidence, is on the brink of declaring martial law. If that happens..."

"Then they will break the alliance with Vasyllia." The Dar finished the sentence for him.

It was part of the old agreement between city-states. Only Vasyllia had the right to declare martial law for any of the Three Cities.

"What if Vasyllia pledges her own armies to fight this nomad danger?" Otchigen asked.

"We would need incontrovertible proof," the Dar said doubtfully. "Judging by everything you have already told me, I would not send anyone to Karila. You will forgive me, Sagynduk, but it sounds like your city is merely chafing at her collar. Would you suggest that your people have just found an excuse for something they have desired for a long time?"

"You mean separation from the so-called Brotherhood of Cities? I am no politician. But you may be right."

For a long time, no one said anything, every man lost in his own thoughts.

"What is it that the tales say?" said Otchigen, attempting a lighter tone. "The morning is wiser than the evening? Sagynduk is tired from his journey."

"Yes, of course," said Dar Antomír, visibly relieved. "The best steam room of the palace, a chamber of your own in my personal tower. You will dine with me as well, I insist."

Sagynduk looked about ready to explode into a tirade of contrary words, but he nodded placidly.

"We also have the old saying. The dawn is wiser than the night. Old wisdom for an old problem. It is proper."

"Good. Otchigen, you will stay?"

"Highness, I beg your leave. My wife..."

"Yes, I had heard, my friend. Forgive me. Give all my love to your lady. Tell her I await her wit and her beauty at my table as soon as she can bear spending an evening with an old bore."

Chapter 5

Fires in Vasyllia

Rushing back and forth through the third reach, back and forth—it happened often enough since Otchigen's appointment as Voyevoda, chief warrior of the armies of the Mother of Cities. But today, more than ever before, the way stretched before him, endless and tiring. It was as though the moonlit path grew longer as he walked, not shorter. Otchigen cursed loudly, imprecating himself, the Heights, his extended family.

In such moods, it was better if he remained out of doors, away from the comforts of home. It would not take much to light the char-cloth in his chest, always dry and always ready to catch at the faintest spark.

Aglaia's expression as he misjudged the wounds on her body flashed through his memory. No, he did not dare spend even another minute away from her. Without realizing it, he had started running.

Each step of his booted feet sounded loud, even ponderous. Bell-like. Each step raised the dry dust of summer, and with it rose the foreboding in his gut, reaching for the abyss in his heart, filling it up.

Suddenly, lightning flashed, as though from a clear sky. But no, he remembered now. Burly grey-black clouds had been gathering all day, far taller than the mountains of Vasyllia, as though the Heights of Aer revealed themselves, greater and more terrible than the Vasyllia of earth. A second bolt flashed, and with it came the thunder, sounding to his beleaguered mind like the cracking open of every mountain peak in Vasyllia. A third bolt flashed, and he saw his estate in the distance, for a moment stark, as though it was on fire.

No. It *was* on fire.

Lightning flashed not one hundred paces from him. The shock of it knocked him off his feet. With a sound like the unmaking of creation, fire burst up from the ground to his right, on the lands of Sudar Gartanían. No, not just his lands. His house burned as well. Otchigen stopped in horror, turning about in place as the acrid smell of smoke reached him. Three houses—now it was five, not including his own—were burning like the beacon-fires on the border between Vasyllia and Nebesta.

What are you doing standing here, you idiot? Your house! Your family!

He bolted forward as the third reach came alive around him, people erupting in droves from the houses like ants from a collapsing anthill. Some called to him for help, but he looked nowhere but ahead, where he thought he could still see the stark outline of his own mansion burning in the flames.

Then the wind came.

It roared as though it were a ravenous mountain lion attacking a pack of wounded goats. The cries of the third reach rose with it, as any hope of stopping the fires was lost. Now all they could do was contain it as much as possible.

And yet, through all the chaos, through the screaming, through the flashes of lighting that blinded him for moments on end, he heard a whisper of a thought somewhere far away in the depths of his mind.

Your house was on fire before the lightning struck.

It was not his own thought, he was sure. It was suggested to him. But he had no doubt of its truth.

His feet hardly seemed to touch the path any more.

Before he reached home, the rain came—a hot, summer downpour that together with the wind could break trees with its power. He was drenched in less time than it took to draw his sword. But the discomfort was only momentary, as he realized that the immediate danger of fire was past.

His realization was confirmed as he approached his two-story, three-gabled sprawling house that even from the ground looked like some huge dragon ready to pounce. The smoke from it rose, mixing with an evening mist that had come with the rain. Only one of the forelegs of the serpent—a wing added during his father's time to accommodate his grandmother's strange passion for clay pottery—was badly damaged. The rest of the house looked merely scorched, with some of the gilding on the eaves gone and one section of the roof slightly caved in. Quickly, he tried to guess which part of the house that was.

His stomach twisted. It was the bedroom he and Aglaia shared. He was sure of it.

As he came through the cherries, which were shedding pale blossoms in the rain as though the trees themselves were weeping with the heavens, he saw Lebía, wrapped in what looked like five heavy blankets, her hair sticking to her scalp. Her face was red and wet, and he suspected it was not only the rain that drenched it.

He scooped her into his arms even before she realized he was there, eliciting a yelp and a frenzied attempt to escape, followed soon after by a tight embrace. She had not hugged him like that in months. Now he was no longer sure his face was only wet from the rain, either.

"You're not hurt, Lebía?" he boomed, trying to make himself heard over the continuing din of the wind and the rain.

She shook her head, but then erupted into a fresh torrent of sobs.

"Papa, Papa. It's Mama. She's gone!"

The hours that followed were little more than a series of sounds and images, barely joined together by anything other than the ever-present sense that the world was about to end. If not the whole world, at least his own. The door to the wine cellar, torn off its hinges. Her Lardship repeating, over and over again, "What will become of us?" Three young third-reachers caught in the act of trying to burn down Otchigen's house, tied roughly together and thrown like sacks of cabbages into the middle of the hearth-hall. Two menservants watching over them, armed with metal pokers. The whinny of a horse in fright. Lebía's huge eyes, red-rimmed from tears and fear.

Nowhere did he find Aglaia. Not a sight, sound, smell of her. No one knew where she was.

It was near dawn when he came back to his rational mind, awakening from some kind of stupor to find himself on his rocking chair, with Lebía sleeping in his arms like she used to when she was a baby. It was so domestic a scene, so perfect, that he turned to the front door, expecting to see Aglaia there with her quizzical half-smile, so redolent with yearning, holding a branch of the season's last rowan-berries. But the door was shut and barred. Its edges were still smoking.

He realized then that someone was speaking to him, and probably had been for a long time. He turned to the voice and realized, with some confusion, that it was Otar Gleb, a young priest only recently raised to the clerics from among the second reach. An ugly man, almost grotesquely so, with a misshapen nose and large eyes too closely placed together. The softness of his curling, blond hair—which would have looked beautiful on a young woman's head—only accentuated his ugliness.

"You may be inclined to blame yourself, I know," said Otar Gleb, his voice gentle and soothing. "But I do not. There is a place for that kind of ferocity in the fighters' pentagon. And Adonais knows that Nevida committed a breach that should, in all fairness, see him exiled to some pox-infested land on the far side of the Steppes."

With some effort, Otchigen remembered that they had been speaking for at least half an hour about the events of the past few days. They had only now begun speaking of the fires. Otar Gleb had brought news that only some of the fires had been naturally caused, while a few had been part of a plan by some friends of Nevida. A puerile act of revenge against Otchigen and the families who supported him in the Dumar.

"I think they were emboldened by the prince's support. That spiteful boy! And all because he didn't last the Ordeal, while my own Voran…" Otchigen couldn't finish the sentence. Voran had been inseparable from his mother. What would he do when he came out from the Ordeal?

"I'm sure Mirnían did what he thought was necessary." Otar Gleb smiled, and it was like a sunrise after a dark winter night. His ugliness softened, and his eyes shone. Otchigen had been wrong. Otar Gleb had his own kind of beauty. "Be sure to add it to your daily devotion, Otchigen, that you have the right—the grace, even —not to play both sides in a quarrel. Mirnían does not have that luxury."

Otchigen found himself at a loss for words, trying to untangle what he had imagined from what had actually happened. Otar Gleb leaned forward, his smile now no more than a dimple on each cheek.

"I understand that Lady Aglaia's disappearance is… not connected with the fires. That the servants had noticed her absence earlier in the day? At least we can be sure she did not perish in the flames. That is some comfort, no?"

It came back to Otchigen like a sudden wave that overwhelms and pulls under at the same time. Aglaia gone. Without a trace. As though she had simply vanished into thin air. No one had so much as seen a shadow of her since he had spoken to her that morning.

"Yes, Otar Gleb, I suppose you're right." Though nothing of the sort was true, of course. Naturally, her disappearance could have nothing to do with anything but the most important thing —their quarrel. "Though it's more of a comfort to Lebía, I imagine, not me. I will not be at peace until I have found her."

"You believe she has left then? Of her own volition? Or do you suspect foul play?"

The only foul play is my own.

"The circumstances of her disappearance are... strange, to say the least. I don't know what to believe any more, Otar. I only know I will not be capable of rational thought, much less a warrior's worth, until I find some word of her."

Otar Gleb nodded thoughtfully, but before he did, a very clear expression flashed across his face. It said a great deal, though it ended in a moment.

"You suspect I have done something to her?" Something of the growl returned to Otchigen's voice.

Otar Gleb's eyes opened in genuine surprise. "No, of course not! Though... I do imagine there are some who would suggest it. Even before you punished Nevida, you were unpopular with a certain kind of third-reacher family. But you already knew that."

Otchigen did. There was a worrying trend among some of the newer third-reacher families who had been raised to nobility for services performed for the Mother of Cities in the last hundred years or so. Most of them had a disturbing—and completely mercantile second-reacher—tendency to prefer cunning and compromise to honor and righteousness. He made it part of his daily responsibilities to extirpate those unworthy qualities, sometimes in public ways. He felt no qualms about it—it was necessary for the virtue of the Mother of Cities. But they didn't appreciate the public nature of it.

"Well, Otar Gleb, I hope you will do what you can to stifle any sort of rumor. Especially when I am gone."

"Where will you go? Have you any indication of where she might have gone?"

"I have none. But there is one who may."

Otar Gleb smiled with genuine pleasure. "Ah! You go to have tea with the stylite. Excellent! Do give him my love, and tell him that I can smell his unwashed holiness all the way in the third reach."

CHAPTER 6

THE PILLAR-DWELLER

Pushing his shuddering legs those final few steps, Otchigen held his breath and leaned against the stout quarterstaff he held in his right hand, given him as a final blessing by the Dar himself. By this time, four days into his journey, calluses from the rubbing of the oak-wood had formed over the soft, blistery flesh—an embarrassing reminder of how much of a city-dweller he had become. Many were the days in his youth when he had spent weeks in the wild, hardening his body in preparation for an ordeal. Now, even his sword-hand had become soft. He hadn't realized it, not until these days in the wild. It made him think that perhaps he knew even less about himself than he thought he did.

Finally, he crested the peak. It had taken him most of the day to slog up this last rise. The footpath reached the cairn marking the summit, then twisted around it. Otchigen stopped for a moment to consider the cairn, then he fell on his knees before it and kissed the ground, closing his eyes and wrapping his fingers around the first stone that he happened to touch. As he rose, he placed the stone—a smooth pebble the size of his fist—on top of the cairn, making sure not to topple the entire structure.

This was the custom for any who would enter the valley of the stylite. His name was Semyon, a strange hermit who lived on top of a pillar of stones he had crafted with his own two hands, probably more than fifty years ago. Though there were some in the first reach who swore by all that's holy that he had built that pillar over two hundred years ago. The story went that he had only come down from it once to visit Vasyllia in person. The reason for his visit was disputed, and the best version Otchigen heard was that he had taken violent offense at learning that Dar Antomír had canceled a rarely-celebrated, esoteric feast day honoring the dendrites of Cassían's reign.

Until he heard that story, Otchigen hadn't even known what a dendrite was. Thinking it was a species of river fish, he was astonished to find out that it was a kind of hermit who lived in the bole of a tree, never leaving it until he died.

However that may be, he did know for a fact that Dar Antomír, in his youth, had wanted to simplify the Temple Calendar, removing some of the less-attended feast days entirely or combining them into a single day of greater solemnity. He had done it with a few, but the Day of the Dendrites he had left alone.

Otchigen thought he understood the impulse that caused the hermit to abandon his pillar. He stood for the old order of the days of Covenant. He understood, as did so few Vasylli these days, that once you begin to undermine the traditions that had buttressed a civilization for centuries, even for perfectly logical reasons, you were laying cracks to the foundation of that civilization. If Otchigen had been in his place, he would have done more than simply come to Vasylli to voice his displeasure. He would have challenged someone to an open battle in the pentagon. The most ancient of rites—the ordeal by arms.

Perhaps he and the stylite would get along, after all.

Otchigen stopped to catch his breath, agog at the valley sprawling below him. The summer air that day had the peculiar quality—rare in other seasons—of giving everything in the distance a sheen of unreality. It was as though he looked at a very realistic fresco. The river snaking through the grassy valley, the tufts of willows on the banks of the river, the stands of alder and birch and aspen surrounding the crooked pillar of stone that looked like it would topple at any moment, and finally the hovel made of sticks, bark, and moss on the top of it—it all looked too concocted to be real. As though he could extend his hand to it all, and it would ripple away under his touch like a reflection in water.

Instead of wiping away the view, he started the steep way down—it was half footpath and half broken-down staircase from some lost age when such things were actually carved into the mountains.

As an entirely new group of muscles began to complain at the strain of the descent, Otchigen wondered if he hadn't made a mistake coming to Semyon.

The stories about him were varied in the most spectacular ways. Some said he was a kind, gentle soul who spoke little, and when he did it was all nonsense anyway. Others insisted on his spectacularly bad character as the reason for his living so far away from everyone. The one common thread in all the tales was his clairvoyance. And that vision was what Otchigen needed. To know where Aglaia was, no matter how far away.

He had spoken to the infrequent travelers on the Dar's road and the even more reclusive woodsmen living along the footpaths —none had offered up any information as to the possible where-abouts of Lady Aglaia. None had so much as heard of a fine Vasylli lady traveling outside the city. What would a fine lady like she be doing out in the summer heat anyway, they wondered? And a few of them had turned away from Otchigen with doubting looks that seemed to suggest that perhaps it was better for the lady that this hulking shadow of a man would not find her, after all.

It was possible, he admitted to himself, that he imagined those looks. He trusted his senses and his impressions less and less. A foggy dimness often descended on his waking hours, so that he could walk for hours on end without realizing what sort of land lay around him. Once or twice he actually missed a crossroads, forcing him to turn back and take the same road twice.

It worried him, but he tried not to think of it. It was becoming more and more difficult to think through anything. All he could hold in his mind clearly was Aglaia's pained face after their last argument. That was enough to force him to continue moving, even at night, when he should have been resting.

And so, as he approached the pillar of the stylite, he had to force himself to remember the exact words he had planned to use when speaking to the enigmatic hermit. From the many different versions of the tales, he had learned that upon a first visit, one must address Semyon as "Your Pillarliness." The second address could be either "great lord of the stones" or "great stone of the lords"—the accounts were confused as to which. But all agreed that a studied civility and conventionality in speech were necessary if the old man were to speak to you at all.

Something plopped against Otchigen's cheek. He felt it with his fingers and examined it. It was brown and it smelled foul. Otchigen stopped in mid-stride, shocked. Another gift came from above, landing on his left shoulder. He looked up at the top of the pillar.

"Just making you feel at home, my dear!" The screeched words came from a wizened old man with a beard so long it was tied in five knots just to keep it from tripping him. "I could be wrong, of course, but I believe you hark from the city of dung itself, no?"

"Your Pillarliness!" began Otchigen, but he could say no more. The old man had laughed so uproariously that he actually fell over and out of sight. Otchigen wondered if he had fallen off the pillar entirely.

"Pillarliness! Ho-ho-ho! Oh, that's good! Precious! The things the dung-heap-dwellers come up with these days!"

"I come from no dung heap," Otchigen said, his voice rising in annoyance. "I come from the Mother of Cities herself."

"The mother of shitties, more like!" And he cackled and

hooted again. "I know why you've come. And I have no answers for you. Go home, raven-man. None of your blood-stained hands here! Your smell has preceded you for days. Blood and rot and filth. Go! Away with you!"

He disappeared.

Otchigen's mouth was open in utter shock. Though plenty of the stories described him as odd, none had said that Semyon was a madman. Still, the words he spoke echoed in his mind. If he hadn't known any better, he might have thought that the man spoke with the power of prophecy.

"Master, will you not at least tell me one thing? I will be on my way presently."

"One thing?" The hoary head popped into view again. "It was only one thing that led to the fall of Vasyllia. It was one thing only that caused the rotting rust to eat away at the relic of Karila. It was one thing alone that burned the fair lady of Nebesta to ashes. Or wait..." He cocked his head like a curious blue jay. "That hasn't happened yet, has it? Any of it?"

His eyebrows, bushy even from this distance, lowered so far down his brow that it seemed they might fall off his face entirely. He studied Otchigen, then his face softened.

"Not yet. No. And for all your stink..." He left the rest unsaid.

"Semyon!" Otchigen decided to discard all the stories and speak to this strange person man to man. "Surely you have loved a woman in your life. Surely you have felt the emptiness when she is lost. All I ask is information. A word. No more."

"Oh Heights! It's all so distressing sometimes. How does the Most High do it? All laid out before him, as on a tapestry, I imagine. A tapestry in constant motion, with every thread like a vein full of pulsing... events? Faces? How does he do it? I can hardly manage a shadow of it. Now for the poor creature. The poor wolf-woman."

Otchigen's patience was quickly reaching its end. Before he started screaming at this poor idiot of a man, he tried a last time.

"You may have heard from a traveler come to visit your holiness. The Lady Aglaia. Has she come here? Has anyone heard of her whereabouts?"

"Is it just an unbreakable inner focus? I have too much to scatter me, even here, even alone. If only there were some way to bore a hole in the Realms. Jump through it down into the Heights..."

The space inside Otchigen where the abyss gaped caught fire, and his fists clenched so hard he was sure he would find bloody marks from the nails on his palms.

"A pox on you! What Otar Gleb sees in you, I will never know. Though he was right about one thing. Your obsession with foul smells. He asked me to pass on his love, and to tell you that he smelled your unwashed holiness all the way from Vasyllia."

"Gleb! Oh, the rascal! He would say that, he would." And he laughed, but it was a sane laughter this time, with a note of a fully rational old man, a bit weary perhaps, but not mad. "It is good that you value his friendship, Otchigen. If you two lived in a different age, perhaps you might have found peace. But now..."

The face disappeared again for a time. It sounded as though he were rummaging though something in his hovel. Then Otchigen heard, to his surprise, the sound of scrabbling, as though someone were climbing up rock. Or *down...*

Surprised, Otchigen walked around the pillar. He saw Semyon climbing down the pillar with the skill of a mountain goat kid. He hardly looked down at all, as though his hands and feet knew exactly where the best ledges and holes were. In a few quick minutes, Otchigen was faced with a short, remarkably dirty old man whose holiness, as Gleb had said, if measured by magnitude of smell, was truly monumental.

"Yes, I know," said Semyon, sniffing loudly, then scratching his nose. "Well, not much time to wash if you know the end of the world is coming soon."

He said it with the same flippant tone as before, but then he seemed to notice something as he looked at Otchigen, and his eyes went a fraction wider than before. A slight movement, but

Otchigen sensed that it revealed much. His tone from that moment was entirely serious, even commanding.

"Tell me, Voyevoda of Vasyllia. What sort of madness causes you to leave your hearth and your home right after a fire that could have wiped out the entire third reach of Vasyllia?"

"How do you...? So you *have* seen someone from Vasyllia, then? Did they have word of Aglaia?"

"Otchigen, tell me. Has anyone suggested to you that you are going mad?"

Something itched in Otchigen's chest, like a blind mole looking for soft spots in the earth to burrow. Otchigen didn't answer.

"No, I don't suppose anyone would brave that temper of yours. That thing you call warrior virtue." Semyon scoffed. "Warrior virtue indeed. A noble aspiration, but only if tempered. And not with your temper. So, madness. Yes, well, what else would you call it? The third reach burning, at least partially from the ill will of its own sons. A daughter with a broken heart, abandoned in hallways that still stink of smoke, without even her brother to look to her. A champion for the ages—your own words, I believe —in potential danger so obvious that a child could see it. And yet, you wander the wilds looking for the woman whom you drove out her own house yourself. Yes, I believe that is what you call madness."

Otchigen was so shocked by the exactness of Semyon's information that he forgot, for a moment, to be angry. By the time the mole in his chest had grown into a rat scrabbling for a way out of his chest, Semyon was speaking again.

"And the lapses in attention. The strange thoughts whispered in your ear, as though by another. Madness, I tell you. You are a danger to Aglaia. Why do you pursue her when it is so clear that she is better off without you?"

That was the final drop.

"I am not mad, pillar-dweller! Though I suppose if anyone were to suspect me of it, it would be someone as mad as you."

"It would indeed," said Semyon, his expression guarded, his eyes slitted as he watched Otchigen.

The rat in his chest was throwing itself madly against his ribs, biting, clawing, ripping its way out of him. How dare that old man suggest such a thing? Otchigen had been traveling for days on end seeking nothing but a bit of consolation. And this was what he was to receive? After so many years of unflagging service to his family, his nation, he was to be lectured in loyalty by a man who had abandoned the world to sit on top of a pillar and stare at nothing? This was unbearable.

Otchigen's hand shot out, grabbing the old man by the throat.

Break his windpipe!

The thought was so sudden, so sharp, so sweet on his mind, that Otchigen gasped. But he did not let go.

Semyon's face didn't change expression, even as it turned bluish-purple. His hands didn't come up to defend himself. He even seemed to smile a bit.

Break his neck!

Yes! I will! The foul canker on the earth's face. Deluding people with his words of so-called wisdom. The world would be lighter for his being taken off its surface.

Lebía's wet face flashed on his mind. Aglaia's expression of despair. Voran's calm, infuriating resolve. Karakul's laughing eyes.

With a groan that seemed to come from underneath him, from the rocks themselves, Otchigen dropped Semyon.

The old man tried to take a full breath, but it wouldn't come easily. As he twitched on the ground, looking like an overturned beetle trying to find its legs, he kept his eyes on Otchigen. Finally, with a sound like a wooden spoon being dragged against a washboard, he breathed in fully and landed on his knees.

"Not madness, no," he wheezed. "Something else. Something that the great enemy desires. Your capacity to love, turned inward. Your powerful anger, turned outward. Two forces that, when linked, can break the world."

Otchigen, his hands shaking, fell onto his knees before the old man. Shuddering sobs had replaced the gnawing in his chest.

"I... forgive me... what happened to me? I've never..."

"Voyevoda of Vasyllia, can you see now? How you have made choice after choice that condemns not only you, but everyone who is attached to you? Can you not see that it is likely that Karakul is already dead? Killed in his own bed by his so-called brothers?"

"No... certainly things are not as bad as..."

"They are a great deal worse. You know this. You, of all men the most eager for the virtue of your city and its people. You, of all men most focused on your own honor and virtue. You, who have had such a tight control over your own thoughts and emotions that hardly a stray thought passed through you? And yet, who was it that beat Nevida to a pulp?"

"I don't ... I don't understand." A strange thought formed itself into words. "Am I the infection?"

"No, not you, my dear one. It is in Vasyllia, boring its way to the city's very bones. But it may be that you will carry it deeper still."

"But all I've ever wanted is the good of my ... You said it yourself..."

"If that were so, why do you abandon them all when you know full well that Aglaia is not only safe, she is better off where she is now? Away from Vasyllia. Away from the taint that infected her so badly that it broke through her skin in lesions."

His body shuddering sporadically, Otchigen fell on his knees. He hadn't considered it until this moment. Could his lapses in memory and Lebía's sickness both be expressions of a rottenness at the heart of Vasyllia? Was such a thing even possible?

"Something is going to happen to Vasyllia, isn't it? Semyon, tell me! What must I do?"

The stylite finally spoke without a wheeze as he stood up. Though he was a small man, he still loomed over the crouched figure of Otchigen.

"I am but a man. I see things, yes. And what I see is horrifying. If you go now, if you do not stop on your way home, you may —it is only just possible—delay the coming of the darkness to Vasyllia. But I do no know any more. Gamayun, the teller of all fates, sings to me in riddles, and the images in my dreams are soaked with blood and tears."

Otchigen, in a sudden flood of emotion that seemed to break every carefully crafted guard he had placed over his heart and mind over the many years of his military discipline, embraced the old man.

In that moment, he saw something that was not real. A flash of a scene so vivid, it left a trace on the back of his eyes, similar to the spots children see after they stare at the sun for longer than their parents allow.

It was this valley. The pillar had toppled. The body of the stylite was splayed out on one of the fallen stones. Thick metal pegs were driven into his hands and feet. His chest was slashed open.

Someone stood over the fallen stylite, holding the knife high as it dripped blood, dark in the fading light of an autumn sunset.

The man holding the knife was Otchigen himself, though he was emaciated, most of his hair had fallen out, and his expression was not his own.

"This event... I have seen it often over the years," said Semyon, banishing the vision. "I used to think that you did it willingly, for hatred of me." Otchigen let go of the old man as though he had splashed scalding water on him. "But now I think that you will no longer be in control of your own will at that moment. Know this, dear one. I have outlived even the span of life, even of the elder men of Lassar's day. And for one reason alone."

But he would not say what that reason was.

Otchigen, heedless of anything but his own terror, turned and ran.

I am my own man, he thought feverishly. *I have my own will. No one will take it. No one.*

CHAPTER 7

VORAN

Otchigen hardly stopped to rest at all on his way back to Vasyllia. Only when his legs buckled under him and his eyes closed, heavier than the lids on iron pots, did he simply fall over in place for a brief repose, sometimes on the path itself, sometimes a little way off it. He met no one, or at least didn't remember meeting anyone. He hardly noticed anything, need driving him to move forward. Occasionally, he thought he saw the sun glinting off the steel of a spear or a helm—perhaps a scouting party from Vasyllia or a merchant guard—but there was nothing more than the glint.

He was more and more sure that he was going mad.

When the first vista of Vasyllia opened up before him, he was shocked. At first, he believed it to be a delusion. He had not even realized at what point he had left the woodmen's paths and rejoined the Dar's road. And yet, there it was. And it grew nearer with each leaden step.

As he approached the plateau stretching before the great mountain city, bursting with the green of new growth and the foaming heads of wheat, more and more of his perception returned to him. His sour stomach twisted hungrily with each step, and he was shocked to find that his breeches hung loosely on him, as did his travel tunic. Had he eaten so little during his journey? His legs ached so deeply that he thought his bones might shatter at a breath of wind. His back groaned, twisted into a bent-forward shape that his military training decried. Even his fingers looked more like weathered wood than the muscular, veiny hands that had been smeared with Nevida's blood only a week ago.

With the return of his body's sensations came a storm of jumbled thoughts, as though they had been held back by a feeble dam that had only just collapsed.

They rushed over him so fast that he couldn't hold on to a single one of them. Instead, he focused his attention on the silvery path through barley fields leading directly to the twin gates of Vasyllia, set within an arch of marble carved to resemble two trees leaning toward each other to embrace at the point just above the peak of the gates. It was still early morning, so he was surprised to see the gates open ahead of him as he approached. Already carts full of wares were making their way back to Karila on the Dar's road. The merchants and their serving men hardly paid him any attention as he walked. Only a few of them seemed confused when they looked at the sword hanging on his hip. One of them had eyes that kept darting back and forth between Otchigen's face and his sword. Only on the third pass up and down did recognition come to his eyes. But it was a shocked recognition, nothing warm or familiar about it.

They think I have something to do with my wife's disappearance.

The thought made him laugh bitterly.

"You there! That is a fine sword for a vagrant like you to bear. Stole it, I imagine."

Otchigen faced the man who accosted him. As he had thought, it was Rogdai. He had not recognized Otchigen either.

Forcing his wood-stiff back muscles to straighten, Otchigen unsheathed his sword and raised it over his head in the ceremonial challenge. In a voice cracked with the dust of the road, he said, "Who would challenge the Voyevoda of Vasyllia? Let him name the time and place for a public airing of his grievances before the Dar himself and the Dumar assembled."

Rogdai blanched and stood rooted to the spot, his mouth open.

I must look even worse than I imagine.

"I... forgive me, my lord Otchigen. I did not... Lord, I am told to watch for your arrival. The Dar awaits your convenience."

"When were you given this command, Vohin Rogdai?" Otchigen's heart lurched forward in sudden terror. Was it Lebía? Had something happened to her? Was Karakul still alive?

"Just this morning, my lord." He looked quizzically at Otchigen. "Of course," he said, more to himself than to Otchigen. "You couldn't have known. Voran has successfully passed the Ordeal of Silence. The first warrior to do so in one hundred and sixty-seven years."

To Otchigen's rising guilt, his first thought was not of Voran at all. It was worry about Karakul. But he stifled the question. No good for Rogdai to know that he seemed to care more for a Karilan foundling than his own son.

Without another word, he hurried by the fastest roads to the third reach and home. The Dar would have to wait.

Otchigen examined Voran's face, not sure what he expected. It was still roughly oval in shape, his hair still the dark, almost black, color that his own had been in youth, though straiter and less unruly. The first semblance of a mustache hung on either edge of his upper lip, and a puff of dark fuzz hung on by his chin for dear life. His eyes were different, though not by much. They seemed slightly haunted. But that could have been the news of his mother as much as any supernatural wisdom attained during the Ordeal of Silence. He still looked no older than his sixteen years.

Otchigen kept waiting for some emotion at the thought of his own son completing an ordeal that no warrior had managed to overcome in a century. He should be proud. He should be embracing him right now. Not standing stiffly before the dining table, his hand lightly resting on the back of one of the chairs. Voran, for his part, seemed not to expect much more from his father. Otchigen didn't know what was worse—the reality of his unfeeling or Voran's expectation of it.

Instead, Otchigen's heart beat with fear for Karakul. Was he well? Was he even alive? Why would no one tell him?

"I am... proud of you, my son," said Otchigen. It sounded even more forced than it did in his mind a split second before.

"Yes," said Voran, his eyes somewhere else, in some unfathomable deep that Otchigen would never reach. "Well, it's not as difficult as all that. Or perhaps it just suits my temperament."

"That it certainly does," said Otchigen. He couldn't prevent a note of derision in the laugh that followed his words. "I mean, certainly a hot-head like Mirnían was never cut out for it."

"I wonder that he even tried, to be honest," said Voran in that remarkably assured way that so many took for conceit when it was simply a lack of self-awareness. "Still, he has nothing to be ashamed of. He lasted longer than most."

"Yet he is to be Dar. I think it might rankle a bit more than you think."

"I don't see why it should," said Voran, with a tone that intended no more continuation of the present subject.

"How is Lebía?" asked Otchigen.

Voran's eyes flared for a moment. There was real anger there. Otchigen almost rejoiced to see it.

"As well as can be expected. She is only eight, you know. And she has been without any family member for the past *week*." So much suppressed blame in his voice! Otchigen wished he would let it all out in a torrent of anger. It would do both of them good.

"I found no word of your mother," he said, trying to change subject. "I did have a very..." he wanted to say terrifying, but settled for "interesting ... encounter with Semyon the Pillar-dweller. You've always been one for the stories, yes? Well, you might be disappointed to hear that none of tales about him are even close to the..."

"My lord," said Voran, his voice like a white-hot metal poker. "I believe you are tired from your journey. The Dar is expecting both of us to appear before the afternoon bell. I will have the servants prepare a quick meal for you, you need not worry. Perhaps the steam room as well? Yes, of course. You need not worry about Lebía. She is with the Dar's family for the day. Rest, my lord."

"Voran, one more thing. Semyon suggested something would happen to Karakul..." He felt too embarrassed to continue.

"Oh, you had not heard! The day after you left, Karakul was attacked in an alley in the second reach. Four men, hired by Nevida's family. He killed three of them. He is a little shaken, with a few bruises and slashes. But he is well."

Otchigen's relief must have been evident, because Voran pursed his mouth and turned stiffly away. A wave of jealousy seemed to pour off him.

"My son..."

"Rest, my lord. We leave in two hours."

The setting sun painted the Chamber of Counsel with shifting shades of red, orange, blue, and purple, making the flames on the Covenant Tree dance as though Otchigen and Voran were facing the actual tree, not a fresco. This time, the Dar sat in his own throne of marble. He was robed in a deep red mantle fringed with gold that caught the light from the colored glass and sparkled. The effect almost distracted from his sudden aging, but not nearly enough.

Look at the pair of us, thought Otchigen. *Both of us are half what we were only last week, but dressed in more finery than we'd ever put on if we had any say in it.*

Voran was serious, even stately, in his cohort robe of black cinched with a forest-green belt. It was adorned with a brass buckle wrought into the shape of a falcon in flight. Mirnían, who stood across from Voran, was in the pure white of his princely office. He studiously ignored Voran. Voran didn't seem to notice, still lost in his thoughts.

The bulk of the official proceedings was over. Voran had been honored by the Dar with a drink from the Dar's own toasting horn. Voran had accepted it with a look at the Dar that had more warmth in it than Otchigen had ever felt come in his direction. He tried not to feel hurt at it.

"My dear friends," said the Dar. "I must soon call the Dumar for deliberation. They will call for an open declaration of war against Karila. The mood has been restive for a while now, and, for good or ill, Vohin Karakul's victory over the third reach's boy darling has not helped."

What he did not say, and what Otchigen had heard from Voran on the way to the palace, was that Segynduk had had to go into hiding after two attempts on his life. He and Karakul were at the moment packing their things for the journey to Karila.

"I would have kept Karakul here for as long as possible, but his victory provides us with an unexpected advantage. He has sworn his oath of loyalty to our person this morning. I do not doubt him. Otchigen, do you have any reason to doubt his word?"

"I do not, Highness," said Otchigen, trying to keep his tone neutral.

"It is as I hoped," said the Dar, sighing. "He will lead a small detachment of warriors who will go ostensibly as protection for a special embassy of Vasylli from all reaches. Segynduk will go with them. He has promised me that he will do everything in his power to defuse the fear at the rusting of the blade. With the blessing of Otar Kalun, I am providing Karila with a cutting from the Great Tree itself. Segynduk will carry it himself in a lantern specially crafted to withstand heat. It is my hope that the flame on the cutting will remain, even after removed from the city."

"That is a great gift, Highness," said Voran. "What of the rusted blade? Surely it should be removed from Karila?"

"Karakul is charged with bringing it back. Ostensibly so that our Otars can see if there are any measures that can be taken to restore it."

Otchigen winced at the Dar's apparently unthinking admission in his use of the word "ostensibly."

"You cannot entrust such a task to a new Vohin, Highness," said Otchigen. "He may not yet have the necessary... well..."

"Shall we call it authority?" offered the Dar helpfully. Otchigen nodded, feeling his cheeks get warmer as he felt Voran's gaze intent on him.

"I should go with Karakul. It will be good for him, and the Karila will surely see this as a fitting expression of our continued unity."

"Yes, I agree," said the Dar. "It will do you good as well."

Voran shifted in his otherwise perfectly straight stance.

"Does Voran disagree with the decision of the Dar?" It was the first time Mirnían had spoken. His voice was replete with scorn. Voran seemed genuinely taken aback by it. Poor Voran. He had much to learn about the world still.

"Highness," Voran did not look at Mirnían. "I understand why so little has been said of my mother's disappearance. It is inexplicable and strange, and even Semyon the stylite had little to helpful to say, as I am told. But in spite of that, surely you can see that my sister needs her father at this time? My time will be split between the study rooms and the pentagon as I enter the final years of my studies. Surely my father would not want me to flag in my warrior training?" He did not look at Otchigen, though the rising pink in his cheek betrayed much.

"Voran, my dear boy," said the Dar. "Your concern is commendable. We will get to the bottom of your mother's disappearance, I promise it. But surely you can see how comfortable Lebía is with my daughter Sabíana and the rest of the women? She must stay here for the foreseeable future."

"This morning, she seemed content with Sabíana," Voran admitted ruefully. He shook his head, stubbornly unconvinced. "Of course, it must be as your Highness wishes. You have always been like a father to this family."

Only then did he look at Otchigen for a moment, before turning away. On the surface, it was only a straight glance. But the pleading there was strong, containing what Otchigen suspected was many months' worth of thoughts and contemplation in the silence of the ordeal. For the first time, Otchigen realized that enforced silence could have driven a lesser man mad.

He was almost surprised to realize that he was proud of his son. Perhaps something would come of him, after all.

Chapter 8

The Embassy to Karila

They made a strange company—twenty mounted warriors, led by Otchigen and Karakul, a young diplomat and his wife with ancestral ties to Karila, seated in a merchant's cart laden with wares, the merchant himself guiding the two packhorses, and Segynduk on a spirited pony so small it could have been specially made for children. His legs hung almost to the ground, comically. But one look was enough to show how much the old Karilan valued the little beast. The merchant, Otchigen was pleased to note, surprised every stereotype of the second reach by being both skinny and morose. A motley company, but certainly not a boring one.

Otchigen found the days passing quickly, even pleasantly, in his conversations with Karakul and the young couple, both of whom were well-educated, with a subtle wit. More than that, Otchigen was warmed by the easy intimacy of their personal conversations, even when he couldn't hear them. Clearly, they were not long married, or if they were, then their bond was a rare one. Not that different from the bond shared by him and Aglaia not so long ago.

He tried not to think of Aglaia, though her image never faded from his heart.

About two weeks into their journey, when they were already in the heart of Nebesta, the jagged mountains of Vasyllia started giving way to the gentler, more feminine landscape of the Nebesti ranges. Crags still jutted out from the rare carn, but mostly the hills rolled like the waves following a longboat's wake. That day, Karakul had been quieter than usual, more thoughtful. The young diplomat had tried to engage him in conversation several times, but Karakul hadn't even seemed to hear. Otchigen knew him well enough to wait for him to begin speaking when he wanted.

It came unexpectedly, when Otchigen himself was lost in memories of the storytelling at his hearth when Voran was still a wide-eyed, impressionable boy of four years old, and Lebía wasn't even a thought in her mother's mind.

"My Lord Otchigen," said Karakul almost diffidently, as though he didn't want to break into Otchigen's reverie. "You haven't said anything about your meeting with the stylite. I would be honored if you shared some of his wisdom with me."

"Wisdom?" Otchigen scoffed. "Yes, I suppose there was some of that. But if I told you the pattern of his speech, word for word, you would think I was making a bad joke." The memory of the old pillar-dweller cooled him unpleasantly, but even stronger was the impression of the scene of his death. *Which had not happened and never will if I can help it.*

"There was one thing he said to me that remained with me, Karakul. If most of what he said would make little sense to anyone but me, this, I think, you will understand. He suggested to me that the capacity to love, turned inward, coupled with a powerful anger, turned outward, are a force for destruction." He would not say that Semyon suggested that those particular failings in Otchigen could break the world apart.

Karakul seemed to guess something of the like in any case.

"It's an interesting thought. What does the Wisdom of the Warrior say? 'A love so hot that it can melt the blade of your opponent'? But that love is not a love turned inward. It is a love for family and city-state. I suppose that the same force of love, when centered completely on the self, could be a terrible thing. But a force for self-destruction alone, I would have thought."

"I agree. But coupled with a powerful anger? Why would that make it an externally destructive force?"

Karakul smiled, then shook his head. He said nothing, though his glance was knowing.

Of course. "I apologize, Karakul. Certainly that is exactly the kind of thing that caused Nevida's failure in the pentagon. But I still think it a sign of weakness, not a force for destruction."

"And yet," Karakul seemed unwilling to continue, pushing the words as though against an internal obstruction. "It can be destructive in the darkness of lies and treachery. For they nearly had my head on a platter, my Lord."

Otchigen said nothing, confused into silence. Was he capable of such actions? Or did Semyon mean something different? And would the reverse—a love turned outward, an anger turned inward—then be his saving grace? But how? Was not his anger turned inward making him a pitiable fool already? One who abandoned his loved ones for a fruitless search in the wild?

He could not fathom it.

He kept thinking about it until they made camp under a stand of old oaks, huddling near one of the mountain springs that crisscrossed the entire landscape of lower Nebesta. As he had during this entire journey, Otchigen eschewed putting up pavilions. He had had enough of his pampered life.

Lying under the stars, too numerous to even contemplate in the nearly moonless sky, he did not hear the hoofbeats until they were nearly on top of his small company. When he snapped into awareness and sat up to see, torches already defaced the tranquil darkness. At least twenty torches, and the shifting smoke between each evenly-spaced flame roiled, hiding the exact number of riders, but giving the hazy impression of a large force.

"Karakul!" Otchigen snapped in his commander voice. "Get the men up. Horsemen approaching from the South."

Karakul was up, his sword buckled and his helm strapped on in less than a minute. The rest of the warriors took longer.

"No time to ready horses." Otchigen swore into the fog that streamed from his mouth into the chilly night air. "Well, brothers. Time to put your training to the test."

By that time, the rest of the party had awoken in the ruckus. Otchigen arranged his men in a semicircle around the cart and the civilians, enough of a space away to at least try to control the angle of attack. Though if there were as many horsemen as he suspected, that would be nearly impossible.

"Try to keep yourselves between the horsemen and our civilians," Otchigen barked. He looked around to see intent concentration on the faces of each man. No fear. No shuddering moves. Nothing but contained ferocity, waiting to be unleashed. Only Karakul shifted from foot to foot, though there was no laxness in his body. He was storing energy to be expelled like an arrow from a bowstring.

Before he could finish that thought, the torchlight expanded, so that the distances between each fire increased. They were going to try to outflank them. Damn. That's exactly what he would have done.

"Circle the cart! Go!" Otchigen commanded, and every man obeyed as one.

The moment they took their new stance, a sound ripped the air around them. As the small hairs stood up all over this body, Otchigen realized, horrified, that those were human cries. They were wilder, more unfettered than any wolf's howl.

One moment, the torches looked a hundred yards away. Then, suddenly, they were only a stone's throw in front of them. Otchigen had just enough thought left to realize that these attackers had shuttered their torches partially to make it look like they were much farther away. A brilliant tactic. There was a cunning mind behind these attackers.

Arrows fell like a summer hailstorm, and the torches retreated a few steps. In a blink, five of his men were on the ground, killed by arrows in their eyes. Not a single arrow had missed.

"Heights! What is this?" Otchigen growled, his palm sweating as he gripped his longsword.

Five more arrows flashed in the light of the torches . Five more men fell dead, arrows in their eyes. In half a minute, Otchigen had lost half his fighting force.

"Karakul, don't wait, attack!"

Otchigen and Karakul ran at the retreating horsemen, who had now turned back. Arrows sped past Otchigen's head, not striking, but close enough for him to feel the wind sliced in half. A quick half-glance to ensure Karakul was still alive, and he hurled himself at the nearest horseman. He slashed with his longsword, but the horseman's curved saber parried it easily and his horse rode past him. Otchigen, almost in desperation, grabbed the rider's kaftan and pulled him down to the ground. The man fell awkwardly, but rose up again as though the ground was bouncy. He was short, but even through his mail, Otchigen recognized a frame of wiry muscle, like a young stallion. He lunged again.

The flurry of blows was quick, but the saber was no match for the longsword. Otchigen impaled him and pushed his limp body off, clearing his blade. He had just enough time to turn around when something struck him on the back of the head, something heavy and blunt. He was on his knees, his vision dimming, before he knew what was happening. Through the dimming haze, he slashed at two horses circling him and hamstrung them. They screamed, and the mounted warriors jumped off their backs, landing on their feet like cats.

Otchigen couldn't believe his eyes. He had never seen such agility, such prowess before.

Something hit him again, and the darkness swallowed him up.

The world swirled around Otchigen wildly. He saw faces leering at him as strange rat-a-tat voices chattered in a half-bestial tongue. He saw the bodies of his warriors being laid down on the ground in tidy rows completely stripped of both armor and clothing. That brought him back into full realization. The throbbing racked his body, beginning in his head, ending in his feet. He tried moving his hands. They were unbound. He was unbound. So was Karakul next to him. That was strange.

The rest of the company, except for Segynduk, was dead, he saw after a quick glance around him. Even the young woman. She was also laid out, stripped, and not even next to her husband. Several of the attackers had eyes for nothing but her naked form, even though she was clearly dead.

He tried to focus his splitting vision on the attackers. There was something of the Karilans in them—similarly angled features and rounded faces, but in more exaggerated fashion. And their skin was darker than the Karilan paleness.

Segynduk was on his knees, holding the jar with the cutting of the Covenant Tree. For a moment, Otchigen was relieved to see that a feeble flame still played on the leaves. Then he realized how foolish he was.

Segynduk was speaking with the attackers in what seemed to be their own tongue, his tone still sharp with disapproval. One of the larger ones, dressed in a brown kaftan of similar make to Segynduk's own—the only difference being the wildly-colored sash of what looked like silk, which exactly matched a silk bandanna wrapped around a black fur-rimmed cap—listened to the old Karilan with amusement.

Something moved with blinding quickness in the corner of Otchigen's eye. Karakul, in full battle readiness, had run up to the vessel with the cutting and grabbed it from Segynduk. In a quick movement more reminiscent of a leopard than a man, he threw it against a stone monolith that sat in the earth like a rotten tooth of a giant. The vessel shattered and the fire flared for a moment before going out.

"You'll wish you hadn't done that," said a voice behind Otchigen. All the warriors and Segynduk had eyes only for the speaker now. Fear came in waves at Otchigen from behind. He tried to will himself to stay in place.

He turned around slowly, as though a giant hand had taken the crown of his head and was spinning him like a child's toy.

What he saw made him gag. It looked human. Or at least, it may have been human at some point in the past. There was little on that former man except yellow-brown skin stretched like a tanner's leather over jutting bones. The face had no more nose or ears, and the eyes were more red than white, bulging, as though they might fall out of the socket at any moment. The figure lay on a litter placed on the ground, swaddled like a child in furs.

"Karakul, isn't it? I've had my eye on you for a while. Yes, you'll make a fine vessel."

Karakul seemed rooted to the ground, though none of him was tied in place. He had a vacant expression in his eyes, and they kept rolling back into his head as though he were about to fall asleep or pass out.

"You're young and strong. You should manage the process of transfiguration well enough." The lips hardly moved on that skeletal face. It seemed as though the voice sounded inside everyone's head, not coming from the dried-up lips. In fact, the face had no lips to speak of any more. Just withered bits of flesh.

"It is only fair you should know in advance. I am the Raven. You Karilans may know me as the Great Changer. To be chosen as my vessel is the greatest honor offered to those who inhabit the Lows of earth."

Otchigen's eyes went dark for a moment. Then, vision. The same intensity as when he stood before Semyon. Karakul standing on the palace turret of Vasyllia. All the people of the city assembled before him in a crowd as thick as an anthill. Karakul raised his arm, and it had a faint outline extending from it just beyond his vision, as of a monstrous raven's wing. Grey-helmed soldiers ran into the Vasylli crowd and began tearing infant children from the hands of their mothers...

"No!" Otchigen snapped back to awareness. His chest was filled with fire, but a different kind. A sureness that he had only one deed to accomplish in his life. A desperate hope that it would be enough.

He lunged at one of the attackers who stood near Karakul, grabbing the knife at his belt so quickly, the man barely had time to twitch.

"Stop him!" bellowed the Raven's voice in everyone's head.

"Karakul," said Otchigen as he plunged the knife into Karakul's heart. "I love you. You are my son."

Chapter 9

Possession

At the command of the half-dead man, the soldiers did unspeakable defilement to the corpses. Otchigen watched it all, willing himself to remember it all. He didn't know how, but he would make these warriors pay for what they did.

Suddenly, there was not one heart in his chest. There were thousands.

He retched and lost consciousness.

You may think you are your own man. You are not. Your anger is futile. Nothing can save you. You are not you any longer. And soon, you and I will be so intertwined that there will no longer be a you or I. Far better, I think, than the intimacy of the marriage bed.

Not one flesh. One will. One mind. One desire.

To devour.

Otchigen stood in the stylite's valley. The pillar had toppled. The body of the stylite was splayed out on one of the fallen stones. Thick metal pegs were driven into his hands and feet. His chest was slashed open.

Otchigen stood over the fallen stylite, holding the knife high as it dripped blood, dark in the fading light of an autumn sunset.

"I used to think that you would do it willingly, for hatred of me," said Semyon.

Otchigen's sense of self returned, and he felt only one heart in his chest. He screamed as he fell on his knees, clutching the knife as though he could never let it go.

"Fool!" hissed a voice to Otchigen's left. A towering figure, at least eight feet tall, dark grey like slate. It *was* made of slate, or so it looked. A man's chest on a man's pair of legs with a man's set of arms coming from the shoulders. But it had a feathered head with the crest erect, a man's eyes bulging from above a raven's beak, curved like a pair of sabres joined at the tips. Two jagged wings extended out from behind the bestial creature. It clicked its beak.

"He is mine. I have already eaten most of his will. The rest I keep for myself, so that he will know what he does in Vasyllia. So he can see the blood of his children spill in the streets."

"You have no power here, Raven," whispered Semyon, his eyes losing focus. "He would indeed have been yours forever. And your victory would have been complete. But for one reason alone."

Otchigen tore his eyes away from the monster on his left, thirsty for Semyon's words like a man traveling the desert for a week.

"Do you think you have enough power yet, Raven, to kill me? In my own valley? You are still formless. Only fools believe that the illusion of that monster-form is real."

At that word, the monstrous giant-raven shimmered as though he were a reflection in a pool.

"No, Raven. You may yet topple worlds, subvert nations to

your cause. But you shall not take my life. I, however, give it. Willingly. Not to you. To that poor wretch."

He raised his head feebly, the muscles on his neck seemingly barely holding it up.

"Otchigen. There is just enough left of you in there. Remember what I told you. And use it. You may hold off the utter darkness yet."

Then, the thought, so, so feeble.

Can a love turned outward, an anger turned inward be my saving grace?

"Yes, it can," answered Semyon in a barely audible whisper. "That creature inside you has only one use for you. To kill Voran."

"Why?" Otchigen wheezed, barely able to get the words out. "Voran is no great warrior. Why should it want his death?" He felt, with every breath, his own will collapsing as the will of the Raven clawed its way back into his heart.

"Voran is the key. It is not by accident that he fulfilled the Ordeal of Silence. He has a part to play, a very important part, in this great story."

"He is nothing more than a rusted blade," growled the bird-creature at Otchigen's left, becoming taller and more substantial by the second. "As is this pitiful vessel."

Otchigen gasped as he felt himself slipping out of his own control.

Otchigen hobbled on the road before Vasyllia in a crowd of ragged beggars. He was one of them. It was the feast day of Holy Poverty. The one day that every beggar in the outlying villages of Vasyllia would be given entrance into the first reach of Vasyllia, where each of them would receive a single coin from the hand of the Dar himself.

Voran would be there with the Dar.

He was supposed to kill Voran. He wanted to kill Voran.

The Dar seemed to float through a sea of ragged forms in the first reach. He was only a stone's throw away from the shuddering form that had once been called... what was it? Otch... something...

The Dar and his retinue were only two beggars away. A knife appeared in the beggar's hand. He no longer wondered at such inexplicable things.

Two young people walked behind the Dar, their eyes filled with pity. The young woman, a dark-haired beauty with piercing brown eyes, extended her hand to touch every finger that lifted toward her black velvet gown. The young man next to her had the eyes of a much older man. They were wet with tears. He threw coins to every person on whom his eyes rested.

He was...

His name was...

Voran.

The man he had to kill. He had to kill him. If he did, he would finally be at peace. His heart would be his again.

The beggar's eye fell on the young woman again. He knew her. Sabíana. The Dar's daughter.

She and Voran held hands. The ring of betrothal sparked on her finger.

They were promised to each other.

Kill him!!!

The thought was inside him, but it was not him. He hated that voice. He hated that thing inside him. He unleashed the full force of his hatred against himself for having that thing inside him.

It screamed. He felt as though every drop of blood in his body has suddenly boiled.

The dagger fell clattering to the rocks. No one noticed.

The beggar remembered himself. He remembered Voran. His son. Tears filled his eyes and he quietly wept.

Voran. I bless you. I bless you as your father. I, Otch... Otchigen. I love you more than you will ever know. Care for your sister. Find your mother. I failed you all.

The thing inside him roared with fury, and Otchigen, the former Voyevoda of Vasyllia, doubled over in pain.

He was in a pile of garbage outside a public house. It stank. He stank.

It was the deepest part of night, but even a moonless night couldn't hide the towering figure of the Raven before him.

"You think you've won?" It growled. "I will find another way to kill Voran. And now that you defied me, I will not obscure your mind from the horrors your body will perpetrate. You will see everything. Every death. Every treachery. Every drop of innocent blood. That is my gift to you. It is what you deserve."

The beggar with no name awoke to a world transformed. Outside his hovel of sticks, assembled on the wind side of a garbage pile on the second reach, the trees were encased in ice. Branches, like freshly-minted blades, beat against each other in a military salute. The beggar stood up, every inch of his body searing in pain. The hundreds of hearts in his chest thrummed, threatening to burst him from within.

The sun breached the distant lines of the Vasylli ranges, and the ice-encased branches glowed from within. A song rose inside him with a vast crescendo, then faded again. It stopped his breath short like a punch to the chest.

"Ammil," he said aloud, remembering something.

Where had he heard that word before?

The sun's morning sparkle through hoarfrost, said a young woman's voice, as distinctly as if she were standing next to him. There was something familiar about that voice.

It was the voice of Lebía. His daughter. He was... Otchigen.

Otchigen, his heart full of the memory of the song that he did not understand, fell on his knees before the sun and begged.

"Most High," he whispered. "I am not a praying man. I am not worthy of anything you can give me. I do not ask for my will. I do not ask for my body. Only take my mind. Leave the rest for the Raven."

He heard the voice of Lebía again.

That's how the Old Tales call it. Ammil. The blessing of the Most High, you know.

He knew...

It was the last thought of Otchigen, former Voyevoda of Vasyllia.

THE CURSE
OF THE RAVEN

RAVEN SON: BOOK TWO

To Adrian and Emilia

In the year of the Covenant 1066, the great city of Vasyllia, the very heart of the known world, was betrayed to an invading army of nomad Gumiren by its own people. What many did not know, but suspected, was that the invading southerners were no more than a tool in the hand of Vasyllia's ancient enemy. He has many names, that demon. The Raven. The Great Changer. The Bringer of Darkness. But as often happens, in the moment of the Raven's ascendance was the seed of his demise planted. All that remained was for at least a few Vasylli to remain true to the Old Ways until the time of reclamation. But when the Healer returns, will he find any true Vasylli left?

From "A New History of the Covenant" by Dar-in-Exile
Mirnían II

CHAPTER 1

LLUN THE SMITH

Llun the Smith gazed into the fire. The bellows blew, and the sparks exploded before him like a shower of fireflies. He breathed in. The smell—soot, sweat, dross melting from pure metal. It was as near paradise as anyone could get in Vasyllia. Especially after Vasyllia fell.

"Smith Llun! How much longer?"

It was the fifth time Garmun had asked the same question in the last half hour. The old fool. Llun was continually amazed that the fat man was the most sought-after master builder in Vasyllia. All he ever seemed to do was sit in Llun's smithy, covering most of it with his belly.

"It's coming, it's coming," growled Llun. He didn't mind Garmun sitting around while he worked. But no one...no one was allowed to break the hallowed moments when the fire and the metal fused to become something new, something sacred.

"By the Great Father, Llun, I only asked for nails, not works of art."

Llun twitched at the name. *Great Father, my muscular left bicep. Why is the Raven renaming himself now, of all times? Does he imagine we've forgotten how he took everything from us?*

"What is it about you master builders? What ails you? Too many children?"

Garmun turned purple, opened his mouth to speak, then choked on himself. He had no wife, but his illegitimate progeny filled half of Vasyllia's first reach. Crude people snickered that being so fat was normal after so many pregnancies.

"Peace, Brother Garmun," said Llun. "They're all but done. And I promise you they'll be the hardiest, longest-lasting nails you'll find in all Vasyllia."

And the only ones with a raven etched on the nail's head. May his memory be forever cursed, and may every hammer stroke hasten the time of his demise...

"You mean the most *exquisite* nails in Vasyllia, no doubt," the fat man complained. "I've never seen anyone so taken with his own talent. Don't you know that your little frills and personal touches make no difference? Competence! Competence! That's what the market wants."

"The market, with all its frippery and cheap wares, can burn in the fires of the land of the dead for all I care." It slipped out. Llun hoped the hammer would be distraction enough. But he had never been blessed by fortune.

"Your talk smacks of the Outer Lands, you fool. Be careful no one in the Great Father's good graces overhears you."

"Overhears what?" said a new voice from the doorway.

The stranger who walked in was the antithesis of Garmun—short and wiry like a ratter. Everything about him suggested potential action—his smile, just on the verge of malice, his hands, holding his thick belt as though it were someone's throat, the sharp line of his cheekbones, suggesting some nomad blood. His physicality was so overwhelming that it almost distracted from the dog's scalp hanging from his belt.

So this must be one of that new department that the Gumiren—those filthy nomad invaders from the South—had concocted for collaborators. What was it called? The Consistory, yes. The secret police of the Raven. Dog-men, the commons called them. A kind name for a traitor against his own people.

"I'm not open to new customers," said Llun, trying to keep his tone light.

"That's a relief," the stranger said, with more gentleness than Llun expected. "No one will bother us, then."

He closed the door and dropped the black curtain over the door-window.

"What a pleasant smithy you have here, Brother Llun."

Llun stiffened as the stranger began to look around the smithy. Like a bitch on the scent, the stranger's pointed face bore down on the cluttered left counter of the smithy. He pulled out two interlacing shields of iron leaf-work tracery so fine they almost looked woven. Each held a heraldic icon of a raven in flight.

"Well, that's..." He didn't finish, but to Llun's surprise it sounded like he was about to say "beautiful." What? A Raven's man actually admiring beauty for its own sake?

Llun's stomach churned. It was all wrong: there was genuine admiration in the stranger's eyes. He appreciated the shields as things of beauty, not as objects to buy or sell. That wasn't supposed to happen. The Raven's men followed a script. They were supposed to ask where Llun was going to sell these useless trinkets, and when he hemmed and hawed about beauty and artistry, they would threaten Llun with something horrible.

Llun had seen enough of the Gumiren's work to know that the threats of the collaborators were never idle—weavers with one eye burned out just so their depth perception would no longer be of any use, sword-wrights with their right hands chopped off at the wrist, potters with broken feet.

Damn them all, he thought bitterly.

But this one was admiring decorative shields that had no practical use whatsoever. Llun had made them merely for the sake of beauty.

"What possessed you to make such a thing?"

Llun's hammer stopped in mid-air. It was the choice of words. "Possessed." No, this was no mere inquisitor. This man understood the creative process. What it means to make something, and how it feels to be taken by the hand of the Maker.

"It made itself," said Llun, hesitating. "I was just the instrument."

The stranger gasped with pleasure, as though Llun's words had given him a taste of something he hadn't felt in a very long time. Maybe this was an impostor? A motley fool who put on the dog-scalp to ridicule the Consistory? But such people did not walk the streets for long before their bodies were used as decorations for lamp-posts.

"Llun," said the dog-man, and looked Llun directly in the eyes.

The lack of the "Brother" before Llun's name frightened him more than the direct gaze. This collaborator was something new. Yes, he was likely an artist. An artist of torture and death.

"Llun, you stand there, gawking like a fool, telling me you made something for the sheer pleasure of artistry?"

The stranger's right index finger caressed the outline of the raven, as though he could memorize shapes better with his finger. Could he see it, the *true* picture? The hammer slipped in Llun's hand and almost landed on his thumb. *Careful...*

"Yes." Llun's voice didn't remain as steady as he would have liked. The stranger noticed. His smile was an adder's smile.

"Who taught you to waste your time like this?"

So they had come to it at last. The stranger wanted Llun to be an informer to the collaborators, a friend of the dogs.

Not on my life.

"No one," said Llun, continuing to beat the nails. "Don't think I use my work-time on these things. I give all the Great Father's time to my customers, as anyone, even fat Garmun here, will tell you." The builder looked like he wanted to kill Llun and run away from him at the same time. "I do this...art...in my own time."

The stranger raised his eyebrows slightly, faintly amused. Llun immediately realized his mistake. He shouldn't have said anything about having the luxury of time for himself.

"What a shame," said the Consistory man. "You should *rest* during your free time, Brother Llun. It will help you make better nails and horseshoes and braziers. *Useful* things. Will you accept a gift from the Great Father? A gratis pass to one of the houses of rest?"

The dog-man leered. Llun flushed, embarrassed. Did the dog-man really think that sort of thing appealed to an artisan? How typical. The smith working off his frustrations with a romp in the hay.

Llun struck the nail so hard it cracked in half.

"I don't fraternize with prostitutes," said Llun. His finger bled where the cracked nail had pierced it. *Concentrate!*

The Consistory man smiled, gentle as ever. "I didn't say a thing about *fraternizing*. And why use such a crude word as prostitute? I believe I have heard them better described as purveyors of pleasure."

Garmun chortled, then tried to disappear. For a man of his size, that was not easy.

"Anyway, I don't have time for that nonsense," said Llun.

"Nonsense? It is all sanctioned by our Great Father himself. Are you suggesting that anything his greatness allows is not worthy of your time? I will not say coin, because I have already offered you a gratis pass."

"That is not what I meant to say." Llun stopped hammering, put the hammer down, and wiped his hands on his apron, which only made them dirtier. "I'm sorry, I don't believe I have the honor of your name, Brother?"

That should bring matters to a head, whether or not Llun's head would be the cost.

"Ah, my mistake! My name is Aspidían. You may have heard of me."

Oh, *Heights*. Aspidían? The right hand of Yadovír, the traitor who had opened the gates of Vasyllia to the invading army of Gumiren. Some even insinuated that Aspidían was more than his right hand. By all accounts, he was a monster that had killed over one hundred true Vasylli with his own hands.

"Brother Llun." Aspidían's face no longer showed interest in anything. He leaned against the wall in assumed fatigue, the very picture of a man who had seen too much and wished merely to be left alone. "I would be most honored if you would come to the Consistory's halls on the morrow, perhaps at three hours after sunrise? I would like to employ your skills in a most important matter. Good day to you."

"As you say, Brother Aspidían."

As soon as he left, the forge coughed, the bellows sighed, the anvil begged to be struck again. Everything in the smithy heaved out a relieved breath. Garmun was near to tears of hysteria.

"Brother Llun, Brother Llun," he whispered, as if expecting the inquisitor to be eavesdropping just outside the door. "Do you know what this means?" He threw his hands up above his head. "Who will make things for me now? Don't you know you are the best craftsman in Vasyllia? Have I ever told you that, Brother? Have I?" Both sweaty hands, fleshy and fat, wrung Llun's arm, kneading it like bread, though even his massive hands hardly encircled the width of Llun's arm, hardened by years of the smithy. "Why must it be you? I know the Great Father needs an occasional example for everyone's instruction, but ... why *you*?"

"Calm yourself, you fat fool. Why not take the man at his word? Perhaps there is some manner of work to be done?"

Garmun guffawed. "You madman of an artist! Don't you know what they do to people like you? Have you forgotten Dashun?"

Llun tried to stop the grimace, but failed. Why did Garmun have to mention Dashun of all people? Llun was sure he would never forget the sight of Dashun's mutilated body. But what was worse? The torture, or the way he had publicly recanted all his beliefs and convictions? He had read aloud a text prepared for him by the Raven. Then he had collaborated with them, even uncovered a conspiracy against the Gumiren. And still they killed him horribly.

"You exaggerate," Llun said, coughing to cover the quaver in his voice. "I'm no danger to anyone. I am simply an odd, self-absorbed craftsman."

"Brother Llun, do you know *anything* about Aspidían?" He raised both hands, palms out. The gesture to ward off evil.

"Your nails, Brother Garmun."

"Brother Llun. Oh, my dear friend." Garmun wept, blubbering like a woman. Perversely, Llun remembered the jesting commoners and the purported pregnancies. He couldn't help himself.

"There, there, Garmun. I know it's common enough to cry more than usual when you're pregnant."

Garmun turned purple again. Shoving Llun back so that he nearly flew into the forge itself, he pointed a finger thick as a blood sausage at his nose. "You ... you ..." He huffed out like a passing thunderstorm, taking his bombast with him.

Llun remembered to breathe.

"You can come out now," he whispered. The entire left side of the table heaved. "Did no one teach you discretion, you little idiot?"

"Llun," said the girl of thirteen who finally managed to extricate herself from all the bits of metal. "Did you mean what you said to Garmun? Or did you just make him mad so he wouldn't be associated with you when you're trussed up like a chicken on the spit?"

"Which do you think, Mirodara?"

Mirodara's face went white. "I wasn't serious, Llun."

"Never mind. I'm not that worried. I'm not nearly as important as your father was."

"Dashun is *not* my father. I have no father. Not after he collaborated."

"You can't wash his blood from inside you, girl! Why do you think they've been after you all this time?"

Llun's breath caught as he realized how close the girl had been to death only a few moments ago. Was *that* why Aspidían had come in? Was someone blabbing again?

"Anyway, I don't even look like Dashun. Everyone knows I'm my mother's—"

"Don't!" Llun's voice cracked. The last thing he wanted was to be reminded of Vatrina.

"I'm sorry," said Mirodara, her face switching from red to white and back to red with dizzying speed. "I know you don't like to talk about her. But she was my *mother*, Llun. You're just her brother."

"You don't have any siblings, Mirodara. You don't know. You just don't know. I never knew either of my parents."

"Yes, yes, and now I'm the only one you have left. Blah blah blah. You won't talk me out of it."

"What do you hope to accomplish, anyway, with these...what do they call themselves?"

"The Sons of the Swan. We're going to reclaim Vasyllia for Darina Sabíana, the true queen of all the lands. She's still alive in that palace. I *know* it."

Llun laughed.

"You laugh? You're about to be thrown into the middle of it all. You think they'll let you stay on the side, uninvolved?"

Llun sighed and stretched his aching shoulders. Mirodara, for all her silliness, was older than her years. She had no choice. All the children had grown older the day Vasyllia fell.

"You'll stay here tonight," said Llun, the tone of finality clear in his voice. Mirodara looked like she wanted to argue, but nodded and extended a hand to Llun.

"Peace?"

Llun embraced her, trying hard not to weep. She did look just like her mother, his sister.

Please, Adonais. If you still listen to us who failed you, don't let them take her. Not her. She's just a girl.

On the day of blood, a day when the sun turns black and stars fall as flames from the sky, those walking the streets of the Great City will seem alive. But they are naught but the hordes of the dead. In that day, the swan's wing will be broken, and the falcon will be too far to hear her cries of pain. The earth itself will moan for the Healer. But the Healer is lost in the maze of his own doubts...

From "The Prophecy of Llun"
(The Sayings, Book XXIII 3:1-3)

Chapter 2

The Consistory

The early morning light showed Llun's smithy off at its best. The prevailing colors peeking through the soot-grimed windows were gold and orange. No customer came this early, and as the sun rose, the true, hidden beauty of the place came to life. In the light of the fire, the smithy danced with shadows, but the morning sun, which coddled like a mother and warmed like childhood memory, showed the things Llun made in their true aspect.

He picked up the decorative shields that Aspidían had so admired. Only now could their secret be told, their mystery uncovered. They were not ravens at all in the tracery. The morning rays, coming through the window at a very specific angle, revealed the ravens to be two falcons. The dancing fire-light of any house's interior was intended to trick the casual observer to think they were ravens depicted flying at the observer, head feathers curiously ruffled by the wind. The figure was made so that it shifted in the mind's eye after long contemplation in the light of morning, like a difficult sentence in a book that rewards the slow reader. Then, the ravens transformed into falcons.

Llun wondered if Aspidían had read the riddle in the tracery.

Was that why he was so astounded? Or was it true appreciation? It was bad enough not to have any visible representation of the Raven in his smithy, as was required by the so-called Great Father. But to blaspheme him by association with something as unclean as the falcon—the sigil of Voran, the Healer and the great enemy of the Raven—that would be reason enough for a high inquisitor to pay a visit to the first reach of Vasyllia. Or was it simply that someone had reported Llun in hopes of gaining his smithy as a reward? Llun knew of too many such cases to consider it impossible.

Too many thoughts. Like someone banging an iron pan with a wooden spoon inside his head. Llun decided to take the long way to the Consistory.

He looked in on Mirodara sleeping in the back room. She was sprawled on the floor, snoring. As though she had not a care in the world. He couldn't help smiling, though that only brought back the pain of memory. The way her nose bent slightly to the left, giving her mouth a soft quirk, as though she were always on the verge of laughter—that was her mother's most obvious feature. Rubbing his eyes until the stars exploded on the inside of his eyelids, he hurried out into the street.

I will not be maudlin this early in the morning, he thought.

He still thought of his smithy as belonging to the first reach. Only a few houses down, Siloán the potter's home stood, now even smaller-looking than usual after the mead-house had swallowed two neighboring houses to become the largest building in the reach. The roads were as meandering, the refuse as omnipresent. The poor still bickered at street corners, fighting for the rights to an intersection as though their eternal soul depended on it. But it wasn't the first reach any more, he reminded himself. Just a few roads down was the new merchants' quarter—part of the "Great Father's" efforts at equalizing opportunities for all citizens. Or some such unintelligible nonsense.

The walls that had stood between the three reaches of Vasyllia for centuries had been torn down. The stairways joining them together now seemed naked without the walls buttressing them. They were a pitiful sight, and most Vasylli instinctively avoided the stairs, preferring the new, wide gravel roads that joined all reaches in stark, over-straight lines, so counterintuitive to the gentle roll and sway of the mountain's side.

In the other direction from the merchants' quarter was the other great equalizer—the pleasure quarter, as it was officially labeled. Llun flushed with sudden disgust, remembering the dog-man's offer. The air of the first reach had always been redolent with aroma. But it had been good and clean, for all its earthiness. The first reach had had its problems, but people had been princi-pled, keeping to a code that separated them from the corruption of the upper reaches. It had been important before, to keep oneself clean of the base and the vile. Now, worker and noble alike drank sour ale in the wide anterooms of the whore-houses. Equality indeed.

The former second reach was now a shambling mess. Most of Nebesta's refugees still lived there in tottering canvas tents. Every hundred paces or so, a pile of those tents was set apart from the next by a line of spears stuck into the earth, their points directed at the people in the camps. Guards with longbows patrolled the spear-lines constantly. Whenever they passed, silence fell.

Cutting into the silence like a knife into flesh was the sound of children. Two Nebesti boys, dressed in barely anything but loincloths, chased a much smaller boy through the pile of tents, screaming something menacing. The small boy turned directly toward the lines of spears. Llun felt his vision go dim as he saw that none of them were stopping. Two grim Vasylli warriors converged toward them. One of them grabbed a standing spear from the ground and pointed it at the children, shaking it menacingly.

The children tried to stop, but their momentum was consid-erable. The first one—a ratty-haired boy of about six or seven—

managed to dig his heels at a suitable distance. But his assailants, who were both muscular and seemed large for their age, were not as quick to stop. They scratched and pulled at each other, trying to stop in time. At the very last moment, even the Vasylli guard paled. But he didn't move.

The small boy, pushed toward the spear, managed to twist aside at the last minute. He wasn't impaled.

But his side was slashed open. There was a lot of blood, even from the distance where Llun stood, clutching his chest for horror. A young Nebesti man ran into Llun's field of vision, his hands shaking in those ridiculously expansive gestures that all Nebesti indulge in. Behind him was a young woman. She stopped as soon as she saw the boy. Her sunburned face blanched, and she screamed.

The warriors tensed as the Nebesti man approached them. The warrior who had not hurt the boy stood in front of the one who had. His fists were bunched, and he yelled at the Nebesti to back down. The father did not. His eyes' whites grew, and his hands waved more and more frantically. All the while, he moved toward the spears. The second warrior drew his sword, yelling. Llun couldn't make out the words in the general mayhem of women and children screaming. The stricken boy moaned not at all, which was even more frightening. The father shoved his face into the warrior's face, his raspy torrent of words turning into shouting. The warrior's eyes bulged, and his face grew red. He kept repeating something again and again. Not once did he look at the boy.

Something twanged by Llun's ear. The boy's father twisted back unnaturally and fell to the ground. An arrow shivered in his shoulder.

"Move along!" A rough voice yelled near Llun. A huge Gumir, his face twisted into a grimace, making his already angled eyes disappear in the folds of his dirt-brown face. "Not your concern, Vasylli. Great Father's business. Move along."

Llun looked away and moved along. As he walked, he heard the familiar laugh of the Gumiren as they closed in. Then the thudding began. The sounds of fists on flesh and bone. Gritting his teeth, Llun ran on.

Where the Covenant Tree had once stood, a pile of kindling reached as high as a two-story house. It stood as a dour reminder of that day Vasyllia fell, when the Gumiren had nearly thrown the children of Adonais's faithful into the fire. It had been a cruel joke of the Raven. Deny your divinity, your Adonais, he had said. And I will spare your children. And for what? For an existence of fear and no hope of a brighter future? Perhaps it would have been better for the children to burn.

Above the pile of logs—it obscenely resembled a huge raven's nest—was the Raven's totem: a stone obelisk that branched out into a pair of jagged wings. It was black as obsidian, but without that stone's glass-like sheen. Whatever it was made of, the material seemed to suck light in, making it not so much black as absent—a hole in the fabric of the world shaped like an obelisk.

Llun stood before it, his hatred a hair's edge from boiling. He forced himself to move on toward the third reach.

Of all the former reaches, the third was the one least affected by the Gumiren. Most of the damage of the battle for Vasyllia had been quickly repaired, as the Gumiren took residence in the mansions of the wealthy third-reachers. Many of them had kept the nobles as their servants. More like slaves, in fact, especially the women. Some old noblemen had been quietly dispatched during the now-infamous "night purges" that the Gumiren conducted every so often. Llun had heard that the purges continued, but now it was not the Gumiren, but turncoat Vasylli who would rat out their own brothers for a chance at a better set of table knives.

Seeing the mansions still sparkling like the jewels of great Vasyllia that was—it gave Llun vertigo. For a brief, brilliant moment it seemed that everything—the Gumiren overlords, the horrors of the nightly purges, the baseness to which everything had sunk—was just a dream. After all, wasn't the palace of the

Dar still standing, its seven towers like beacons of hope leading toward a glorious future?

Except now the palace was the dwelling place of a demonic Power who had the brazenness to call himself everyone's father.

The gates to the outer courtyard of the palace, which now housed the Consistory, used to be open at all times as a sign of the Dar's closeness to his people. After the fall of Vasyllia, the gates had been shut. So, when they opened to admit Llun, he had the sinking feeling that he was being invited to step into the gullet of a hungry monster.

He had been inside once only, during the matriculation ceremony of the warrior seminary. In the old days. He, as one of the preferred swordsmiths of the seminary, had received a place of honor in a front row of the viewing gallery. It was an impressive sight—the pentagonal courtyard filled with silent, unmoving, black-robed warriors, all with their swords drawn. At the whip-like calls of their cohort elders, the hundreds of warriors had demonstrated, as one man, every step of the sword-forms. It was like a dance, and it had taken his breath away.

Now, he was struck by the emptiness of the square, save for a few scurrying forms of servants. Instead, his eyes were drawn to the huge banners flapping on the walls of the keep—the red raven obelisk on a black field. Like a bad joke, Sabíana's sign of the gold sun on black field flitted small and insignificant from a pole jutting up above the smallest of the seven towers.

Perhaps she is alive, he thought. The thought did little to comfort him. What was a crippled young woman with no army behind her supposed to do to change the fortunes of Vasyllia?

"What, you as well?" Aspidían materialized out of nowhere. "It's the strangest thing, Brother Llun. Whenever one of you old Vasylli come up here (oh, it's rare enough, I grant you) their eye is always drawn to that pitiful banner. I wonder why?"

"Brother Aspidían," said Llun, bowing in greeting. The wiry inquisitor was dressed in simple linen trousers with a billowing linen overshirt—the picture of leisure and relaxation. Only his eyes still smoldered behind his smile.

"Come, Brother Llun. I want you to meet someone."

They took an unobtrusive door in the keep's wall that led to a twisting staircase. It was dusty and disused, and Llun was sure that this was where he would be suddenly attacked from behind and thrown into a dungeon. Instead, at the top of the staircase, Aspidían opened another unobtrusive door. Facing the golden light that streamed into the stairwell was like staring into the sun. When Llun's eyes adjusted, he saw they were in a vaulted chamber covered in frescoes. Every inch of the curved ceilings and walls burst with giant-sized fancies on the theme of flowers and birds. Bumblebees painted with actual gold leaf seemed to buzz on purple and red petals of peonies. Strawberries and blueberries burst from the confines of their green and yellow leaves.

"He likes it. How pleasant."

Llun's stomach lurched at the sound of that voice. It was more than one voice. It was like a voice with a hundred echoes, coming from one mouth. When he saw the speaker, it took a strong effort of will not to cringe.

He was...well, beautiful. Flawless skin, like polished ivory. Soft eyes, almost lavender colored. Long-fingered hands, the nails reflecting the golden candlelight in the room like polished metal. Llun had heard that Yadovír, the Mouth of the Raven, had grown younger and more pleasing to look at in the five years since the fall of Vasyllia. But the beauty was somehow... wrong. As he stared at Yadovír, unable to look away, it seemed to Llun that something shivered in his face. No, *under* his face. Like his entire surface—skin, face, hands—was an elaborate costume for something foul underneath.

Yadovír cocked his head to one side and slitted his eyes, assessing. "You're a bear of a man, aren't you? But my friend here says that you have talent."

"That he does," said Aspidían, coming close to Yadovír. *Too* close. Llun felt sick to his stomach.

Yadovír's eyes wandered over Llun, from head to foot, lingering. He smiled, a predator's smile that was not his own. Llun had the sensation that he was being judged as potential food.

"For all your strength, Brother Llun," said Yadovír, with a hint of a growl. "You are rather soft, aren't you?"

Aspidían chuckled, and they both turned away from Llun and walked to a strange contrivance in the middle of the room. It was so out of character with the general opulence that at first Llun didn't understand what he was looking at. The he realized it was a hole. In the floorboards. In that hole was a hearth, the simple kind that you find in a first-reacher house. There were pillows around the hearth—simple, red pillows of no especial value. A small table stood by the hearth. Three goblets and mead. Mead? Llun couldn't understand what he was seeing. Why, in this palatial room, was there a sliver of commonness more appropriate to Llun's own back room behind the forge?

Aspidían and Yadovír sat on two of the cushions, leaning into one another in a way that bespoke more than casual intimacy. It was unsettling. The whole picture was unsettling. Was this part of an elaborate plan to confuse him so much that he would somehow stumble into revealing some dangerous truth? Did they know about Mirodara?

"Why do you gawk?" Aspidían guffawed. "Sit. That cushion's for you."

Llun did as he was told. Yadovír continued to look at him hungrily as Aspidían poured him the mead. Llun tried to focus his attention on the cup, and once again he lost himself in the quality of the work. The wrought iron tracery woven like ivy around the wooden goblet was exquisite. It nearly rivaled his own abilities. Then he drank the mead and nearly drowned in the pleasure of that taste. He had not had good mead—hearty, first-reacher bread-ale—in years.

Laughter jolted him out of his contemplation.

"You're right, Aspidían," said Yadovír. "He really is...an artist."

Llun felt his face get warm, and suddenly he was angry. Sick of it all. His teeth creaked as he tensed his jaw.

"What do you want of me?" he asked, surprised at the audible growl in his own voice.

"Oh, how disappointing," drawled Yadovír. "No small talk? Cut straight to the heart of the matter, eh? Artists." He sounded faintly disgusted with the idea.

"You never understood us," said Aspidían. "We operate on a different schedule than most. Don't we, Brother Llun?"

Llun refused to be included in the offer of intimacy. He had no desire to be named the kind of artist that Aspidían was. If they wanted something of him, they would have to pry it out of his hands. The thought gave him shivers.

"As you wish," said Yadovír, putting his cup down, then yawning as he stretched against Aspidían, who still seemed amused by everything. "We want you to take on a commission. For the Consistory. In fact, we want it to be the last commission you take."

There was a double meaning there, Llun knew it. But he pretended not to hear it. "You want me to be your exclusive smith? But why?"

"We have a...sudden vacancy." Aspidían's eyebrows came together, shadowing his eyes.

Llun picked up his cup and offered it to them, significantly.

"Yes," said Yadovír. "These cups are his work. As you see, he was very good. But he had an unfortunate slip in judgment. He can no longer help us."

"You killed him?"

Yadovír looked disappointed. "No, of course not. They only took his hand. The Gumiren."

"So...wait, I'm not sure I understand. Are you saying that you and the Gumiren are not...on the same side?"

Aspidían's eyes were no longer smoldering. They burned.

"Now *that* is a comment unworthy of you, Brother Llun. What makes you think any Vasylli would willingly collaborate with those animals? No. Compromises were made, yes. Necessary ones. But never think, not for a moment, that we do not anticipate with great joy the moment when we can slaughter them in their beds."

"What about the Raven?" said Llun.

Aspidían tensed, and his hand went to his boot. Something gleamed there.

"Do...not...utter—" he whispered menacingly.

"Oh, don't worry, Aspidían," said Yadovír. "He's brave, for all of his goggling at the fine things in life. Perhaps not as soft as we thought." His smile stretched his face. "Brother Llun, I'll let you say it once. But never again. The *Great Father*, for your information, is well on his way to becoming a figure of speech. Soon the Vasylli will forget about the Raven. Just as he would want it. His desire is not Vasyllia itself. It is something else. He has promised me that, soon, we will have Vasyllia back to ourselves."

"How can you trust him? He seems willing enough to turn on those he needed to get into Vasyllia in the first place."

"I don't trust him, you fool," said Yadovír. Something shimmered in the shadows behind him—a suggestion of huge, jagged wings. Llun's heart plunged to his ankles. "I'm useful to him. And I'm making the Gumiren less so. Soon, their time will be over."

"And high time too," said Aspidían. "They've all become so fat and complacent. The Ghan himself can hardly walk now, he is so round. He must be carried around on a litter."

Llun's curiosity got the better of him. "Is it true, what's been said in the first reach? That there are troubles in the Gumiren ruling council?"

Aspidían put on an entirely new face. Intense concentration, with a hint of anticipation. Llun had a suspicion that was the sincerest Aspidían face yet. "Do tell, Brother Llun. What sort of gossip are the commons bandying about?"

Llun resented the tone, but forced himself to speak evenly. "Well, in the first years of the occupation, the Gumiren were everywhere, weren't they? Patrolling streets, eating at the public houses, propping up the spear lines in the refugee camp. But over the years, fewer and fewer of them were seen in the lower reaches. Then the rumors started that the Gumiren had taken to Vasylli luxuries. Particularly wine and mead. Not surprising, given their nomad bloodlines. And they were willing to give more and more of the ruling responsibilities to the collaborators."

Yadovír smiled again, and Llun realized he had said "collaborators" out loud. *Focus, you idiot!*

"Then there are the rumors of diseases among the Gumiren. Some sort of pox, some say. Others are less...compassionate in their guesses."

"Yes, you could say that," said Aspidían, snickering. "Why are you so afraid to say it out loud, Llun? Your tongue won't be polluted. Say it. 'Venereal diseases.'" He mouthed it, slowly, as if he could taste the syllables.

Llun scowled.

"To answer your question, Brother Llun," said Yadovír, "yes, the Gumiren are growing complacent. And soon, soon the time will come when we will take back Vasyllia for the Vasylli. I ask you now. Will you help us? Will you help your people?"

This was not collaboration with the enemy at all. This was... well, this was exactly what Llun wanted. But not with Yadovír. He was there during the battle for Vasyllia. He remembered what Yadovír had done. Yadovír had orchestrated a pogrom of clerics of the cult of Adonais to cover up his own crimes, his own treachery. The thought propped up his cold hatred, and the words tumbled out of his mouth even as he thought them.

"And what about the Darina? Where is she in all your plans?"

The silence hissed, so complete that Llun heard the squelching sound of Yadovír's feral smile stretching across his gums.

"She is...instrumental."

"She is alive, then?"

"Oh, yes. Very much so."

"I don't believe you."

Aspidían got up, slowly, his muscles so taut that it looked like an invisible hand lifted him up, like a marionette. "You don't seem to understand, Brother Llun. Here we are, extending you a hand of friendship when you know very well that we could be extending a corkscrew to separate your nails from your hands. And you spit on this hand of friendship? Is that wise? Do you not understand who it is that sits before you?"

Llun's breath quickened. His head buzzed. He had had too much of the mead. Or was there something in the mead? Something to make him more...malleable?

"I...forgive me, Brother Aspidían," said Llun, nearly whimpering, and hating himself for it. "I...why me? Why choose me to be your exclusive smith? You have seen my work. It is good, yes. But I do not work fast. And if you need a swordsmith for an uprising against the Gumiren...well, you would not have many swords..."

Aspidían relaxed back into Yadovír's side. "He has a point, you know," he said, conversationally.

"You forget one thing." Yadovír looked at Aspidían. "Who he *is*."

"Ah yes!" Aspidían's eyes sparkled with mischief as he crossed his arms across his chest. "You are related to key members of the Sons of the Swan."

And there it was. The trap snapped shut. Llun almost imagined the sound, like a big bear trap chomping down on his ankle. He nearly panicked then and there.

"Dashun is dead," Llun managed to say, barely containing his fear within. "His infection has been cut out of Vasyllia. I am not of their mind. I do not seek what they seek."

"No, but Mirodara does," said Yadovír.

"She is a *child!*"

"Children will grow to be men and women, a new generation of rot at the heart of Vasyllia. Until every Son of the Swan is killed, no peace will ever last here or anywhere else in the world."

"Unless..." Aspidían cut in, his voice reasonable and kind. "We are prepared to overlook her involvement with the Sons as ... a youthful indiscretion. But only if you take up our offer."

Llun sighed. "Am I expected to give an answer immediately?"

"No, no!" Aspidían waved his hands placatingly. "Take your time. Just ... not too much of it."

The dawn of hope rises. From the dirt of the tree's roots will arise a sleeper of ages. She will be braver than many men, stronger than myriad warriors. Her age is not counted in years, but in the bitter days of pain and loss. Her death will bring forth life. Her sleep will make Living Water flow again in the wasteland...

From "The Prophecy of Llun"
(The Sayings, Book XXIII, 5:8-10)

CHAPTER 3

MIRODARA

Llun hardly remembered the way he took back to his smithy. It didn't help that most of Vasyllia was hidden in fog, dropping the early summer temperatures down to what they had been in late spring. The kind of weather that obscured one's thoughts and deadened one's limbs.

Bacon. The smell shocked him back to awareness. He was nearly home, and the bacon-smell, to his amazement, was not coming from the mead-house, but from his own smithy. He laughed with pleasure. It had been a long time since he had eaten bacon.

Mirodara.

Idiot girl. Is this your idea of being unobtrusive?

He rushed into the smithy, and the smoke attacked his eyes and mouth. He choked as the pleasing smell of fried pig transformed into the sickly-sweet smell of burnt pig.

"If you're going to let the whole neighborhood know you're here, at least don't burn the bacon!" He smiled as he saw Mirodara blowing on a thin, black piece of something that could have once been edible. She breathed out in exasperation and offered him a bite. He shook his head and laughed.

"I wanted to make you something nice," she said, never more like his sister than at that moment.

"If you really want to do something nice for me, you'll sit down and listen."

She straightened at the change in Llun's voice. Nodding slowly, she threw the charred bit of meat back into the pan on the hearth. It sizzled, as though hurtling a final insult at her.

"So ..." she began, "what sort of false promises did they make, the vipers?"

"Stop." He raised his voice just enough for her to curl in on herself a little. "I said listen. Open mind, yes?"

"Fine." He saw that she was working very hard not to sulk.

"They know about you. Not about the Sons in general. About you, Mirodara."

"Then why am I still here?"

Llun sighed and looked away from her. He suddenly, ridiculously, really wanted to eat that bacon.

"Oh, I see," she said, her voice husky. "They're using me to force you to do something. What, exactly?"

"I'm not entirely sure, to be honest. They say they need a swordsmith. But I can't imagine why they'd want me for that. Unless Yadovír wants a family heirloom he can hang over his door."

"Yes, you do take rather a bit more time than necessary on ... well, everything. Even nails!" She chuckled.

"I think there's much that they're not telling me. But one thing I know for sure. If you do not stop your silly association with the Sons of the Swan, it'll be the end of both of us."

Mirodara took Llun's paw of a hand between her own. They were so uncalloused and small. Like a mouse holding on to a lion. Llun's heart felt stretched to a breaking point.

"Llun, let's be honest. They're going to get us, sooner or later. Whether or not you help them. Whether or not I ever so much as speak to a Son of the Swan again. At some point, in the middle of the night, you'll be taken in your sleep. Me too."

"Don't speak like that. I'll—"

"What matters," she said, not listening to him, "is what we manage to do before they stop us. What have either of us done in our lives that is worth remembering? Hm? But now, when our world has already ended, now ... well, every decision of every person can have huge consequences. Don't you understand that? Every person who capitulates to the Gumiren and their collaborators is guilty of treachery before our whole people. But every single child who refuses to bow down...How can I make you understand? Every sacrifice...it matters. Even if it seems pointless. It *matters.*"

"When did you grow up, my little cub?" He tried to smile through the tears that now fell. He wiped them off. "But what if I were to tell you..." He lowered his voice to a whisper. "There are rumblings ... that the collaborators are preparing to throw off the Gumiren. To restore Vasyllia to the Vasylli. Even to restore the Darina to her place."

"You believe them? They'll say anything, Llun. Have you forgotten what they did?"

"I haven't, no. *You* were too small to remember, I would have thought."

"I was nothing of the sort. I saw the warriors ... *our* warriors turn into beasts. I saw them attack defenseless women who tried to reason with them, to prevent them from hacking down every priest in sight. You don't forget such a sight. Not ever. And these are the people you entrust the safety of our city to?"

"You're right. I just can't fathom losing you."

"You'll have to fathom a lot more than that. Don't you understand? This isn't the battle for Vasyllia. It's the battle for the soul of Vasyllia."

She breathed deeply, as though considering whether or not to divulge something.

"There's something else," she said. "It's Voran, the son of Otchigen."

"What about him?" Llun couldn't help the bitterness coming

through. Voran, Darina Sabíana's intended and the supposed hope of Vasyllia's reclamation, had been exiled years ago. But rumors had trickled into Vasyllia that he had found Living Water and that he was using it to heal those who had fallen to the Gumiren onslaught. Others suggested that he was gathering an army to reclaim Vasyllia. Probably all of it was rubbish.

"The Sons have it on excellent authority that he is finally coming back to Vasyllia. And he has Living Water."

Llun couldn't muster the enthusiasm necessary to believe her. He found he had run out of things to say. She hugged him.

"I want to go out in a blaze of glory. I want to do something so mad that the Heights will have no choice but to bow down again before my act of courage. You'll see. It'll happen soon. Everything is going to change very soon."

How horribly have you grown up, my little one, Llun thought. *Can I expect anything else, when all you've ever known is fear and death?*

The Day of Blood will be dread and awful. But it is not the end of the tribulation. Hear my voice, O faithful of Vasyllia! There will come a time when brother will slaughter father, for he will not recognize his face. Brown-faced Gumir will attack white-faced Vasylli, but he will be stabbed in his back. No one will know the face of his enemy in the darkness and the chaos. Nor will he know the face of his friend.

From "The Prophecy of Llun"
(The Sayings, Book XXIII, 2:4-7)

Chapter 4

The Sons of the Swan

After Mirodara left, Llun could not face his thoughts. He opened the smithy and threw himself into his work with the kind of abandon he had only really felt in the early days, when his body hardly noticed the strain of smithing. It was a surprise to him when he looked at the window to see that it had gone completely dark.

He allowed his forge to sputter and die. The shadows at first faintly resisted their inevitable end, then they lay down to a quiet death. He went to his rest in the back room, bare as always but for the bench lining the back wall. The barrenness was a comfort, clearing the mind, especially in its contrast to the clutter in the smithy itself. Llun lay down on the bench, not bothering to undress. In spite of the buzzing of his mind, he could not keep his eyelids open, and only a few moments later, he was asleep.

When his door tore from its hinges, he woke with a start. There were five men in his room, dressed in black, a shriveled dog's head hanging from the belt of each. In the absurd confusion of the just-awoken, all Llun could think of was how disappointing it was that the promise of bacon had not lived up to the reality. The intruders gave him no time to reflect. They all fell on top of him like the dogs that they were.

He struggled, but it was soon obvious that any sign of resistance meant an excuse for them to inflict unnecessary pain. But pain was an old friend of Llun's. He fought them back as furiously as a cornered rat. They were in *his* smithy. He knew better than they where the most painful weapons were, if only he could get to them.

Two held Llun's arms pinned to his back, while two more demonstratively took off their gloves. Underneath, Llun saw black metal between their fingers. This was not a mere arrest, then. He was to be made an example of.

Not in my smithy.

He made a feint of losing consciousness, forcing the two holding him to lean down to keep him pinned. As he leaned hard against the shin of the man holding his right hand, he twisted into him, catching his foot under him and pushing his knee back. Llun felt it crack, and the man howled. Before the others could restrain him, Llun lifted both his attackers up with his huge body and threw them at the rest of their fellows.

Under his sleeping bench, Llun kept a half-done war hammer. It was too heavy for most men to lift, but in the heat of the struggle he lifted it like a dry twig and swung with all his force at his assailants. Something gave way behind the blow. More wailing. For the briefest of moments, Llun saw a way through the five attackers as they tried to avoid his blows. Dealers of pain were always the worst at bearing it themselves, he knew. Llun rushed past them, through the broken doorway, into the smithy proper. It was still dark, except for the gaping hole where the butchers had broken in. Llun ran through it, but stopped dead in his tracks.

Unaccountably, it had snowed last night. The moon being full, the thin layer of pristine white seemed to give off its own eerie light. In the dark, there were smears of black all over the snow. Blood. A lamentation of swans lay like an unholy sacrifice before Llun's smithy. All their heads were cut off. He understood. Yadovír and Aspidían were not waiting for his answer. He turned around and ran back into the smithy, a red haze before his eyes.

The dog-men must have felt it, because they hung back for the blink of an eye. It was enough. Llun crashed onto them like a wave onto a cliff, and they scattered before him. One swing of the war hammer, and two came down with crushed heads. One tried to lunge under Llun's attack, but Llun had a knife in his left hand, and he plunged it into the man's arm before he could reach his body. With the back hand of his hammer-arm, he crushed the man's shoulder into his backbone. The man screamed.

Only one left.

The last one turned and ran away. Llun put his hammer on the ground and took the knife in his right hand. Balancing it on his fingers, he felt for the center of heaviness, remembering his occasional training from the old days, when he had forged for the warrior seminary. Then he flipped it forward. It landed in the man's neck. He fell, spluttering.

Llun picked up his hammer and rushed toward the nearest of the new roads.

Once in his life, Llun had seen a beehive overturned by a bear. It had been in an outlying village near Vasyllia, where his favorite great-aunt lived with her woodsman husband. The bees, normally sleepy and gentle, had frenzied into a mass of death-dealers that could no longer distinguish their caretaker from a marauding bear. After the bear was done, his aunt had come out—wearing chainmail for good measure. For the first five minutes, they had swarmed her as though she were the bear's consort. Only her stillness and her crooning song had eventually calmed them and allowed his uncle to begin the work of rebuilding the hives.

But she was not here in Vasyllia now to calm the masses that roiled in the streets of the first reach.

Madness seemed to have taken over. It was too dark to make out much except that everyone seemed to be attacking everyone.

In brief snatches of focus, Llun saw what looked like Gumiren warriors, judging by their kaftans and silk-sashed caps, attacking and hacking and burning everywhere they went. But there was something wrong about them. Then he heard it. They were speaking Vasylli to each other.

Without another thought, Llun plunged into the swarm, brandishing his war hammer over his head and screaming at the top of his lungs. To his own surprise, he remembered how to use it. It had only been a few lessons with Elder Pahomy of the warrior seminary, years ago now. But he had taken to the weapon like a babe to its mother's teat.

The false Gumiren had not expected any serious resistance. That was clear enough by how they fled from Llun's wrath. But he was fast, in spite of his size. And some kind of war-madness was on him. He had heard a name for it: the war-wind. It was said to make dark gods of men. Well, perhaps Mirodara was right. It was far better to die like this than to continue merely existing in the Vasyllia of the Raven.

The false Gumiren were like sheaves of wheat, and he was the scythe. At fourteen, he lost count of the ones who fell under his war hammer. Before he knew it, the swarming had stopped. Everything was silent, save for the lingering ringing in his ears. Then the sounds of the after-battle began. The crying and the wailing. The wounded. The beloved of the wounded. The war-wind still blew within him. He could not stay here, could not bear to listen to the groans of the weak and fallen.

He ran on, toward the second reach. The Nebesti refugee camps were on fire. Mounted figures rode back and forth, black and demonic against the dancing flames, screaming and whooping. These were not Gumiren. The flopping sacks on their belts—no, they were dogs' heads—revealed them to be warriors of the Consistory. What was going on? Who was attacking whom? Why?

Suddenly, a wave of armed people—they were not warriors,

for there were women and children among them—encircled the mounted Consistory men. Banners fluttered among this rag-tag army. In the smoke, it was difficult to make out much, but then the firelight exploded as a tent collapsed, and Llun saw Sirin and other High Beings embroidered on the banners. These were the Sons of the Swan.

His war-wind fled at their sight. So many of them were children! What were they hoping to achieve? Was all this madness of their doing? Is *this* what Mirodara meant when she said that everything was going to change?

Llun was frozen in place, torn between a desire to run and save Mirodara and a gut-deep need to see what was happening in the third reach. Something was going on. Something vital. His hammer could prove important here. But he needed to be near the palace. At the center of everything. He needed to *know*.

With a groan, he wrenched himself away from the sight of the child-army. Running past the Raven's totem, he found time to spit at it. No Gumiren stood guarding it. If he had time, he would have defiled it properly. But no time. Up the gravel roads he ran, the pebbles barely holding him up as he flew with unnatural speed for his bulk. Blasts of fire seemed to be everywhere, exploding even out of bare earth. Then, the rains came. Smoke belched up in black, choking billows. Llun lost all sense of direction, but continued to push upward. Bloodied people ran past him, down into the first reach. Screams burst from in front of him, then behind him, then from the left. Then the screaming was *above* him. He stopped, completely lost, his head spinning, his throat raw from the smoke. He coughed, and it seemed his coughing was adding to the smoke choking everything around them.

The rain fell again in gusting sheets. Then the wind, a gale from the mountain. Everything cleared in Llun's vision suddenly, and he couldn't understand where to look to get his bearing. He fell on the ground, thinking it was the sky.

"There! The smith. Over there!" Vasylli voices. In seconds, black figures surrounded Llun. Dog-men. Llun growled.

"Take care. He's taken many already." The voice was unfamiliar, but unmistakably of the Consistory. It had an emotionless quality about it. Nothing personal, it said. We have to kill you, because it is our business to kill you. Llun raised himself with difficulty, his head still spinning. He tried to orient himself by the tallest tower of the palace, which was directly ahead of him.

He froze. Something was hanging from the turret. A bloody and battered body, hanging on a rope attached to its neck.

Oh, by the Heights. That's... Yadovír!

Something struck him in the back, and searing pain spread across his shoulder blades, hot and prickly. Then something hit his head. Blackness.

Water splashed over his face. For a moment, he couldn't breathe. Then he woke up.

Llun was strapped to some sort of metal post, tied down with both chains and leather. He couldn't move anything except his head. His back tingled with nagging pain that seemed to slowly bore into his backbone. The water splashed over his face again, and he gagged.

"Enough!" he bellowed when he managed to shake the water out his mouth and face. Three dog-men surrounded him, swords drawn and pointed at him. Beyond them, Llun saw darkness. The only light in the dim space came from a table directly ahead of Llun. A single candle, barely illumining the cave-like interior. Three thin, weasel-faced men with salt-and-pepper beards sat there. They were second-reacher, merchant class, judging by their mien and the luxurious fur ringing their felt hats. The hats were red. But the rest of their clothing was black. Black kaftan, black shirts of rippling silk, black vests with silver buckles. Very fancy. One of them, the central one, had dead eyes that latched on Llun's face like a leech on an exposed leg.

"You are Smith Llun, yes? Brother of the traitor Dashun?"

"Hrrmph." Llun's mouth was caked with something sticky. Probably blood. Though his tongue was too swollen to taste it. "Brother-in-law."

"Ah, yes. How stupid of me. Brother of the traitor Vatrina. Even better."

"Worse, you mean," said Llun, under his breath. He had the absurd desire to antagonize that man. To really annoy him.

"Yes, I do," said the man, without expression. "Smith Llun, do you understand why you are here?"

"I may have killed some fifteen of your fellow dog-men."

The man looked down at a parchment before him, as though he had not heard the insult. Then he leaned over to another of the dead-faced inquisitors. None of the three, he now saw, had any expression at all, just blank faces. Not even boredom.

"Twenty-two, by our last count. So, you admit to this treachery and murder of your fellow citizens."

Llun laughed. One of the guards slashed his face with a knife. It left a burning gash—not deep enough to cause serious damage, he felt. These men were good at what they did.

"I do no such thing. I charge you, dog-men of the Consistory, collaborators to the invaders, of treachery and murder. I charge you with impersonating Gumiren to start riots in Vasyllia. I charge you with instigation of violence against your own people and against your unlawfully placed ruler. I—"

This time, the guard punched him with the pommel of his sword in his gut. It was studded with blunt nails. Llun couldn't breathe for a minute, and when he coughed, his stomach lurched in a way that suggested something may have been torn.

"No matter. Your admission is not necessary. Are we in agreement, then?" He turned to one dead-faced inquisitor, then the other. They both nodded, and continued to stare into empty space ahead of them.

"Smith Llun, you are found guilty of conspiring against the state and the person of Yadovír, the Mouth of our Great Father. Your sentencing will be held at a later date."

He waved at the guards, as though he were waving off a mosquito. One of the guards put a bag on Llun's head. It smelled rank. He saw nothing, but suddenly the ground was the ceiling, and his hands were his feet, and...

I have always been fascinated by the effect of pain. Not that I found any particular pleasure in dealing pain. No, that sort of fetish is base. Not worthy of an artist. Rather, I explore how the subject's mind and body twist and mold themselves in incredible ways in response to pain. I have also found ways to control that twisting and molding, to make the subject into something that I can use. That is the true art. To create, as the commons call him, a dog-man. The perfect perpetrator of justice, for he has no conscience of his own. Only the need, bone-deep, to be found worthy in the eyes of his handler.

From the personal notebooks of Aspidían, Grand Inquisitor of the Consistory

CHAPTER 5

A DEAL WITH THE DOG-MAN

Llun awoke. His head throbbed as though separated from his body. He couldn't understand his body's position. He did not feel his feet. Rather, they were there, but not solidly established. His arms were wedged behind him, and something cold pressed against his face. Slowly, concentrating through the throbbing pain, Llun made out that he hung inside a metal cage, his face leaning against one of the bars. He opened his eyes. Nothing changed. Total blackness.

Something whispered far above him, like a soft wind rushing through a narrow passage. The temperature plunged. Something licked his face. He recoiled in terror and disgust, but it kept licking him, like tens of small, ridged tongues, like a cat's. But that wasn't right. No. It was...was it possible? Snow? But he was inside, he was sure of it.

Soon there was no mistaking it. Snow pelted his face. Gritting his teeth against the pain, Llun managed to yank one of his arms out from behind him. He groped across the chain, trying to understand its shape and make. Then he reached further out with his hand. It met stone. Cold, dry stone. Not weathered. No, he was not outside. Then how could it be snowing?

He shivered. Every shudder of his muscles sent arrows of pain from the center of his back. Something crunched there, like broken cartilage or a ripped ligament.

The temperature fell again. Now it was ice pelting his face, not snow. Wind howled, just like it did during a blizzard. Was he going mad? No, the cold was very, very real.

Then, an explosion of light and heat burst from above his head. He jerked his head without thinking. It struck the metal grating, and his ears rang.

He sweated, his skin tinging where it was encrusted with ice just seconds ago. It was momentarily pleasant. But the heat kept rising. He forced his eyes open, and through the reddish firelight he saw that he was in a tower with no bottom to be seen. Just above his head was some horrifying kind of chandelier, but the heat from its torches was unbearable. He watched with horrified fascination as the hairs on his arms curled up, thickening into deep black, then smoke rose from them as they singed. The smell was sickening, mixed as it was with his own sweat and something far worse. Something rotten and musty and sickly-sweet.

His skin puckered and twitched. It bubbled. Llun closed his eyes, unwilling to see it through to its end.

The light went out. The darkness was so sudden and complete that Llun thought he had gone blind. Something scraped above him—the sound of metal scraping against metal. Cold wind blew in. Hard, sharp snowflakes followed. On his burnt skin, it felt like fire.

It all happened again—the snow, the wind, the biting cold. Only it was a hundred times worse. Then, just when sleepiness began to pull at his eyelids and he was ready to succumb to it, the strange chandelier returned with its blazing heat. Then again it was replaced with the winter storm inside the tower.

At some point, it all blurred into a monotony of agony. Llun must have lost consciousness for a long time, because when he woke up, he was in the throes of a chest-deep cold with a fever so hot, he could probably fry eggs on his forehead. Everything was hazy, and he was sure he had begun to hallucinate. After all, where did that hole in front of him come from?

It was a monstrous emptiness in the stone wall. The sight outside it was so elaborate a deception that Llun decided it must be real.

He had never seen such a sunrise. The clouds were striated like brushstrokes, each layer a deeper red the closer it was to the horizon. The tips of the trees were gilded, while the shadows underneath were a rich nightshade purple. Llun couldn't help himself. He chuckled. This was the perfect torture for an artist. In this place, at this moment, it did not seem absurd that Aspidían had ordered the sunrise especially for Llun. The beauty of it seared his mind, to remain there forever—far more a torment than a relief.

A strange sound reached Llun's ears. It sounded like ... market day. But surely not! Vasyllia wouldn't go back to its daily routine, not after everything that happened. Or ... how long had he been hanging here? At the thought, a hunger so huge it was like a living creature inside his stomach started to claw at him. A long time, then. But still! Had Vasyllia become so depraved that it could just go to market? After all that happened ...

Something cracked inside his head, and he screamed and shook the cage with all the strength he had left. The bars bent, but did not break. All he got for his pains was bloodied fingertips and a headache that felt like two hot pokers pushing his eyes out of his head.

Llun leaned forward, hard. The cage creaked and moved just enough for him to catch a glimpse of the accursed marketplace. It sprawled over the former Temple to Adonais. The ring of red-barks glittered with hundreds of lanterns, but no longer were the lanterns symbols of the flame in the heart, the inner striving for the Heights. Now, they were a convenience that allowed the market to remain open far into the night. This morning, the clearing seethed with brightly-colored dresses of brocade and silk, tall beaver hats, fur-lined mantles sparkling with golden embroidery. The resplendent walking dead.

How dare they! Their own people were being slaughtered in the streets only days ago. By other Vasylli. But still, the market thrives!

Llun's thoughts were interrupted by the sound of footsteps. Many men in a rush. After endless clanking of old keys in even older locks, a sickly light shone far beneath him. Steps echoed through the tower, which Llun now saw was narrow but immensely tall. The figures below him were no bigger than mice. At the head was Aspidían, gesticulating in a manner suggesting, to Llun's surprise, extreme displeasure, directed at a man to his left, apparently the keeper of the tower cells. The man had the air of a dog expecting a beating.

Suddenly, at a strange signal from Aspidían, three of the dog-men behind him grabbed the jailer, who screamed. They dragged him, though he bit them and flailed with his legs so hard Llun was sure his back would break. Another cage lay unused on the ground. They threw him in, so hard it must have broken some of his bones. His screams of defiance quickly changed to supplication, but Aspidían, busy working a rusty winch, ignored him. The chains all clattered at once, then the man's cage began its slow ascent toward the window. To Llun's amazement, his own cage descended at the same time.

Aspidían's face, as it came into focus, was a study in inscrutability. On the one hand, he had the air of a foreman exasperated with his workers, but on the other, something glinted behind his eyes that suggested bestial enjoyment at pain. He smiled.

"Brother Llun!" He raised his hand, as though they were old acquaintances running into each other at a popular market-stand. "You must forgive me. There has been much confusion after the failed coup. I had no idea you were here."

So there had been a failed coup. Or at least, that was what Aspidían wanted Llun to think.

Aspidían led Llun out of the cage with his own hands, and when his legs failed to support him, he grabbed the huge smith by the waist and forced him to lean on him. Llun was reminded of those snakes from travelers' tales that encircled their prey in a warm embrace before squeezing the life out of them. But he had little strength in his legs, and so he submitted to his torturer.

"Come, my brother," said Aspidían, as cordial as a viper. "Have a drink with me. You look awful."

Llun spat on the ground. But nothing came out. It was like he had been sucked dry.

The long hallways seemed endless. Endless curling staircases, endless rows of black doors. Endless smoking torches jutting out of stone walls that seeped with dark and fetid moisture. The sudden end of the dark was replaced by jagged light. But Llun had grown so accustomed to those changes that he didn't even bother closing his eyes. He just waited for them to adjust.

Aspidían took him to the same room where they had shared mead with Yadovír. Now Llun saw that there were three arched windows looking out directly over the marketplace. He also noticed that the false-commoner hearth had been wiped out of existence. There were new floorboards in the space where it had been. Strange.

Aspidían slumped into one of two extravagant chairs facing the windows and motioned for Llun to do the same. He did, but he nearly fell backward when his muscles failed to hold him. Aspidían laughed.

Between the two chairs stood a short table with a long-necked urn and two squat clay cups.

"I never liked those elaborate goblets," said Aspidían, answering Llun's unspoken question. "And I find clay brings out certain unexpected flavors in the wine."

Llun said nothing, feeling the tension behind Aspidían's words, even through the haze of his burning fever. "Brother Aspidían," whispered Llun. "Who did it? Who killed Yadovír?"

Aspidían turned on him, and for a moment Llun thought

that he was going to bite him like a rabid dog. Breathing like a bellows, Aspidían steadied himself.

"You know who," he said.

"The Gumiren?"

Aspidían nodded. "And not only they. The Sons of the Swan. They colluded with the Gumiren. Can you imagine? After all that talk of evil collaborators and traitors to Vasyllia? They did it themselves!"

"That's not possible." It came out before Llun could stop it.

Aspidían smiled, but it was poisonous. "Oh? Enlighten me then."

"There were Vasylli dressed as Gumiren in the first reach, killing and destroying everything in their path. And..." His head spun, and he had to cover his eyes with shaking hands. "It...it was Consistory men who burned down the Nebesta refugee camp."

Aspidían shook his head and sighed. "So much madness. So much confusion. Everyone pretending to be someone else. We need... we need to purge the filth from Vasyllia. For the last time."

"How will you identify friend from foe?"

"Oh, we have ways." He smiled, probably contemplating some especially subtle form of torture. "Shall I demonstrate?"

Aspidían jumped to the windowsill. Llun was surprised to see that the arches were open to the air with not even a thin layer of parchment against the elements, though how no wind or cold blew in, he couldn't understand. Aspidían whistled and nodded. A drum rolled. Easily visible through the arched windows before them, lines of spear-bearing Consistory men surrounded the market from all sides. The bustling people, without even think-ing, all stopped their purchasing, haggling, gossiping and stood still, as though they were hoping that they wouldn't be seen if they didn't move.

"Brother Llun, I know you do not think highly of the new way of Vasyllia. But I will show you how effective it can be. It is winnowing time."

Llun stood up from his seat, his head spinning for a moment

before his body found its place, and put a hand on the arch to better see. His hand was thinner than he remembered, and the sight of caked blood on it confused him. In the haze of the fever, he had almost forgotten the torture. Had it actually happened? He shook his head, trying to clear the mist from his thoughts. The hot pokers behind his eyes prodded him, and he saw stars. He almost fell, but the wall caught him.

Aspidían braced himself against his side of the arch, looking at Llun. He was done with pretense, it seemed, though his posture was casual, even languid. He even seemed faintly bored. Again, Llun had the sense that he was stuck in a dream where the details were terribly clear but made little sense when put together.

"People of Vasyllia!" Somehow, Aspidían's voice echoed through all Vasyllia below them, as though the mountains caught his voice like a child's wooden ball and threw it back and forth for their own amusement. Every face in the crowd craned upward, listening intently. "Please forgive the intrusion into your day of rest and pleasure. After what we have all been through, you deserve it. But we now have clear evidence. Yadovír, the man who is so dear to all of us, who has made the transition to the new order as bearable as possible, was betrayed by his own people. Yes, the Gumiren killed him. But we now know that he was delivered to the Gumiren by those vipers, those hawks wearing dove's tail-feathers. It was all an attempted coup. By the Sons of the Swan."

The crowd seethed as people began to whisper to each other and push each other and gesticulate. From this distance, it looked like an anthill disturbed by the stick of a small boy.

"Yes, my people," he shouted over them, arm outstretched for silence. "I know your anger, your frustration with these cowards, these degenerates, these postulants of a retrograde idea. It is time to winnow them from our ranks. I charge you. If any of you know of a friend, a neighbor, or even a family member who is of the Sons, you must come forward. The doors of the Consistory are at your disposal. Come. Let us cleanse the foulness of the Sons from our Vasyllia!"

He turned back to Llun, his face a careful blank. "As soon as I hear of Mirodara's involvement, I will bring her here before you. You will sit there and watch as I kill her. Slowly. Would you like to hear the details of my process? It is quite...artistic."

Llun's hands shook, and his head spun wildly. He was sure he would faint. With an effort of will, he straightened himself and looked down at Aspidían. Such a small man. He would be able to crush his head with a single hand. Yet he had so much power in him.

"I will be your man, Aspidían. But you must promise not to touch Mirodara."

Aspidían looked away from Llun, a slight smile playing at the edges of his lips. Swift as an adder, he backhanded Llun across the face. Hot, wet blood spurted. He had struck him on the place where the dog-man had sliced him during his mock trial. Llun looked at the blood on his hands, and could no longer support his own weight. He fell on his knees, the sobs racking his stomach. He released them, and a blubbering groan came out of his mouth. He hardly recognized it.

"Don't imagine you can haggle with me, vermin. You will do what I say."

Llun breathed deep. His heart slowly calmed, and he looked up at Aspidían. Deep inside, there was still something left of his strength. He shook his head.

"No, Brother Aspidían. You let too much slip. I don't know why, but you need me. And I will kill myself before I help you, if you so much as scratch Mirodara."

Aspidían held his gaze for an endless minute. Then he collapsed into hearty, chesty laughter.

"Oh, Llun! I'm so glad I met you. It's impossible to be bored with you around."

He snapped his fingers, and two dog-men appeared. They picked Llun up and carried him back the same way they had come.

"No," whispered Llun.

"Oh, yes," said one of the guards, flashing his eyebrows up and down at his companion.

They took Llun back to his cage.

I do not know if this letter will ever reach you, my beloved. I know that you are doing everything you can to come back to me. And I know that the forces arrayed against you must be strong indeed. But Voran, my love, I do not know how much longer I can hold on. I lost my body on the night of the Fall. I can hardly feel it any more. I fear my mind will be next. They say that you have become a Healer. Come to me, my love. Heal me. I need you.

From an unsent letter found in the apartments of Darina Sabíana of Vasyllia

CHAPTER 6

———

THE DARINA OF VASYLLIA

The first night, the cycle of cold and hot repeated five times. The second night, the cycle repeated six times. By the fifth day, Llun had trouble distinguishing day from night. It may have been a month, it may have been a year. The fever in his body reached some kind of critical point, and there was a period when Llun remembered nothing. He came back to consciousness with a strange sensation of being that he had never before experienced. He felt every fiber of his body separately. He moved individual muscles with a clear understanding of where they began and ended and how they worked. At the same time, every breath was an unbearable agony. It was as if there were two of him.

"There's more to this than mere torture, you know," she said. "There's a foul magic at work here. Not something I understand. But I've seen it at work in others already. They're preparing you. Reforging you, if you like. To be able to withstand the horrors that you will perpetrate on others. And, possibly, for something even worse."

Where did she come from? And how did he suddenly get from his cage to this garret? It looked like an unused attic room, the kind where all the unnecessary bric-a-brac of a great house was

534

placed in piles that were once orderly, but had long ceased to be so. Immense mounds of fabric, bits of metal, broken chairs. But then there was the wooden throne, its every inch carved into shapes of Sirin and wolves and giants and vila that came out of the wood like ripples on water. It was illumined with a dappled firelight that...yes, it was fragrant. Like roses.

"I will not be like them," he said to the figure on the throne, whom he could not quite see, though he didn't understand why.

"No, I don't believe you will. But there will be a price to pay."

Something about the voice enchanted Llun. It awoke forgotten images of sharp mountain peaks and waterfalls at dawn, images associated with a childhood longing that flared in his heart whenever he listened to his mother sing a ballad of Old Vasyllia.

"I will gladly pay the price of my life," said Llun.

"You do not know what you are saying," said the figure. She shifted in the throne, and the light also changed, so that he could see her more clearly. She was a young, dark-haired woman in chainmail, a heavy wolf fur draping her shoulders. Across her chest flew a black swan embroidered on a snow-white field. Her expression was still, but joyful. It was almost as though she were laughing at Llun, except her eyes were so old, deep as a lake with no visible bottom, that Llun was certain she was incapable of mocking others.

"What if you did give them the gift of your life to save your niece? Mirodara, was it? You would be able to bear it, perhaps, but only because you knew you would die eventually. At some point, all the pain will end. Perhaps you even keep suicide in the back of your mind as an extreme measure."

She sighed and shook her head. Her hair shone in the firelight, mesmerizing Llun with the play of dark red and brown and even purple tints.

"But you don't understand what the Raven is. His eternal quest is for endless life. And if he does find the source of endless life, whether in the form of Living Water or in some other unknown form, then imagine what they can do to their dog-men.

Given a few centuries of constant atrocities, a few centuries for the mind to hide their atrocities under a mental scar, they will be capable of any evil. Not just capable, but confirmed in it. Any internal change will become impossible. They will not think twice about murder, rape, torture. They will no longer be men."

"Why are you telling me this? And who are you?"

"Can you not guess who I am?" She smiled mischievously, patting the black swan on her chest with her forefinger, with an expression that said, "Can it be any more obvious?"

"You are Darina Sabíana? But they say you are bed-ridden. Unable to move."

"Yes, that is all true," she said, faintly annoyed, "but you are also in a cage, are you not? And yet you stand here with me."

Llun opened his mouth to retort, but found nothing to say.

"Have you never wondered," she said, "why your name is Llun?"

The name was a rare one, it was true. "I always thought my mother wanted to be unique."

Sabíana rolled her eyes. "Not much imagination, for an artist. No. Have you never considered the importance of names before? Why, for example, there are so few Cassíans and so many Lassars in Vasyllia?"

"Oh," he understood immediately. "It's the old superstition. You need to give your child the name of a person who was successful in life. For good luck. Name a child after a martyr, and ..." He chuckled significantly.

"No, no, no," she waved her hands in frustration. "That's the ... No ... There is something profoundly important about naming. It's not a matter of luck. The name does, in some ineffable way, reflect a person's place in the Universal Harmony. Have you never wondered why in some of the Old Tales, you have different characters with the same name living in vastly different circumstances, yet in all of them, the same events keep happening? It's not an accidental pattern. It's part of the fabric of the creation."

"But Llun. He was a mad prophet, wasn't he? His writings in

the *Sayings* are incredibly arcane. More interpretations of his prophecies exist than the prophecies themselves. What does that say about me and my name?"

"Llun wrote of a terribly important event. A time of blood, when the dead would walk as though living, but with no souls to speak of. He said that he, Llun himself, would bring this time about as a punishment for Vasyllia's iniquity. But…"

"Oh, you mean he could have meant that I am the Llun that will bring divine retribution? How?"

"I cannot say for certain. But Aspidían has been studying Llun's prophecies for years. He even comes to me in my bed of misery to speak of it. He finds no one else who believes him. But he seems to think that a smith is necessary. You are to make something. Something rather banal, I think. But with unexpected uses."

Hardly helpful. "Why are you telling me all this, my lady?"

"It's the only thing I have left, you see," she said. "And it is why I linger here in Vasyllia. I am given to help those who are needed at Vasyllia's sticking points. Yours is coming. You may have to make the most difficult choice of all. To abandon everything. Not only your own life, not only your own death, but even Mirodara."

"No. That I will not do."

"And yet, the alternative will be far worse than you can imagine."

"I will not!"

The pain in his back grew and arched and exploded into stars that danced before his eyes, before they pulled him back underneath into the darkness. He felt turned inside out, and once again his legs were clamped in place, his arms hanging useless outside the cage that was too small for him. He closed his eyes and tried to sleep.

And I, Llun of Vasyllia, will bring down the retribution of the Heights on fallen Vasyllia. The stars shall weep blood, the immortal one shall hold the lifeblood of the worlds in the palm of his hand, and the Realms themselves will hold their breath for utter terror. But in that day, the truth will become known at last. And the fireborn will brave the seventh baptism to demand vengeance from the Throne of the Most High himself.

From "The Prophecy of Llun"
(The Sayings, Book XXIII, 10:3-6)

CHAPTER 7

THE CHOICE

When Llun came to himself, he was no longer in the cage, but in a simple prison cell. He lay on a straw pallet on a wooden ledge. A pitcher of water was at his feet. He attacked the pitcher, spilling much of the contents on the ground in his haste. His hands shook, and he was unable to stop them. His hands...they were blackened with soot, thin and brittle-looking. How would he ever again manage to create anything with his hands? Why did they do this to him, if they wanted him to become the exclusive smith of the Consistory? Or had they now abandoned all that?

Still, despite his shaking hands, he felt clear-headed for the first time since the ordeal began. He groped his chest and arms, trying to see how much muscle mass he had lost. It was not as bad as he thought. About as much as he would have expected after not eating for a week. No, they hadn't been torturing him for months or years, then. Only days.

It was then that he realized that, outside, some sort of commotion had been going on ever since he had woken up. He listened, trying to understand. Lots of pushing and jostling, by the sound of it. Scraping metal. Gumiren voices, angry, yet without that note of defiance that usually characterized their speech. These voices sounded...yes, frightened.

So, the pogroms have begun, then.

He was too tired to feel any emotion accompanying that thought.

For the next few days, he was brought heaping plates of chicken and boar meat. It was unseasoned and not very well made, but these were the tastiest meals of Llun's life. Almost in the space of hours, he began to regain his strength. His hands stopped shaking. He found the courage to try to scratch off the scorch marks on his skin. All that came off was a layer of dead skin. Underneath, everything was smooth, almost baby-like. Strange for a man whose skin was more like leather after a lifetime at the forge. But it would harden again, soon enough.

A few days later, Aspidían himself came in the morning, bearing a tray of roasted ribs. Even from a distance, Llun smelled the rosemary. This was a king's meal, not a prisoner's. Behind Aspidían came a host of servants bearing trestles, stands, plates, crockery, spices, and wine. Urns and urns of wine. Llun's mouth watered at the sight, even at the clinking of the cups on the makeshift trestles.

"What are you doing?" asked Llun, his voice hardly more than a croak.

"Your last meal," said Aspidían, smiling. When Llun's jaw clenched, Aspidían laughed. "Your face! Even after all we've put you through, you're still as innocent as a babe in swaddling clothes."

Llun didn't know whether to laugh or cry. Aspidían poured wine for them both. It was blood-red, almost viscous.

"I wasn't lying when I said it was your last meal. It is. From this moment, you will be something else. It will be your choice, what you will be. But not Llun the smith of the former first reach of Vasyllia." He raised his cup. "To the new order."

Llun hesitated a moment, then drank. There was something different about this wine. It burned him on the inside. Llun suspected that there was more than just wine there. But Aspidían drank it with Llun, so it was not poison. At least, not the kind that kills.

"New order, you say?" croaked Llun. "One cleansed of both the Gumiren and the Sons of the Swan?"

"Oh yes," said Aspidían. "You would not believe how willing our Vasylli were to rat out the Sons. So many traitors in our midst!"

"You do realize that people will say anything to keep themselves from being implicated. It proves nothing."

"Yes, yes. But that is well and good. It doesn't matter who remains in the new Vasyllia, really. As long as they understand the new rules. As long as they are the ones who will resist external influence to the last drop of their blood. As for the Gumiren, we've killed most of them already. The Ghan escaped with a small band of his elite warriors, but they have nowhere to go. They'll be found in the mountains soon enough. If not, they'll have a surprise waiting for them at the border with Nebesta." He chuckled. The expression on his face left no doubt that whatever it was, it would be painful and probably fatal.

He snapped his fingers, and the servants began slicing the ribs apart. The meat practically fell off the bone. Llun's hands shook again, and it took all the will he had left not to attack the food. Aspidían watched him the whole time and seemed pleased with what he saw. Finally, all the ribs were separated and placed in a pile in the middle of the table. A servant tossed herbs over it, and another poured sauce that smelled strongly of onion and beer.

Aspidían inhaled deeply, eyes closed in pleasure. He sat there, savoring the smell, for what seemed an eternity.

Llun could wait no longer. "Tell me what I want to know," he said. He knew that he risked losing this meal, possibly the most elaborate and well-made meal of his life. He didn't care anymore.

Aspidían inclined his head and smirked. "Yes, Mirodara was turned in. I've kept her safe, for now. I was waiting to see how you'd do in your ordeal. And you did surprisingly well, considering the ordeal lasted almost two weeks. Do you know how many postulates to the Consistory survive it? Less than half."

"You risked losing your exclusive smith?" Llun said, with a hint of mockery.

"Yes." Aspidían became deadly serious. "Enough games, Llun. The Great Father needs you for a frightfully important work. I know you are squeamish about serving him, but you were never a particularly devout member of the cult of Adonais. You weren't much of anything, really. But we live in a time where half measures have no place. I think you know that now, and not merely with your mind."

Llun nodded. His body would never forget the lesson.

"You are more important than you know, Llun." Aspidían pulled out his table knife and speared three ribs through, then dropped them on Llun's side of the table. "Eat, O important one."

Llun did. Somehow, he managed not to transform into a wolf on the spot, but ate with admirable restraint. Or so it seemed to him. Aspidían shook his head with a smile, again in his faintly amused persona.

"Brother Llun, have you ever read the prophecies of your namesake?"

So she had *been real. The warrior-Darina who spoke to him from her throne.*

"Of course ... when I was a child. Everyone reads *The Sayings* at least once."

"Ah ... you have not *read* them, then. Have you ever heard the idea that names are not accidental? That when one takes on the name of another, especially an illustrious name, he takes up some of the qualities of his namesake?"

"I have not given it much thought, to be honest."

"Well, you would not be the first. But your name. What a name! A rare one. And with good reason. 'The Prophecies of Llun' is the strangest book in *The Sayings*. So many contradictory interpretations. So many phrases with no apparent meaning. Until now."

Llun's back straightened as he listened, unwittingly enchanted by Aspidían's voice. The pain was there, but now no more than an ache. Amazing. Sabíana was right about the body's ability to heal itself. Or was it perhaps something in the wine? Something with the appearance of goodness, but actually dangerous?

"There is a series of images that keeps popping up," continued Aspidían. "Most of them involve fire and a night full of stars in the constellation of the sword. The stars begin to weep. Then the tears turn to blood. By themselves, these images make little sense. But there is a mathematical precision to the prophecies. Certain images appear at regular intervals. Every seven verses, every twelve verses, and every four chapters, these central images repeat. I won't bore you with the calculation, but I have managed to make a cipher of the prophecies. They speak of a moment in Vasyllia's history when the lifeblood of the worlds will come into the hands of an 'immortal one.' At that time, the key to life and death will be revealed, and the dead will walk as though alive."

"*As though* alive? Animate corpses walking around Vasyllia? Sounds horrifying." He thought of the people in the market and realized that part of the prophecy may have already come true. They were no better than animate corpses.

"I do not jest, Llun. I am speaking of something monumental." His eyes widened, his eyebrows shot up, and he spoke in hushed, awed tones. "I have the ear of the Great Father. He has helped me to understand the true meaning of everything that has happened. All the suffering Vasyllia's been through. All the troubles. Nothing more than a cleansing. A time of ordeal. We are about to embark on a new age for Vasyllia. One unmatched in glory in the history of the world. Man will not lord it over man.

Everyone will be equal. Opportunities to rise in the world will be given to all. Every person may choose what he or she would like to be. And the might of Vasyllia will become legendary. Then we will be a beacon, a city on a hill, truly. Other nations will seek alliance with us, and we can choose with whom to associate. No more need to pander after the pitiful Nebesti or worse, the Karila.

"At the heart of this new world will be the ultimate gift. Eternal life. Even now, the Raven is at the cusp of finding it. But it will only be given to the chosen. Only to the men of the Raven. They will live for all time."

Sabíana's warning about an eternity of atrocity rang in Llun's ears like a bell. Truly, she was right. If the dog-men had millennia to live, they would be no different than changers or any other evil Power.

And yet...

"Brother Aspidían. I hear you. I am moved by your words. But I am a simple man, not given to theorizing. Tell me, simply, how I am to help in this new age of Vasyllia?"

"You will be one of the Consistory. But not yet. After a time. First, a test. There is a trinket that the Great Father would have you make for him. A simple thing, really. A metal flask that a man can wear on his hip. To hold wine or mead or water, even."

Llun was taken aback. He had expected something elaborate. But a flask? And a metal one, to boot? He had never seen such a thing. Why would anyone want to drink water from a metal flask? What was wrong with leather skins?

"Is there any design the...um...Great Father would prefer? Any details he would like included?"

"He wants you to...be possessed by your inspiration."

Again, Llun shuddered at the use of that particular word. It tainted his enjoyment of the rest of that meal. It didn't help that though his mind registered how superior the cooking was, his heart ached with worry for Mirodara and fear for what he would have to do. Aspidían was content to allow Llun his silence, though he talked the entire time. Llun had only a faint recollection of what he spoke about, but it left a sour taste in Llun's mouth.

To Llun's surprise, Aspidían led him through the Consistory back to the outer courtyard of the palace.

He's not letting me go home, is he?

At the gates, Aspidían embraced Llun and hugged him warmly. Llun stiffened, not sure whether to be afraid or uncomfortable.

"I am giving you this day and night as a gift," said the dog-man. "For you and Mirodara. Use it well. For both your sakes, help her understand the way that is best for all."

It has been the source of some debate—where did the essence of the Raven go when Yadovír was killed? Some survivors of the wars for Vasyllia insist that, a few nights after the death of Yadovír, they saw the presence of the Raven hovering about a smithy in the first reach. Impossible to confirm now, of course, since that smithy no longer stands...

From "A New History of the Covenant" by Dar-in-Exile
Mirnían II

CHAPTER 8

THE CREATION

Mirodara lay curled in a ball on the floor of his back room. She did not budge at his call. She shrank from his touch on her shoulder.

"What did they do to you?" he asked, shaking with the suppressed desire to kill everyone who would dare to so much as lay a hand on her.

She uncurled slowly, like a flower opening over the course of a long morning. Her eyes were hollow. Not a sign of tears on her face. Just horror lurking behind her eyes, like a parasite that had invaded her body. She would not look him in the eyes. The closest she managed to get was somewhere near his left eyebrow. He waited for her to sit up, giving her what he hoped was enough space to feel safe, without the distance he feared would clam her up even more. He wanted to enfold her in his arms, to hide her in his bulk, to never let anyone else see her.

"Not much," she said, but it sounded like she had forgotten how to speak. Her own face looked surprised at the sound of her voice. "It's what they did to the others. They made me watch." Her face turned green, and her hands went up to her mouth as she retched. But nothing came out. She dry heaved for almost a minute.

Llun went outside to the well and pulled out a bucketful of water. He nearly threw it on her head in his haste and in his desire to make her better. She had to calm him down by taking his lone wooden cup and dipping it in the cold water. Her eyes closed at the pleasure of the water.

"You must have some bread. I have a little. I think…"

His bread box was nearly empty, and what was there may have been a feast for the mice in the last few weeks, judging by the suspicious looking crumbs in the left corner. Sighing out his exasperation, he took his table knife out of its sheath on his belt—he still couldn't believe the dog-men had given it back to him—and cut a thin outside layer off the crusty, black rye bread. Without much hope, he looked in the apple basket for last year's shriveled apples, few of which had survived the winter. He was shocked to find one tiny, shriveled, but bright red apple hiding in the far corner. He picked it up. It smelled like autumn.

Mirodara took both the bread and the apple and looked at them for a long moment, not understanding what they were, or what she was supposed to do with them. That, more than anything else, cut his heart. How could he go through with it? They'd already damaged Mirodara, possibly beyond repair. She was not strong enough to survive what was coming.

But the food gave her obvious strength. Her breathing slowed and deepened, and a spot of warmth touched her cheeks, though they were still far from a good color. It was as though the blush of healthfulness had gingerly approached her cheek, had even tried to warm it, but ultimately scurried away like a skittish deer. Still, she looked much better for the food and water.

"Why?" she asked as he brought her tea, the last of his precious hoard, probably never to be replenished now.

"Why what, my cub?"

"Why are you and I here, now, speaking to each other? Is this a test? Are they waiting outside, waiting for you to lull me into a sense of security, so I can let slip some vital piece of information about the Sons of the Swan?"

She looked at him with such a strange expression—anger, distrust, defiance, exhaustion. And yet, they had not stamped out the hope, deep within her eyes, no more than a fading ember.

"It is a sort of test, I think," he said. "But not the one you think. This is the last chance you and I have to lead a normal life before everything changes. I am to become one of them. To save your life. And maybe even to save your death."

She stiffened. "Oh, Heights! Has the Raven found it, then? His immortality?"

"No, not that I can tell. But I think he is close. The Consistory wants me to make something for him. I don't understand it, not quite. Aspidían did a very bad job trying to make it sound unimportant. But what the Raven would want with a metal flask, I haven't the faintest idea."

Mirodara's eyebrows gathered in confusion. "That's...unexpected. One of the Sons was deep inside the Consistory, and before the last purge, he managed to find out that the Raven is burrowing *inside* Vasyllia. Inside the mountain, searching for some elixir, like the Living Water, but possibly something else entirely. I know, bad information. It's the best we have."

"It's clearly important. Maybe the flask is intended to hold this elixir. But wouldn't it have to be a magical artifact then, to hold a thing of power?"

"Perhaps you have magical powers you weren't aware of."

It was a joke, though she barely smiled as she said it. It made Llun smile and nearly exclaim in joy.

"Llun, you must do what you think is right. But let me say one thing. I don't know why, but I think that this object will be your last as a smith. Your work is too beautiful to be allowed by the Raven. And I think that you need to be very careful when you make it. It's going to be not a battle, but a war."

He knew what she meant. Every *thing* he made was made with pain, in a process of battle with himself and with forces outside himself that tried to stop him—tiredness, lack of inspiration, a sense that he was incapable of creating beauty. Only after it was complete did the sense of synthesis, the joy intertwined with intense grief, come flooding over him, threatening to overwhelm him. In that moment, he and the Heights were one, until once again the hunger for creation overtook him, and the process began anew.

If, instead of the usual, natural antagonists, the Raven and his dark Powers interfered with his work or tried to subvert it to their own desires, the struggle would be a hundred times more intense. It might even kill him.

But what better way to die, than in the creation of a perfect piece that would never, not over his dead body, belong to them? After all, nothing created through the mediation of the Heights would ever be corrupted. It would simply be. And even if they later used it for their own vile ends, its beauty would be a thorn in their side, a reminder of their eventual failure and end. For nothing evil can last forever, not unless it were already the Unmaking of the world.

"Yes, Mirodara. You will have to help me. There will be times when I will want to stop. Or when my creation will try to wrest itself from my hands. Be my cold water. Be my conscience."

She smiled, and the ember of hope in her eyes lit up.

"Our last hurrah. Yes. It will be glorious."

"I must do it in my forge. And I need Mirodara with me."

Aspidían had come to the first reach with a full honor guard, and he looked a little offended at being thus greeted. But that quickly passed, as understanding crept in. Again, Aspidían surprised Llun. He had expected at least something of a fight.

"I understand," said Aspidían. He looked at Llun, his gaze slowly boring into him as though he were pushing a knife into his eye, waiting for it to come out the other end. He dismissed the guards with a wave of the hand, still looking at Llun.

"Only know this. This is a concession. My final one. After you join us, you will not come back here. In fact, I intend to destroy this smithy. I know about the foulness that you perpetrated here. Those decorative shields. I did not see it at first. But later, after the benefit of some...external aid," for a moment, the mask slipped, and Aspidían's pain shone in his eyes. Was the inquisitor the recipient of the tender mercies of the torturer himself? "I recognized them for what they were. I should take both hands from you for that. And both eyes for good measure."

"I understand you, Brother Aspidían."

He met the inquisitor's gaze. It was terrifying, but already Llun felt the beginning of the inspiration. The process of creation. He could not be gainsaid by anyone when in this state. Aspidían began to smile his adder's smile, but he stopped in mid-smirk. His eyes softened, and a face Llun had yet to see manifested itself. It was terrifyingly, heartbreakingly sad.

"Brother Llun. It is my great regret that we did not know one another before ..." He choked on what he almost said, before his eyes filmed over with their usual expression of assumed boredom. He turned and followed the honor guard back to the Consistory.

For a moment, Llun watched in wonder. Was this last, sincerest version of Aspidían the greatest lie of all?

But the forge called to him like a lover after a long absence. And Mirodara's gaze was burning swirls into his back.

"I'm ready," he said.

"I don't think you are," she said, but she was deadly serious.

A shudder ran up his spine. She was right.

Llun took the piece of iron like a mother taking her child from the midwife. Llun folded the iron gently into a thick block. He cut the block into two billets and placed the two halves on top of each other, with the grains perpendicular to each other. Then, he forged it into a thin sheet, so thin, he was afraid it would crack in multiple places at the smallest stress. But it held.

As soon as the sheet was ready to be shaped, it began. The heaviness in his mind. Usually it was no more than a kind of fog that pushed him to stop, to lay down his tools to wait for a better moment, when his heart would be more into the process. But this time, it was like a voice in his head.

You are weak. Why do you labor? You know that it can never be appreciated for what it truly is. It is going to be twisted out of shape and out of its intention. Better give it up. Come what may.

He was already sweating, but now it poured like rain down his body. His breathing hurried, and the heat on his face was more than just the forge.

"You don't matter," said Mirodara. "*You* don't matter. This thing you make. It matters more than you or I or my mother or anyone else. It may be the last thing of beauty created in Vasyllia."

He breathed a sigh of relief as the enthusiasm caught at the wave of his shame. He began to shape the iron around a rounded wooden block. It felt like butter in his hands, supple and easy. So easy. He could do anything he wanted with this. Would he be remembered for this creation? Would Vasyllia sing the praises of Llun the smith after this final, wondrous thing he made?

A flask?

Truly, an insignificant, pitiful thing to make as one's swan song. Why not change it? He could use this metal to make a weapon so fine, so strong, that it would make even the dullest swordsman brilliant. Why not? Surely such a gift would be acceptable to the Great Father.

Great Father? Have you gone mad?

Something chuckled behind them.

"Don't look," said Mirodara, her voice shaking. "He wants you, Llun. Not as a smith. They've been lying to you the whole time. He doesn't want your flask. He wants *you* as his..." Her voice squelched, like someone were holding a wet towel over her mouth and throttling her by the neck at the same time. Llun nearly turned around. Something kept him firmly in place, working the sheet around the mold.

The presence in the room was unmistakable, its malice so palpable it was akin to a smell of something rotten, like old eggs or a week-old corpse. And yet, there was a kind of energy in that presence. It fueled Llun's manic activity. His hands worked faster than they ever had before, with as much, or more, control than he had had since his early days. Already he saw the decorations of iron he would place on the flask, fine as embroidery.

No! Not for him. Not ever!

There were two Lluns in that room. One was already finished with the creation of the flask—a marvelous thing that sparkled even in darkness, that was light as a feather but virtually unbreakable. A perfect receptacle for an elixir of power. The other Llun was still in his human body, sweating, aching, laboring over the sheet, which every second threatened to break apart into splinters of iron. This Llun was tired. He wanted to give up. The other Llun, the one in his mind—how he wanted to be him already! To rush past the drudgery of the work. To stand at the completed stage, the state of synthesis, to feel the joy of it.

"I can give it to you," said the presence in his mind, *"all you have to do is desire it with every fiber of your being."*

"Is beauty without suffering possible?" asked a new voice, strong and regal. Sabíana stood before him, half-insubstantial, her eyes dancing in the shower of sparks Llun sent up with each blow of his hammer. "Is it even preferable? You are the last true artist in Vasyllia, Llun. Not because of some talent given by the Heights. You are the last in the tradition of the old masters. The ones who understood that the secret of beauty is pain. Only through birth-giving can the miracle be brought forth."

The presence in his mind laughed. *"Yes. Listen to the woman. She is a pitiful creature, chained to her bed. I offer you the way of fulfillment. It is also the path to power. Never again will you be subject to the whims of the Consistory. You will rule them."*

"You have no power here, foul thing," Sabíana cried. "This is a place protected by me. It is given to me from above, this protection for my chosen few."

Again, the laughter, only now directed at her. *"And what if I told you that everything you think you know about your precious Power, your Adonais, is a lie? What if I told you that your entire existence is a mistake, but one that is mercifully coming to its end? What would you say to that, eh?"*

Sabíana's eyes filled with tears and she shimmered for a moment, then faded.

"You see? She cannot protect you. Only you can protect yourself. And Mirodara as well. Save her from what the Consistory will do. Become the Consistory."

Llun breathed deeply and closed his eyes. He stilled his breathing and focused on the beating of his heart. It began to slow. He waited until the beats were regular and unhurried. He breathed again and smiled. Everything hurt. His mind, his body. Everything. And he loved it. He would have it no other way. He would make this thing. This last thing of beauty.

But not for you. Begone, you foulness. You have no place in the creation of the beautiful.

"Llun? Are you well? What happened?"

Mirodara touched his shoulder.

"Is it...Can I turn around now?" He asked.

"Yes. I think it's over."

Llun turned to look at her. She was unharmed. Only a little pale. He nodded at her and turned back to his work, suddenly sure that the time needed to create this thing properly would not be given them. With a speed he never expected from himself, he created something... remarkable.

He puffed like a bellows after it was done, cradling the thing in his hand like a child. It was a flask, but it did not even look metal. It looked like a dark flower enfolded in leaves at midnight. It was the most beautiful thing Llun had ever seen. And he recognized that it was not *he* who had made it. He was but the instrument.

"Mirodara," he said. "Go. Take it. You are its only hope. It must never fall into the hands of the Raven. Find a way. Leave Vasyllia. Seek the true Vasylli out there, in the wild. If you find Voran the Healer, tell him to hurry. There may not be a Vasyllia left if we wait much longer."

The doors to the forge flew open. Aspidían stood there, his gaze expectant. It quickly turned to disappointment, then anger, then horror.

"What...? What have you done, Llun? Where is Mirodara?"

"I am ready," said Llun. "I am ready to be a dog-man."

Aspidían gestured, and the guards behind him swarmed in and seized Llun, pulling him out of the smithy on his knees.

"Turn him around," said Aspidían. "Make him watch."

Ten dog-men with torches stood in a semicircle around Aspidían, their eyes red in the fire-light.

"Burn it," said Aspidían. "The whole block."

And it came to pass that the sacrifice was offered, and it was found acceptable by the Most High. And he deigned to bend down from the throne of his greatness to confirm the sacrifice, and to give a final gift. But his words were terrible. Thus saith the Lord, the Most High: "For the last time I grant the fallen a boon, until the fire-born braves the final baptism and stands before me in his transfigured flesh."

From "The Prophecy of Llun"
(The Sayings, Book XXIII, 4:1-4)

THE ESCAPE

Mirodara dropped the flask into the first canvas pack she found lying in a heap of rubble in Llun's smithy. It tied over her shoulder well enough. She hoped it wouldn't look conspicuous in the first reach. She must do everything possible not to attract too much attention to herself on her way out of Vasyllia.

She stopped at a food stand and bought three breads and some dried meat. Enough, she hoped, to get her into Nebesta, where she would try to find some gainful employment while she searched for Voran. She had nothing more concrete than that as far as plans go. Some very reasonable part of her, deep inside her mind, nagged at her that the lack of a plan was no plan at all, but she was too excited by her forthcoming adventure to listen.

Only when she was halfway to her destination—a side gate in Vasyllia's wall that was usually undermanned and filled with merchant wains entering and exiting—did it fully hit her. She would never see Llun again. She sped up her walking, if only to force the hard cobbles in the streets to rattle her out of her desire to sink to the ground and weep like a baby. It was no use, not any more. Yes, she was an orphan, but she had gotten over that (or so she kept telling herself). Now she had no one left. But the world was ending. What difference did it make if there was no one to share it with?

Focusing on the ground before her feet, she almost didn't notice that she was at the gates, even as she joined the line of people leaving. Her good fortune held strong. Several caravans of merchants were lining up to take the shorter, more difficult routes that skirted the mountains and led out to the lands that used to be taboo to the Vasylli. Magical lands with monstrous creatures with many eyes that spun silk out of their own saliva. If the stories were to be believed. Mirodara certainly believed them.

She tried her best to blend into the gaggle of merchants, some even with their families, as they prepared to take a journey that could last them years. What sort of hopes animated them? How did they survive in the new Vasyllia? Were they not also affected by all the madness? Perhaps they did well to leave, hoping beyond hope that things would be different when they returned?

A little boy of two or three saw Mirodara and started making faces at her. She did the same, and he laughed with pleased surprise.

"What's your name?" she asked him quietly.

"Adarin," he said, sheepishly.

"I'm Mirodara," she said. "Do you want to play a game?"

He nodded, eyes sparkling.

"I'm going to hide under your father's wain, under here. But I have to get there without anyone noticing me. You can help me, right?"

"I want to hide with you, too," he said.

"But then we'll both get in trouble, won't we? I'll tell you what. If you help me hide now, I'll let you come down with me for the rest of the trip. I just need to be under there when we pass the gates. Got it?"

Adarin looked dubious, but he obviously wanted to play. He nodded seriously, then started to scream bloody murder. Every adult within earshot was completely absorbed by his screaming. Mirodara slipped under a wain and held on for dear life. As soon as she did, Adarin stopped, as though it were the most normal thing in the world to scream one second, then stop the next. Mirodara had to bite her lip to keep from laughing aloud.

Just as they approached the gates, Mirodara heard the stomp of booted feet. Many booted feet.

"Stop the wains, stop the wains!" Someone called from behind.

"What's the matter, sir?" asked someone Mirodara assumed to be the warden of the side gate.

"Political prisoner. Escapee. Young girl, thirteen maybe. She has something of value needed by the Consistory."

"We'll keep a watch out for her, sir."

Adarin. Please don't say anything. Please don't say anything.

He didn't. They passed without so much as a peep from the boy. To his credit, he waited until they were well beyond earshot before he crouched down to look for her.

"Well? Can I come down now?"

Mirodara laughed, dropped and rolled out from under the wain. She hopped up and ran away from the merchant caravan. A few surprised merchants reached out to catch her, but she had always been fast. She managed to squeeze past them. She ran down into the deepwood without stopping or looking back.

This part of the Vasylli mountain woods she knew like the back of her hand. Even as a child, her—she almost thought "father," then realized she *had* no father—"treacherous person who raised her" took her often into the woods for days at a time while he would find the best kind of wood for his carpentry. So, finding the backwoods paths that eventually joined the Dar's Way to Nebesta was easy enough.

She ran with inhuman speed all the way to the border of Nebesta. Three days and three nights of nearly constant running and walking, with only short naps for rest whenever she felt like she couldn't go on any more. The rough mountain tracks she followed were well-worn, though strenuous. But she found unexpected reserves of strength inside herself. She ate less than she had expected, and she traveled farther, faster than she had thought possible.

When she joined the Dar's Way, she was sure some sort of alarm would blare the moment she stepped onto the pavement. Nothing happened. At least, nothing she could detect. But there did seem to be some kind of unseen energy that hummed on the level of emotion, just beyond sound. She was unsure if she had caused it, or if it was some devilry of the Raven. It left her stomach queasy. But she resumed her easy pace without any hindrance.

She knew that just before the Way crossed over into Nebesta, it would rise up onto a ridge, then fall away steeply into a shallow valley walled by two tree-covered hills. If there was going to be an ambush anywhere, it would be there. So, she took her time cresting it, listening for the slightest sound of pursuit or ambush. But she heard nothing at all. Not even the sounds of animals. That frightened her, and as she crested the ridge, her breathing became shallow and spots danced before her eyes.

On the downslope, a wall blocked the Dar's Way. It was not very tall yet, clearly in the process of being built, though it was dark and imposing. Menacing, even.

The moment she stopped to stare at the wall, she heard it. Horses behind her.

She ran to the wall and tried to find a handhold to launch herself over into Nebesta and safety, but her hand shot back in pain as though there were tiny barbs all along the wall. She looked at her palm, and it was bloody. Her arm pulsed with pain. Had she just poisoned herself?

She turned around to face whatever it was that was coming after her. Three horsemen. Gumiren. They were bloodied and their eyes were wild and hungry. She would get no quarter from these. They looked like they had just escaped one of the latest pogroms.

"Why you out here, Vasylli girl-child?" asked the central of the three, the youngest.

She said nothing.

He talked to his neighbor in their rat-a-tat tongue. They quickly came to a consensus.

"Your hand." He pointed. "It bloody."

"Yes?" she said. "The wall. It's..."

"Pricked...yes? Keep you in. Keep others out. We guard the wall. All who touch it are for to be executed. You not know this?"

She gulped hard and shook her head. These Gumiren had death in their eyes. She supposed she should be grateful it was only death she saw in their eyes.

"Well, it sad for you. But law is law."

He nodded at the Gumir at his left. In a smooth motion, he pulled a knife from his belt and threw it at Mirodara. It struck her in the chest, the blade going in all the way to the hilt. She stared at it in fascination, before the spots began to dance in her eyes and her knees wobbled. The ground reached up and grabbed her. No, it was the Gumiren. They hoisted her above their heads, she thought. Then, the sensation of weightlessness, followed by the earth falling on her body. No, it was she who fell on the earth. Why was it so hard to concentrate? Everything hurt, especially her left leg. Strange. Why her left leg? She felt at the thing that tugged at her chest. It was knobby. That didn't belong there. She wrenched it out, and a fountain of red poured up and out of her. It was mesmerizing.

Then she realized it was her blood. She seemed to be drowning in it. But no. It wasn't just blood. There was a great deal of water. And it smelled...like...roses.

Voran and Aglaia—he still had trouble thinking of her as Aglaia when she was in her wolf form—had been traveling toward Vasyllia in a straight line for a week. It was the first time they had done that since the fall of Vasyllia, almost ten years before. At every step, Voran expected that the road would fade, that he would fall into a different realm, or that reality would shift around him, and he would find himself where he had started a week before.

Returning to Vasyllia was impossible. He had tried it. Hundreds of times. But someone—whether Zmei and his brothers or the Raven, Voran didn't know—had made the lands before Vasyllia a warren of hidden doorways and traps. Time and time again, Voran took a step toward Vasyllia, only to find himself in the Lows of Aer, or displaced hundreds of miles farther away from Vasyllia. Something was doing everything in its power to prevent anyone from approaching Vasyllia.

It also didn't help that he hardly had a day when he wasn't running away from Zmei or his giant brothers. It didn't take him long to realize that they had noses like hounds, and they were nearly always three steps ahead of him every time he made his way toward Vasyllia. A few times the encounters had been close to fatal. When his mother Aglaia had joined him in her wolf form, it had actually gotten worse. The giants had bound her to her wolf form in the first place, and somehow her presence made them seek him out ever more ferociously. But she had refused to leave him. She still bristled if he so much as mentioned it.

There were other reasons Voran didn't come back to Vasyllia earlier. One was that Voran had been healing everyone he could find. As Zmei had predicted, the power of the Living Water only lasted for some time. Voran learned to supplement its lack with a thorough study of herbs and medicines from every leech he could find, in whatever village he happened to be at the time. Those travels had taken him as far as Karila, even to the edge of the Steppelands border. He had become a competent enough healer with his hands alone. But sometimes, rarely and never according to his own desire, an echo of the old power came out of his hands, and people were healed by his touch. That alone had been enough to make his legend travel ahead of him. He hoped that it had reached Vasyllia by now.

A year ago, something had happened that made him seek

Vasyllia with renewed energy. Lyna stopped coming to him. He realized in the pit of his gut that she was upset with him for not managing to return to Vasyllia. For not accomplishing his calling, so to speak. He felt he had had little choice in the matter, but her lack was like a knife slowly cutting a hole in his chest. He needed her like he needed to breathe. So, he and Aglaia had braved the most obscure paths, some of them nothing more than pure deep-wood, with little more than pressed-down grass from the passage of some wild animal.

It took much longer than it normally would. Finding food was a problem, even for Aglaia. But they had done it without even a whiff of giant-stink anywhere near them. Somehow, either the traps had faded in power, or they had managed to evade them. Finally, they came to a sharp ridge of mountains. In them was a narrow pass, hardly noticeable to the naked eye, beyond which lay a hunter's track that connected with the Dar's Way near the border between Nebesta and Vasyllia.

The trek over the pass was difficult—it was late spring, and the cold and ice were omnipresent—but they made it over with only scrapes and bruises, not broken bones. Voran was continually astounded by the unseen grace that protected him in the wild. Sometimes it was just a whisper of a thought that kept him from falling into a crevasse in the night. Sometimes, it was more obvious, like the gust of wind that had actually lifted and carried him and Aglaia over a gap in the mountains that a mountain goat couldn't have jumped. Voran was sure it was no wind, but possibly even a Majestva, one of the higher Powers of Adonais. But he kept his thoughts to himself, and Aglaia had not commented.

Finally, they were within visual range of the border.

A wall towered between Nebesta and Vasyllia, uncommonly high. Higher than the red-barks in Vasyllia, without a doubt. Voran didn't think human beings could build such things. Perhaps it was the giants?

As usual, it was as though his mother had read his thoughts:

"No, that doesn't smell of giants, Voran. Very clearly Raven-made."

"Not Gumiren?"

She sniffed the air for a long time, her head bobbing up and down hypnotically. She did this for more than a minute. Then she huffed and sneezed.

"Some Gumiren. But I think it's an old smell. Very little human smell at all, actually."

They approached it carefully. Voran unsheathed his sword, and Aglaia's hackles rose in concert. Her low growl made the ground shake. It gave Voran the needed push of courage.

Nothing stopped them as they approached, their eyes fixed on the wall. Voran could see no way in or out. He could see precious little at all, as though this were not a wall, but a single, strangely-shaped piece of stone that snaked along the border. It stank of dark magic, even to him. Aglaia's nose wrinkled more and more with distaste the closer they came.

Then, sudden as a sunrise in the middle of winter, the smell. Tube-rose and lavender. Even a hint of orange.

"Is that...?" Aglaia ventured, her tail out straight behind her.

"Yes, it has to be," said Voran. "Only Living Water smells like that."

The road bent leftward, just before rising toward the first ridge of the Vasylli mountains. As they turned the corner, Voran saw the strangest thing he had ever seen. And he had seen some very strange things.

It was a dome-topped square building, similar to the kind of chapel to Adonais that rich merchants liked to build on cross-roads in the wild. But it was built entirely of thick vines with vaguely heart-shaped leaves. Tiny purple-blue flowers exploded from the vines at regular intervals. The dome was an interweaving of some fibrous, root-like material that from a distance looked like an oversized onion. It was tipped with a single white blossom with eight petals, larger than any flower he had ever seen.

"What in the Heights...?" Voran said.

"The smell..." said Aglaia, "it's not coming from that edifice. It's from *inside it*."

Voran's hands shook. But it wasn't fear. It was the overawing sense of presence that he used to feel in the Temple in Vasyllia in the old days. A sense he had not had in the wild for many years. It almost physically pushed him down. He felt the need to approach it on his knees.

The vines moved with the slight breeze, revealing a chamber within the strange edifice.

"There's something inside," said Voran, a little lamely.

Aglaia chuckled. "You always become so painfully obvious when you're in the presence of the grace of the Heights."

Voran smiled.

He pushed aside the vines, and a light shone from within—warm and yellow, like a firelight. He climbed in.

A girl lay on a bed of moss and leaves. Her hair—wavy and strawberry blond—reached to her ankles. Her hands were crossed on her chest, where they barely covered a wound from a very wide knife-thrust.

"She's alive! Look at her nails," said Aglaia.

She was right. Her nails were long and curled, as though they had been growing for years.

"But how? That wound would kill a warrior, much less a girl like that."

"I think she's been here for years," said Aglaia, ignoring him. "This place smells strange. Fresh and old at the same time. Only one other place has ever smelled like this. The barrier between the worlds."

Voran reached for the girl's clothes, and realized they were wet through. Her hair remained strangely dry. What sort of place was this?

A compulsion came upon him. He recognized it. It was the same as the push he had felt the night he first heard the Sirin in the forest. He turned the girl over to reach at her back.

She wore a pack made of old canvas, from which the ivy that

made the walls grew. This was the source of everything. He opened it gently, and the smell of tuberose inundated him. His hand touched something metal. He pulled it out and gasped.

"That is gorgeous," said Aglaia. She had turned human again, her eyes filling with tears.

The object shimmered in the strange light inside the room. It looked like a budding flower erupting from a nest of leaves. Only it was metal. As he turned it over, he saw that one side was smeared with blood. He tried to wipe it off, but it seemed to have welded to the metal itself. Suddenly, the flask grew heavy in his hand, as though filling with water.

"What in the Heights?" Voran dropped the flask, and it fell down on the girl, overturning its contents of what looked like, and smelled like, Living Water. He picked it up again, and it was once again full.

The girl gasped and sat up, eyes wide.

"I died," she said. "You brought me back." She looked at Voran, then at the flask. "I think I understand."

"I don't," said Voran, crouching down to the girl, examining her chest to see that there was nothing, not even a scratch, left from a wound that was surely fatal.

"A final gift," she said, her voice not quite her own. "for the Healer. It is the final sacrifice of Llun the smith for the sake of the reclamation of Vasyllia."

A song like wind whistling through reeds sounded all around them. Lyna the Sirin showered them with her song. The ivy burst apart in flames that were warm, but not burning. The sun streamed down on them, far too warm for this time of year. The girl's eyes opened wide and she laughed.

"You are real!" she said. "The Sirin. You are real!"

"You came back," said Voran, his voice shaking with the joy-pierced sorrow that he had not sensed for what seemed an eternity. "Thank you. I can breathe again."

"Yes, my Voran. I come to confirm this blessing. But it is one laden with pain."

"Is it ever not, Lyna?" Voran laughed ruefully.

"This flask contains Living Water. An inexhaustible source. But it will only remain as long as the Healer heals. If you leave your path, your chosen calling, it will empty and not fill again. And your path does not lead to Vasyllia. Not yet."

And so, Voran walked away from the wall, away from Vasyllia, away from his beloved Sabíana. His heart was a stone inside him, the flask was a burden on his hip. He turned back to the wall a final time.

When will I see you again, my Sabíana? Voran thought.

The girl stopped next to him, staring up at him with eyes that had not yet returned to the mundane.

"What will you do now?" she asked.

"I will do what I'm supposed to do," he said. "Ready the rest of the lands for the return of Vasyllia. Stop the internecine war that's raging among the city-states. Prepare the soil of people's hearts for the bond-fire of the Sirin."

"You will do all that? You're only one man."

He laughed bitterly. "Sometimes, there is only one man left who is willing to do what must be done." He sighed. "Where will you go, little thing?"

Her expression clouded, like she was trying to remember something important.

"She's coming with me," said Aglaia. "We're going to find her a place to rest and heal. Maybe Nebesta, maybe farther away."

"So, you're finally letting me out on my own?" he asked, smiling.

The wolf sniffed loudly through her nose. "You have to grow up someday. Might as well be today."

About the Author

Nicholas Kotar is a writer of epic fantasy inspired by Russian fairy tales, a freelance translator from Russian to English, the resident conductor of the men's choir at a Russian monastery in the middle of nowhere, and a semi-professional vocalist. His one great regret in life is that he was not born in the nineteenth century in St. Petersburg, but he is doing everything he can to remedy that error.

The Raven Son Series
The Song of the Sirin
The Curse of the Raven
The Heart of the World
The Forge of the Covenant
The Throne of the Gods
The Rusted Blade

The Worldbuilding Series:
How to Survive a Russian Fairy Tale
Heroes for All Times
A Window to the Russian Soul

Russian Fairy Tales and Myths:
In a Certain Kingdom: Fairy Tales of Old Russia
In a Certain Kingdom: Epic Tales of the Rus
In a Certain Land: Wise Fools, Cunning Dragons, and Baba Yaga

Children of Vasyllia:
The Son of the Deathless

The God Wars Cycle
Cantos of Arcadia